CRUSHER

vs.

The Empire

The first book in the "Geronimo's Revenge" trilogy

by Mike Palecek

For all those group home workers,
who dream of blowing something up,
or burning something to the ground.

CWG PRESS

Published by
CWG Press
1517 NE 5th Ter #1
Fort Lauderdale, FL 33304
www.cwgpress.com

ISBN 13: 978-0-9906714-5-9

Printed in the U.S.A.

Also by Mike Palecek

Fiction:

SWEAT: Global Warming in a small town,
and other tales from the great American Westerly Midwest
Joe Coffee's Revolution
The Truth
The American Dream
Johnny Moon
KGB
Terror Nation
Speak English
The Last Liberal Outlaw
The Progrrressive Avenger
Camp America
Twins
Iowa Terror
Guests of the Nation
Looking For Bigfoot
A Perfect Duluth Day
American History 101: Conspiracy Nation
Revolution
One Day In The Life of Herbert Wisniewski
Operation Northwoods: the patsy
Red White & Blue
Welcome to Sugar Creek

Non-fiction:

Cost of Freedom (with Whitney Trettien and Michael Annis)
Prophets Without Honor (with William Strabala)
The Dynamic Duo: White Rose Blooms in Wisconsin, Kevin Barrett, Jim Fetzer &
the American Resistance
Nobody Died At Sandy Hook (with Jim Fetzer)
And I Suppose We Didn't Go To The Moon, Either! (with Jim Fetzer)
Nobody Died At Boston, Either (with Jim Fetzer)
America Nuked on 9/11 (with Jim Fetzer)

It is forbidden to kill; therefore all murderers are punished, unless
they kill in large numbers and to the sound of trumpets.
— Voltaire

So you're sayin' there's a chance.
— *Dumb & Dumber*

The bums will always lose.
Your revolution is over.
Condolences!
My advice to you is to do what your parents did.
Get a job, sir.
— *The Big Lebowski*

... "The Revolution" was a villainous stable in Total Nonstop Action
Wrestling (TNA), consisting of members James Storm, Abyss, The Great
Sanada, Khoya, Manik and Serena Deeb.

... Revolution invests in people and ideas that can change the world.
Our mission is to build disruptive, innovative companies that offer more
choice, convenience, and ...

... The Revolution is an American health and lifestyle talk show with
some reality television components. It aired weekdays at 2:00pm on the
ABC network from January 16 ...

... The Revolution
Changing Lives
"We teach agents with agents who do it every day
and do it big."
Mark [ ], Owner, CEO and, Most Importantly, Producer
Mark Is one of the most successful producers of fixed index
annuities in the industry. Over the last decade, he's written more than
$250 million in personal production and consistently writes well over
$20 million a year. In March of 2008, after years of success, Mark
noticed a tremendous lack of resources and training for independent
producers. It was at that time that The Revolution was born. A company
with a proven sales system created and used by Mark personally, an
actual producer rather than someone working behind a desk. A sales

system designed with hands-on training and step by step instructions, from filling up the seminar room to closing the sale. This system, coupled with our hands-on training, has propelled The Revolution to over a billion dollars in premium with under 200 producers. A history making accomplishment and further proof that The Revolution's sales system is a complete game changer for serious producers.

· Revolution Supplements
www.Bodybuilding.com/Store
Save On Revolution Supplements Today at Bodybuilding.com! Shop Now
• Shop Deals on Supplements
• Multivitamin Supplements
• Free Workout Plans
• Get Discounts- Join Today
The Revolution FMO
www.revolutionmo.com
info@revolutionmo.com Pause Video Terms of Use ... The Revolution FMO, LLC. All rights reserved. For Financial Professionals Use Only- Not For Use With The Public. ...

The Revolution (TV series) - Wikipedia, the free...
en.wikipedia.org/wiki/The_Revolution_(TV_seri...
The Revolution is an American health and lifestyle talk show with some reality television components. It aired weekdays at 2:00pm on the ABC network from January 16 ...

Revolution Tea
www.revolutiontea.com
We're Revolution. We make tea for drinking both hot and over ice. It matters because we know it's really all about the ingredients, full-leaf teas, select herbs ...

· Homefront: The Revolution - GameSpot
www.gamespot.com/homefront-the-revolution
Homefront: The Revolution throws players into a near future dystopia where catastrophic events have brought the United States to its knees and enabled the Korean ...

· An American Revolution - Wikipedia, the free...
en.wikipedia.org/wiki/An_American_Revoluti...
An American Revolution is a former advertising campaign used by American car manufacturer Chevrolet. First introduced on New Year's Eve 2003 in the United States
to ...

· <u>Revolution Media - Marketing Strategy-Media...</u>
revolutionmediainc.com
A strategic media agency integrating marketing strategy, media planning, media buying and analytics to ensure your advertising connects and converts

Let's face the fact, this country needs a revolution every bit as much as Hasni Mubarak's Egypt needed a revolution.
The question is, what will it take?
— Dr. Kevin Barrett

Feed the birds, tuppence a bag,
Tuppence, tuppence, tuppence a bag.
— Mary Poppins

Always believe that something wonderful is about to happen.
— *widespread meme, kind of*

If we go, go insane
We can all go together.
— Lindsay Buckingham by way of *Northern Exposure*

A note from your narrator:

While you get situated, here's something that we in Minnesota have that you don't. There's lots of things like this, so I guess get used to it.

Anyway, from "The Prince Hope Show" — *A Letter In A Boone's Farm Bottle*, some notes we've received from readers by email, chatroom, telephone, telepathy and telegraph.

"Just glad to finally be in Minnesota, where it's safe, sane and serene. Just arrived at the lake, the resort, the cabin, so much to see and do and just forget about things in the stupid place that I was. Found this book here and can't wait to just sit in the sun with my toes in the water and read and relax! Minnesota! Professional baseball! Money! Lakes! Smart people! The University of St. Thomas! Small towns! Cities! Woods! Bears! Summit Avenue! Ely! Good beer! One fucking gigantic lake and ten grand more! Fuck yeah!"

".... *A Letter In A Boone's Farm Bottle*, some notes we've received from readers by email, chatroom, telephone, telepathy and telegraph."

Go at it boldly, and you'll find unexpected forces closing round you and coming to your aid.

— Basil King

Yeah, right. — Lara

INTRODUCTION

Nice weather.

I'm just reading this electronics manual as I am wont to do.

I find it fascinating, and unnerving, complicated, dangerous, enticing.

I've always wanted to know how this works, and I can never really quite get it, try as I do.

I'm just reading here: ... three main properties make electricity work: voltage, current and resistance ... these properties work inside a circuit ... yeah, yeah ... allowing electricity to move from place to place.

Well, that doesn't do it for me.

I want to go to the root, as many do, to find the deep-seated, interstitial power, the motivator. And sometimes, some times, there is none. Things happen, shit happens, people do things, maybe they haven't thought about it beforehand as much as you think you might have ... and there is not satisfactory, cleansing, what is that word I'm searching for? ... Cathartic. Nope, that's not it either.

It is what it is, that's what it is.

What I want is to know how to make a good bomb. I've wondered for a long time how that is possible.

They often do not turn out good.

Anyway, hello.

I'm a reporter, a writer, of sorts and I've done, written, a story. That is I'm working on it and here it is, parts of it. I'm not done. I'll keep working while I tell you and in the meantime I've got this electronics, electricity manual I want to look at.

And here we go. At least, I'm going.

Shall we?

No, wait, wait just a goddamn minute.

No, sorry, just wait.

I'm being followed by a moonshadow, moonshadow, moonshadow ...

1

and if I ever lose my legs all my feet north and south, oh if I ever lose my legs, moonshadow, moonshadow.

I love Cat Stevens, best ever, ever, well, yeah, Natalie, but it's like John Prine said about that music that comes on right after the movie, it's like, woah, where did that come from? It doesn't necessarily follow. It's poetry, it doesn't make sense, but it works, two different components, just let it be. It's all right. Be cool. Be calm and fish from the shore, everything's all right, or it will be all right. Just give it time.

It's like the '70s trying to catch back up to the '60s, it wasn't going to happen, frustrating, hopeless, but still, it's morning and you have to live the day. Like trying to live Nov. 23rd. You just do.

Nice to meet you, by the way.

Most people are totally invulnerable. You can't get to 'em. But some, well, they are uncomfortable, when they are young, in their thirties, when they grow old, not all the time, they operate, they buy gas, but they are vulnerable. I like 'em.

Would you rather be in a family that's kind of stupid and laughs a lot at a lot of stupid shit and so they look happy, or in a family that doesn't laugh so much, but isn't stupid. They had that question once on "The Price Is Right." No, of course they didn't, you fucking, oh, nothing, forget it.

Just sayin'. But of course you realize what it is, not this or that. You could have a stupid family that does not talk, or a smart family who is so happy you feel so bad that you are not like them and you of course wonder what is wrong with your family, but then that is the question and answer of the whole universe, of the heavens, and we are not there yet. We are just at the beginning.

But also there is this to consider ... I really should have an editor, but I don't, it's just me, mostly.

"And there's nothing you will ever say for the rest of your life because we will be there and we will know it." ... "perpetuating a camouflage story that has taken on a life of its own and goes forward like a Dickens novel, simply on inertia." ... "Jesse Marcel went back to work as if he'd never held the wreckage from the strange craft in his own hands."

I just read that shit. A lot of what I do is wait. I think that's any job or any family. If you listened to a recording of an office or a home I think a lot of what you would hear is silence, just sayin'.

Anyway, that's *The Day After Roswell*, and I think it's interesting. Nobody believes that shit but I kinda do, depends on the day.

But think about it, yeah, the family thing, whatya gonna do? What can anyone do? One foot in front of the other, that's all anyone can do. I know, right.

But the alien thing and the War of the Worlds. Just think about it for once. They faked that radio show, or it was faked as entertainment, whatever, and found out it could be done, easy as fucking pie, right?

And that's the same as all this other shit, Dallas, all this shit.

They make it up, fool us, then keep adding on to the story, and who fucking knows where anything is true, right? Right? *Fuck* you, then.

No, wait, I'm sorry. C'mon.

And then those who really know, they tell 'em they will fucking kill their family if they say anything and they don't and so nobody knows the truth.

And so nobody talks and it's all shit.

And that has almost exactly nothing to do with what I am about to tell you.

I am certainly not one to let a dogged allegiance to the truth get in the way of a good story.

This is a good story. At least I think it is.
And that's the truth.

Pleased to meet you, hope you guessed my name ... what's puzzling you is the nature of my game.

— The Rolling Stones

Unfortunately, there is no alternative. The USA MUST do an investigation of the JFK assassination to the satisfaction of all American people. Not to discover who did it or how it was done but to restore global confidence in USA justice. To say, "It was probably...", "We may never know..." or "It's in the past" leaves the world believing that the USA considers corruption to be okay as long as you don't get caught but the problem is that it isn't. The JFK assassination showed the elite that they could get away with any crime as long as they make all information concerning it "top secret" as a matter of national security. And so began a covert war against the American people. This case laid the foundation stones for lies, false flag operations and crimes against humanity and what they failed to realize is that the repetition of lies has made the American Government a laughingstock and those desperately arguing that "Assad and Putin are the monsters are doing so because they NEED their government, their flag and their identity to be good. It is time that the American people stood firm.

— Internet article, *from the comments section*

ONE

He startled as the wood popped like a gunshot just as he began to talk. Jim ducked, looked around, turned a little red in the cheeks and kept going.

... The police man he didn't have no head, he said.

I write it down.

The policeman he didn't have no head.

I'm talking to Jim.

"That's what I remember about him," says Jim.

"He was drawing like he always did and he was working on a *police* man and there was the *police* man and there was The CRUSHER and the policeman was shooting at The CRUSHER.

"And the *police*man had no head.

"He was really a pretty good drawer.

"And he was The CRUSHER. He loved that Walmart costume. We got it the day before that one Halloween. He didn't have money and that's all he talked about so we put our money together and, we weren't supposed to, but we did, we bought him that CRUSHER costume. He didn't go out trick or treating, but he put that costume on the minute he got home from work, wore it through supper and he gave out candy that night, huge grin on his face, talking to all the kids.

"His name was Napoleon Ulysses Custer.

"And he liked it if you called him Geronimo.

"Yeah a Native little dude named Custer. You can't make that shit up.

"Some parents with disabled children, probably most of them, all of them, except this one I guess, give their children the most normal names possible, they don't want them to stand out any more than they already do, just hoping for some kind of normal life for their fuckin' kids.

"Disabilities people die earlier I guess. Let him die and get to heaven and be who he really is. He was already who he really is, way more than any of us are, more than me.

"Why didn't he like police? I don't know. Usually people like that love cops and army guys they call them, but then again he was native, and wrestling, definitely wrestling, every Wednesday and Friday night, seven o'clock. And they get really worked up about it, serious. You can't really joke about it, because to them it's real. And it's not just retarded guys who like wrestling, lots of people do. I don't. To me it's fake, but lots of people do, like it.

"The fight for justice. He was just always talking 'bout that. Maybe he heard it on wrestling or Spiderman, the first one, or something else I don't know.

"He would definitely have done that, made everything right for everybody, if he had a chance.

"There was a lot in there, inside his head, and his heart. A lot more than you could see at first by lookin' at him. And that smile, wow.

"I saw him once sitting alone in the living room, wearing his CRUSHER costume and watching Mary Poppins, again. And it was the part about feeding the birds and the, ya know, fuckin' decision they were forcin' that little kid to make about putting his money in the bank to be rich or spending it on a little fuckin' feed for the birds.

"And he's singing along to himself, feed the birds.

"That's actually what started all a this.

"He sort of inspired us. It all came from him. Things are going big now, well, kinda, were, not now, but it took us a long time to even get started, let me tell you.

"We all worked at the home, the group home. Well, I did, for a while, and then I worked at the workshop. I don't think they call 'em that anymore. Maybe you're s'pose to call it a facility. Gerry, Geronimo, you weren't supposed to call him that when there were supervisors around, supposed to use his whole real name Napoleon Ulysses Custer, they said that's what his mom wanted, but seriously, there really wasn't time, to always be sayin' all that.

"I'm not fuckin' sure how it all got started. Let me think, how did it I wonder? We talked.

"And I guess somebody, probly Evey, said she would feed the fuckin' birds. And whoever was workin' that night, we all said would we put the fuckin' money in the fuckin' bank or would we feed the fuckin' birds, ya know?

"And yeah, I was definitely gonna put my nickel or whatever the fuck a fuckin' tuppins is, in the fuckin' bank. I wanted to fix my fuckin' truck and get a new gun.

"But, yeah, that's how we got talkin' 'bout it. And we even argued about it the next day. I remember that, because I thought it was pretty much over, move on, right? But what I remember is everybody kept fuckin' goin' on that.

"And then it went from Mary Fuckin' Poppins to other shit.

"We never even thought about starting a revolution, not this revolution. We thought about whether to fight. We talked about that a lot. But I knew nothin' would ever come out of it. That's what I thought then.

"I think it was because there was so many of us interested in it, ya know, that it kept on goin'. If it's just one person or two, it ain't goin' nowhere.

"I started to read, a little, others a lot. We researched. We pretty much took our time. We kind a knew that if we ever really got started, that was it, no goin' back, and so, at least for me, I wanted to kinda know what all I was gettin' my ass into, ya know?"

The wood creaked.

Like the trees poppin' in January, Jim said.

"Must be new wood they're usin'. Probly birch. Oak, maple, that's good wood. I'm not complaining. Like complainin' 'bout bein' hanged with a new rope, huh?"

He asked about Kaitylyn and Lara.

I said that I would pass along his hey.

"Oak, maple," he said.

His grandfather and then his dad used to sell it by cords out of a pickup, same pickup, different years.

"It's not cheap. Not like birch.

"They made pretty good money."

Martin Luther King, Jr. was killed because he was about to lead 500,000 people to Washington, D.C. and start a revolution. That revolution is long overdue — as every American who learns the truth about "deep events" like the 1960s assassinations, 9/11 and false flag terrorism, election fraud, and other suppressed issues will surely agree.

— Dr. Kevin Barrett

TWO

I went to see Lara.

I have to say that she looked horrible. She'd lost weight and, wow, lots of weight. Her hair had not been washed. She came in wearing no socks, just like shower shoes, picking her fingernails, looking as if she were wondering where she was.

Snot dripped from her nose. She wiped it with her sleeve, then searched the floor for something.

She sat, but not even close to me. I had to get up and move to sit next to her. She scooted away and then there was the concrete wall and she couldn't go any farther. I thought about just leaving, but then she said something, in that deep, husky voice I remembered. I'm pretty sure by the look on her face she did not remember me. I can't see how that could be.

"You talked to Jim?

"How's he doing?

"Of course I remember him, whatya think?

"Oh, so, yeah, I see. One of us is the agent and, yeah, well, it's not me and it's not Jim, you can see that. Right? Anyway, fuck you if you don't see. Can't see. Won't see. Just fuck you."

Something caught. Some gear, some synapse fired and she looked as if she remembered why we were here. She held her hands in her lap like a lady and dusted something from her lap that remained filthy despite her attempt at tidiness.

"We looked at revolution like the wardrobe, wondrous, magical, and then, when you get there. I've been waiting to tell someone that line for a long time.

"Why did we care? That much? All young people care, probably that much. And they are ready to risk it all, but most don't get a chance before they are caught and then once you're in the trap you can't get out and the more you struggle the worse it is. That's just how it works.

"But for some reason not with us, we escaped, at least that.

"You do know what I'm talking about, don't you? I mean otherwise there's no reason for me to go on, if you can't understand, won't.

"You do?

"You think you do."

She looked around and looked as though she were ready to get up and pace, but saw we were not alone and arranged herself in a sort of straight line on her uncomfortable perch.

"The Terrible Tough Twelve. A stooopid name. That was who we were I guess. What a name. It didn't last anyway. We were CRUSHER. Even got tattoos."

She showed me.

"It could possibly have been worse. It was supposed to be like the Marvel comics characters, you know? Oh, you do. I suppose you would.

"Yes, the policeman had no head.

"I suppose Jim would remember that."

She swept again at her lap, this way, that.

"Of course I remember Gerry.

"No, The CRUSHER is not a Marvel character. Not really. You need to not be so, reactive."

I had said nothing.

"There are layers to this. They, the clients, had a club, let's say. They called it Men's Group. I think Ben might have helped them start it and then some of the other guys took turns, facilitating, hanging out. They'd have supper and then supposedly discuss an issue like money management or fitness or marriage and family, and then it would eventually meld, devolve, into putting on costumes or taking off their clothes to get to the costumes they wore underneath and watching wrestling on TV. That's really what they were waiting for.

"Yes, I'm getting to that. There's was no doubt I was going to feed the birds.

"And Jim, poor Jim. He didn't want to feed any fucking sky rats as he would say. He wanted to play guitar, play pool, and fuck. And he ended up doing some of the most serious shit and look at him now.

"And to decide to actually start a revolution. Isn't that your next question?"

Actually.

"How connected were we to liberal thought and knowledge of past and current efforts, and don't you need those bona fides to do this?

"Fuck no. Maybe a little, maybe a lot. I probably knew more than I let on, others too. Maybe less than I thought.

"And didn't we need that background to carry out something like this?

Like I said, I don't know. Maybe yes, maybe no. Maybe all that was just in the water and we already knew it and it was part of us. No, you're right.

"Well, actually we actually didn't talk about Marxist or revolutionary theory from other people. We talked a lot about our own, our own lives. I know we wondered how to go to war, you know, do battle, actually fight, and some people looked it up, got some books from Amazon and they sort of taught the rest of us, flanks, maneuvers, punches, training, like that. We actually did a lot of training. I liked it. I hoped the training would never end because I knew we were all going to die.

"I know you didn't ask about this, but here it is.

"And it has absolutely nothing to do with what we're talking about.

"Remember that old song, be happy?

"Landlord say your rent is due? All that? That one? Yeah.

"Well, it just popped into my head. It's something Brooke used to say, pretty much all the time, too much, anyway. It was just a bunch of nonsense, but then it ended, 'don't worry, and then be happy.' Like, do your to-do list, and then be happy. She'd make up a bunch of stuff. Mow your lawn, bathe your dolls, plant your dope, parachute from Mars. And then be happy. Like that. Sleep 'til noon, fix your roof, sit in the street, wear red clothes ... and then be happy.

"You know about Brooke?

"The thing is. It's hard to do.

"What? What were we just talking about.

"Brooke, yes Brooke, but what before that?

"Exactly.

"And then be happy.

"No matter what you do, it's not going to be enough. She made it funny, but I think she was also saying you could make that list as long as your arm and you can never-ever just sit there and be happy. At least she couldn't. I think that's what she felt.

"Me either, I don't think.

"Maybe I'll find out now.

"What's it like being here?

"I don't know, how's that for an answer. It's the only answer you deserve. Anyone who is not in here right now with me does not deserve an answer, that's how I really feel. You are scum, you are vermin, you are weak and stupid. You wanted to know about me, right? You think I'm angry you should talk to, ummm.

"In a way it's like being in school.

"In my area, long aisles, there's these alphabet stickers or pictures on the wall, capital letters, small letters, each has a drawing of a different flower or plant and the letter has nothing to do with the plant as far as I can figure. The other day I stared at that wall and those letters and thought about school. I remember being in grade school and snow-flecked boots lined with heels touching the wall and the smell of eraser and the contour of the plastic chair bottom, trying not to be distracted by the scene outside the row of windows that went the full length of the room.

"And later discovering what we had not been taught. The poor teachers didn't know though. They hadn't been taught either, or their teachers before.

"So, yeah, has anyone told you about Brooke? Yes, of course I just mentioned her, but there's more.

"Brooke.

"Well, she was something.

"We were besties. Why didn't they kill me, too? Well, I'll bet your little mind is whirling trying to figure that one out, am I right?

"How is it going out there?

"Oh.

"Yeah, Brooke.

"Well, she was something.

"She was a secret agent. Yeah, a spy. I think someone else is also a spy, I can't remember. I never wanted to be one. I don't think I'd be good at it. Brooke was, very good, very sneaky, that one.

"Yeah, I guess not sneaky enough.

"One time, I remember, we were back in school, that same classroom with the long line of low windows looking out onto the front lawn of the school, all very suburban-soccer-mom-chic mostly. Proper, designed to put us on our way.

"We didn't think much of Mrs. X, that's what we called her. We thought she was kind of stupid. Brooke's brother, Brett, he found a German swear-word dictionary online and was feeding them to us.

"Ficken you. Ich will ficken.

"Me and Brooke, we were inserting those German swear words into our casual conversation to see if Mrs. X would say anything, and she didn't.

"Kuss mein arsch.

"We were sure she would get that one and we would be in so much trouble. We'd say it as we walked by her on our way out for recess or if someone asked us to borrow paper or a pencil. Nobody knew what we were saying and we thought we were so clever. One time Mrs. X asked Brooke to come up to the front and raise up the little flag on a pole thing as we said the Pledge and Brooke smiled and said "kuss mein arsch" as she walked up to the front.

"Nothing happened.

"I s'pose looking back on it, the intent of those windows and that school, was to put us into those houses we could see across the street, with the lawns and the golf carts and the flower boxes, tractor mail boxes, yippy lap dogs.

"Hmmm.

"Anyway. Back off."

I scooted. My chair made a squeak. The person in the hall looked to see if I was ready to leave. I held up my hand and shook my head.

"Anywaaaay ... me and Brooke, Brooke and I, said fikken that very early on, not because we knew anything really, we were just girls who thought a lot of ourselves.

"As it turns out we had every reason.

"No. Of course I didn't kill her. How can you ask me that? But I could have. She drove me crazy sometimes.

"We didn't get to some of your questions, but I'm sure you can ask others, if they are still out there. Are they? Oh.

"You should talk to Korey, he would know more about Brooke. I mean, I knew her, but not lately, you understand?"

She dusted herself about the lap and shoulders like a prize dog preparing itself for the show.

"Good," she said as I began putting things away.

"You must go, they must be coming."

QUOTE REMOVED BY ORDER OF DHS, UNITED STATES DEPARTMENT OF HOMELAND SECURITY. [DHS US2FA]

From the narrator:

Since I started writing this story I have somehow been receiving these by group email. I decided to include them, some guy in Iowa.

THREE

Geoffrey,
    With Mike here, we have without planning it come together early for dog walk to the river, daily. Mike ever is talking the most, Kelly second. We are not abreast but more strung out, and Mike is a fossil hunter now. Primarily I am wanting to get the walk done, for Choyota, return for ax workout or deadlifting, then to drink. Forty degrees is fine for Jazz, big lab pup, to fetch sticks in the river. On his better days old deaf Bo will trail us. That I in backseat returning from HEB on the fourteenth, Blackbird brothers had this yelling argument about reality and Obama, probably matters little, seems like I am angriest.

Mike the scientist is so out of it, what he calls politics though he will "vote Democrat of course," he considers probably Oswald is lone nut, says he looked into it, he said some amazing shit, on way back from, I sketched a bit of lately in Postings, to Steve V., Bix. Who else? If I go look now I will lose my above. Like "pipedream," I forget exactly. Too though, Kelly is incredible.

Kelly has read some books "Bill's friends" have sent, LBJ, JFK. He is ok there, till Obama. A phenomenal disconnect. I had thought, he had grasped 9/11 was a fake story, till Obama, who covers it up. Then, Sandy Hook, all this. I had way back from HEB reminded him I had liked Obama, and he jumped at that: Yeah, you were glad to see a black president. I said: Sure. Then he began killing kids with drones every day and all his 8 years and he has not done shit otherwise. Obama is a liar and a murderer. On the way back from HEB sometimes my brothers were yelling at me the same time. They need to believe Assad gassed his people. Were Assad insane, why destroy Libya? Blank. My brothers have a craving to believe Corporate News,

15

that it is Assad and Putin killing women and kids in Syria. Presently, do you know or not, the killers of kids are being killed by Putin and Assad. Assad was voted in, I think by 78%. These killers they kill, and have on the run, are supplied by NATO,C.I.A. etc. I am sure they are taking out some USA special-forces while at it.... Good stuff....

Everything changes by the day, and couple days back when I punched latest Sane Progressive, at YouTube, all these videos popped up, several tremendous journalists, mostly female, from Europe. They boldly gave truth. Called USA/NATO bald face liars.

Obama has done naught for USA black people. Naught for poor people. Obama Care is no good. Ask the poor people. Our economy is fake. Alternative News is wildly growing.

Mike and Kelly do not grasp Alternative News. Nor "Bill's friends" in a past decade. BLANK.

Here is a phenomenon. I see Steve Vaughn is not doing well at it, Kelly said on the way back Steve agrees with him Obama is best USA president ever. BLANK, eh.

I do get tired. NOBODY DIED AT SANDY HOOK is the only book ever banned at Amazon Books, because nobody died at Sandy Hook. BLANK.

I do not care if Obama is gay and his wife was born male. He has not helped any people anywhere and the crowd who wanted to nuke Russia who killed JFK who was secretly communicating to Khrushchev have been with us, breeding. They fear they might not control Trump, rich lout. Get Trump now, keep Obama, easily managed, Hillary is a basket case.

Then, there is Pizzagate. Well, hell, more the phenomenal, fantastical.

I am reading yet this book from Novak , when I am not too drunk to remember everything, F.B.I. got MLK, proven in court by author William Perry, mid book are photos of burned Vietnamese orphans in the street dying, kept out of Corporate News. VIETNAM WAR had sickened MLK. "The US is the largest purveyor of violence on earth." Our nation does this. They got Iraq and Libya and nearly Syria, for oil, for Merchants of War. My brothers: DISCONNECT. Each day of Obama Merchants of War and Big Oil is murder. Obama is shit. Kids bombed all the time, in 7 nations etc.

Geoffrey, after Steve and son Shade breezed through here and agreed with Kelly Boy's fantasy, which is Mike's, which is your mother's, I wonder how does your mind now work.

Just ignore me, fine. Flapdoodle I turn angrier. Do not

fuck with me. Our civilization kills kids. DISCONNECT. Ignore me or not. I am ready to get awfully pissed. Heh, as in Sane Progressive....Ah... worse than that now....
    Love,
        Bill

    PS DO NOT TRY TO PLACATE. You might change subject. USA is most evil nation in official history.

Blood-soaked earth that you call home; Close your eyes but don't sleep; We comin' like peoples army; For the people who can't eat; Who work with no sleep; For the child; With no shoes on their feet; A generation who flash heat; Who roll up on the banks; For their cash see; You're the criminal? You got the nerve to ask me; Tear mics till my voice get raspy; Faced flame for five centuries; And if L.A. were Baghdad we'd be Iraqi; With our straps in the backseat; Next to a general tied up; With shit in his khakis; Best leave my mic alone I'm full grown; And I'm off to the green zone.

After dark my city's a fuse; One day I say today we live as a lion; And when our cubs grow; We'll show you what war is good for.

— Rage Against The Machine

FOUR

Here's Korey.

He's bruised, mouth swollen, like he's got cotton in his gums and cheeks, a cut on his chin. His knuckles are red, his nose crusty, there's a white film around his mouth and dried blood in his ears.

"No, man, no speak English," he said, squinting in my direction against the light through the window over my shoulder.

"Geezuz," I say.

"What?" he said.

"Geezuz, Korey, it's me."

"Hey, man.

"What? That bad? Where's a mirror?"

He touches his face.

"No, you're fine, you're fine. Here, sit."

He recognizes me, but he can't remember my name. I see that in his first glance after scanning the room for the mirror.

He stinks. Or maybe it's me. As subtly as I can I pull up my arm and smell myself.

We look at each other. That's the most eye contact I've ever seen from Korey. His clothes are worn miles past trendy. He's dirty, hands, face, jeans.

"Good to see you, man," he says.

I nod.

"Good to see you, too."

"Well, we don't have that much time," I say, and pull out my notepad, cross my legs to get into ready position.

"How did you get to be a guerilla leader?" I ask and right away realize I'm nervous, too. I already know about Korey and all that, mostly. I let it go.

"Your dreams," he said, and I write it down automatically.

19

"Aren't any more weird than anyone else's," he said. "You think they are, that there's something wrong with you, or you're special, but they aren't."

"Okay," I said.

"Yeah," he said. "Guerilla?

"*This* is a drag."

With Korey I got the feeling that he never really felt at ease, anywhere.

"She did that thing with her mouth ... Did you ever? Anyway ... she'd twist her lips to go different directions and her jaw and sort of cross her eyes when she talked about a mistake she'd made or something. Disasters of the mind, that was another thing, you know? Like if you're driving and you imagine, what if I swerve and crash into that tree or go off that bridge, what would that be like and I have the power to do it, right now. She thought that was interesting."

"Who?"

"Brooke."

"How are you?" he asked.

"I'm fine, Korey."

"Well, in a way, it's exciting," he said and I try my hardest to focus and follow him wherever he's going.

"Can you imagine, having enough guys in your neighborhood one Saturday to play war and you are in charge of it all and you plan an assault from six different angles and it's all working and you are part of a team. That's fun. But that's not all."

"Yes."

"Brooke died. I'm almost sure of it. Yesterday I almost joined her. I wanted to.

"We both just graduated from the U and we got jobs. I was at St. Joe's ... Home for Children. She ran a group home, that's where she met Jim, Lara, them others. And we had money, and a car, and a place, stereo, surround-sound. Everything was looking like it was gonna click. She always said that security comes with a price, and it's not real. I didn't care. I wanted to live my life as a young dude in the Twin Cities, to have fun. She wanted our lives to have meaning.

"Whatever. Hell with that I guess. My parents said stay away from her. I guess now they get their wish.

"Well, after all that went on to have the idea, talk it over, plan it out, well ... and Camp Sweaty ... you know about that?

"Yes, but tell me again ... please."

I ask Korey to speak up.

"Camp Sweaty, I said, you heard of that?"

"Yes, you said Camp Sweaty?"

"Yeah, our top-secret training camp."

He uses air quotes.

"Anyway, after we did all that, well the idea was how to start, see? So now we're really kinda doin' it. I don't think we ever actually decided to do it, it just started, how to get guns, these Orange Crush uni's, and we read all kinds of shit, got about nine hundred books off Amazon, really, I'm not shittin', read about strategy, John Brown, flanks, columns, hand to hand, Viet Cong, Quantrill, mortars, bayonets, Persian wars, Civil War, Chinese philosophers, how to kill, all that shit."

We stop here. Korey is either having a seizure or he's lost in thought, or he's fallen asleep.

We're back.

"Decided to do it at Prince Hope's last show. You know him? Yeah. Very famous, the whole world. He was on TV, USO tours, the Olympics, the White House, the Minnesota State Fair, Iowa State Fair, Ohio State Fair, all that, and he started here, always had his own show here, a radio show, golf jokes, airplane food. He's from here. We used to go to it, a lot, my family, my dad loved Prince Hope and to be able to be right there in the audience while the show played over the whole world. He thought that was so cool.

"Well, his last show, was right down here, over about ... I don't know ... in The Minnesota Theatre, old place, pretty cool, chandeliers, all that stuff. And we all got tickets. Brooke or Lara and Kennedy had to be right online when they went on sale and make sure we could fuckin' get in.

"He's powerful. They say he pretty much runs the whole country. An entertainer. And you don't get that way without paying attention to details, I'll bet. I'll bet he checks everyone to see who's going to his shows.

"And we did, not great seats. Somebody was bitching about that.

"Prince Hope wore his white suit and his red tennis shoes and that long pitch-black hair, even when he got old. And he's tall. Tall people think they own the world. No, really, they do.

"Yeah, we screwed up, big time.

"How did we mess up? Just a lot. Yeah, just think of all you would have to do if you just right now decided you were gonna start a revolution.

"Yeah, uniforms. You know, I thought we were just making fun of hunters, you know, but actually, the Roman armies, ya know, with the big red feathers, plumes, on their helmets, that's to make them look taller, bigger, formidable. It's called posturing, and so these bright orange uniforms, they're more like janitor or, yeah, jail uniforms, but they're supposed to scare the enemy, like all the janitors in the world are rushing at you. And yelling, yelling helps too.

"Sure, yeah, you got to go through all that why fight stuff and then ninety nine point nine percent of the time you go get jobs at Target or something after that, but if you do go on, that's when the fun starts, let me tell you.

"And yeah, just think, you got to get (He holds up a fist and releases fingers. One. At. A. Time.) people, people to join you, right? Weapons, guns, for sure, you got to have some guns. Somebody to fight. Who you gonna fight? Are they right there in front of your apartment? You want to shoot that old lady and call that the revolution? Or what? And you got to have a way to get to your war and some food. There's lots to consider.

"How's Jim? Yeah? Those your notes? See 'em?

"Popping wood, yeah, just like the trees popping in the winter up north, that's where he's from. It must be fresh wood they're usin'. Birch? That's good wood. Nah, I don't know shit about wood.

We looked at revolution like the wardrobe, wondrous and magical and then, when you get there.

"She said that? Weird.

"Yeah, here ya go. I don't really need to see all that.

"You want to get a good interview, talk to Blake. He's an angry, crazy, mad dude. Out of his mind. But I'd say he's got reasons.

"Yeah, and then that show, Prince Hope, yeah. Well, yeah, we had good seats, not great seats, but pretty much all together and they're doing the last bows, all holding hands and everybody is standing, cuz it's the last show ever, except for a few more, like the state fair, but they were calling this the last show anyway.

"Yeah anyway he keeps coming back for his encores you know? And the one plan was for Jim and me and Blake, Reuben, Hector, to jump up on the stage and take him away, out the back door, into the alley. We had a car waiting. We'd take him away and out to this one cabin and we'd talk all about the revolution to the press and it would be a big deal, right?

"But he keeps comin' back for more fuckin' encores and singing these Lutheran church songs. There were like senators and the governor there so it would have been cool to take him right there, but we had our little "primary" plan and we had to stick to it, and that was to walk up the side stairs all real cool as he walked off and then whisk him away like we were his entourage and into the car and nobody would know until later they found out we had him. It was Kennedy's plan.

"But Blake went and did it. I could see him getting all antsy down the row from me and I was just hoping he wouldn't do it, but he did it.

"The tall ... fucker ... in the white suit came out *again* for *another* big goodbye and Blake he just couldn't take it. He climbed up onto the seat in front of him, and I swear to God, he like walked over rows, like five rows, hitting all the seats just perfect and he musta looked like he was ten feet tall and he jumped up off that last row and onto the stage — he was a state champion freaking long jumper at Eden Prairie, no, seriously — and he hit the stage and Prince Hope was singing some Lutheran church song and Blake jerked that microphone right outa his hand and he screamed, just fucking yelled, '9/11 was an inside job! You all know that!'

"That whole theater went dead fucking silent. I'm not fuckin' shittin'.

"And that Prince Hope just stood there and he smirked. He took another microphone from somebody else and he just stared at Blake and smirked and he walked right up to Blake with that microphone by his mouth, but he didn't say anything. He was famous for making up these nursery rhymes on the spot. You know, nursery rhymes don't make any sense, but they do, back in the day they were actually a way to talk about political stuff back then, he did this all the time and he was famous for it. And then he said something, I don't remember what. The crowd went wild though. They stood up and cheered and clapped and then he led them in *The Star Spangled Banner, America The Beautiful* and another one I can't remember and Blake just stood up there with him like a busted ornament, like he was being hanged right there. And we all stood with everyone else and we even sang. It was so weird.

"But you know what?

"You know what?

"After all a that, all of that, we still did it.

"Everybody sat down and Blake was still standing there, dying. He let his microphone drop and it banged like a gunshot aimed nowhere, and I think that kind of woke me up that this didn't have to end this way. And I nodded down the row to Hector and Reuben and Lara, Kennedy, Jim, all them, and they all nodded back and I got goose bumps down my back.

"And the tall fucker finally went to the side and we quick got up and excused ourselves down the row and ran up to the little stairs to the side of the stage. We grabbed his ass and hustled him out, into the car where we had two people, and we took him to the cabin, and we did all that, Kennedy's plan, and the rest of it went pretty well, but nobody could stand Prince Hope, stand being around him, so we took him back, right to the same back door of that theater.

"That's how all this got started.

"We maybe shouldn't not have done that. I don't know, but we did."

Well, Korey got up and left. He returned and shook my hand and then he left again. I'm sure he enjoyed talking. It sure seemed like it. Like a wound-up doll he talked until his batteries wore out. How often do people ask? Who really has time to listen, takes time.

I'm alone again.

Which is okay I guess. Not that great, but whatdya gonna do, huh?

Well, as they say, that was then, this is now.

Whatever.

It's good to see Jim, Lara, Korey again, or not. More like horrible.

I wish this were over. It's never going to be over, that's what I'm afraid of. But I've still got my job to do.

Let me just go ahead and tell you about me going to see Evangelina.

Yeah ... but first I want to see if I can get ahold of Ben, Blake, or Kennedy.

Moncada stands in revolutionary history as a great example of defeat transformed into victory. It's a perfect symbol: The attempt itself, not its immediate outcome, is what's important. The mere fact that someone was willing to go up against Batista's guns inspired other Cubans to join the revolution.

— *Underground: SDS and Weathermen (1968-1970)*, by Mark Rudd

... two wires crossed. This small accident completed an electrical circuit to a detonator cap, which in turn must have set off the dynamite.

Young audiences are hungry to know this history, sensing its relevance today. They seem genuinely amazed to learn that once there was a group of young white kids from privileged backgrounds who risked everything for our anti-war, anti-racist and revolutionary beliefs, to act 'in solidarity with the people of the world.'

— Mark Rudd

FIVE

These were the three the others mentioned, but I'd never met them before. They were in the CRUSHER revolution and then they were out.

I wanted to know why.

I found Kennedy at the grocery store, in the cereal aisle. She was pissed.

"How did you find me?

"Get away from me! I'll call security."

"This is just like, a grocery store, c'mon," I said, looking around.

"I'm not sure if they have ... but I'll just go, it's all right. I'm gone."

So, I sort of waved and left her with her screaming fuckin' kid in the cart, her face red, watching me, so pissed.

Blake was nowhere as far as I could find, though someone did say something about him doing something in Europe, maybe London, but Ben was around, that same person said.

He was coaching football at a high school not that far away, in the west suburbs. That trip I could do.

From the age and the description he was the stout man on the thirty yard line, whistle, sweats, ball cap, shouting at some linemen for doing things not quite right.

I found my way to a gate in the fence and to where I stood behind the man I thought was Ben.

During a break where he had sent the players off to another form of torture I approached him, tentatively, I have to say, because I was pretty sure he wanted to talk to me about CRUSHER about as badly as Kennedy had.

"Ben?"

He jerked around with furrowed brow.

"Yes. Can I help you?"

I said I was a reporter, gave him my name, held out my hand to shake.

He shook and said that this was practice, not the time for this.

"Can you call me? You got my number?"

"No, I don't, but this isn't about football."

"Oh?"

And he seemed to get it. He lowered his head and walked down the sideline. I walked with him.

He said he was in CRUSHER, yes, and he smiled when he mentioned Geronimo, and Lara, Jim, Korey, Evangelina, Hector, Reuben, yes, yes, he remembered all of those, very well.

"It just wasn't for me," said Ben.

"After awhile I figured that out. I just couldn't do it. It's not for everyone."

He said that there were a few of them who were really against the idea of violent revolution.

"Killing."

He stopped and looked right up at me.

"Can you imagine?" he said.

"You and I right now talking seriously about going out and killing someone, with a gun, or a knife, on purpose, for any purpose, no matter how good? To save puppies. If we felt we had to kill someone to save a basket of fourteen puppies, could you do it?"

"I doubt it," I said.

"Yes, exactly."

We walked on and he mentioned a couple of names out of the blue.

"What?" I said.

"Really? Them?"

"Yep," he said.

"They were so not in favor of killing. They threw a fit, said it made them actually vomit to think about it. They left. I wonder whatever happened to them?"

Note from the narrator:

From "The Prince Hope Show," in case you're not from Minnesota, that is, which you probably aren't, but we are:

Tonight's show is sponsored by "Left Behind Adult Diapers."

If you're a conservative Christian who did not get raptured up, you're probably wondering why. We're here for you, Left Behind.

The duty of every revolutionary is to make the revolution.
— Che Guevara

You know, something very troubling has just happened. A friend in the Bolivian government sent us a package: it arrived yesterday. Che's hands, his very hands, preserved. Before they destroyed his body, they chopped off his hands to prove they had him. They were definitely his hands, I recognized them. I don't know what to do with them.
— Fidel Castro to member of Weather Underground, in Havana, *Underground: SDS and Weathermen (1968-1970)*, by Mark Rudd

SIX

So, yeah.

We've talked to Jim, Lara, Korey, Ben and that's how things stand now, at least for them.

Let me now tell you how I first got started in all of this.

No, I shouldn't.

I just won't tell you everything.

Didn't Hemingway fucking say the most important parts of the story are the ones you leave out?

Well, this wasn't the first thing I did when I started this story, trying to find out about CRUSHER, but that's where I'm going to go next in this recounting, my trip to talk to Evangelina.

I hope you like the story, but if you don't, well ...

You thought I was going to say, fuck you, didn't you.

Nope, I'm leaving that part out.

So, I am looking now for The Sidetrack Tap.

This is the Iron Range.

I want to find Reuben, Evangelina and Hector, the triplets. And I want to talk about some things I have written down here: tactics vs. strategy, hammer and anvil, Alexander, Hannibal, Caesar, Frederick the Great, Napoleon, weather and terrain, all those details of battle that I think are interesting.

In any case, here I am headed into ... The Café in Mount Iron.

I have my window seat and Wi-Fi, which I cannot believe. According to Wikipedia:

Mountain Iron is a city in Saint Louis County, Minnesota, United States; in the heart of the Mesabi Range.

U.S. Highway 169 serves as a main route in Mountain Iron.

The city's motto is the "Taconite Capital of the World".

And it doesn't say this, but it's "soon to be destroyed, burned to the ground, but the fighting has not yet reached this little Lake Wobegon island in a sea of hot burning oil."

Folks take a look at me and then return to their conversations. All round tables, no window booths, which I prefer, but life goes on. I am waiting for something, not sure yet what, something even moreso than the coffee and four pancakes. Of course the waitress has given me the consumer warning, have you seen our pancakes, and I tell her I will take full responsibility. I want to take advantage and so I research the history of the Iron Range, Dylan, Italians, Slavic, Nordic, hockey towns, Fargo accent, Wellstone crash near Eveleth. The fighting here will be hard sledding in winter, but maybe winters aren't what they used to be.

We're to meet at the family home. The mother and father are there, too. But it might be awhile. First I'm gonna tackle Mount Strawberry-Walnut.

There's the landmarks, no other house in sight, the ridiculously worn sign for Hamm's Beer across the road, the big guard tree out by the old mailbox on the wooden post, a narrow dirt path leading from the gravel road, another large clump of trees and bushes, a larger tree seeming to grow out of the house, protecting the rear, the right flank exposed except for a large, neat garden. I pull in. I can see just the nose of a car peeking from behind the white house. It's grassy around, low brush, maybe swamp, not woods like a half mile away.

After I park I go to lock the doors and decide no. I hear the bugs first and then see them right in front of my eyes. A dog with its head down, tail wap-wapping, trots up to see me and I feel welcome. Crows tell them I'm here and a creek begins to bubble. There is movement in the front window, a curtain. I put a foot on the first step of the porch, going slow, paying homage to the reds, greens, purples, yellows in the flowers on both sides, surrounding the Virgin Mary shrine and the battered, wrapped in dirty plastic, framed, black and white photo of Pancho Villa on a donkey.

I make my way by clomps up the steps of the little cement porch. The inside door opens. A small young woman pokes her head around the screen. She smiles and says that I must be me. She opens the door wide and I see she is wearing a knife and a pistol on her sides as if she has been playing war in the backyard and a white T-shirt that shouts: Sobchak For President: Nothing Is Fucked.

We sit in the living room, thick comfortable '50s style chairs with flower prints. I smell something, exotic? And I feel the texture of the chair arms, so many things going on. I try to notice everything. Small details are fun and important. The young woman hurries to finish something she was doing, brings back a vase of new lilacs, offers them to my nose and I smell. I smile and say nice.

I'm making my notes, not daring to write, just making lists in my head that I hope I won't forget this time. The wood floor, oh, man, the walls of family photos. The exotic is ... candles burning, like church, and there is something hot cooking. I do not notice until now that I am running my finger around the flower print on my chair. There are stairs going up, going down, doors, so many wooden doors, headed practically everywhere. We talk, about the drive, the weather, the garden, and like a play the others begin to appear, sitting at the dining room table, peering around a corner, standing back in the kitchen holding a knife.

The back door slams somewhere off stage. I spot three more candles, very vertical, with Virgin Mary, angel, Jesus pictures. A recurring old friend of mine is present, the feeling that I don't belong here, that I am out of place, an imposter, need constant validation. Like someone who must lug around an oxygen tank.

I wait for the young woman to offer a soft drink.

She sits down opposite me, knowing I am here for her alone. She sits straight. Her hands are folded on her bare legs. I'm trying to see her tattoos. She gets up and walks over to show me, smiling. I smell bug spray.

As she sits, the man is there behind her, in the kitchen doorway, not tall, old, but solid, forehead and shirt spotted with sweat, thick grey eyebrows pointed right at me, staring, now nodding, going off to search for something in the drawer, nuts and bolts and screws clatter.

I can imagine what they will say. They don't want their children to die, to fight, someone else should, but they know when someone must fight. Sometimes interviews take an hour. That's how long an interview takes, but sometimes you just know it's going to be longer, that there is more to this than that.

Of course Mr. and Mrs. Zamora fought long and hard to get here, to this old rental in the middle of nowhere. Just look at their hands, their eyes, the lines running from the corners of the eyes off the steep cliff of sharp high cheekbones.

But I'm thinking that's pretty much where the once-a-year Cinco de Mayo feature story stops.

I point at one of her arm tattoos, the woman in the headscarf showing her muscles. I tell her I recognize that. She gets up again, comes over, leans down and shows me that under hers is one word: Muerte.

She also shows me her hand and looks right into my eyes. Should I look at her tattoo, her brown eyes or read the words on the palm of her hand, written in ink, spreading with sweat: *Talk later.* I nod. WTF? Okay. She sits again and we talk about the weather. I wonder. Her parents don't know what is going on? As she prances around the house wearing a knife and a pistol? While her brothers are gone? With fucking Pancho Villa in the flowers?

Let me show you the garden she finally says.

I nod, gather, try to hold all my shit and follow her, through the rest of the house, more wood floors, yet more candles, into the kitchen, a neat, nice '50s kitchen that I wish were mine and I were a child again, lots of whites and reds and greens and yellows, and bright vegetables on wood counters, fresh, strong smells.

The older woman, mom, I guess, grandma? almost smiles at me, but mostly averts her gaze. The old guy is gone. When we get outside there are bugs and lilac smell and the old guy way over there, fixing something with a tree. I later discover he is building a fort, an outer defense, in the grove. It will look like a deer stand that someone put a lot of work into, but it's not.

So, she says, now turning to invite me to walk with her.

We walk past the garden, but I notice. It's got stakes and the seed packages to show what is what, and no weeds and it's taken a lot of work and will take a whole lot more, but we move past it.

She is small, perky black hair, shorts, tennis shoes, no socks.

I picture the dead photos I've seen on the internet of Bonnie & Clyde, Che, John Dillinger, Butch Cassidy, Sundance, how they died in the movie, not sure if that was real, but anyway, Jesse James, Billy The Kid. They all die. They can't live in this world.

She finds the spot, the perfect spot, under a big tree, three comfy cane chairs, a circle of charred rocks with used wood in the middle. She points at a chair and waits for me. I sit.

"What do you want to know?"

She asks as she smooths an invisible wrinkle in her shorts as if she is wearing an evening dress for a warm summer night.

"Why did we need to come outside?"

"It's nice out here, so beautiful," she says, swatting bugs.

"Yeah, but your hand, don't they know?"

"Yes, they know, but they don't know everything. I don't want them to know. They can't know, but they are so nosey, so curious. If it were up to them they would go to the mountains. I won't allow it. Information is dangerous. They worked hard to get here, many years, they must live."

"Fair enough," I say and look around for mountains.

"Nice place."

"Livin' the dream," she says.

I don't know what to ask, and I panic, but I hope it doesn't show.

"You are nervous," she says.

There are a million things I want to ask, but what would be good enough, smart enough, relevant enough, enough to the point and ... she is too good, too good for me. We are not lovers, would never be lovers, can't be, but oh, my god. I would go to the jungle and die with a bullet in my stomach right now if she ... I look around for jungle and see a duck waddling straight toward me, not caring how fast it goes, just knowing it will arrive at its destination sometime. I wish I could think like that duck ... *aaand* I'm thinking too much.

"Why do we fight?"

She begins and I swallow.

"Why not have lives and allow the normal USA to continue."

I nod exactly.

She looks away and refolds her hands in her lap as she crosses her legs perfectly, easily. She has long, yes ... rifle earrings, silver. Just fucking amazing.

In order to concentrate superior combat strength in one place, economy of force must be exercised in other places. Economy of force requires the acceptance of prudent risks in selected areas to achieve superiority at the point of decision ... she recites and she has lost me.

She looks back at me and I don't think she realizes she has been talking.

"I don't know why," she says.

"It just seems like the right thing to do ... it is the right thing to do, don't you think?"

"If that's what you think? Is that what you think?"

"Yes. ...

"Yes, definitely.

"Yes, of course."

She moved her chair closer as if someone might hear. I looked around and saw her mother peeking out a curtain in the living room and her father with his head around the corner of the house. I imagined the rabbits and squirrels pausing from their frantic business to listen and eagles circling overhead, looking down.

I am in a unique position and I am trying to understand what I should do, she pretty much calmly explained as she sat there not speaking.

What white teeth she had.

I wonder if she is still alive.

"Yes," she continued, "I know more than most people. How does that sound? It sounds terrible. But I do, what can I say? I spent years on the internet, studying. If you do that, you will know. Most people watch TV and talk to others who are watching TV, reading newspapers. They say those newspapers and TV shows are controlled. Of course they are controlled. That is not a theory. Try being at a job, talking about things that matter. You won't be able to. It's money. People have to live, they like living a certain way and you can control how you think, what you say. You cannot control how other people give you their money for doing a job.

"But, I try not to hate people for being stupid. I try to be like Zen or something and accept what I have as a sort of gift and deal with it, with grace and humility, not hate.

"Does that explain to you why we do this? No, of course not.

"You think I'm crazy, you should talk to Blake. You have? Haven't? You should.

"Oh, that whole CRUSHER thing, you probably want to know about that, too, right? Yeah, the guys and their farting. I would just listen to them watching their wrestling and talking.

"They got such a kick out of farts.

"I am Fartacus.

"You make dumper stickers.

"Mr. Thunderpants.

"No. I am Fartacus.

"They also did serious things on their Men's Night, they called it. They watched *The Mask You Live In*, and they talked about what it means to be a man, and then they talked about wrestling and farting again.

"And they did this one thing, where they would put on their capes and they had this idea that if you stretch your arms out and jump out, parallel to the ground, just go for it, that you could fly. They'd all line up, put their hands out and then maybe one would jump, a little, but keep their knees in for cushion and nobody ever flew, but they wanted to."

Sometimes you don't have to talk during an interview. Some people just keep going. Some people, you have to ask them questions frequently, they just stop. But not Evangelina.

"We went to Walmart for their Halloween costumes. Sometimes they made their own, not that one year. And Gerry sat with me one night, in his costume, and he read me his essay about what he wanted to do.

"The essay. I remember it, parts.

"I want to, how did it go? ...

"I want to save the world and risk my life ... Oh, there's more, I don't know.

"So cool, I cried. Well, I knew that he would never do that. You are not supposed to say that. They are supposed to be able to have any dreams they want, but if you think about it for even a minute you can see that these guys are going to be watching wrestling and making fart jokes just like this ten years, twenty, thirty years from now, until they are sixty years old. That's just the way it is.

"We are their advocates, as they say. Their helpers, and if they want to save the world, we must help them. That's just what I thought. And what I should have done is forgotten about it, I s'pose, and gone back to school in the fall and put that essay — I made my own copy, you're not supposed to — in a bible and pulled it out thirty years later to show my children and maybe remember cute little Geronimo Gerry for a moment and then go back to our Slip N' Slide outside.

"But I didn't. I have rifle earrings."

She plunked one.

"And it goes on from there, I guess. I'm not sure if that was before or after we all were talking about revolution.

"Well, we just came from Camp Sweaty, before the Prince Hope action. We were all there for that, and then we got all that press because we had Hope up at Sweaty and were getting lots of volunteers who wanted to join. We had this whole constant, and I mean never-ending, conversation, dialogue, about beginning a shooting war, an actual revolution. Some of us figured the Hope thing would be it, that's enough.

"But Buster brought all these war books, military, textbooks, about generals and battles and flanks and fronts, and he kept talking about it and making us all read that. Hope even read it. He read some of the war stories to us. He's got a beautiful voice. He really does. I can see why he's famous.

"Camp Sweaty?

"It's a cabin, somebody's cabin, on a lake. I can't tell you who. It was their grandparents and then their parents and now them, her cabin, with some land. It's beautiful, there's canoes and a sauna, and a dock. Her family just always called it that.

"We used it for a training center, too, and swimming.

"We trained in the woods. We really did. We took it serious, tried to get lost, get un-lost, stayed out all night, did maneuvers, used walkie-talkies, somebody had a gift certificate from Christmas from Gander Mountain. We did pushups and learned how to take off your glasses first when you spray your face with bug juice. And we looked for Bigfoot sign in the woods, tree leans, X's. Not sure why, but we did that. Well, for a while there was some talk about staying in the woods, and being like the resistance that nobody knows about, that people don't know is really real. But then we didn't do that.

"It really all happened pretty quick.

"So, how did we really get started? With all this?

"Well.

"We decided to go to war. We talked about how to get guns.

"Wawakane. Try saying that four times fast. We had to, as part of our training, so people will think we're from around there.

"Getting started. That's the hard thing, isn't it? Once we are moving along at a certain pace, in life, a routine, that's when we don't want to adjust, to change. Maybe ... maybe that's why younger people are pretty much the only one's who would ever do this shit.

"Oh, my God, when I think of it ... attacking a July 4th parade, my God. I'm so scared.

"And then Gerry he always loved the Fourth of July Parade, the big trucks especially, fire engines, semi's.

"And we talked out around the campfire at Sweaty. About how sometimes you just have to change up your routine, your tired way of thinking, acting. Have to be like the fluidity of water. Try it, changing things, it's hard. In relationships and in life. There was so much drama going on, too, on top of it all. I don't know how we ever got started.

"But we did, eventually. Or we are. We are.

"We're getting there.

"It was those first guns at Sweaty. Jim and Buster and Korey brought them in the pickup, Buster's truck, never heard how they got them, some said they robbed a pawn shop, but I could never see them actually doing that, or they bought them, or they were Jim's uncles' guns, whatever, we had guns. And that's when it started to get real, you know what I mean? And bullets, lots of boxes of shells, bullets. We held them up, ran our hands over them, shoved our hands into the bullet boxes, ran our fingers through them. They were warm on top, cooler down below.

"Lebowski T-shirts? Yep. We all had brand new. Actually, that was something we waited for. We ordered them on a card on Amazon. The UPS delivered right to our cabin. It was like a little league team getting real uniforms, pretty cool.

"I love it," I said.

"Well, I'll tell you, we've got time, right?

"Okay then. One year I was in charge of planning the summer carnival. I had committee's and daily and weekly meetings and memos up the ying-yang, and I thought I had it all nailed down, but when it came to that day, it seemed like everything was going in slow motion and it all depended on me to get every little thing moving, the water in the pool for the duck thing, the bottle toss, pies in the face, sidewalk chalk, but finally I got a little help and we actually had the thing running for a while out there in the parking lot and people had fun.

"That's exactly what it reminded me of.

"And yeah, another thing, remember when you were a kid out in the neighborhood playing war? Running around, jumping fences, hiding in the deep grass, how fun that was? Well, at least for me, that's kind of what I expected.

"It's not like that.

"Once Gerry and I were sitting out on the deck. A fly landed on my arm and I swiped my hand, caught it, squeezed it and let it drop. Oh, the look in his eyes! He got down on his hands and knees and picked up that crumpled fly and poked it, trying to get it to wake up. He cried and I cried. I felt so bad.

"So, she said that about Narnia?

"We all read that in school.

"There never was a time when animals could talk. That's what they will tell you, what they want you to think.

"We really were fighting the empire. We were Gerry. We were all The CRUSHER, the little guy in his orange outfit coming out of his house in that outfit his mom made him, to take on the whole world.

"Except you were wearing Walter Sobchak T-shirts."

"Yeah.

"It was each of us alone against the army, navy, marines, air force, the Pentagon, overseas bases, military bases here, recruiters in every small town, billion-dollar defense contractors, American Legion, churches, Democratic Party, Republican Party, CBS, ABC, Fox, CNN, New York Times, every local paper, thousands of them, almost everybody in every big city and little town.

"There really wasn't anybody on our side, who thought like us, just us.

"But then, somehow we actually kidnapped Hope and people heard about us and we got to tell our story, and then we actually got this revolution, this war started up here. And we are actually going to attack a Fourth of July Parade in a small town in America.

"The news made it look like a little thing by a bunch of crazy people, like they do with that, like ranchers in the desert, you know what I mean? Yeah? You do?

"Well, we started loading up to leave Camp Sweaty. And I remember, maybe it was to keep our spirits up, we talked while we worked about what all that parade means, the wars, the stupidity.

"On Friday morning, last.

"The parade is next Saturday.

"And so we headed out from Camp Sweaty toward Wawakane.

"They've got the camp all set up. I'm going back up there soon.

"It's actually kind of beautiful. You go through small towns and the names of the stores have Italian and Slovak and other names. It's not just what you think it is. It's rolling hills and woods and lakes, trout streams, doesn't really put you in the mood to kill people.

"But, it's not Wawakane anymore. That's the original, first name, but then the town voted to change it to Lake Wobegon, officially. They voted and did it.

"That's the hardest part, by far, killing people.

"Nobody likes to do it. Well, maybe some, yeah, definitely some, but not most.

"You have to go through some real psychological hoops to get yourself into being able to do that. But if you don't, how else are you going to change things. You can't.

"Some of the guys had played football and they told us how the coaches got them in the mood, to be mad, to hate the other team, even though they probably didn't know anyone over there, maybe even had friends on the other team.

"Well, what you do is you make it like you are going to die almost, it's this or nothing. You don't die in a football game, probably, but if you were fighting somewhere and you were afraid of dying you would fight a lot harder, right? And you have to make it like your team against everybody, they all are against you and your team, that helps, too.

"And some of the guys, Bill, Jim, Lara, too, they were always reading, trying to figure this stuff out. And they knew that in war, usually the ones who are fighting don't want to kill the other guys and there is all this psychological shit that comes in, it's really interesting really. When people are actually put into that, what they do is they yell to scare the enemy, or they wear big hats or have banners or they pound their feet or have music or they chant. That's all because they are scared as shit themselves and they want to scare the other team, or whatever. And like, animals, if they fight, they don't want to die and nature doesn't want them to die, so they will like, ya know, bare their teeth or like a cat arches its back to make it look big, stuff that they do so they don't actually have to fight, and then there's submission. A dog will lie down, or maybe a lion, and then there's fleeing, running, that's another way to not die or kill.

"So there's all that shit and it's in you, you can't help it, and we know it. We're prepared. But it's not gonna be easy.

"So, yeah, you have to keep telling yourself there is a reason for putting your head down and charging at those other guys, trying to hurt them. That it makes a difference if they cross your line or you cross theirs."

Well, that's all Evey wanted to say. I wanted more, but in a way I can't blame her. She had spent a lot of time with me already.

She dropped her head and itched her finger like she wanted to wear it away. The more she itched the worse it got. That went on for a while, and I touched her hand and got up to go. I waved to her mother in the window and her father peeking around the corner. They waved and smiled, glad to see me go, I'm sure.

I walked away and didn't look back even though I wanted to.

Note from the narrator:

From "The Prince Hope Show" ...

Tonight's show is sponsored by "Razor Wire Dental Floss," for Americans. It's good for you, really.

QUOTE REMOVED BY ORDER OF DHS, UNITED STATES
DEPARTMENT OF HOMELAND SECURITY. [DHS US2FA]

SEVEN

Billy: syria is such a mess, cant tell rebels from ISIS anymore, as they defect. ISIS gassed the people it is thought. They confiscated the wmd gas from Iraq and used it on Syrians and Curds and rebels. Bashar Assad supported ISIS. Russia supported Assads election and now are 'supposed' to be fighting Isis. What a fricking mess!

Billy have you ever realized that you praise alternative media in an effort to legitimize the bad guys and delegitimize the good ones? Their 'word' is not gospel.

Islam has always planned to infiltrate every country, reproduce like rabbits, and take over the world with their Sharia Law. They are filthy, illiterate and lazy people, just like the so called Palestinians. They dont belong in the western world.

Steve,
I should have printed your longhand note yesterday, was too busy with my vodka and water.

Bill. It is my opinion that no U.S. president has had any real power since (maybe) Truman. Ike (no favorite of mine) warned and explained this. Since Truman the president is a mere stage hand, a symbol hired to reassure us in our myths about ourselves. All real geo-political decisions are made by the military-industrial corporations. They decide who dies.

Given this reality, Obama is my favorite symbol. Black, beautiful family,

41

great dignity. He could try to buck this system, he (and family) could die.

You ascribe to Obama powers he does not have.

Love to all,

                    S.

Well, I mainly agree with your note. Though I see the last president is JFK, who is strong. Truman for me is a man of murder, a murderer of   innocents. He let it happen without protest. We now understand Japan was trying to surrender, etc. So Obama is this. I see no dignity. His fake tearing for Sandy Hook was pitiful.

Yes, he can be killed, his family can. But he is with Big Oil. Not guts enough to risk speaking up for those at Standing Rock. Who are not even "illegal." At least Amy Goodman is doing that now. She has asked him to. She had been terrified at 9/11. I had liked her before that. Too, as said, I had liked Obama earlier.

Further,

                    Bill

Bix,

We are closer to World War III than I have seen it before. Read my last two Postings, to Steve and to Caryl. I said to Caryl, punch in Sane Progressive - YouTube.   Punching in Debbie's latest will then pop up many YouTube videos, very many there showing facts on Syria. Some great female journalists now.

The Truthers are winning. Are you not a Truther. I recall some years back, before your phone quarrel with Packy, your telling me of your bringing up to him that 9/11 is inside, and he responded as he does with his small sneer: I know that....

Yesterday Mike and Kelly were blathering at me. Kelly: Who do you know who believes like you!

I did not enable to finish many sentences in return. You know, I have hoped to get some backup with my siblings - maybe keep the noise down a bit.

The Obama administration is the most violent, conquering pack of fascists in the nations' ugly history. My siblings disagree. I wonder what do they think 9/11 wars are. I wonder what of decency do they imagine Obama has done. When Steve and Shade passed through, Steve and Kelly at least, agreed Obama is best US president ever.

Sure, I would like to talk with you, even without presence of any of my siblings.

I feel Choyota and I have to stay here, be safer here now.

Further,

Bill

Hey Bill,

I think I have not received your Postings the past few days though I did get your note asking about it. Who knows? I shut off nothing as I would not want to or know how.

I enjoy Caryl though she is perhaps a bit unhinged.

Aren't we all. Regards to all. S.

Steve,

This with the asterisk does not get its last word: Nancy says this is fixed - blanked by the postal stamp. Nancy your wife or Nancy Jean?

Either way. This morning early after punching in yesterday's on this subject from Debbie Lusignan, there is then made available just a lot of videos on the situation of Syria, Standing rock and etc., related topics.   Therein are many honest journalists of Alternate News, here and abroad. This is easy to tell. I am not going to remember names or numbers. TRUTH OF SYRIA is breaking through.   TRUTH OF STANDING ROCK. These are the same folks.

Mike and Kelly and I did an HEB trip to Borne just now.

Kelly said you agree with him Obama is our best president ever.

Alright. I had liked Obama. I could find no excuse for the drone attacks on unhostile civilians, 7 countries.

Mike and Kelly cannot speak to this. I know you cannot. Kelly said your recent visit you agreed with him Obama is USA best president. But, his second administration, I got off of that shit, Steve. Went to looking at 9/11, excuse for all this bombing non-combatants. I saw zero logic of claimed reasons. Real reasons is terrorism. Obama pretends 9/11 is done by these guys with box cutters. I wonder if this might even register in your mind. We 3 went round. They can't hear. Maybe you cannot. They want to blather all this at me, can't hear me can I get in a sentence.   Kelly Blackbird: Who do you know who believes like you!

I would begin. Bix (Bix's late mother is a Truther) and Packy are in the closet. I would attempt some statistics - Truthers are bigger in Europe but growing in USA.

I tossed in some politicos, Wesley Clark, Kusinage (sp), Ron Paul, Jesse Ventura. Willie Nelson. I can slip in a sentence, hither thither. UNHEARD ALWAYS, Mike Blackbird giving me his mad library equation of how aluminum can possibly penetrate steel and concrete. Remember 9/11 TRUTH IN 9 MINUTES? Naw.

This is nuts. Pitiful. Obama is a liar and bomber of children his entire term daily.

Asked Kelly did he yet believe Assad gassed his own people. Kelly and Mike believe it.

Why would Assad?

Because he is insane.

Mentioned what I got today from clearly honest and humane journalists at Alternative News. Steve, there are many. Educated, humane, real. Growing. Truthers are growing. I asked insane Mike Blackbird how he thinks I can study this over a decade and have my opinion.

Mike Blackbird: It is your pipedream.

Me: What for? What do I get from this?

Mike B: Pipe dream is like an opium dream....

Do I need an opium dream.

Talk of different languages. They had not explained why would Assad "gas his own people."

They live without explanations.

It is necessary to understand who benefits.

This tale is condensed.

Hard to get in any of my sentences.

Steve, I have been at this many years. I really do not know a soul smarter than I am, more objective when I need to be. My feelings are too subjective, that my very siblings are wantonly ignorant, believe I am the more ignorant.

Truthers gain ground past mind control. Happening by the day, maybe you should understand your sons will in time be no longer fooled. You should know about Europe.

If your sons have been, fooled. Thought Shade was interested. Maybe not this year. I sense Gabe is.

We will do as we like. I have offspring and they will not be owned. Coming on the 18th.

Past the Frogs, Bill

Bix,

Thank you to know you like this second EY, PACO. In my daily alcohol struggle I think End Times whatever, I should have in my Postings something going of focus though still Postings, and Packy is perfect. He needs to be the center, and let him complain, as the generally loose other Postings will in themselves continue. AY, PACO will all be kept, a seed, the kernel, for he is perfect. Hope he lets his desire for attention eclipse his paranoia.

Last night like three o'clock I reflected I did not know how to store anything in my computer. Never got back to sleep.

Mike Blackbird after dog walk sat in here to see about setting it up for me, but was too unfamiliar with my computer, kept saying he did not like my computer, not to matter I tried to inform him John helped me select it. Mike was taking it personally, and I would say Mike, this is not enemy soldiers, and he would hear the humor, chuckle then snarl and go at it. One time he called it "cocksucker," first time in my life I have heard him use that term. Well, if I am not too drunk when I finish this note I will call Madrea, who works in her kids' school cafeteria, is day and night busy attentive to her kids. Tell her about it, can she preserve Druthers, Dec. 6, and Characters, Dec 11, for me to not worry about losing the start of a potential book, AY, PACO.

Who-o, just took wine down the windpipe, been doing that. Never used to do that before this month. This week.

Anycase, Madrea does know a bit, and she and Cynthia and kids will be here soon, for a few days - she will be having to return to her job. I need to hear again when they expect to be here.

Further,
Bill

"Col. Andy Tanner: [*using a crude diorama, the Wolverines prepare for an assault on the Calumet Drive-In, which is now a Russo-Cuban Re-education Camp*] All right. Four planes. Cuban bunker, Russian bunker. Munitions dump, troop tents. Four machine gun bunkers. Back here by the drive-in screen are your political prisoners. We'll cause a diversion over here... cut holes in the wire here, fire on all these machine gun positions. The B-Group comes across this area in a flanking maneuver... and when you reach this bunker, you lay down grazing fire on this defilade. I think that's pretty simple. Anybody got any questions so far?

Aardvark: What's a flank?

Toni: What's a defilade?

Robert: What's grazing fire?

— *Red Dawn*

EIGHT

Well and so I left Evey there, with her parents, in that house, with her tattoos and garden and candles that will one night burn the house down. That's what waits for poor, honest people.

The Battle of Lake Wobegon: Well, I went up there to see it first hand.

Which I did, and I'm gonna tell you all about it, just a minute. I also stayed up there afterwards and talked to some of the people to get their take on it all, so we've got that, too.

Evey, she told me about how they traveled the almost vacant little highway to Wawakane in a caravan of vehicles. They left Camp Sweaty in intervals spaced ten minutes apart so they would not draw attention, but then there was hardly no traffic so eventually they all bunched up together anyway.

They were coming to Wawakane for July 4th, an old-time celebration.

They'd scouted ahead and went straight to the campground in City Park. There was another park out by the river, but it was out of the way. It would have given them some privacy for more training, but they didn't want to be the strange people way over there, so they thought being right in the middle of the action would be a better cover.

So that's what they did, found a spot for the pickup, cars, tents, pulled a couple of picnic tables together, had a fire ring, a grill, played Frisbee, walked down to the creek with their poles, all that stuff that people do.

Jim and Lara had found a University of Okoboji banner at a rummage or something and they strung it up between the pickup and the main tent.

They kept the guns put away.

They got there early and were able to watch people pull into the campground. They walked about in two's and three's around town to check things out. They saw a young woman running around with a clipboard over by the ball field and Kylie guessed that's where the parade

47

was going to line up. That was good to know and another woman over by the school was welcoming her helpers and getting metal tables all lined up for something, and there were some people in shorts, hats, carrying gloves who might have been getting ready for a game.

Reuben, Hector, Evangelina, Jim, Lara, Joe, Brooke, Ariel, Morgan, Zima, Kaitylyn, Sara, Korey, they were all here for this first one. They'd let Prince Hope go by then, and were actually hoping he would do his part and keep talking about them. They needed to get the word out and any publicity at this point was good.

Evey had told me that she made a point to find Brooke at this time, to get her alone.

She saw Brooke walking by herself over toward the playground and she followed. Brooke sat down to swing and Evey plopped into the swing next to her. They kicked their legs and smiled and the movement made it easy to talk, like I remember sometimes talking to my son when we shot baskets or played catch. I remember.

"So," said Evey.

"We're gonna do this."

"I guess," said Brooke.

"Umm, killing," said Evey.

"What!" Brooke shouted as she swang high, then skidded her feet to stop. Evey stopped with her.

"I said, you ever killed anything, shot at anything ... alive?"

"No, you?" said Brooke.

Evey said she had chopped heads off chickens and she used to blow up anthills during Fourth of July with Hector and Reuben. She said it quickly as she could to get it out of her mouth.

"Oh," said Brooke.

"Well, things will be better, if we do it, if we just get started. It's got to happen."

"I know, right?" said Evey.

So later — *this is after the battle that I'm going to tell you all about that I witnessed in person* — afterward, see, I went to the Koffee Kup café.

I knew the town was now rebel-free in the popular parlance, and there would be lots of folks willing to talk. Also, the local newspaper had already published the blow by blow battle story, so there were really no secrets, I didn't think.

So, yeah, I walked in and looked around and saw a table with a few older gentlemen, with an open spot. Against my nature I went right for them, asked them if they would mind if I joined them.

They said yes, and one of them asked me if I was a reporter here to talk about the battle.

"It's that obvious?" I said.

They all grinned and took sips of coffee, then set down the white mugs, looked me in the eye and waited on me to say something smart.

I asked if they were there, what is was like, things like that. They didn't mind talking.

"It was those kids down at the park," said Walt, the man in the blue "Veteran" ball cap.

I nodded and looked at the guy across the table, Fred, in the camo hunting cap.

"They started it all. I think they wanted a fight. They weren't here to celebrate. That's what I think."

The man directly across from me in the striped railroad cap just shook his head and stared into his coffee cup, which he had surrounded with both hands.

I asked him what he was thinking.

He looked up with sad eyes.

"I just never thought something like that would ever happen here," he said.

They told me all they knew as I sipped a coffee and finished off an amazing plate of eggs, pancakes and sausage. I thanked them and walked next door to the newspaper office and asked for the reporter who wrote the battle story. The front desk person said she wasn't in right now, but if I had time I was welcome to wait. I said, sure, thanks. I sat by the window, admiring the classic small-town newspaper shop. The young woman brought me the three editions of the paper in which the battle story ran.

"Thank you much," I said.

She smiled and returned to the other side of the front desk and continued her typing.

I began to read "War In The Northland," Three-part series, *Banner-Herald* exclusive, by Abby Inquvist.

The first story took up most of page one on the tabloid and jumped to two full pages inside. I was about halfway through when the front door jingled and a tall, fit young woman with long black hair in a ponytail bounced inside wearing a smile. She laughed and talked with the front desk person who nodded my way.

Abby said hello and invited me to her office.

Abby was the editor. She graduated from college and started at a smaller weekly, then came here as the sports reporter. Now she had two other young people as her reporters and a few older stringers from town.

Anyway, it's just interesting, the whole small-town reporter gig. I miss it. I really do. I could talk about that for a while, but I won't. Abby was very helpful. She told me all about that day.

"I see you already are reading the story," she said.

"Yeah, and I just want to try to get a feel for it by talking to someone who was there, if you don't mind," I said. "If you have time."

"Oh, okay," she said, looking at the clock on the wall, a big one, that you heard tick off each second.

She hurried out and said something to, Susan, I guess, out there and then clomped back with her long strides on the wood floor.

"I can talk," she said, sitting straight in her chair, folding her hands on her desk.

Abby kept referring to her story, but what I wanted to know were there things, I don't know, more things she could tell me.

She began rolling a pen around in her hands, clicking it like Morse Code.

Tina Tolleson, she said. She's a very good friend of mine, very.

And so now I turned on the little recorder I held and set it in front of her on the desk. I didn't ask.

So, Tina's home for the summer from college. She's studying to be an elementary teacher. She and Abby went to high school here together. They played basketball, volleyball, softball. Tina was working at a group home and also volunteered to organize the parade for the Fourth.

And Jeremy, she said, he's a single parent, two kids. His wife died in a car accident not that long ago. He didn't play sports, more of a gear head, liked to mess with cars. Now he owns a local bar and is kinda this up and coming town leader, a real doer.

And Rachel, she also told me about Rachel. See, this is the stuff I really wanted. Rachel was in charge of the pie-eating contest, blueberry, cherry, raspberry, all the really messy ones. She's kind of shy and didn't really want to be involved as the head of anything, but she loved to bake and actually, I guess it was Tina who got her to join in. And now, I guess, she was kind of loving it, getting to talk to everybody and plan things out.

And so, here we go.
I'm not that good at this. I hope I am not confusing you too much.

As I am writing this the battle has already taken place. I am sitting at home. I have my notes and I have talked to the rebels and to the boys in the Koffee Kup and I have talked to Abby Inquvist.

Now I'm going to tell you the story of "The Battle Of Lake Wobegon."
Well, what a beautiful day.

The sun comes up early, probably around five. Some clouds over there, way over there, but they would not dare to come over here, preferring to watch, from way, way over there.

The rebel campers are all up already even though they were up late, sitting around the fire, smoking cigarettes, nervously going over details. Then it was Evey who was up first, putting the old metal coffee pot on the still warm coals, getting that all going. She had packages of rolls set out on the picnic table in case anyone was hungry.

Brooke came out of her tent rubbing her eyes, putting her hair behind her ears like she did. She gave Evey a side hug.

Jim walked to the edge of their area, turned his back to pee. Evey laughed and Brooke told him, not here.

And so, the sun came up over the trees guarding the river. No clouds.

"Boom, boomboomboom ... boom, boom!"

And then everyone was up, crawling, charging, stumbling out of the tents and the vehicles.

"Fuck is that!" said Jim.

Korey was pissed that somebody else got there first. He thought that some other group had the same exact idea and now they were skee-rewed.

"Goddammit!" he said.

Lara said she would walk over toward where they thought the gunfire came from. Barb, Reuben, Jim and Kaitylyn jogged to catch up and go with.

Korey sat down to poke the fire with one of the marshmallow sticks, nibbling the end when he thought nobody was looking.

Evey worked on the coffee and re-arranged the packages of rolls so maybe people would eat.

"I think it was fireworks, firecrackers," said Korey when he saw the group coming back, across the field.

Lara was smiling as she got close, the others spread out toward the coffee and rolls.

"Peach?" said Sara. "Isn't that special."

"It was the thirteen gun salute at dawn," Lara said.

"They had uniforms, costumes, you know," she said, making a triangle atop her head.

"That's what we need."

"Oh!" said Kaitylyn.

She hurried away and came back with her arms full of the T-shirts, the bright orange shirts with the words: CRUSHER across the chest.

"This is so stooooopid," said Hector.

"Shhhhh-shoosh!" said Evey, pointing her finger.

Somebody groaned.

"I thought we were wearing Lebowski ..."

It had been agreed upon and discussed and now was not the time to have a problem with the fucking T-shirts.

"C'mon," Brooke motioned with the peach roll from Kwik Trip in her hand to get everyone around the picnic table.

Jim set down the big map of the town they had secured what seemed like years ago. He smoothed it over the rough table, gouging the paper.

"Shit!"

They went over the hammer and anvil strategy that someone had thought would be a good idea ten weeks ago.

"That's stupid," said Hector.

Evey shooshed him.

Hector stood up.

"Well, it is," said Hector.

"We don't need fancy tactics."

He used air quotes even though there was now an unofficial sanction.

"We need a plan," said Lara.

"We need to know what we're doing," said Kaitylyn.

Well, they were going to have one group kind of like charge at the parade and then another group would come around the side, in a flanking maneuver I guess. Nobody really understood it, but they never thought they would get this far.

Reuben stood up next to his brother and told the others what he and Hector had been talking about during the night, about how they really thought this should go.

Reuben stared hard at Jim.

"Dude," said Jim.

"I could give a shit. Let's just get this done."

Reuben picked up the pencil lying on the map and began to draw, arrows, lines, stars.

Tina jumped when the guns went off. Nobody told *her*.

She actually thought it was the fireworks box exploding or something. She dropped her clipboard on the cement.

People were already starting to come in through the gate to the ball field parking lot, so she's checking off names. She recalled asking Elmer Tuttle what was that? And then she checked his name and smiled as he pulled in with his Tuttle Realty float with the giant doll houses and all that.

Tina flipped her page and checked her list to find if she can accept any more entries, sixty-three was supposed to be her max, but then Marge Klancy called her last night and asked if there was still time to get her dance studio in, they'd been practicing all year, she forgot to enter, she thought they could just show up, I thought you just showed up? That's how they do it in Gilbert.

Well, that was not how they did it in Wawakane, Wobegon, whatever, but if she said no she would be on Marge Klancy's shit list for life. Well, she wasn't going to live here her whole life, so what did it matter, but those girls had been practicing.

For a moment she just stood there, in the middle of the big lot, full of rocks and dips, watching Elmer roll over all that so carefully so not to knock off any of the houses or the balls of spray-painted Kleenex. She thought about her mom, probably not awake yet, sitting back there with her dad, having to sit with him every day because if she doesn't he can't remember where she is and he gets scared.

And she wondered if she would see Tim today. He said he'd be here. He wanted her to ride with him in the antique pickup, and he wanted her to move in with him, into that two bedroom he just bought and fixed up, and stay here forever and run this parade for the next forty years. In lots of ways that wouldn't be so bad. In a way that would be heaven.

Tina smelled wood smoke and saw it came from the campground, that bunch of tents and vehicles, the art students from the U, here to draw the parade and the other stuff, for the project they got funded through the state arts council.

She smelled gun powder now drifting from the thirteen-gun salute, and blueberry pies.

She breathed deep and looked for Abby, who said she had to be there early to take pictures of practically everything.

"Toast is readyyyy!"

Jeremy stood with one foot on the steps to shout as he always did. He listened. Nothing.

"We need to get a move-on!"

"It's nice outside! Beautiful day!"

Still nothing.

Time to go nuc-u-lar.

"Your cousins will be there. You can enter the pie-eating contest I guess, I don't know. ... They throw candy at the parade this year."

He stepped down and out of the way as a herd of elephants clomped on the floor above and down the narrow steps, leaping, falling, sliding like rock stars.

They didn't throw candy last year because some kid in Pennsylvania had been crushed by a semi-truck.

First though, they had to go visit the graveyard, like every year. She died on the Fourth of July.

That could be why they didn't want to get up.

One giant drop of sweat ran down Rachel's cheek.

She stuck her nose into the air to appreciate the baking apple pie and cinnamon over-filling the already thick, hot air in the school kitchen. She stood for a moment in the middle of the airstream flowing from one open door to the other, raised her arms and closed her eyes.

Pans banged and ladles clunked over the sound of the radio tuned to the local station announcers already sitting on main street.

Rachel's helpers, all wearing the "Lake Wobegon" special T-shirt, laughed and hustled around.

Rachel's bare feet found traction by the moist flour spread around on the tile.

She went again to check her list taped to the yellow wall with plenty enough masking tape.

She checked her ovens and high-fived someone, wiped her brow with the back of her hand and moved to stand in the doorway to watch things. So much going on, well soon enough they would be right in the middle of the action. She went out to count her tables again, sitting right on the school front lawn. They were on a bit of a slant, but it could not be helped.

She had not heard the guns and she had wanted to, well next year.

Like an idea whose time has come, more and more people began showing up, walking, in cars, floats, wagons pulled by horses, little wagons pulled by children in cowboy costumes.

Rachel walked along the metal picnic tables, counting with her hand the spots for the contestants who would eat the pies, faces down, hands behind backs. That's how Rachel got her start in the celebration, as a kid, second place, raspberry, mmmm.

The rebels put on light jackets, hoodies over the orange T-shirts, not wanting to be too much too soon. They would carry their weapons inside their pants, jackets and carry rifles inside artist tripod field easel cases. Long folding knives fit nicely inside pockets.

They checked again the schedule taped to the wooden picnic table: Parade at Eleven, Pie-Eating at Noon, Ballgame at One.

"Time-check," said Blake.

"Seven, oh-seven hundred, seven in the morning, aye-aye, cap'n, " said Korey.

"Shut the *fuck* up," whispered Lara as she poured coffee for herself.

Rachel checked her time, her ovens, said hello to more volunteers, so happy, showing off their T-shirts.

She would be ready way too early.

Maybe they should have started at nine, or eight, but she didn't want to have to hurry, this should be fun, and it should be done right. Well, the pies would cool, for four hours. They would melt in the sun, disintegrate.

No, it would be all right.

Everything would be all right.

There had been a not so small controversy over the town changing its name.

Steve and Wendy, station WWKW, set up at the card table on the reviewing stand, across from the ball field and high school, had a clear view of Rachel standing in the doorway to get some air, Tina working the parade contestants in the parking lot, and Jeremy now heading over toward the ball field with a bat filled with gloves thrown over his shoulder, followed by two children taking their sweet time.

And, so, yeah, Steve and Wendy wanted to keep it all upbeat and came up with some trivia for Wawakane history.

"So, yeah," said Steve.

And he told about a postal carrier one time, or many times actually, see, using a horse drawn wagon. Her route was many miles and she did that through snow, too, see?

And then they milked that for as long as they could, ya know, asking people to call in or stop by and tell them how they knew that postal carrier or their grandparents maybe did.

Wendy told the story about the famous bank robbery. It wasn't right in Wawakane, but over in Duck Falls, about three, maybe four miles. It's a ghost town now, they have 'em up here, when a mine shuts down and the school closes, something like that.

So, well, the rebels they had to wait. At seven, seven-thirty they were all up and ready to go and the parade wasn't until eleven. They couldn't go sit there now, though some people did that, put out chairs to reserve a good spot, but usually just chairs, they don't sit in them all that time.

That gave them all the time they wanted to go back over the map and the plans and the different events going on, where to drag their wounded, how they were going to get away, what if they don't get away, what if they're all dead or captured. They even went back over all that stuff from the way beginning of why they were doing this and why they shouldn't just quit right now and write a group signed letter to their congressman or hold a sign in front of the federal building.

There was also all that talk in the newspapers about who were the kidnappers of Prince Hope and where did all the money go that they stole from him, and of course there was no money, and so they worried about that, too.

Kaitylyn wasn't feeling well, so she went and lay down in her tent, stretched out and went right to sleep, she had one of those air mattresses.

"Well, I s'pose I'll get the fuckin' fire goin' a little," said Jim.

"Why?" said Korey. "We're goin' soon, why?"

"Well ...," said Jim.

And so he didn't get any fire going, just sat on top of the picnic table working his phone.

Brooke and Evey and then Lara decided they wanted to brush their teeth so they took their plastic bags and headed off toward the school area, right across from the downtown, the radio station setup.

"Sorry, man."

Korey went over and sat by Jim.

Jim hopped up and walked away.

Brooke headed straight for the ball field. She thought that was where the smell was coming from.

Evey shouted, "Hey, let's go over here!"

Brooke kept going, not looking back.

Lara had begun her own mission, the three National Guard vehicles parked in a line in Tina's lot, a tank, a Jeep and a big truck.

"You guys sit here."

Jeremy, anxious to get the weight off his shoulders, let the bat and gloves down to the ground and pointed to the bleachers. His two children immediately squatted in the weeds and rocks, looking for bugs, as if they were bred for it, like retrievers for hunting.

"Hey!"

Jeremy looked back and saw Brooke sitting with them, picking up the colored rocks, examining them like scientists, then tossing them like grenades over the bleachers.

"Boom!"

Evey saw before her the entire battlefield she had been studying for weeks. The primary streets, the high school, ball field, the rolling hill gently leading to the high school. She saw vehicles, people streaming, headed like ants toward where they knew they needed to be. The sun had gained a substantial position with no clouds to be fought off, not yet.

Lara walked right up to the tank, stood in front of it with her hands on her hips.

A green-helmeted head poked out of the top.

"You're gonna have to move, ma'am."

Lara laughed.

"Ma'am? Where you headed? Move? Am I in your way?"

The soldier pulled out of the tank top, and in one motion removed her helmet, revealing dangling tank earrings.

"Nice," said Lara, tweaking her own ears.

"Thanks."

Evey saw it all as a canvas, a moving painting, a scene in a famous book. She put her head down and charged in, stepping right in front of a glorious float.

She stepped back, smiled and waved at the pickup driver pulling the flatbed.

Evey crossed the little playground and headed up the hill to the high school, where Rachel stood, hands on hips surveying the scene, not happy at all with the slant of the tables on the hill.

"Hey," said Evey.

"Hey," said Rachel, looking away from the tables for only an instant.

"What are we lookin' at?" said Evey.

"It's all on a dip," said Rachel.

"Yep," said Evey.

"This is for the pies," said Evey.

"Yu-up."

"And you can't have them sliding off the ends of the tables."

"Yup."

"Sooo, what can we do about it?" said Evey.

"We?"

Evey reached out her hand.

"I'm Evey, with the ..."

She pointed toward the campground.

"The artists," said Rachel, using air quotes, now looking back at her tables.

"Okoboji, I been there."

"You have?" said Evey. "It's a place?"

"Yu-up."

"You don't think we're artists?"

"I didn't say that."

"You did this."

Evey made air quotes.

"Oh, did I?"

"I want to have kids," said Brooke.

"They're pretty cool," said Jeremy.

Brooke thought about her short life and watched over Jeremy's shoulder across the street, way over past left field and beyond the chain fence where some guy was leaving his house and getting in his car, dressed in a suit, on such a hot day.

"Look at that," she said.

He couldn't see. The sun was bright. She described what she saw.

"Yeah, workin' on the Fourth, that ain't right," he said.

"I wouldn't want to."

"No," she said, "me neither."

"Yeah," said Jeremy.

Brooke hopped up and walked toward Jeremy. Her eyes were light blue, a little too focused.

"With all that's going on in the world and people just go to work like nothing," she said.

She stood close. He stepped back.

"I know, right?"

He tried to smile. He leaned his head to check on his kids around her shoulder.

"We comply. Wash the dishes, take out garbage, put on deodorant."

"Yeah, I know," he said. "Well, I got to get going."

"It's disgusting," said Brooke.

"Yep," said Jeremy.

He picked up his kids and put one on each hip.
"Okay, well, seeya."

"So, you're a, a soldier. You been to Iraq?"
Lara stared up at the silhouette on the tank.
"No, but I want to."
"What?" said Lara.
Tina walked over, staring hard at her clipboard. She stood next to Lara and shielded her eyes with the clipboard as she looked up at the soldier on the tank.
"You do?" said Lara.
"What?" said Tina.
"She wants to go to Iraq," said Lara.
"Why?"said Tina.
"Money, dinero," said the soldier as she began to climb down.
"An extra thirty thousand for combat pay would come in handy."
"Yeah, I guess," said Tina.
"And it's what we need to do," said the soldier.
"Right? We can't give in to terror."
Lara smiled.
"Terror? You don't really ..."
"What a beeyoooteefullll day!"
Tina interrupted.
She stretched her arms up as far as she could.
"Isn't it hot in there?" Lara asked.
"Yep," said the soldier, running a hand through her wet hair.
"It's double-time though, and I've never really been in a parade."
"Don't run anybody over," said Tina, moving away with her face in her list on her clipboard.
"That's the plan, ma'am," said the soldier.

"I wanted to go to art school in Minneapolis," Rachel said.
"Why didn't you?" said Evey.
"Just didn't work out."
So, Rachel told Evey all about her failed artistic career. Not failed yet, said Evey.
"You're an artist," said Rachel.
"What's it like?"
"No, not really. It's great, just great. How about we put them in a line?"
"No then they stretch out too far, everyone's not together. There's really no flat spot. It's just not going to be perfect."
"Yep."

Back at the camp, folks were beginning to gather again around the picnic table. The sun had climbed to ten o'clock. The chirping birds had spread out for the day.

"Hey, look at this."

Korey walked in with a poster of the day's activities. He found a tack on the picnic table and put it on a tree.

Two historical speeches
Thirteen guns at dawn
Bicycle, horse and foot races
Softball tournament
Barbecue/Beer Garden
Fireworks
The classic car show w. root beer floats
Corn on the cob, apple pie
Fire trucks, honor guard, high school band, dance team, guys in little cars
The honor guard
Choir

Kaitylyn scanned it with her finger and dashed off to the edges to both knees to throw up.

Evey and Lara walked back together wearing red, white and blue buttons that said "July 4, Celebrate With Us."

"Where's Brooke?" said Hector.

"We have to go, can't wait, show time. Move out!" said Jim.

Where is Brooke! I don't know! We have to go!

"Wait! Just stop!"

Lara jumped onto the picnic table.

"Everyone over here."

They walked her way and she jumped down.

"We said we would have a go, no-go discussion right before," said Lara.

"So."

They stood all around the picnic table, holding rifles, easel cases with rifles, handguns in holsters on hips, knives in sheaths on shoulder straps, orange shirts, shorts, camo pants, tennis shoes, boots, ball caps, no hat, bandana.

Some nodded, some just stared, some looked at the ground.

"Listen," said Evey stepping to the front.

"This is important. We have to each one of us say yes, or no. No voice vote. We said we would do this."

She pointed at Hector.

"Yes," he said.

She pointed at Lara.

Lara nodded.

Evey nodded at Kaitylyn.

"Yepper," said Kaitylyn.

Evey went around the group, looking each one in the eye, getting an affirmative from all.

"You," said Reuben to Evey.

"Me?" said Evey.

"Well, if Brooke isn't here, technically."

Evey searched the eyes for permission for this cup to pass.

She bowed her head and just stood there, breathing deep and slowly.

Others lowered their heads, some others looked around.

Evey looked up.

"Okay, let's go," she said.

"Let's do this."

Red, yellow and green chairs held spots for industrious folk on the parade route, a right turn out of the ball field parking lot, straight down Lake Street, and then left at Oak.

Steve and Wendy kept up the cheerful banter, giving away prizes every fifteen minutes, pouring on the trivia and announcing the schedule of activities and providing weather updates.

Rachel beamed as she set the last of the pies out to cool on the table inside the kitchen. Outside the tables were laid out in red, white and blue, with streamers and tablecloths and centerpieces. Volunteers signed-in participants and gave them their American flag bibs.

Tina jogged along the line of floats, checking the list, making sure everyone had showed up before she handed it over to Steve and Wendy on the reviewing stand.

Kaitylyn, Korey, Evey, Lara, Jim and the others walked up to the edge of main street and set out their red, white and blue plastic folding chairs. Korey laid his easel case with his weapon on the grass, pointed toward the street. The others did the same. Everyone had a case, everyone had a handgun on a belt, concealed under the orange T-shirt all ordered a bit too large. All carried knives and wore Bluetooth devices on their ears.

After they spread out over one whole section of the north side of the street, they divided up to play Frisbee.

Evey sat in her chair, working her phone, trying to find out about Brooke.

Jeremy kept an eye on his kids. Some friends running the concession booth had volunteered to watch them, but every fifteen or thirty seconds he made sure to be able to see each of them. He also had a list and a clipboard, checking off names for the Patriots and Redcoats.

The uniforms were awesome, red stripe and blue stripe, red hats, blue hats, red gloves blue gloves, shoes, bats, bases. The committee had gone all out and everyone was going to love it.

The teams spread out in the foul areas and the outfield, playing catch.

Abby arrived in the press box and talked to the person who was going to announce the game.

Brooke moved a chair to set hers next to Evey.

"Where were you!" said Evey.

"I was just here," said Brooke.

"There. I was just walking around, such a beautiful day. It's a shame we're all going to die."

"Don't say that," said Evey.

"I know, right?" said Brooke.

A Frisbee whizzed over their heads and landed in the street. They both jumped up to retrieve it.

"No, you. Go'head," said Evey.

Brooke sprinted to the Frisbee, skidded on the pavement, picked it up, turned and tossed it all in one motion. It spun and flew, curved and just like on the videos, a big dog jumped and caught it in the air and ran with it.

By now every space on both sides of the street was filled in two rows deep.

The rebels in the bright orange T-shirts hurried in, excusing themselves, to take their seats.

Steve and Wendy, behind their card table and microphones and piles of notes, stood as some drums rat-a-tatted and the honor guard headed their way.

Jim leaned forward to see down the street.

"Everyone get ready," he said into his headset.

"Hold your fire."

"Jim," said Lara.

"You are not the general. We've talked about this."

"Then who is?" said Jim.

"Practically nobody," said Kaitylyn.

"We've discussed this."

"Consensus," said Evey.

"Consensus fucking sucks," said Hector.

"I know, right?" said Reuben.

The drums rolled and the honor guard approached, four older men carrying flags, one not so old and one in his early twenties.

The rebels stood with the crowd.

Nobody would be able to reach a rifle then, but they stood anyway.

Tina stood sentry at the gate of the parking lot, holding each entrant until there was enough space.

"Okay, go, go," she said.

It was her goal in life that there be no giant spaces, but that there also be enough room for each float to get its share of glory.

Jeremy stood with the red and blue captains at home plate, along with the two umpires.

He dug in his pocket and found a quarter.

He held it up and turned it over so they could all see it was not a magic quarter. The captains and the umpires leaned way in to examine closely.

"Who's gonna call it?"

The red captain nodded.

Jeremy flicked the quarter as he had been practicing for the past ten minutes. It rolled over and over, gaining its apex, then falling.

The honor guard passed and everyone sat.

"Okay, now what?" said Jim.

A few of them leaned forward to see down the street.

Someone unzipped a case.

Korey thought about the revolutionary war. Jim thought about Che Guevara. Lara thought about the girls in the Manson family and likened herself to them and didn't want to. Evey felt her stomach rumble and Kaitylyn remembered what she had read about the Weather Underground and also about the Berrigans and what she had heard about non-violence, Ghandi, and she didn't want to. She just wanted this to be over. Whatever it's going to be, just be over with this part.

Without telling anyone, Jim raised up his easel to his shoulder and pointed at the Realty Float and the smiling man in the Uncle Sam costume in front sitting on an old barrel. The tall man waved and smiled and when he saw the easel case he lost his smile and fought to get it back.

Lara jumped in front of Jim and putting on a very fake smile asked him what the fuck he thought he was doing. She made a very public game of him and his easel case gun and he put it down and those around them laughed a little and wondered what that had been and then went back to watching the parade and oh, my, god, here comes the actual Lake Wobegon High School Band with the actual new name on the banner.

That is so cool!

Everyone stood again and the band stayed right there to play *God Bless America* and everyone sang along with hands over hearts and caps removed including the rebels with the sidearms and the knives, growing sorta angry and bloodthirsty.

Everyone must think reasonably well of themselves to keep going. People cannot think they are evil when they brush their teeth and go through all the things one has to do in a day. You have to think, I am good, I am doing good things, or you cannot go on.

And so Evey went along because she had been trained, and she had been one of the starters way back at the group home and she had her tattoo, and she couldn't think of everything right now because now was a time to focus and remember just a few things, see the ball hit the ball, but she knew what she was doing was the right thing and this thing had to be done because nobody else was going to do it and what the fuck else were they going to do, just become a part of this, it almost had them already, it all looked so good, the pies and the parade and the little kids and little houses and having a nice life and then there's the graveyard, what else do you need. I *need* this. I need *this*.

She took a deep breath and smiled at Brooke next to her and that didn't seem appropriate but Brooke grinned back while reaching up to tie her long hair back into a ponytail.

The little cars with the guys in the maroon fez's whizzed past and another band and bicycles and dancers and the bakery float and the Chamber, the school, and none of them seemed like they needed shooting apparently, so the rebels just sat and clapped, stood, sat down. Somebody went to get some of the free popcorn and carried back as much as she could carry in her arms.

What else is left?

Yep we should have done the honor guard.

Here, firemen.

Somebody shoot the fireman.

No.

Jeremy waited with his ballplayers watching the parade from the first baseline because they were ready to go, just as soon as this was over. They weren't going to wait for the pie contest, shit, we're ready.

Rachel and her crew lovingly cuddled pies in their arms and brought them out to the waiting contestants all ready to go, along with the photographer from the paper. The gooey winner shot would probably go on the front page. It did last year.

The Bluetooth mumbling was fast and furious by now.

What are we gonna do?

Who's got a schedule?

Shoot the announcers.

They are lame.

You got it.

No.

The National Guard trucks! There we go. Here we go.

The tank.

Jim. Shoot that girl on the tank.

You got it.

No! said Lara.

No. No, tanks.

"No tanks," said Korey.

"Is that supposed to be funny?" said Kaitylyn.

"None of this is funny," said Max.

So, yeah, now the classic cars, shoulder to shoulder, about ten deep, and then after that would be the church association handing out free root beer floats and that's about it.

But the world came crashing down now on Tina's shoulder as one of the cars would not start and this giant thing, this gap grew and grew in her parade.

Evey leaned forward and unzipped her gun case. She snatched the megaphone up from Lara's feet and walked into the middle of the street into the gap.

She drew the folded paper from her back pocket and flapped it open.

She stood facing the crowd, with her back to the opposite side. She appeared unsure how to stand.

Evey read the manifesto, the explanation of what was about to happen. It took ten seconds, as they had planned, too long for some, not long enough for others.

She then ran, she did not walk, back to her gun. She saw that nobody was moving, not the rebels, not the people. Time stopped. Only the old cars moved. They roared, in order to make up for lost time, they bounded down the street like old lions, because the fucking ice cream was fucking melting behind them and they had to go now.

At least somebody has to shoot.

At least we should shoot.

There must at least be shots.

Evey drew her rifle from her easel and it took her longer than she wanted. The gun was too long. It took too long. Everybody was looking at her, as if she were on stage, all playing their parts, happening in slow motion.

Slow is smooth and smooth is fast, she said in her head.

She stood and snapped the rifle to her shoulder. She aimed down the site as she had done a dozen times.

She placed the white corvette driver in her site and raised up, over his head.

Breathe, let it go, empty your lungs, consistent shoulder pressure, keep your head down and married to the stock through the shot, press do not pull.

Evey saw one horse raise up, children slap hands to their ears, old people reach for the ground.

And she saw where her bullet flew.

She ran toward the pie contest.

Lara and Kaitylyn grabbed her arms and pulled her back. Evey's legs kicked at the air.

Jim, Max, Jack, Hector, Reuben drew their rifles and threw up covering fire over the heads of the crowd, the floats, the reviewing stand.

Sirens cried out and lights flashed.

The National Guard tank turned around slowly and headed their way.

Rachel's blood mixed with the green, green grass, Christmas colors. She lay on her back, looking up, smiling, wondering what everyone was doing all around her, then she was tired and closed her eyes.

People ran away in groups, they cried, they screamed, they dived for the ground. One whole band hid under the ball field bleachers.

Two cowboys on horses chased after the rebels running for their waiting vehicles.

Abby and Tina sprinted toward the little slope at the pie-eating contest. Jeremy found his children playing with rocks by the concession stand, picked them up in his arms and fast walked toward their car.

Steve and Wendy, after getting down to the review stand floor when the shots began, crawled to their chairs and got back on the air, describing the scene.

The attackers, the terrorists are running from the park.

This is the city park, pretty much right in the center of Wawakane.

Lake Wobegon.

Yes, now officially Lake Wobegon, yes.

We can see them being pursued by two, maybe three men on horseback, one tank and now we see one police car, lights flashing, siren blaring, rushing after them.

It seems the attackers are getting into a line of vehicles waiting along the campground.

Three vehicles, four.

Five.

Yes, five.

And they are headed this way.

Get down.

Yes.

And now they are here, right here.

One went north on Highway 44, now two go that way. One straight, one south. All headed different ways.

That is what it appears like to us.

QUOTE REMOVED BY ORDER OF DHS, UNITED STATES
DEPARTMENT OF HOMELAND SECURITY. [DHS US2FA]

NINE

Caryl,
I cannot open up this one from you this evening, hopefully I can in the early morning. Or hopefully on the fourteenth. Though I doubt I am missing anything if I do not open it.

I have heard of this child torture for many years, and books have been written.

Now, "fake news" is a term from the Alternative News people, but lately the MSM who originally are the fake news are pretending this is their original name for Alternative News.

Alternative News should be sincere but this is a large body of journalists getting larger, thus among them will be many who do not understand or like all the others. Some are spies.

If you have no patience for Jim Kessler and his large gang of intellectual humanitarian friends, educated but sincere sorts, and he himself is a retired Philosophy of Science professor, whose subjects included Logic and yet Computer Science, then don't bother with my amigo Kessler.

I have for years heard of this from many other individuals - way before contact with Jim Kessler. I would hear this, and move on. Suddenly we have Pizzagate, which takes in the Clintons, the Bushies, and very many others. They believe in satanic power. Their scared flunkies have been giving us the original Fake News, for years, many years. And I ask, have you seen this fifteen year old girl talk, I had told you of her. Says she was kidnapped age of two. I have seen her mother talk. Her lame mother saying her marriage had crashed and she felt incapable in her emotional breakdown to take care of her child, thus the age two child was given to the mother of her poor spouse, however idiotic this is, people are often horrible idiots

67

you can agree. This mother of spouse was criminally insane and let the worse than criminally insane of child torturers buy the kid, age two, or says the fifteen year old who is visually traumatized from infancy, but yet, she can communicate, answer questions.

If, you were to look at this over many years as I have, we are joined in our shock and sorrow. I do know you.

My conservative brother Kelly tells me he is past year hearing of this, from his MSM. He agrees it is international. Interesting to me, MSM speaks anything on it. But now times we have muddy water.

Kelly and Mike and Bonnie cannot handle 9/11, Sandy Hook, Boston Bombing, bombing kids in seven countries entire Obama administration, and on and on. My siblings freak out on me.

I conclude: Ignore them, they must some day wake up.

Can the kiddie rape and torture and murder then cannibalism, in occults worshiping evil, be as some say ruling all else in a word of shrill horror, well, I think not. I am wanting to know. what this is. Understand, the philosophy of satanic rituals is it gives power to the broken soul.

Can James Kessler and his friends who speak passionately be themselves utterly insane? My sense... is they are not... utterly...insane....

There is no cash for them, no fame. Maybe Kessler and other intellectuals he knows are this year of 2016 one huge gang of crazies. There they go, running and shrieking down the street at midnight in their underwear, or something like that.

My sense is something awful for years and years has broken the boil, via the Net. The pus runs out the ripped mind of a species.

Evil, sure but we have to do more than label it.

And I shall try to get to this place you have given. Though it sounds like MSM jerks. We'll see.

Love,

Billy

Note from the narrator:

From "The Prince Hope Show" ...

Join us next time for "The Adventures Of Troy The Town Cop," when we will find Troy being called to a high school kegger in the woods and finding only a crashed '69 Chevrolet Lunar Lander and a lonely alien sitting on a stump singing "I Am A Lineman For The County," drinking Boone's Farm Strawberry Hill.

If I had a rocket launcher.
If I had a rocket launcher.
If I had a rocket launcher, some son of a bitch
would die.

— Bruce Cockburn

Time to take a shot, rise up.

— *Hamilton*

TEN

He sat tall at the window in a wicker chair, his long legs crossed, a coffee cup submersed in his lap, a third filled with red wine from downstairs.

Prince Hope looked out over downtown Saint Paul, at the people walking two stories below on the sidewalk. The window was open. He heard them talking.

This was his office. The whole building was his. Not the whole building, this half of the building. There was a wall between this half of the block and the other half, which was a warehouse for plumbing supplies, with loading dock in the alley. This half, with the corner office area looking out over an expansive four-way stop, was "The Lonely Lutheran Bookstore & Lunch Club" with the logo of the silhouetted man in the rowboat to show to all the cars stopped and all the people on the sidewalks.

Except there were not that many people on the sidewalks.

That was the problem.

Saint Paul just was not that lively some days, even Saturdays in the summer, even with the new baseball field and the fancy hockey stadium and the soccer stadium coming, well, maybe that would be the ticket.

Prince Hope swirled his wine in his white coffee mug that said "Lake Wobegon/Wawakane."

The downstairs front windows were filled with blackboards and colored chalk writings about tonight's special and also Hope's three biggest books: *Golf Jokes, Airplane Food Jokes*, and *When Birds Collide*.

He sat silently looking out the window while the rest of the people in the room waited.

Hope wore a straw hat, stylish beard, white shorts, white T-shirt, red tennis shoes, no socks. The shirt had a yogurt stain with signs of being dabbed with a wet towel.

I was there. My reporter's I.D. bounced on my chest. I stood because the chairs were all taken. I was in the second row. There were three rows and some in the doorway and down the hall.

We were there for any news of the beginning of his writing his next book, rumored to be titled "The People That Live in Hiding."

Prince Hope remained seated, facing the window, his legs crossed, his coffee mug of wine in his lap.

In the other chair, not wicker, by the window, sat Korey, from the rebel group.

At one point Prince Hope removed his straw hat, uncrossed his legs, sat forward, leaned in, indicating, apparently, that Korey should also lean forward, which he did.

Prince Hope actually put up the straw hat to conceal from us what they were saying, or if they said anything at all.

Then the hat came down, both chairs swiveled around, squeaking in Korey's case.

"Any questions?" said Prince Hope, looking around among us to see if there was anyone either he knew or respected, is what it looked like to me.

A young woman with black hair raised her hand and spoke at the same time.

"Shouldn't that be "who" lived in hiding?"

"But it's not," said Prince Hope, just as he looked back over his shoulder at something somebody said on the street below.

"Who is this?" someone said, indicating Korey.

"This is Korey," said Prince Hope.

"And what does Korey do?" said the woman with the black hair.

He doesn't *do* anything. He is. He is one of the ... and then he looked back out the window as if he was so done with this. See, none of these reporters believed that the people who lived in hiding, well, it was going to be this book, but it was also ... a thing. That nobody believed in, but it was still real. Ask someone about it and they know what it is, but they don't believe in it. Like that. And having Korey sitting there was like having Bigfoot sitting there.

And so, yeah, Korey started to talk.

And at first it was like Korey was a traitor to the people, that's what I was thinking, but then I knew, or I thought I knew, that he was there because the people wanted to be known.

And so he told the story about Geronimo, Gerry, and the group home.

"But why are you talking about them? Didn't they kidnap you and hold you for ransom? Why are you on their side now, Mr. Hope?

"I'm not. They should be stomped out like bugs, of course," he said as if he meant it. "But they do exist and people should know that as well."

Korey scooted his chair to be closer, and then he stood, and he smiled and he talked to people while Prince Hope remained sitting and watched for a while, then turned his chair around to the open window, his straw hat shoved back on his forehead.

Korey told all about the young people who worked at the group home and how they got started talking about revolution and they were inspired by Geronimo and then how it evolved and they kidnapped Prince Hope.

"Aren't you afraid of being arrested here?"

There were a couple of older reporters there, wearing like beach clothes, sandals, big guts, not that much hair. They were standing together and like giggling. I was standing close to the one, and I heard him making a moo sound like a cow. An inside joke, I assumed. And that made the other guy laugh.

"Yep, a little."

And Korey, he started to talk about one of the group home workers in particular.

"Moooo," went the other guy, not the guy I was standing next to. And then it broke loose like dawn into the barn. Moo. Baaa. Horse whinny. And I watched Prince Hope, and of course it was confusing Korey. But it seemed not really connected to right now, to this, but more of an inside joke going back decades. .... And when Prince Hope whinnied for a brief moment like a horse I just felt completely dejected and out of the loop and not part of the group.

"One who gets out of going to workshops, other things, he just likes to see what he can get away with, while others just hope to be able to cling to their jobs and their lives for a while longer," Korey was giving more information than we wanted.

"And he was working with Gerry in the shred room, where they shredded documents and then the workshop gets money from the different businesses.

"And Gerry found this one, thing, some stuff that wouldn't go through the fuckin' shredder teeth they had to show to whatever fuckin' staff was workin' and turn it over. Well, this was like a receipt, a document with a bunch of color and Gerry could have shred it I guess, but he brought it over to Jim just to fuckin' show him, ya know?"

Comes now a remnant moo, probably the last one.

"And it was a red, white and blue boarding pass for American Airlines, and it's fuckin' Flight 77 and it's for fuckin' Sept. 11, that fuckin' year."

"Two-thousand-one?"

"Yeah, yeah. And Kaitylyn was like, do you know what this is?"

Prince Hope looked around to look us over, our eyes, to see if anyone got it, the nut graph, then looked back out the window.

And then some reporter asked Korey to explain guerilla battle strategy or some shit and the whole subject got like immediately fuckin' changed as Korey went into talking about minuet ambush strategy, constricting cordon and triangular defense.

Where is the ticket? I asked.

Again.

Oh, I don't know, maybe he's still got it.

Who? Who's got it, the ticket.

I don't know, maybe Gerry, said Korey as he began to gather his things for exit. He looked around, over the shoulders of the reporters, still hoping to get away clean it seemed.

I raised my hand and my voice to ask another question and Korey excused himself and sidled past. I thought at that moment that I could just put out my foot and trip him and wondered where that thought had come from.

After Korey crowded through the journalist gauntlet we all looked to be going as well, but someone noticed that Prince Hope still sat at the window looking out onto the street. It looked like the reporters in front were staying and then because the rest did not want to allow them their scoop we all stayed, found what chairs we could or leaned against the walls or stood, again, throughout the little room, the doorway, down the hall. Except now those who had been in the hallway had decided they had had enough of that shit and stepped into the room making things even more intense, like a pen of some sort and I felt an unstated moo remaining in the air.

Prince Hope sat there as if he were alone, or a painting.

And when he did turn around he did not appear shocked to see us, or annoyed, but more as though we weren't really there.

Someone asked a question about the new book, and another asked if the underground tunnels really did exist and how could they live there, you know.

"Have you heard about the Vietcong?"

Prince Hope looked up and at that particular reporter and then away again as if he had answered that question now and for all time.

Hope worked at a little desk, John Kennedy in the oval office, and we were his little children allowed to stay if we will be as quiet as mice. We listened to the rustle of his straw hat, the scratch of his pen. And you could tell definitely that he was now pulling his bare feet out of one tennis shoe in order to use the barefoot to scratch the other calf.

And then he pushed back and smiled, for what reason we all wondered I suppose. He apologized for us standing and tried hard to find a way for all to get comfortable.

He told stories ... about his capture, imprisonment, kidnapping as if it were one of his made-up stories of life in Minnesota.

He talked about the native way and I wondered if he possibly had some native in him. He told about how Bigfoot is also a known unknown and noted some Ojibwe list of spirit animals.

"Pancho Villa," said Hope.

"The man, the myth, the legend.

"He was a peasant, wasn't he? An unlikely hero, legend. He was a klutz, a stumbler. But he had big ideas.

"Traffic like a buncha bees.

"The kids said that was one of Gerry's great sayings.

"Their brigades have names and costumes, named after clients, not that they are violent or would condone killing, but to honor them. They used to get together to watch WWE and that's where we got the names."

I quick asked for more about the airplane ticket and scribbled down what he said. He said he didn't know anything about that, but that was strange, I thought, because when he was their captive up there for all that time, it sounds like they talked about everything. He even did shows for them, told stories, sang songs, told jokes. That's what I heard.

And then Prince Hope stood in front of his desk and stretched like he was in his own bedroom.

He yawned and scratched and scrunched his face and told about his own perceived megalomania, how he has a theory about how he only does things because he needs to be big, the rush, just to overpower his sense of not being enough.

He sat.

And he told about the rebels as if they were friends and he wished them well as if he kind of hoped their revolution would succeed and this all came tumbling down. But then he also added that he was sure the police would appreciate any help we might give in aiding with their capture and imprisonment.

And we kind of thought we were done, but then he leaned back, way back, crossed his legs, and he looked, no, not really at all, like Mark Twain, with his white shorts and straw hat and the lazy Saint Paul downtown meandering in the background like a river on a hot summer day and you just have to try to appreciate it for what it is.

"Well, they all worked at this group home, or a couple of group homes, maybe same company, maybe a couple of different companies, I can't remember."

He pushed the hat back with a thumb, inviting us along on a journey that we could either choose to believe or not to.

"They, or some of they," he began, and for a while, thankfully, a short while, he affected a drawl that came from who knows where, but no matter, soon he tired of that.

"They believe the whole war on terror is rooted, rotting in fakery.

"They also believe you can't win a fight you are not in, and though we are all so accustomed to sitting in the watch seats, it should not be unheard of to climb up through the ropes and enter the ring, feel the real canvas in your souls.

"Well they are Super Heroes, Marvel, DC, but they don't know how to sell it. They completely lack any art or acumen in marketing for either marketing's sake or the greater good.

"But that's what they pay me for, as the man said. No, that's just not true. They have nothing.

"I'm telling you about them so that when they are caught, captured, corralled, when we, I, get our man, that it will not be on page six. It will take considerable effort and expenditure and it should not go for naught.

"There are many, but only a few what we might call leaders, I suppose.

"And there is no general, of that I am certain, having observed them for some three weeks and more. It takes them that long to decide who should go to the store for coffee, why it is good they should go and which route to take.

"Anyway, Jim. He robs banks. That's what he wants to do, that's why he joined I'm sure. He wants to steal. Yes, from the rich and ostensibly for the poor, but largely just to steal. He talked a lot about Jesse James, Bonnie and Clyde, Dillinger, and I believe, I know, after some three weeks of day-long gab session, that he saw himself as a populist hero, though he could not have used those terms.

"Well, at least I can give you the names, some of the names. You know, writers, reporters, that is, are not wholly useless. Without reporters how would the people in the east have learned of Geronimo. The first one. Right? Think about it.

"On to Lara. Good friend of Brooke. Very funny in a quirky way. Brooke not Lara.

"Korey. Well, he talks in question sentences. If you know what I mean? And he actually said once without apparent irony that he was destined for great things. I was sitting with him and a roomful of young women at the time and I just wondered to myself if I could imagine any woman ever saying that.

"Kaitylyn.

"Small as the name suggests.

"She worked at the group home and also a restaurant, in Northeast.

"She made the chalk menu there, many-colored chalk, very creative and was asked to make the menus of other diners as well. Not sure if she ever did. You will have to ask her, though you would soon be asking a short, perky little cadaver, in my opinion. *IMO*. They have their own texting shorthand that they liken to Samizdat. I doubt it's that original.

"Kaitylyn, Kate, said she had seen me once at her restaurant and that we talked. I don't recall.

"Oh, yes Brooke. Long hair, plait, stunning.

"Why she would waste her life. She had evidently read a book. And so now she believed in this massive schism, in time, a space between the United States pre-JFK murder and following.

"Whatever I suppose.

"She was always taking notes and so some told me, in confidence, they thought she was a spy and I told them right out that no spy takes notes right out in the open and then I told them as we both poured skim milk on our cornflakes at midnight that for sure I was a spy and if I ever leave here I am going to tell everything I can remember, to everybody. But they still let me go and here I am telling you.

"But Brooke, well I guess by and by she really is a spy and I say good for her.

"American culture after the JFK murder, nobody sits on front porches or goes bowling ... some shit like that. She was always ... taking notes ... people thought she was a spy. I don't think spies just take notes? Do they?" And he looked right at me.

And at this point I started to look for seating.

"What should one say about triplets? Evangelina, Hector, Reuben. Quite a lot.

"Evey is at home now, that's what I have heard. Hector and Reuben in the Iron Range Mountains, yes, Virginia. The Embarrass Mountains. And when I asked ... I think it was you ... about the Vietcong that's what I was referring to.

"How's that?" he smiled from under the straw hat, with sweat covering his forehead, and we understood and we thanked him and we left, though it took some time. On the sidewalk I looked up and there was a brim of a straw hat with the hint of a red band, facing out onto the street – looking at the bank across diagonal – the time and temp because he left his own gold watch at home – or he had given it to the rebels.

When they come to your front door, how you gonna come, with your hands on your head or on the trigger of your gun.
— The Clash

The death of a single human being is too heavy a price for the vindication of any principle, however sacred.
— Daniel Berrigan

I'm wondering where the lions are. — Bruce Cockburn

ELEVEN

Some reporters get breaks along the way, certain things that make a career. Some reporters push and make those breaks happen, and I suppose some are chosen and some just stumble into the door at the last moment and find themselves at The Last Supper when things are happening. I think this is what happened with me.

After everyone else left, I realized I had forgotten something. I hurried into the store and up the wood steps down the narrow wood floor hallway to his tight little room and he was still looking out the window.

But now he was standing. And Korey was back in the room as well as a couple of others and they were talking. I started to interrupt them to ask about my thing, whatever it was, I forgot as soon as I got there. They looked at me and then away and kept talking and I sat. They looked at me as if I was the younger brother and I was here every day and they were bored with me.

And for a while they, the people in the room just muddled around, like housemates in the morning, not talking, just doing what they did.

The hallway door opened, inward, and I actually sat up straight and scooted my wooden chair over the wood floor, back up against the wall.

And in stormed four guys in suits. They looked like pissed-off salesmen, storming into the house to demand to talk to dad about some damn insurance.

The four sat down in front of the desk. The other two stood against the wall and Prince Hope turned to talk to them.

I thought for sure Prince Hope was in big trouble. Maybe that was why I was here. Somebody was going to tell the story about Prince Hope's pedophilia or his tax fraud or his real estate market manipulation, and I don't really do complicated stories.

Korey had been in the corner and now he came out to stand next to Prince Hope, both silhouetted by the bright light of the fucking window.

"There never was a time when animals could talk, Narnia" ... we read those in third grade. We all did."

I recalled the words of Lara as I sat there, the fly on the wall.

"So, yeah," said Prince Hope.

He nodded at Korey and Korey sat down as Prince Hope once again turned toward the window, perhaps lamenting he was not a stoplight or a traffic cop. I don't fucking know. He just loved that fucking window.

"So, yeah," Korey said.

And he began to talk as the four, like choreographed swimming pool swimmers, removed little notepads from their jackets and began to take notes.

He told them all about the revolution, the group, how they started, what they had done, what they were going to do.

I couldn't believe it.

I didn't want to, but I wrote too, frantically, trying to keep up, but it was mostly a review so I stopped.

"He's like Pancho Villa," said Prince Hope to the window, as if talking through a headset to the young woman down there on the corner waiting for the light.

"He's a stumbler, a klutz, but he has big ideas."

Korey looked back over his shoulder and the four looked up for a brief moment, pausing their pens and just like the sun momentarily peaking out from the clouds, they returned to staring intently at Korey as he spoke.

Korey stopped talking.

The little notebooks, blue, green, red, I remember, went back into the inside pockets of the coats.

The two against the wall left, the four, Prince Hope along with Korey and there I sat.

What the fuck?

I sat there, wanting them to get a lead, and forget about me.

I got up slowly, looking back at the door, walked behind the desk, looked on the desk at the scattered notes, crumbs, pens, cups, with music playing in some loose ear buds, buzzing, connected to a grungy iPod.

I turned toward the window and looked out, and saw Prince Hope walking alone across the intersection, on the green light, his straw hat, his red shoes, white shorts, long strides.

And I saw a small black man sitting on a white five-gallon bucket, banging on two other buckets.

That night I watched Prince Hope on The Night Show on my hotel television.

He came out and sat on the sofa, in his white suit, red tennis shoes, his big beard and long, sleek, coal-fired black hair, with the same straw hat.

He joked back and forth with the host, told some inside jokes.

"So, yeah," said Troy or Brad.

"Yeah," said Prince Hope, messing with the hem of his pants.

And the crowd wanted to hear about the kidnapping, the imprisonment, the torture, that Hope had endured as a prisoner of CRUSHER.

You could hear the studio crowd pushing forward, the crush of corduroy over the seats.

And they both just kind of looked around.

Troy or Brad nervously smiled and Hope stared, then looked out into the crowd, into the camera. Troy or Brad looked at his desk, probably at the notes on his desk, what he had coming for the next commercial break. He looked around, at his producers, very close to panic.

Ask the question, everyone in America screamed inside their heads.

But Troy or Brad did not have it in him.

"What about your capture?"

One man hollered.

Troy or Brad pretended not to hear.

Prince Hope heard all right, but still messed with his pants, probly stalling for the break.

"C'mon!" another male voice called out.

"Yeah!" shouted a woman.

And then the chorus rained down.

"Tell us!"

"We want to know!"

"Cru-sher! Cru-sher! Cru-sher!"

The chant filled the studio as well as ten million living rooms.

Brad or Troy grinned and shrugged his shoulders.

Prince Hope smiled.

He raised both hands to quiet the ruckus.

"Okay!

"O-kay."

And he told the story I've already recounted about being abducted from the theater into the alley. And then taken on back roads.

"Blind-folded," he added, as if it were cliché.

"They must have seen a movie. They do not read books."

The people laughed.

To a cabin.

He used air quotes, as people do.

"Really, a trailer.

"And kept prisoner."

"For over three weeks," added Brad or Troy.

"Yes," said Prince Hope, "three weeks and some odd days."

"Very odd days," interjected Troy or Brad.

"Yes, very," smiled Hope.

The people laughed.

And so, yeah through the next three breaks and probably during the breaks when the cameras weren't on, he talked to the audience, even getting up to walk around and talk, he recounted the long days of his imprisonment by the rebel group called CRUSHER.

He told stories about the tedium, helping to prepare three meals a day without really adequate utensils or supplies, sitting in the same kitchen, playing cards, talking to the same people, some other few who came and went.

"You do get to know them," he said.

"They become friends (air quotes), of a sort, I suppose.

"But they are still terrorists. They each and every one deserve the death penalty or life in prison if they are not shot in the wild, for what they did on the Fourth of July."

The crowd stood as one and cheered.

"Six-four!

"Six-four!

"Six-four!"

"It's actually the seventh month," Hope raised a hand and cut in.

"Seven-four!

"Seven-four!"

And then Prince Hope led them all in singing *America The Beautiful*.

Tears flowed down Brad or Troy's cheeks as he pointed a long, straight finger at camera number one to take them to break.

Note from the narrator:

From "The Prince Hope Show" ...

Now we ask that you sit back, relax, maybe enjoy some popcorn and a beverage, and listen to another episode of "Steve and Sally Storm: We Were Weathermen."

"We Were Weathermen" is sponsored by *Global Warming Popcorn* — just put it outside. You don't need the microwave anymore, with *Global Warming*.

Get a butt-load of *Global Warming* today.

What is so important about this that after 50 years they have to keep making this effort to cover it up?
[Barrett]

[Pepper]
Though individuals have passed away, nevertheless the agencies survive. The agencies of government that function on the basis of public credibility and public funding for their work continue to require that their credibility be maintained, sustained, enhanced because they continue to serve the interests of the ruling class in the society. If the ruling forces are to continue and be perpetuated in power in the way that they have been for so very long these agencies are there to make sure that that is the case, that is the way, that is how their rule, their control is perpetuated, and if the agencies who are doing this come under attack and lose public support then the whole system begins to shake and begins to perhaps come apart at the seams and begins potentially to begin a revolutionary atmosphere within the society itself.
— Dr. Kevin Barrett, William Pepper, on No Lies Radio

TWELVE

"Why are some people poor?"
"Because some are rich, colonialism, industrial revolution, breakup of feudal system where farmers, peasants were protected."
"Just like Max said."
"No, that's not it."
"What is it then."
"I don't know, but it's not that."
Are you going to sit there?
Yes.
For how long?
A long time.
How long is that.
Depends.
On what?
Your idea of time.
You are crazy.
We are digging tunnels. Holes in the ground. Rabbits.
Rabbits don't do that.
Yes. They do.
You know this or you believe it?
Does it matter?
Shit no, with you, it doesn't.

Hector and Reuben sat in the dirt or rather to be specific Reuben knelt in the clay throwing a short shovel back over his shoulder and hurling it like a javelin into the bank.

They smelled the pine thistles, heard a plane, feeling a bit sick and a bit giddy, everyone was after them, everyone knew about them, how could they not find them, right here, in about two seconds.

It was their charge to dig, dig, dig. It had been planned and talked over earlier and this was just how it would go.

They would build tunnels and fight this part of the war like the Vietcong. They had plans and diagrams of the old VC tunnel layout, how they had sleeping areas, ventilation, and meeting rooms and even kitchens underground.

And so they knew it could be done, and it was a proven way to beat the United States.

So, yeah.

If anyone finds them they are to say they are digging for agates or they are to shoot them. Their rifles lay in the grass close-by.

Hector tossed clay and sticks at Reuben. He farted. He lay on his back and imagined what the clouds looked like.

So, yeah, I told you about the buried treasure, right?

Yeah, you sure did.

No, really.

What treasure?

Hector took out his wallet and pulled out the treasure map.

That's a map?

It's not even old.

Pretty old.

Hector smoothed it on a rock.

"This treasure."

He pointed at the "X."

"You never told me, said Reuben.

"I'm telling you now."

"Why didn't you tell me."

"Why do you have to be difficult."

"Really, man you have a treasure map and you don't tell me.

"It's not real."

"How do you know?"

"It might not be real."

"Yeah, but it might."

"Yeah, it might."

They sat awhile on the palms of their hands.

"How'd you get it?"

"I can't tell you."

"Why can't you tell me?"

"Who can you tell."

"No, not just you, anybody. I just can't, that's all."

"No, that's not all. Why can't you tell me!"

I said I wouldn't.

Said to who?

I said I wouldn't say that either.

You are pissing me off.
I'll let you have half.
Half the treasure?
No, the map.
Which half.
Just half.
It doesn't matter.
Maybe it matters to me.
Okay, that's half.
That's not the half with the X.
I know.
Okay.

They both started to dig with the two small shovels made for foxholes.

Reuben looked and then Hector looked at the X on the map, as if at a blueprint.

They heard flies buzzing and swiped at the sound, smelled the sweet thistle and grinned at the purple flower. They looked up at the drone of an airplane, around at the buzz of highway traffic, wiped their foreheads with the backs of the hands and imagined SuperSize Pepsi, with automatic refills.

Reuben adjusted his digging a little bit. Hector kept going the same way he had been, for a while, and then angled his chops and scrapes and lunges to coordinate with his brother, who he thought was going a little kittywompus, but he wasn't going to mention it, at this time. *Let him go the wrong way, the treasure will be mine.*

In that faithful heart are you forever 19
Or are you a stranger without even a name
Enclosed then forever behind a glass frame
In an old photograph torn, battered and stained
And faded to yellow in a brown leather frame.
                    — The Greenfields of France

In Latin America, the bearded men who took to the hills in the early sixties were still there in the late sixties, but they had advanced no farther. They controlled mountain tops; the governments against which they fought still controlled the nations; no cities had been encircled ... unable to take over the country from the countryside, the guerillas of Latin America and Asia are now devoting more attention to the struggle in the cities. ... in recent years, guerillas have battled government forces in the cities of Algiers, Amman, Belfast, Calcutta, Caracas, Dacca, Guatemala, Montevideo, Quebec, and Sao Paulo. Other cities throughout the world have experienced milder forms of violence while some, like Santo Domingo and Paris, have been the scenes of full-scale urban uprisings.

No great theorist of urban guerilla warfare has yet appeared. There is no Mao of the city. Carlos Marighella, the leader of an urban guerilla group in Brazil, wrote a manual for urban guerillas, but his death in a gunfight with Brazilian police prevented him from demonstrating that the principles he described would work. Urban guerillas can offer few successes to be emulated by other urban guerillas. They have not taken and held a single city; they have not overthrown a single government. Urban guerilla warfare has not yet been shown to be an alternate means of seizing power. In the absence of any renowned living strategist of urban guerilla warfare or case study of a successful takeover, I have tried myself to distill from a variety of experiences and accounts a strategy by which urban guerillas might take over a city. The struggle could take place in five stages: the violent propaganda stage, the organizational growth stage, the guerilla offensive, mobilization of the masses, and the urban uprising. Each stage is marked by different objectives, targets, and tactics.

(... in conclusion, pg. 18)

... *To fight in the cities, guerillas* must develop an urban strategy. What I have described from the guerillas' point of view is of course a textbook model. It assumes organizational development and a single-mindedness to pursue their objectives that is not yet apparent in existing urban guerilla groups. Some individual, or some group, must develop a practical doctrine and demonstrate that it can be implemented successfully. In the coming decade, the action is likely to be in the cities. We must not overlook both the possibilities and the potential threat raised by urban guerilla warfare.

— Brian Michael Jenkins, *The Five Stages of Urban Guerilla Warfare: Challenge of the 1970s,* July 1971, The Rand Corporation

THIRTEEN

I asked a lot of people about Jim's bank robbery, that's what they called it, why it happened, how, when, so what follows here is sort of a composite of all of that.

It was after July 4 ... 6/4 is what the media was calling it I guess, yeah. And as with most everything else that was happening in those days, early days, all part of a general plan they'd come up with during the planning. Yep.

Jim wanted to go it alone, though there were others who kind of liked the idea, too, I guess.

He'd picked out the First National Bank in Sauke Centre, right on Main Street, like in the book.

The building was old style, a stand-alone brick building, with a stone arch over the front door, with "BANK" etched into the stone, and inside the tellers stood behind beautiful old wood and bars and the floor and ceilings were wood. A big clock hung on the wall next to a steel vault door with the captain's wheel handle.

He got off work at the group home at ten at night and planned to drive all night, get there first thing at nine, rob the bank then get back for his shift at two. Even after the July 4 battle he was still working. It should be okay, he thought. So he had his handgun, a rifle, a bulletproof vest, face stocking hat, camo pants and all he had was tennis shoes, some diet Mountain Dew and chips, one giant Snickers that got soggy because he left it in his car all day but he was still gonna eat it, his phone, smokes.

Well, he started out, pretty much on time, got his radio tuned in to oldies, window rolled down, enjoying the trip.

And then, boom, he was there, Welcome To Sauke Centre, home of Sinclair Lewis, at fuckin' midnight. He didn't know it was that fuckin' close, an hour and a half when he thought it would take all night.

Well, shit. Pitch-dark, small town, probably somebody in their bathrobe like that fucking State Farm commercial calling the cops right now. Put the piece away. *They're callin' the cops, put the piece away.* He had just watched Lebowski for the one hundredth time, a regional record.

So, yeah, he quick shoved all the weapons into the trunk. He got into the front seat, scrunched way down, then stretched out on the seat, put his arm under his head for a pillow. He felt the door handle in his head. And he heard cars and people talking. And because it was so quiet, he listened all the harder. And the sounds he couldn't figure out made him get up and look and he couldn't see a thing, and there was this one sound that kept repeating and it made no sense, like somebody backing up a big truck and dragging the blade of a front end loader over the cement, and then repeating, repeating. How do people sleep around here? It's a very mysterious town.

Jim thought about going back home and sleeping in his own bed, but he had made this big deal about how he was going, now, to do it, let's do it, all that kind of talk.

Well, Jim stayed in his car all night. That's not to say he slept. Every hour he moved the car so that he wouldn't get a ticket and he wouldn't attract attention. He moved from that first spot, which, though he didn't know it because it was dark, was the Sinclair Lewis park or museum. And then he moved downtown, in front of a bar. He thought that might work, but it was loud on the street, so he moved to a residential street, for about twenty minutes because he had the creeps. That time the car wouldn't start and he had to crank it and crank it and lights came on in at least two houses and it scared the shit out of him, but it finally went and he got outa there fast, not too fast, pretty fast.

That last time he was so fucking tired it was all he could do to just steer the fucking boat to the curb without being all out in the street and shit.

He lay down on the seat and actually slept.

The morning light and the sound of someone double locking their car door as they walked away to have breakfast at the café on the corner woke him up and there were some kids looking in, one saying it was a dead guy, and some older women walking past with their elbows all high and shit, getting their morning exercise. Jim checked the time on the dash: nine-fifteen, so he was fucking late.

He wasn't parked that far away that last time. He's been inside a few times and they know him, which, well, anyway. He parks right in front, two spots open, he takes up both so nobody can park next to him. He goes inside, shouts – points – gets them to toss money bags over the top onto the floor, open up the vault, and out he goes, is what I heard. He drove away, and got back in time for his shift, and he was feeling pretty great about it all, but he was careful who he told about it, because by then it was on the news and not everyone at work was all with the revolution and stuff. They'd hired some new people since a lot of the old staff had quit for the July 4th thing, right?

That's how I heard it from those people, is what they said anyway.

So I thought that was pretty cool.

Numbers do not win a battle.
No, but I bet they help.

– The Chronicles of Narnia

FOURTEEN

I should say something about this other guy.

Another guy, the angry guy, really angry – Jake, Max, Buster, some tough name, I shoulda used a recorder but sometimes I don't. It's easier than taking notes, but it takes a long time to go back and write it down.

Someone we haven't said too much about. Let's see, what about him? He can't talk. He signs. Like a goddamn third base coach on the Titanic softball team just as it is going down. I don't see how anyone could keep up. He's a Custerphile. Not many of those left. He knows everything, I guess, about George Armstrong Custer, wears a buckskin or whatever coat with those long tassels hanging from the arms. He's got earrings, not Custer, more like, I don't know, like Slash. He loves to sun tan, always in the sun or tanning booth. I guess, that's what Sara said. She was the one who translated for me.

So, these are the notes I took.

"Angry?

[Waving arms, stands up, sits down, up again, down again, waving arms, tassels flying.]

"Look at the got-damned elections. Rigged. It's all rigged, fixed. It's not fair. If you sit back and take it they will just fuck you again!

"The rich own everything. The conspiracies are fucking real. There is no reason for war, but it just keeps happening.

"We have no rights, no chance, unless we fucking fight."

[Sits down, lights cigarette, crosses legs.]

"He has a heart of gold," says Sara as she turns to me.

"He'd do anything for anybody."

This went on for a while.

He said of course I'm angry. Somebody should be angry. Everybody wants to be nice, to be liked, to not be seen as crazy. But this is bull-shit!

Even with that he didn't swear as much as I thought he would or Sarah just took a lot of that out.

The guy with the tough name turned out to not really interest me.

I'm just going through my notes here.

I should say something about the special unit, those guys I saw in Prince Hope's office.

Well, after I saw them, that day, I asked around and of course I found out nothing.

But somebody said yes, of course, there is a special unit assigned specifically to monitoring and destroying I assume this rebel group. That's all I know at this point.

Well and then there's more from another talk with Lara.

Some bullet points about the July 4 Battle of Lake Wobegon, I guess that's what I'll call it.

She said that Kaitylyn, John and Jim all shit their pants when Evey fired her gun and hit Rachel in the face.

And they, the rebels, the CRUSHERs, were supposed to have music playing that day, you know, encouraging music, like fifes or bagpipes. I guess. It was gonna be on Brooke's phone. They had it all ready to go and then she forgot. Something like We Are The Champions. No, I don't really know.

I really liked Lara. They say they don't have a leader, but it could be her. They don't want to have a leader because they don't want them to be able to kill one person and end the revolt. But there's also something kind of tough about doing a war without a general. I don't see how that works.

But there was silence, somehow, when Evey stood up and aimed. I guess the high school band was too far up the street to hear and everything just kind of stood still, until she pulled the trigger.

And then Lara said something about a loyalty shift for the rebels.

She said all of them of course grew up believing in the United States. Of course. And there were just different individual moments when the loyalty shifted, different things they experienced, or read, or heard about. But none of them had anywhere else to shift that loyalty to. Maybe to a band or a certain song, or a teacher they liked, maybe a TV show. There weren't really any politicians and most of them kinda got it that there wasn't anything there. No Oakland.

But then when whoever first started talking about the revolution and that they were the ones to do it, they all rushed in like someone stuck a pencil into the dike, is how she tells it.

Here's a direct quote, soliloquy, from her:

"We were all so scared. It was fun to talk about it at first, but once we started moving toward it, and then on the morning of the parade, I know there were people puking all over in the woods. Then she shot. Evey. Her real name is Evangelina, not that I'm telling on her, that's just her name.

"And that tall girl up by the picnic tables dropped like a rock and we just ran. We knew what to do 'cause we'd been talking about it for weeks and weeks, but we just ran. I just kept thinking to myself, we killed someone. We killed somebody. Some person who was alive is dead because of us. Her life is over.

"Yeah, we had these red, white and blue bandanas that somebody got at Tarshay. They really tied the room together. We had them around our necks or on our heads and the thing we were gonna do was put them over our faces when the fighting really started, but that didn't happen, and so when we all ran, we ran right through the people in their chairs and on the swings and stuff so I was so sure we were all dead.

"Yeah, we gave up a lot. But the fight comes before family, before life. None of us was really old enough to really believe that, but I think a younger person actually has a better shot at doing it than an old person because the old person gets lazy and wants to save their life and they probably have more to save anyway. But we kept telling ourselves that. It probly came from a book, I don't know, but we said it and we acted like we believed it. Fake it 'til you make it. I really do believe in that. It helped me in lots of jobs.

"Am I the leader? No. I can tell you that for sure. We don't have a leader. It shows, but no, I am definitely not the leader.

"How did we say goodbye to our families? That's a good one. Well, for me, I actually sat down with my parents and told them. No, really. It's not like they were at Woodstock or anything, but they tried to understand. I think my father thought it was just a phase, like wanting to take horse riding lessons, but my mom knew. She knew I was serious, I mean, I had my own gun by then, and she cried and I cried and my dad went out to mow the lawn even though he just mowed it. He mowed it again and again.

"I didn't ask anybody else. I figure most of them didn't tell. They just packed their shit and left. I mean, how can you really talk about that? Hey, I think I'm going to start a revolution against the country, the country you pay taxes to and have a house and a job in, but I want to end all that. I want to bring it down, so hey, I might not be home for supper. It's funny, but you can't. There's just no way. And that's how we almost didn't get started. I mean, it's a miracle we did. I don't see how we did. I think we just always kept moving ahead one step at a time and never really thinking we'd get through all the steps, you know? Talk it over, why do it? Killing? What do we want to accomplish? How can we really fight against a giant country? And then after a few months you're walking through a pawn shop pointing at guns you want to hold, and buying flour in fifty pound sacks. I mean, most of us didn't know what to do with flour, but it seemed like something we should buy, and then we Googled it. You know.

"Korey and Kaitylyn they like wanted us to be all super-prepared, had stuff for us to read, videos we were assigned to watch on YouTube. They'd get pissed if they found out you didn't do it. But there was one video that they told me to watch and I did. It was about some underground group in Yugoslavia or Beirut or something.

"And it meant something. It meant a lot to me.

"They were called partisans, the rebels I guess. And the government or whoever they were fighting killed some and put out the bodies on main street, you know, to show what would happen if people joined the partisans or whatever they were called.

"And they had these undercover rebels, they used to be rebels, but they got caught and the government turned them against the rebels and so they went back and acted like they were still with the rebels and then they weren't.

"I could see that happening.

"And then, I remember this, it said that after three years of fighting only a tenth of the original partisans remained. That's when it really hit me that it wouldn't be over after the July 4th parade, no matter how that turns out. That if we really did this it would take a long time and lots of us would probably die, if we really did it. And we were really going to have to want this to keep going, and I didn't know if I did.

"And they talked about in the video, the documentary I guess about a number of illusions floating around in the minds of the rebels, otherwise they would give in to despair. And I thought, that's exactly right. We're probly gonna have to believe in a lot of stuff that might not be a hundred percent true to even keep going. You know?"

Note from the narrator:

From "The Prince Hope Show" ...

And now, it's time for "The Adventures of Buzz The Space Dog."

"... Oh, crap, thought Buzz, and he pooped on the carpet, then sniffed it."

QUOTE REMOVED BY ORDER OF DHS, UNITED STATES DEPARTMENT OF HOMELAND SECURITY. [DHS US2FA]

FIFTEEN

Ay, Paco,
We begin the AY PACO existential novel.

Kessler's The Raw Deal of 12-06-16 takes one step further, to some Extraterrestrials. To ignore is physical death.

Caryl Jones Connely just then sent me a load of stuff on JFK I must read in the early morning in my limited computer access. But I intend to return to continue AY PACO. Caryl is great, growing now post age seventy.

Interruption, Kat wanted in as Choyota came back in. But Kat does not feel relaxed if I close the door on this trailer heat. He wants in to drink a lot of water. Maybe he can sort of settle in for his meditative very long drink though door got closed. We are existential now. Kat is electric.

Guess Bill must drink a forth cup of vodka and water. Have in here a pile of big skillet - cast iron from Lyla - meat - but am eating less. As they say, getting calories from alcoholic beverage. So it be, the plate awaiting the protein is already piled with raw vegetation, but some cooked rice, feeling like rice, brown sure. Avocado, roma tomato, couple serrano chilies, no more room this moment for onion. Two lbs fried pork coming - doubt I will eat it all yet, not like back at age 60. We cannot all be super heroes but my sense of normalcy is a bad knee, a couple years of the knee already, shall see how this works out. Ah, Kat is up to staying inside for now, inclement weather, he and Choyota share this little two-seat couch ancient thing.

Let's put it like this. Besides Trooper is an abductee, but that is another day. Man, I dig Mingus, and with my other jazz favorite, Duke Ellington, this is independent. Ellington was forced to fire him because of his violent nature. Wow were they sublime, terrific. Anyhoo.

Yas, yas, naturally technology of puny man eventually can work the organic till they slip Time in order to go anywhere on the more or less stable physical plane. Sasquatch being equal to any of this wishes to be let be.

I am of Earth and cannot grasp yet what the Extraterrestrials even want here. Maybe next year or decade.

Earth has become some Hell. This is hard for me to define for the illiterate mob. If an outsider person looks all his life at this dumb shit - I have - once you did so - it is utterly unreasonable. Hell, man, the flying saucers are real and I quit APHS, help us all fucking Jesus. Alright.

It is in TG, yeah, yeah.

Hokay. I should have supper and stop drink for this date.

I am to return to this work.

Far Out,

    Bill

Caryl,

There is fake arguments and other flapdoodle on the Standing Rock

horrific situation, to muddy it up, while this morning where I listen to Debbie Lusignan of Sane Progressive, there are some tv comedian videos where the comics do very well delivering fact to their audiences. These guys come on if you just punch in Sane Progressive/latest Lusignan - you therein get a big selection. As Debbie says meantime, it is Indian land, and the desire is run this pipeline UNDER the Missouri River, which is water these Amerindians drink. Invariably, pipelines leak. Debbie you ought to see, she is true-blue, emotional and has a temper, besides she is just great, smart, informed, one-of-a-kind. You would not like that she has zero trust of Trump, but, it would amuse you she gets worse about Obama, nearly spitting. She ends in some mirth, at herself, still enraged, calling him "Barrack Pipeline Obama."

One sentence of hers did strike me: It is easiest to fool good people.

Think about that.

All this of USA's ugliest cops and present government is undeniable, witnessed. We are in a police state. Gone to get worse.

Do you not imagine the courage and righteousness of people who will face fire hosing in freezing weather and a person's clothes and hair instantly become ice. Besides this is water to kill, it is not purely water.

And rubber bullets fired into faces and groins is purposeful injury.

This morning, well before 8 AM for to get room for videos in my cheapo setup, there was for me new voice, The Hagman Report, of the pit of Hell. Somewhat semi-detached, on the destruction of children - maybe as you have come to see this is happening you have had enough already. I see it is worse than earlier I had understood. End Times stuff provable. This is up to you. Nothing I can possibly relate to my siblings yet.

While they have zero chance of never hearing. I guess, they must think without getting to be angry with me first. Possibly during 2017.

Where are those Extraterrestrials? The Friendlies, the Friendlies, goddamnit.

Love,
Billy

Hi Billy: Brrrr, it's getting cold! Hope y'all are staying warm.

I have read several views about the protests over the Dakota Access Pipeline, yet don't know enough to have a solid opinion. The underground is riddled with pipelines in our country, one would be surprised.

Perhaps good communication would've helped. I am all for oil and gas and all natural resources. Hopefully, we can become energy independent and say goodbye to OPEC. That is my hope.

Why fight an oil pipeline when 10 ft over there is an oil pipeline, a natural gas line and a high voltage power line in the same path? The "Indians" won't tell you that! Anyway, just my thought, for what it's worth.

Caryl

Sent from my iPad

Cynthia,
Good morning. Ho hum. People anywhere in our civilization of dung are shitheads and religion has nothing to do with that, though racism does.Politics makes it worse. Ignorance does too, and politics makes ignorance worse.

ISIS is created and organized and financed by the Saudis, Mossad, NATO, C.I.A., to bring to heel these stubborn Middle East and North African countries, create chaos, to get their oil. Children and noncombatants have been bombed the entire Obama administration and likely this will continue.

Just then I punched in a Posting from yesterday to you, if you care to listen to this video from James Kessler and Scott Bennett, which can blow your mind if you do not mind that risk. I believe you have at least one friend who will take that leap - show it to her - this is an hour and a half. Just plug it in, main thing is the audio.

Madrea has been sad, about Harry too, but wanting you to visit though you haven't a decent vehicle. Well, you know. She is trying to decide when this month to visit with the kids - possibly even before Xmas because she has to return to her job early in Jan. I would like to see you too.

Love,
Bill

Jim,

Past week somewhere, I listened to a present survivor at Standing Rock called into the Dan Bidondi show. She spoke of hypothermia, from the fire hosing of everyone, hair and clothing turned to ice. The water from the fire hosing smells, the chemicals have everyone coughing blood. She said now nobody else will be allowed in or out.

This is like Waco but several fold bigger. It is murder.

Makes me crazy.

Just want to say. Our government will be up for grabs.

Yours,
Bill

Caryl,

This early morning, I went through all of this above you have sent,

which is enough for me. It is incomprehensible, how large it is. Besides Hillary, seems it is Obama too. Interestingly, many politicians.

I am glad it is viral. I think it is in the fourth one above, this 15 year old girl, think the name is Theresa, whom I had come across a couple or few days back, speaks a few words again. She is said to have been kidnapped age of two. I cannot believe she is sane as she seems. Whatever, she is strong, intelligent.

Now I wonder what in hell happens, where does this go.

Political affiliation has nothing to do with child rape/torture/ murder, but what some shock is coming to followers of Hillary, Obama. My siblings have been purely illiterate to Alternative News. And how can MSM get their shit back on track. Frankly, I think MSM is done for. Or am I too logical - New York Times crashes. Wha? How about USA economy? And Paul Craig Roberts puts it, the USA must abandon NATO and jerk all its military bases in other countries, just to simply survive.

While I am worrying about implications of Standing Rock. If everyone coughing blood there will show cancer and die, it is hell to pay. Hell for Big Oil. Rage and blood lust just over the rise now.

I be looking through my window from my little table that is my desk at Kelly's cattle grazing in a little shower on juicy grass.

I have done my short workout now, free to keep drinking.

Kat and Choyota are on this little two person couch thing. I had thought of closing door to punch in my little heating system at 70, but then Kat would feel enclosure and want out. Life can be easier. Yes, evil is difficult to perceive. Something in humanity is wrong and I have nothing else to call it.

Love,

Billy

Caryl,

I do not grasp what is happening, End Times I guess. But how can people get this way, and so frequently they are educated and wealthy.

But why this depth of insanity.

Different subject, if maybe not basically. This morning, I listened to a couple of Paul Craig Roberts audios. If you know who he is, at this moment I forget what he did four years of in the Reagan administration, but he has done very much and Kessler calls him our greatest intellectual.

Paul Craig Roberts is saying we can all die anytime. The whole of the USA government is now mad. Only thing which may save Earth says he, is NATO is abolished, all USA military bases abolished. You know, nobody else has all this. Our nukes surround Russia. What if it were the other way around. Putin is heroically sane. People in the USA government wish to strike Russia first. What if Russia thus hits us first. Paul Craig Roberts as well points out our MSM is entirely dishonest. Mostly USA citizens do not know anything. He says we have been this way since the Clinton administration. Very bad off.

Gee, Caryl, could this nation jerk all 200 or however many military bases, this nation which has been heading down economically since the fifties could be wealthy again. It is not a wealthy nation now, he points out - anybody saying so is working some propaganda.

Anyhoo. What next. Where are these extraterrestrials when we need them.

Love,

Billy

Bix,

Western governments are running out of excuses. Since the Clinton regime, the accumulation of war crimes committed by Western governments exceed those of Nazi Germany. Millions of Muslims have been slaughtered, dislocated, and dispossessed in seven countries. Not a single Western war criminal has been held accountable.

Paul Craig Roberts

James Kessler likes to call Paul Craig Roberts our nation's greatest intellectual.

I think James Kessler is it. He does run his friend Paul Craig often, with some others, at JamesKessler.blogspot.com. Another, presently there now, is this mighty woman, Dr. Eowyn, Ph.D.

Soon more is coming on the child rape clubs. Kessler is getting into this carefully enough at his shorter audio, his The Raw Deal, half the size of The Real Deal. On his Real Deal something went too difficult for me to get there, but Raw Deal still is easy for me and this eventually gets to it all.

Out here someway Janus and I run out our allotment for any speed - in a few days one runs it out, then awaits till next time, in my own case fourteenth of a month.   But, Janus informed me, one can hear videos before 8 A.M., for there is less congestion. I arise early and try to get any newer Sane Progressive. I sometimes hear her twice, or so. But at that location will be this list of videos, and I will judge these, seek honest voice. Snowden, Assange, good here. This morning we have very much on the child rape clubs. Which has been going on for decades, which I knew. I consider it is worse by now.

You have to go see to know what I tell. Thus far Debbie Lusignan has not touched base there. Nor has she brought up 9/11. She is busy though.

I do as I do and expect an avalanche. Tried to help the siblings. What some ghastly shit.

Ha, this morning walking Choyota, Mike B. went with us again. Trying to even outline Standing Rock for him, he tries to tell me. He has no information. Had not known of Standing Rock, has not known of Julian Assange. He might well know naught of Edward Snowden, but our communication is bizarre, difficult. I weary. Who cares has he heard of Edward Snowden, damn, get me out of here. His mouth is a faucet and I lose sympathy for his incomprehensible need of babble. Get me out of here. We all know Mike is a nice guy and I need out of here.

Oh well.

Paul Craig Roberts is good. Google him sometime.

End Times,

Billy Frank the Grand,

                         Bill

Steve and Shade,

I started to include Gabe here, then think to be more polite this time and let Gabe decide that or does he care to send me email address for him, or for him and his missus hopefully. But Shade, just do get me your email address.

Yesterday I had no idea when you fellows would be back, maybe not till tomorrow thought I, thought you were spending the night. I had given up expecting you in daylight and sharing this joint Steve gave me, so smoked it, it made two bowls in my little wood pipe. I am poor on faces but interestingly I would not have recognized Shade immediately. Probably would not quite recognize Gabe instantly. Now I have forgotten where Shade lives, maybe in New York, had though thought Gabe is in the Austin area. I have forgotten how old you guys are.

I cannot remember was it twenty years back I saw you two - seems Gabe was present when late Joy bought me some beer in this Prairie Ridge tavern. But my sense has been you two are not impressed by USA government.

Before 9/11 I knew our national history is twisted lies, the nation sociologically depraved. Morn of 9/11 I had to bike Medicine Dog with leash in Prairie Ridge, just then had noticed on the Brundrett TV that towelheads had sank two skyscrapers, with airplanes, as they were reported to like dying for Allah and getting their harems in heaven. Pulling out on bike with dangerous dog leashed I had to work to not be grinning.

Imagine it, I knew what was being done to poor nations by ours already. Hell, since the sixties at minimum. Ah, wrong again, I knew of USA pillage of Latin America all the 1900s.

Very funny, disturbed Viet Nam vets Bob and Jim could not then give attention to 9/11 fake news - what they did is look at the floor. They did not care to see or hear the irregular - they would look at their dirty floor if any of it came on the box.

My parents in Prairie Ridge could not focus or grasp any of 9/11. My father took some time to die and held grievance and did not want me around, wanted me to get a job, said I had cost him more than the other kids combined, till his mind went a bit more. Slowly, I had to be there, for Lyla, and B. E. went and I and Medicine Dog had a new place to live in. By that point, B.E. had sat on the couch playing solitaire since retirement, glancing at his television programs, game shows, cop shows, very restless right foot of B.E's rubs this large bare spot in the linoleum, it is there today. Except, he could no longer glance from solitaire and follow anything on tv, I learned. He did not squawk if I changed the station. Medicine Dog would want to get up on couch, beside B.E., and did this super slow motion, putting a paw up on couch, then another till he had three on and a hind leg to go, B. E. saying very nicely: You can get on the couch, you can get on the couch. Medicine Dog moved onto his couch before B.E. even went - very funny stuff. B. E. asked me what kind of dog is he. I said: he is a pitbull. Oh, is he. B.E. had forgotten USA commercial shit about pitbulls kill children.

Before my father really began to fade off, he who had believed Oswald killed Kennedy, we then with Medicine Dog got on tv THE MEN WHO KILLED KENNEDY, on the History Channel. A pile of these programs, maybe whole series, was on TV, and B.E. did follow it - it was just before he really began fading out. He learned Oswald did not do it. It was explained this was a coup, still presently so. However much B. E. could follow, before he soon could not even focus on solitaire.

He was a poker player, mathematical aptitude. He was a high school dropout in The Great White Depression. He would win in most of the games with his old pipeline buddies, working at Harbor Island, times the work gang who handled the hoses for the tankers had to await a ship coming in. Lyla said this money is how they built their house, mebbe so, or partly, and his old pipeline buddies also some of them pitched in building our house for Lyla.

I have memory being five years old and Lyla telling friends she does not know where he is - he had not come in. He was playing poker somewhere. Needed some cash. Lyla did not go into detail, she sounded cheery enough, she was busy with Butch (me) and Mike and Bonnie, year or two before Kelly got born.

Hum, I have no recall why I was Butch. Lyla thought I was Nature Boy, she loved this great old song. I chose to be Billy rather than Butch, entered first grade and alien just stood in corners, I digress.

Maybe this is no digression. Adults never impressed me. I would be thankful they were not quarreling like in the movies. B.E. liked westerns and took us to movies and before age 5, I thought all this shit was happening.

But I am spreading out too much. Before long post 9/11, I understood the USA did 9/11. I dug into it. I showed my siblings 9/11 Truth in 9 Minutes. A minor shock, the siblings are too brain washed. 9/11 Truth in 9 Minutes is there right now. Like other stuff, the Brit woman telling USA Building #7 has gone down too, but, she is off the schedule, unknowing # 7 is yet upright, right behind her, one immense turd of USA balderdash fucked dumbest shit. Oh, it went, soon after the Brit lady was gone. Did they fire her. But those who would fire her should be shot for treason.

Along in here I am more short, impatient. Been here my whole life. Wonder am I Sasqquatch. Eh, perhaps just a Texas gunfighter - got no respect. Ah, both.

Official 9/11 any fool can see. My siblings are indoctrinated.

Maybe I should hang up for the moment. I believe people best get down to discussing where went their government. This is it.

I can get a lot from Debbie Lusignan or James Kessler, and others. Primarily my readers do hope to not speak on James Kessler and Debbie Lusignan. For me my readers are not much comprehensible. My daughter is busy with kids but comprehensible - age 32 or 33. Kids is something. We got some kids, man. The hubby had to go and too bad, sad for him.

OK, look, I get carried away. Maybe you two brothers could be more astute.

"Astute," a decent word, what. Argh, I have a bit of homegrown left. I hope we will talk, two/three way talk help us all.

THROUGH THE FROGS,
                    Bill

No one knows if they won't die of some terrible disease, be badly injured in an accident, be killed by an airplane crashing into a building, be kidnapped, be falsely accused, be chased across continents, lose everything. We can't know. We can never have that solace. Fundamentally, we are all terrified. We all decay and die, despite the illusions we create for ourselves.

— Kurt Sonnenfeld

The logic of worldly success rests on a fallacy: the strange error that our perfection depends on the thoughts and opinions and applause of other men! A weird life it is, indeed, to be living always in somebody else's imagination, as if that were the only place in which one could at last become real!

— Thomas Merton

The conductor of the train has been changed, but has the train changed its course? You need to tear up the track.

— Lara

SIXTEEN

The bus stops right in front of the café, little restaurant. It's the Little Bird Diner.

The brakes squeak and the doors whoosh at the same time. People fall out, jump to the sidewalk, look around, excited to be in "the city."

The driver turns and looks over his shoulder into his bus to see who's still there. One silhouette moves forward, dragging a backpack on the ridged floor, picking up gunk.

"So, then," she said.

"How goes it?"

"Oh, fine, fine," said the driver, in a hurry.

"Mayberry," she said.

"Mayberry?" he said.

"This is Mount Airy."

"Yeah," she said.

She hoisted the backpack up onto her shoulder.

She turned and looked up at him.

"You have a good day," she smiled.

She looked, straight up at her new home.

Her nest above The Bird.

Brooke ran her fingers back through her hair and noticed the buildings fitted right next to each other like Legos.

She hefted her pack up onto her back for a better feel.

She climbed the one cement step like Everest, pulled on the little wooden screen and jumped when it jangled. She put one foot in like a deer into the clearing, looked around with wide white eyes, at the people gathered around the little tables who probably knew just who she was.

The lady behind the long front, holding the coffee pot, smiled at her and started to rub the counter top with a rag, evidently signaling that Brooke was assumed to be sitting there, right there.

"Hey, honey," said the older woman, her hair in a bun not fully grey.

Brooke hiked herself up into one of the swivel chairs and dragged her backpack to the chair beside her.

"What can I getcha?"

"Umm," Brooke dug into her bag.

"Coffee," she said, not finding much.

"Are you Brooke?" said the lady.

"Uh, huh."

The woman put down the pot and reached to shake Brooke's hand.

"I'm Judy. I'm your landlady. We talked on the phone. Your room's upstairs, you must be hungry. Long ride?"

"Oh. Yeah," said Brooke.

"Nice to meet you."

"You as well," said Judy.

So, without asking, Judy brought Brooke coffee and eggs, ham, toast. They talked about where Brooke came from, how she was going to work for the city. Then Brooke said she kind of needed a nap.

"You can go up right there," said Judy, pointing at the stairway in the middle of the wall. "Or there's another entrance on the sidewalk, for late at night for a young girl like you."

"Yeah, well," said Brooke, reaching for her backpack.

"Thanks."

"No problemo, Brooke," said Judy.

"You get some rest."

"I'll do that," said Brooke.

She turned and nodded to a table of men and women looking at her who might have been staring at her all the while. She went around the counter and headed for the stairway, between the two deer heads, humped her bag again and pounded up the old wooden steps, creaking, squeaking, so that every person in the café could chart her progress.

At the top she looked down a long, narrow, dark hallway and imagined a young woman one hundred years ago making the same journey carrying an old bag made in eastern Europe.

She looked again at the key Judy had given her and began counting the brass numbers on the old wooden doors, squeaking over the floor. She pictured all the people below looking up, their heads moving as she moved. Some spy, she thought.

"Number nine," she whispered, afraid she might be heard.

She reached to fit the key into the lock and the door pushed open.

Staying in the hall she reached to push again. The door creaked open enough that Brooke saw an old sofa, an old wooden chair pulled away from a small table like someone had just left, two walls without hangings, a door leading somewhere and two windows, a slat wood floor, a bare light in the middle of the ceiling.

She entered as if the first cop on the scene.

At the corner of the living room she put one hand on the edge to pull her head around and saw a bird perched on a nail.

She stepped toward it, carefully letting her backpack to the floor as she stalked. At each step the bird fluttered and worried a little more, not looking at her.

Wow, she thought. She had never seen an oriole before.

Brooke saw one window open a bit.

"It's okay," she told the incredulous orange and black bird as she inched toward the window. She pushed open the curtains, slowly drew up the shade and pulled on the old window that refused to budge.

Looking back over her shoulder she put one knee on the floor then pushed up with both hands on the window and there it came. She stepped back and told the bird, look, go, it's open. The bird became even more worried with freedom at hand.

Finally it pushed off and out the window, swooping over the street and the buildings like a freed prisoner.

Brooke watched it go and saw her town, the little shops and streets.

She had not really watched the old TV shows of the '60s and '70s, but others had heard of them and read about their history and what they apparently meant to their parents and grandparents and this is where they could hit America the hardest, in the gut.

So she was here.

She cried.

Tears poured down her face as she knelt looking out the window. She cried sitting on the floor. She cried sitting on the lone wooden chair at the creepy kitchen table. She cried in the bathroom looking into the mirror to see how sorrowful she looked crying and she cried sitting on the lid of the toilet.

She was all alone in this little fucking town in fucking North Carolina! *Damn!* And this apartment, this room, above a café and her landlady is Judy, and they killed someone. And they are revolting against America! You can't do that. Nobody *does* that. She should have kept that bird. That goddamn fucking shit-ass bird would have been her friend, her best friend, her only shitting friend. And where the fuck was her bed? There's this fucking sofa, and this great chair and this great table.

Brooke let herself down from the toilet seat, crawled to her bare living room, into the ray of sun shining in the middle of the room, tucked her arm under her head, curled herself up, went to sleep and dreamed of kittens in a wicker basket, birds stuffed inside their mouths.

Outside her window, down on the street, people talked quietly and smiled at each other, cars moved past below the speed limit, kids played hopscotch on the sidewalk after having re-drawn the grid over old lines faded by a recent gentle rain.

Brooke's eyes popped open.

She looked out over the long wooden floor, along the straight lines of the slats, extending to the end of the world. The room was lit. A different light from yesterday, a morning glow. She stayed there, her head flat on the floor, not knowing where she was. Was she on her parents floor, a floor from an all night party, the floor of the group home, had she fallen asleep on an overnight and she was supposed to stay awake all night!

She became aware of bird chirping.

Brooke groaned as she rolled over, making the floor creak and she thought again about the people in the café, still looking up wondering who is this strange person sleeping on the floor all night long.

She crawled and pulled herself to the window and saw the oriole perched on a railing. She strained at the window and it was not as hard this time. The bird flicked inside and went right to the nail, continuing to sing, filling the space better than surround-sound.

Her stomach rumbled.

She pulled herself up by the window, found a pencil in her purse to prop it open, and clomped downstairs. Judy was there again. They talked about what she would do today, how she would go to the city offices and tell them she was here, and then they would go for a ride around town in Judy's car to see the sights.

In the afternoon Brooke returned to her apartment, smiling. She peeked around the corner of the living room hoping to see the bird. The curtains fluttered and Brooke went to shut the window, but stopped.

She cleaned, got down on her hands and knees and scrubbed the floors, the bathroom, the little kitchen area, the walls, the windows. The oriole, now named Andy, flitted in and out.

She pulled a small, glass frame from her backpack and set it down on the kitchen table, a drawing of Napoleon The Pig, done by Gerry, with a quote from Napoleon the general: "We had excellent spies."

Beside it she set down the wooden Stratego Spy from Kaitylyn, from Kaitylyn's mother's game.

Judy had offered a rocking chair from downstairs. The two of them had hauled it up the stairs and it sat in the middle of the living room floor.

Rocking, rocking, the motion makes you feel better, like you belong, not standing out so much, even when you are alone. Brooke planned to spend entire weeks like that.

While she rocked and scrubbed and watched Andy flicked in and out she thought of how she liked her landlady, a modern-type woman she guessed she would not have expected in the south.

It was the plan that Brooke would be the advance spy, after Mayberry then the next and the next and she'd always be in the government offices, learn about the police and when they finally got to Washington, D.C., well, I don't know, maybe the White House.

It's like this long weekend of vacation from work.

I can't believe it's here. I struggled so long to get here, thought about it so much and now I don't really know how to do it justice, fully acknowledge it, experience it, give the moment its due. And so I don't. But I still try, she wrote in her journal.

It was the most dangerous job. When they talked at the kitchen table at the group home after most of them had clocked out and they just stayed and talked, went out to the porch to smoke. The PD, program director, was Dolores, and she was cool, so nobody was gonna get fired I guess, not for staying all night and smoking. It helped out the overnight, who was supposed to stay awake all night anyway.

They just thought they should have some spies, some folks who went behind enemy lines. We're all behind enemy lines, somebody said, and somebody said, yeah, but, we need somebody to get some intel.

Intel?

Just some valuable shit, man, and then they tried to go all Lebowski and use Lebowski lines real cleverly and then that ended and they talked normal for a while.

Well, for one thing, somebody who, if we all get caught and killed, isn't dead or in prison, like that, for one thing.

Somebody who knows all this new shit.

But, really, what if we could get some people high up, like the Russians do, or the C.I.A., and well, if we can keep this thing going for a while, we get more and more people mixed in with them and then maybe ...

Maybe some day it's worth something?

Something like that.

And so one night was given to talking about their spy network, even before they figured out how to get guns and vehicles and where they were going to camp at Wawakane.

More fun, I'm sure, to talk about spying.

Anyway, Brooke said she'd do it. She'd loved "Harriet The Spy," seen it a bunch of times.

She knew right away she was going to do it, to volunteer, but she didn't say it right away, at the beginning of the night. She waited until it was almost morning, like she'd been considering it all night. And so, yeah, if Brooke lived through the July 4th thing she was going to be their spy. If she didn't they probly would have just dumped the whole spy thing.

Think of it. In the middle of the night, with your friends. The dark is quiet. Maybe you are sitting on the back deck, smoking cigarettes, drinking a lot of coffee. Things seem so possible, like the '60s, they were possible, they happened, sort of, until someone stopped it. But still they dreamed. They didn't know the details of the '60s. They planned in the dark of the night and they dreamed.

But then the morning.

You have been there as well.

The birds chirp, big trucks begin to move on the highway. On the television in the living room, the wonderful movie switches to the morning news program. Someone makes more coffee, but no matter how much you chug, it doesn't invigorate any longer, burns your stomach.

You might think to yourself, what have I done? What did we talk about. Who was it that said that? It might have been me, but it couldn't have been me.

And then some go home, to sleep, to crash on sofas, others drag themselves to second and third jobs.

Others stay up, take hurried notes on pads perched on their knees, able to see now in the dawning light.

She'd heard around corners how they talked about her. How could someone so smart and beautiful and young go so kinda weird sometimes. I mean, at least a few of the rebels said she sometimes sounded like she was an alien trying to talk human and not really getting it right.

Fuck them royally.

One day Brooke had an adventure.

On a walk around town she began to see characters that she remembered from the Mayberry TV show because as part of their training Kaitylyn made them watch some re-runs: the little policeman, the grandmother, the little boy, the sheriff named after her bird, the gas station man. And she began to wonder what was really going on, until she turned a corner and saw a crowd and a parade to mark Mayberry Days. She took one step to go see and turned back around because she had had enough of parades.

Brooke got started at the city offices. She had her own desk and area. She was in charge of answering phones, relaying messages, various filing and communications.

Weeks passed quickly because she was having fun.

The North Carolina fall was wonderful. After work she often went to walk and sometimes just sit in Westwood Park and marvel at the brilliant reds and oranges. She had made friends, joined a bowling league. She bought apples at the farmer's market and even took a ride around town in the historic black and white squad car driven by an actor who played Barney on special occasions. He ran a candy store downtown and had moved here from Iowa just because it was Mayberry and he wanted to slow down, take life easy.

Things were going so smoothly for Brooke. She was beginning to make friends, to fit in, have things to do after work, to love the town, almost enough to forget she was there to kill them.

And then one day, Brooke looked up to see Karen, the town manager, standing over her desk.

"Good morning, Brooke."

"Hi."

"Well, so, Bobby, he does that sometimes, he has to, was running a check on your computer, just normal, regular, you know. Well and he says you had some emails on your computer?"

"Yes?"

"Yeah and that's fine, that's fine, I use it too, we all do, it's just that, well ..."

Brooke began to slowly turn red. Blotches formed on her neck and her cheeks flushed. She knew it was happening and adjusted herself in her seat on rollers to try to stop it from happening. And she rolled way back and that was weird and she crawled her feet slowly forward to erase that it even happened.

She knew it was the emails with Kaitylyn and forwards from Korey through Kaitylyn. They'd been talking about the "prequel," or the run-up, preparations for the invasion, of Mayberry, only they didn't call it that.

Well, they had this pamphlet.

All this had been planned earlier.

They had this pamphlet because somebody had found this book called "WAR."

And it had pretty awesome red three-dimensional print on the cover and it didn't cost much because at that time somebody had Amazon Prime and there's free shipping. That's how they got lots of their books to learn about how to do war.

Well, this book had great quotes and they just made this pamphlet, for themselves, at Kinko's and it was to just remind them and it gave strategy and it might make them feel better, more connected. It was worth a try because they were actually scared as fuck.

And, Kaitylyn and Korey had been working on the pamphlet and so they sent portions to Brooke because she could get them easily, being at a computer and desk a lot of the time. Brooke had always deleted them, but apparently Bobby knew how to get them anyway.

And so ...

"Yeah," said Brooke.

"I think I know what you're talking about ...

"It's from Kaitylyn and Korey, right?"

She looked over to Bobby, who just stared.

"Yes, I think that's it," said Karen, looking at Bobby.

Bobby nodded.

Brooke typed and clicked to get the emails on her computer.

"Here," she said, pushing her chair back a ways.

"Is this it, see?"

"I've seen them," said Bobby.

Karen walked around the desk, squatted partially to look at Brooke's screen, then stood, then looked at Bobby to ask if this was it.

"Yep," said Bobby.

Bobby typed and clicked to get the emails onto his screen.

"I'll send them to you," he said to Karen.

Karen walked to her desk and sat.

They all sat in a triangle in the city office looking at Brooke's emails.

"Pick your battles carefully," read Karen.

"Create a threatening presence.

"Know your enemies. Control the dynamics. Hit them where it hurts.

"Wow," she said.

"You really can't read my emails," said Brooke.

"Actually, we can," said Bobby. "Since you work here. This isn't just your private residence."

"He's right," said Karen, continuing to scroll through the list.

"Destroy from within?" she said.

"Sow uncertainty and panic through acts of terror."

Karen stood.

"Something's not right here," she said.

"Can you explain these?"

"There's also another bunch," said Bobby.

"About a vanguard, an advance tactical group."

"Oh," said Brooke.

"That.

"It's my novel. I'm a writer. I write. On my breaks, since I don't smoke, smokers seem to be the only ones who get breaks, I just sit here and have my yogurt and I doodle. That's what you're finding."

"Your Stooopid," said Bobby.

"Excuse me?" said Karen to Bobby.

Bobby blushed.

"Not you, that's *her* book, and the title is stupid, it's supposed to have an apostrophe, or You Are."

"No, that's the ... oh, yes, you're right," said Brooke.

"Well, we'll have to see about all of this," said Karen.

"Right now I have a meeting, but I have to confess, I don't know what to think of this, Brooke."

"Okay," said Brooke.

Karen then asked Bobby to meet with her privately in the break room.

"And then I've got to get going," she said, looking at the clock high on the wall.

Karen and Bobby went into the lunch room and closed the door.

Brooke saw them talking and erased the emails from her computer, though it would do no good, Bobby already had copies.

She then fired off another email to Kaitylyn, telling her she was in trouble and to not send any more FUCKIG emails.

"When are they coming? she asked Kaitylyn.

At the same time, Kaitylyn listened to the conversation in the other room through the bug that Brooke had planted.

Karen situated herself at the end of the table so that her back was to Brooke in the other room.

"I have received these directives, these notices," Karen said. "From a federal office."

She opened a manila folder on the table. "They're junk, I thought, for bigger cities, but now I wonder."

Bobby pulled them over with one finger and read. The mailings were on official letterhead saying that a Special Unit had been organized to deal with the recent July 4th attack in northern Minnesota and that any municipality that encounters any suspected activity of the rebel group calling itself "CRUSHER," should contact this office. "We have reason to believe they are in the process of setting up cells across the country."

Signed:CRUSHOP/CRUSHPRO/CRUSHINTEL/SMASHCRUSH STOPCRUSH /SMACHCRUSH

And so, Jim, Lara, Korey, Kaitylyn, everyone then heard that Brooke had been found out because of her emails with Kaitylyn.

"She's working for them!" said Jim.

"I knew it! I told you. Pull her back in!"

"We can't," said Lara.

"Not really. I mean we could ask her. She's kind of on her own. We talked about this. It's kind of up to her."

"I feel soooo bad," said Kaitylyn, putting her head in her hands.

"They're already on their way, right?" said Jim to Lara.

"Yes," she said.

They referred to the vanguard, the advance team headed to Mount Airy or Mayberry.

"I, we, might have to change all that," said Lara.

Lara went to her office, just another room in this downstairs apartment in the neighborhood where I don't even know where it was.

I've always wondered if it was in the Highland Park area or by the Green Mill with that little movie house around the corner. That's a nice area. I've seen cars parked around there that I thought could be theirs.

She put in a call to Team Ernest T. Bass. She could have decided herself to end it, but she wanted Brooke to feel useful and good, so she asked her to find them a good spot on a river.

"How about that place where Andy and Opie are walking up with their poles and they throw rocks?" she said.

They had planned to hit right in the heart of Mount Airy-Mayberry, but with the email debacle in city hall Lara decided they needed to start outside of the city and move toward the city and then take the city like armies do.

They were getting notice everywhere and recruits coming in. Lara had plenty to do in organizing housing, training at Camp Sweaty, uniforms, T-shirts, food, transportation, passwords, phone service, all that.

She expected to battle the sheriff's office, probably the national guard, maybe the special unit.

It won't be easy, she thought.

But, it could be fun.

Note from the narrator:

From "The Prince Hope Show" …

The mind of an American rules the world.

The President? Warren Buffett? Tiger Woods? Katie Couric? Jon Stewart? The Michelin Man?

No, stupid, it's you.

You are king of the world, god, superman, King Midas, all that.

It's you.

You are more than just a legend in your own mind.

You are The Man.

And when the C.I.A. through the C.I.A. propaganda machine called Radio Free Europe or the American Free Press tells you the Russians are coming or the criminals are coming or terrorists or the Iranians or Iraqis of Afghans on nuclear-powered blue donkeys or big bees, and you believe it — well, then, Zeke, that's how the world will go.

You are powerful, the most powerful yahoo who has ever lived in the history of living.

And you are an idiot.

And the world is going to burn.

And that's a bummer man.

That's a bummer.

In response to the killings of Fred Hampton and Mark Clark in December 1969, on May 21, 1970, the Weather Underground issued a "Declaration of War" against the United States government, using for the first time its new name, the "Weather Underground Organization" (WUO); they also adopted fake identities, and decided to pursue covert activities only. These initially included preparations for a bombing of a U.S. military non-commissioned officers' dance at Fort Dix, New Jersey, in what Brian Flanagan said had been intended to be "the most horrific hit the United States government had ever suffered on its territory".

We've known that our job is to lead white kids into armed revolution. We never intended to spend the next five to twenty-five years of our lives in jail. Ever since SDS became revolutionary, we've been trying to show how it is possible to overcome frustration and impotence that comes from trying to reform this system. Kids know the lines are drawn: revolution is touching all of our lives. Tens of thousands have learned that protest and marches don't do it. Revolutionary violence is the only way.

—Bernardine Dohrn

All you have heard about Old Narnia is true. It is not the land of Men. It is the country of Aslan, the country of the Waking Trees and Visible Naiads, of Fauns and Satyrs, of Dwarfs and Giants, of the gods and the Centaurs, of Talking Beasts.

— *The Chronicles of Narnia*, Prince Caspian

SEVENTEEN

" Rebels don't wait."
"Rebels don't wait?"
"Who said that? Fuck's that mean?"

Max, Buster, Joe, Ariel, Zima, Morgan, and Brandon walked along the railroad tracks headed from Saint Paul to North Carolina.

They talked, threw rocks, walked on the rails, looked behind them for the special unit, overhead for helicopters, drones, big drones, citizen drones.

"I don't really know," said Buster.

"It's in the book."

He walked along the rail without looking, reading from the CRUSHER MANUAL *prepared by Korey & Kaitylyn.*

"... English speakers can use the reading skills of Soviet Russians, earlier Chinese and others in totalitarian societies. You read between the lines and pay attention to what is not reported. You translate. For example "so and so said..." Read "said" as "claimed with no evidence". You must be a hard core proud "conspiracy theorist" which requires memory skills of previous events, imagining alternative explanations, assume secret police (i.e. cia/mossad/M15/6) involvement and communicate with known and trusted other people."

"Go on," said Ariel, bending to pick up a pink rock and toss it sidearm.

"No, that's pretty much it."

"And then we need to get started in Hooterville, but we need to get these others going, we can't wait on her," said Zima.

"Hooterville-Pixley," corrected Brandon.

They walked about a mile. It was early morning, just barely light out.

They got tired.

They slumped into the plastic bus stop shelter. Some sat. Max lay flat out on the bench. Morgan hugged a pole, leaned into the street and looked for the bus.

The posters on the sides advertised a play at the Chanhassen.

They had the shelter to themselves. One lone black woman with bags at her feet stood across the street, working her phone.

Max, who considered himself the introvert of the group and was always on the verge of running away, literally, often found mornings, before you are really awake or aware of how creepy you really are, the time when he could talk and then he felt embarrassed later about what he had actually said, said that maybe those creepy Grim Fairy Tales were a way to talk about things that otherwise couldn't be said, you know?

Buster moaned and Max figured he had already said too much.

Nobody responded ... still. It was so still. The whole town shuddered in embarassed silence for Max.

"We did read Narnia, remember that?" said Joe and Max almost shouted *"Yeah!"* But he didn't.

The black woman looked up for a moment, then up and down the street.

"And I'm wondering if I write some modern fairy tales, that might be a way to ... oh, I don't know. I've said too much," Max mumbled.

"Like Shrek," said Buster with closed eyes.

"No," said Ariel.

"Not ... like Shrek.

"That's a good idea, Max," she said.

"You do that."

"They're looking for us," said Joe.

"You think?" said Morgan, "here it comes."

The bus shot up, squeaked short. The seven got all their shit and climbed on, spreading out over the bus. Underneath, they — The Vanguard — wore their Ernest T. Bass T-shirts, but while on the bus none acknowledged they knew each other, each carrying enough gear for hockey players.

The light on inside the bus made the outside darker. Joe and Ariel sat together, with Ariel falling asleep almost immediately and there goes her head bouncing on the window. Buster motioned to Max to come sit way in the back, but Max knew he couldn't stand the exhaust smell so dived into a middle seat. Zima, Morgan and Brandon each found their own spot, taking up the whole two seats easily.

They got their ear buds in, phones out and began texting each other.

Max watched everyone that got on, imagining what they did, what their lives were, what they were headed toward that day, happy or sad.

They were headed for Lake Calhoun, where their vehicle waited on the street. The bus didn't stop exactly there, but close enough, where they would all get off together and take the waiting pickup and topper and drive to North Carolina, to an as yet undesignated campground where they would begin the next phase of the rebellion, the revolution, the revolt against America, The United States, The Empire.

Sounds like a plan, is what I guess Brandon had said when Lara had explained it to them.

"Tell me more about Narnia," said Max to Ariel."

"What do you want to know?"

"Everything."

"Andy and Aunt Bea sitting on the porch on a beautiful quiet evening while elsewhere others starve and cry in agony are bombed in ghettos, in Vietnam. It doesn't change."

Buster texted out some more from the manual.

"Project Ozz," somebody said.

"I was with P.O., for awhile," somebody answered.

"Like Wikileaks, they say."

"Yeah. No."

They made stops at Selby/Dale, Lake Street, 36th, Uptown.

"The military's new program or whatever is called Global Dominance – they don't give a shit what you know, you can't stop them."

"We all will die."

"How do we use the miracle of this flash of light that is called life"

"Fuck you, man."

"I'm serious!"

"Ohmygod," Brooke mumbled to herself.

It was a half-whisper thing she had taken to saying whenever she was encountering someone she thought incredibly stupid. She didn't really think the person she was talking to could hear her, but then again she did not care, she thought.

"Do you want cream with that?" said the man at the coffee counter.

"How many creams? Should we pour the cream in after the coffee or before?"

"Ohmygod, after is fine."

Brooke took her coffee to a window table and hunched over her phone. She is supposed to be doing this, finding out all the little tidbits of information for the vanguard when they get here, but really all she has been doing is making a life for herself, and at this moment she is half-sick about that, not totally sick, how she has cheated the revolution, the rebellion, the whatever you call it with her wanting to be happy, of being more interested in her bird buddy and her bowling friends than the ones arriving here from Minnesota.

So, she searched, frantically actually, on her phone, for information about rivers around here, stuff she should have known a long time ago.

There's Fisher River, Yadkin River, Mitchell River, Ararat, I hope there's no more, she thought, geezuz, they have a shitload of rivers, god.

And then, oh, this is kinda cool, Myers Lake, that's where they went fishin' and threw rocks or stones or ... yeah, but how do you use a lake for an army. That would be cool. That would be where you would want to attack, but ... *I don't know! Fuck!*

She thought and she searched and searched, maps, depth, surrounding towns, all that, as she drank her coffee at a tiny window table in the coffee shop by her office.

"You drive like old people — you know," said Zima to Joe.

"I just want to get their alive," said Joe.

"Like it matters," said Morgan.

"Hey!" said Buster.

"Well, it's true," said Morgan.

"Isn't it?"

"I don't know," said Buster. "Yeah, maybe."

They rested in a roadside park on the Audubon Parkway outside of Owensboro.

The doors of the pickup hung open as well as the door to the topper. They lounged on a bench and swang on the swings. Max and Ariel had gone for a walk to see if there was a river over past the trees.

Zima sat in the shotgun seat with one leg hanging out the open door, on her phone.

"Anything?" asked Brandon, walking over toward her.

"Yeah, Lara. She never stops, fuck."

"What?"

With one hand working the phone she used her other hand to flatten the map on the dashboard.

"We're headed to ..."

She hopped down and moved the map to the seat. Brandon squeezed in to see as she traced her finger along the highways from Owensboro to ...

"Umm, Louis-viiille ... Frank-foorrt ... Lexingtonnn."

Brandon watched the maroon fingernail scratch along the map into West Virginia, Virginia, down to North Carolina.

"We've got a ways to go," said Zima.

"Then whatta we do when we get there?" said Brandon.

"They still don't know," said Zima.

"I guess we find out."

Brooke decided to not go back to the office after her lunch break. She turned off her phone, shoved it into a pocket, went to the park and sat and smoked, her feet outstretched, crossed at the ankles. She watched the orioles in the little tree twitch and chatter and wondered if one of them was Andy telling his friends about this cool chick he met.

Lara fired off texts to Brooke, to Zima, to her mother.
"Nobody is listening to me!" she said.
"People! Fuck! What is going on?"

Brandon pulled the pickup off the little highway onto a roadside park.
There were a few picnic tables under a shelter, an outhouse and a little path that looked as if it led to a river because there was a big break in the trees that must have been the river.
They stopped.
"And so, yeah ... welcome to the revolution," said Ariel.
"Listen!" said Zima, getting out to stretch.
"Orioles," she said.
Shhh! Shush. Just-shush!
Max began telling a story about how his father had taken him to his first major league game, in Kansas City, so he could see a real outdoor field, and how what he remembered were the uniform colors of the Royals and the Orioles, and the deep green of the grass.
And ... nobody cared.
They began to crawl out of the pickup and the topper camper, yawning, tossing rocks, checking their phones.
Ariel and Max headed down the path toward the river.
"You sure this is the right one, river?" said Brandon to Zima.
"I think so," she said. "No."
She continued to work her phone, her thumbs just a pumping.

Meanwhile, Tim Taylor sat in his squad car at Myers Lake.
He had stopped by the city offices on a tip from Karen and then stayed to visit for a while with Bobby before moseying out here.
He got out to walk to the water to check for boats. He tossed a rock sidearm. Nothing but a lone innertube with a swear word written on it meandering along. He'd have to try to find out where it came from.
He walked back and leaned on the hood of his car, crossed his arms, checked his watch, checked the sky. It might rain, he thought, and wondered if he had shut the windows on his house before he left.
Taking one more look around, Taylor climbed back into his black and white to drive down Second Street just to make sure.

"If this isn't right, well just tough shit," said Zima.
"This is where we do it."
She dived into the backseat of the pickup and dragged out bags and tents.

"Fine good," Lara texted back to Zima.

"Whatever."

She crossed her legs, lit another cigarette and frantically texted the others to notify everyone of Zima's position.

Brooke sat for a awhile. She watched Tim Taylor roll past. He didn't see her, didn't even look, usually police are looking all over, staring everyone down. Tim didn't really do that. He had the unusual last name that suggested he was connected to the television sheriff way back, but he wasn't, that's what Brooke had heard. She hadn't really ever met him.

Brooke felt calm and that made her a little nervous. She should be scared. She had nowhere to go. The revolution or whatever you were supposed to call it, was mad at her for getting caught, already, and she couldn't really go back to her job because, well, they could probably go way back in her computer and even see the porn she'd been watching. There wasn't that much to do at her job.

But, mostly, she just didn't give a crap.

And that wasn't good, she scolded herself. At her age she should be excited about all kinds of shit, wanting to go a hundred directions at once, but that wasn't it.

It just was not.

What she really, really wanted to do was to turn into an oriole and join the others over there in that little something tree and hang out and sing and gossip and then fly over there and then fly back. She'd fit in with the oriole crowd.

Well.

She had to do something. She could go home, guess on the bus. Or, she could go back to work and hope it's fine. Or she could text Lara and ask her what she thinks she should do.

She got up and headed over the grass to the edge of the park and crossed the street without looking and opened up the big squeaky screen door to the café.

Brooke nodded at Judy while taking a counter seat.

Judy looked at her with really overly concerned eyes, Brooke thought, while setting down the menu.

She brought coffee and leaned over close while pouring.

"Sheriff Taylor is up in your room, right now," she whispered.

"Why?" said Brooke.

"I don't know why."

"I thought you would."

Brooke looked away and said "yeaaah."

"Why aren't you at work?"

"Oh, I just ..."

She raised her head at the sound of steps upstairs.

"You should either leave or find out what he's doing," said Judy, wiping, wiping.

"Yep," said Brooke.

She slid from the stool and walked past the table with the staring people, then turned right at the end of the counter to head up the steep, old, squeaky wood steps.

She slapped the rail to grab hold and clomped on up.

If we live in a state of constant fear, can we remain human?

— Alexander Solzhenitsyn, *The First Circle*

EIGHTEEN

Zima's family carried a tradition of war, her grandfather in World War II, her father in the first Gulf War and her two brothers in Iraq and Afghanistan. They were fighters, warriors, they all liked to say.

At family get togethers she heard about the camaraderie of combat and how they couldn't explain to her, since she hadn't been there.

The family had relatives in the Civil War too, they had figured by searching online, and that seemed to make them all happy, in fact, people on both sides.

That can't be fun, Zima recalled thinking, having to fight against people you knew, even in your own family, shooting them maybe, killing them? Woah.

And revolution would be the same thing.

You'd be killing people who looked just like you or pretty close, who thought the same thoughts, pretty much, who picked at the same food, thought the same things almost funny, or not.

Lots of things ran through Zima's head as she felt the gravel on her knees as she worked to set up her tent.

She looked around for the others. They were supposed to be working. She heard laughing, splashing, beyond the high weeds, over by the river. She wondered what river they had actually come to. She plopped over on her tent for a moment to dig into her pocket for her phone to try again to figure it out.

Do you see a real revolt ever breaking out?

J. Michael Springmann: I don't think so. I don't think the Americans are politically interested enough to do it. They're more concerned with having their beer and watching their football game and going out to a barbecue more than overthrowing the government. I think they're quite happy as long as they're paid, they have to do whatever they have to do to hang on to their low-wage paying job. They're not going to de-stabilize anything because they're afraid. ... and beyond that you've got carefully managed news, you've got the watching of the emails, the watching of the telephone calls, which would prevent any kind of revolutionary activity. With this you can't meet secretly. You might meet face to face and whisper in somebody's ear, but that's about the extent of it.

Cause finally the tables are starting to turn, talking about a revolution.

— Tracy Chapman

What the world needs now is love sweet love.

— Hal David

NINETEEN

"Well, I don't know, Lupe," said Prince Hope to the laughing late night show host.

"But I can tell you this."

And Prince Hope straightened his long legs, cleared his white pants of invisible lint, and leaned over from the sofa toward the host as if to tell a secret in front of millions of people.

"We will wipe out CRUSHER."

Some people in the audience laughed.

He put up a serious hand.

"No, no. They are not as pervasive or powerful as some people — on the internet — seem to think.

"And I don't mean capture them or prosecute them, Lupe. I mean destroy them, kill them all, before the year is out. I can tell you that. I guarantee it."

The studio audience stood and cheered along with the host.

Prince Hope stood and waved with both hands, as the host yelled as loud as he could that everyone should stay tuned, they were going to commercial.

Four red new Suburbans with dark windows glided down main street, past the sheriff's office, past the city offices, right under the window where Sheriff Tim Taylor knelt coaxing the oriole perched on the nail on the wall to make his escape.

"Come on, you can do it. You can do it. Come on, c'mon."

"His name is Andy."

Brooke clicked into the dark living room.

"Andy?" Tim smiled.

"C'mon ... Andy," he said.

Tim tried pushing the window up a little higher and when he looked back toward the bird an orange streak flashed past his face and was gone, out over the town, darting this way and that, out-smarting invisible, invincible foes.

Tim stood and introduced himself, reaching out a hand.

Brooke did not take it, but chose to stare him down.

"Oh," he said.

"Yeah, I'm in your apartment, sorry."

"My home," said Brooke.

"Yeah," he said, bowing his head, removing his hat.

"Well, we can do that, if we have probable cause."

"I see," said Brooke.

"We didn't used to be able to, well, but since, now we can."

"Yep. I see."

"So," she took a step back, another, to find the wall and put her wrapped hands behind her back.

"It's the emails," he said.

"The emails. The emails at your office, the city office, Karen."

A bit relieved, Brooke dropped her hands to her sides, then wrapped them again at her waist and raised her chin to maintain the stand-off she hoped she was maintaining.

"Okay," she said.

"Well," said Taylor.

"They're not private, I s'pose you know, at your work, government work, that's one thing, just to get that out there."

She nodded.

He took a step closer and she could see his face all scrunched up and curious, and shit.

"And," he said.

"Just what does all that mean? Rebels, revolution ... Carolina, rivers, guns? All that? I just need to know, ma'am."

"Why."

"Well, for one thing, I need to make my report."

"And turn it in to Andy," she said.

He smiled timidly.

"Oh, yeah," he said, pointing his hat back to where the bird had perched.

"Oh, no, you mean, yeah, yeah, we get that a lot, no, what I mean is to higher authorities."

He used air quotes and she thought for a moment she might live, and she got a bunch of ideas of what she would like to do with her life.

"They're gonna want to know, well, what you're up to, ma'am.

"Well, to be true, you're not one-a them, those ... are you?"

"Those?

"Them?"

Brooke looked down on herself as from above, as if she were viewing this from about the level of the ceiling, a southern belle sophisticate, a spy, being interviewed by the local down-home sheriff, and there is no doubt that somehow the nice man will stumble into the truth, inevitably, and he will do his duty, and she will be hanged in the town square, at dawn or shortly thereafter.

"Well, CRUSHER, that bunch," he said.

"I need, we need to know if that's you, ma'am."

He called her ma'am though she was likely ten years younger than he was. She sensed he had gone to the local high school and had dreamed of this job since he could remember.

The four red, husky, new Suburbans with dark windows, like a lost catering crew, winded their way around town, slowly, cameras inside whirring and firing, recording as Max and the others returned from the river, dripping wet, laughing, to find Zima set up inside her crisp blue tent smelling like vanilla-lemon candle, seated at a desk with a rifle propped against it, a giant walkie-talkie on the desk. She wore a camouflage cap and her Ernest T. Bass T-shirt, which had been decided long ago as they had discussed all of this at great length earlier — *and* argued about, the Lebowski or Orange Crusher shirts.

Max saluted, even though he had never saluted before.

Zima saluted back, and that was it.

That was all it took, apparently.

She was fucking serious, man.

This must be it. This *is* it.

Everyone hurried, ran, to get their shit and put things together and in order and get this show on the road.

The four red Chevy Suburbans with darkened windows, with license plates that read:

CRUSHOP/ CRUSHPRO/ SMASHCRUSH now stopped right on the curb in front of the Mount Airy city office, the brick front with the white wood casing on the windows and the lettering in raised gold.

Men in suits and sunglasses, like Men In Black, or F.B.I. agents or things or people you imagine, got out of the car. They did not yawn or stretch or gawk, they put one hand inside their jackets, walked in choreographed motion to secure the scene and also to enter the building.

Brooke imagined as her standoff continued with Sheriff Tim Taylor in her apartment.

She trusted Sheriff Tim Taylor and, she wanted to make something happen. As she had so many times imagined just jumping when she looked off a high bridge or tall building, just to think of what a dramatic human drama she had the power right now to enact – she tells him all.

You can't do that. But I am. You can't. You're under arrest. Citizen's arrest. That's not funny, none of this is. Handcuffed, taken out of the building. Just as four Suburbans, plenty imposing altogether, pull up. They take her. *Landlady texts Lara.*

"That's not me."

He smiled big.

"Well, am I glad!"

He slapped his hat onto his head and shook her hand.

"Now, how about you just tell me what those emails did mean."

He actually pulls out a tiny notepad like Brooke used to collect at hotels when she went traveling with her family.

And she told him a story about how she was a writer and she, you know there's not much to do there?

I can imagine, he agreed. I like getting out. I just can't sit.

They leave together, chatting, laughing, wave to landlady, and Tim Taylor goes out first, just as four new Suburbans pull up.

Brooke looks back at landlady, who points to another exit.

"Go! Hurry! Don't thank me, just go!"

Note from the narrator:

From "The Prince Hope Show" ...

And now... for your local news report, brought to you by Jello Salad, Blue Birds, Baseball Games, Fluffy White Clouds, and also by Powder Milk Democrat Gonads.

QUOTE REMOVED BY ORDER OF DHS, UNITED STATES DEPARTMENT OF HOMELAND SECURITY. [DHS US2FA]

TWENTY

Bix,
Just was talking with Madrea, who now is fixing "Thanksgiving" dinner. I call her on Saturday. Things are ok for now there. Was telling her I miss being there, but there was a couple of fusses with old farts up street, over dogs, and even a cop from Woodville to see me. Dogs get deserted in Ivanhoe and form packs and get shot at and her young hound I liked she named King Dinosaur is vanished.

He had wandered up as a puppy, was out here, loved it here. Her present dog had also wandered up as a puppy, a bulldog, she says I will like him, Bandar, who is as well another personality. She has to keep him chained, or inside when she cannot find time to walk him.

Can't recall maybe I said, recent couple years I reread THE CATCHER IN THE RYE, also in that period read TO KILL A MOCKINGBIRD. Great works these two.

Yeah, Obama is something. Not to go into what is Alternate News now about him, and Michele, besides Killary.

These are cold blooded, murderous. I don't remember numbers, I have read the fire bombings of Japanese cities killed more than the two A-bombs. Germany was saturated bombed, could not get food into their labor camps, thus the myth of the Holocaust. Then we hear more bombs were dropped in Vietnam than in World War II. Lately I understand 70,000 bombs have been dropped on Syria since Jan. I think Jan.

When these subjects involve Obama I am entered Blackbird-taboo-speak. This is insulting. I need not sit around told what to say.

Obama and Trump love Big Oil. My sentiment is kill them.

139

Since the Kennedys and MLK shooting this land is governed by C.I.A., Big Oil, Merchants of War. Mike Blackbird disagrees. He cannot hear shit. No reason to have adult conversation with my siblings. They can't hear English.

I presume Shade and Steve will come in today. I did tell Steve I am curious how hip might his sons be.

Past the Frogs,
Bill

Evening, Bill,

Jack and I make the morning walk along the bay just before the yellow sun yesterday, red sun this morning, an old Vietnamese man fishing every day off the bay wall. There was another old man I'd see every morning, with his little dog, and he'd dig into the trash baskets for cans to sell. They'd walk throughout the town and on occasion I'd see him out on the highway, some miles away. He was a friendly fellow, not clown-like or demented, just nice and friendly, a clear "hello" from him as Jack and I walked past. But he's no longer around.

Yes, Obama has been a huge disappointment. He is a charmer as I watched him hand out Medals of Freedom to movie stars, athletes, etc. He gives one to American Indian woman, reminding me he's done nothing to protect the protesters in North Dakota. Though, I would put Truman as the most murderous President.

Nothing new here, still working out 4 days/week, reading about Salinger of late. Salinger's "Catcher in the Rye" I read when I was 18, visiting the Vaughns. Steve handed me the book, said I should read it. I liked it, read all the Salinger books. He was big for me. Kerouac came next, Hemingway then Algren.

I'll pass on coming that way for now. But hope to drive there some time. Bonnie suggested Christmas, but I don't think so then.

Take care, Bill
Bix

Bix,

Steve and Shade are to come out here tomorrow. Maybe you could too.

Packy is too slow. OK, Packy, you too. Get your shit together. No matter you could not get through officer training in the navy. ALRIGHT YOU PUSSYS FALL OUT WITH FULL PACKS!

Packy would be most welcome, the unseen man.

Either way, I have extra beds here.

I am to not attend gathering with Kelly and Janus where is Blackbird-taboo-speech. I will be here. Perhaps inebriated.

Or not. Well it is some sort of experiment to something. I contend Obama is our most murderous president ever. Trump is a chump....He ain't got shit. Where, each day, of the Obama administration kids got blown away. So far 7 nations.

OK, either reality. My siblings are indoctrinated, unto schizophrenia. Kelly blaming stuff on Trump the Chump before he is in office. But not to matter, for our nation has been schizoid.

Maybe you and Packy could take shifts, one visit with drunk Bill while the others joins in the cum ba ya crowd.

Through the Frogs,
Bill

Geoffrey,

I had thought maybe storms in area are stopping me from getting online, and today it is worse with no storms. I could quit trying to do email, anytime now because of obstruction - is this hostility organized. Hey, look, today is worse than yesterday - no storms today.

I wish to say, in Indian Territory a beautiful age 21 person lost her left arm to cops, a "stun grenade." It is pointed out this cannot be so easily done in the USA street. Big Oil owns Obama, Trump, America. How ugly.

If I can get one more sentence in before I get cut off again: How can it be my very siblings do not know shit. They are hypnotized to think MSM is real news.

Break: Let me see if I am online.

Today is very hard yet in this moment I am online.

Yep, still am.

How can my siblings believe Obama, whose administration has bombed goats and children in 7 countries since 9/11. Can my siblings be stupid. Or is it buffaloed. Can you tell me?

Yep, am still online.

Geoffrey, you see I have no respect for polite conversation. Naturally not.

If I ask a sibling why 7 countries get bombed dogs and goats and children since 9/11 I get a blank. They will try to get away from me. Here is sick. OK, then you explain. Obama is mathematically more evil than Trump.

Wha?

I am cut off again. No Internet.

Perhaps, because of "Bill's friends," how my siblings say it. Bill's friends.

Sad. Traumatic. You don't know.

I expect to get back online this day. If never, I guess I can be a drunken hermit, violent. Be content I have one super daughter and grandkids.

No Shit,

     Bill

PS Meant to tell you, never hurry to respond if at all. You are very busy in different ways.

Bix,

My last note to you looks incoherent. My computer is fucked up and I could not finish Postings, again. This or that jars my cool in drunkenness.

I whack on dry oak, got the torque, from wrists and ankles, whee. Misfit must have something to drink to.

Kelly and I are cool. Something ails him, I don't know. I don't have interest in any MSM and wonder could he and Janus be getting any of the realer Hillary, is it creeping into MSM. Whatever.

Trump had inherited some money and he turned that multiplied, and appears to be a buffoon. He is hiring the wrong people whatever, which is how Barry went wrong we know.

Oh I guess the fix is still in.

I hope Trump can continue friendship with Putin, the great man.

Ah, maybe so.

Far Out,

     Bill

Barron,

What's wrong wi you?

No typo above. I think it is funny. Very common with drunk citizens.

People cannot every day show me much but one day in Austin when I was demonstrating how I have to do palms on floor stretch every day to avoid further back injury, doing it with feet together, you showed me something out of a book or some place,

spread legs and then just dangle from waste. I viewed the value and have ended the daily ham stretch with it every day since.

I have caught on, my not being thrilled with the book EGIL'S SAGA threw you off, embarrassed you with Michele probably.

Hey. People want to comfortably categorize me.

All my life, even my siblings. Mike Blackbird read THE TRUE BELIEVER in 1958 and concluded Bill is a true believer. Then, in as I was an atheist in a definition, as I was no Christian or believer of a sky god, Mike Blackbird saw it his intense sibling Bill could switch, become a born again true believer. Yas, my siblings are always crazy. In 1958 Mike O. still believed in God - not now, he became a scientist, with very poor memory of his childhood.

That book by way is a good read. I found this out years later, reading the author's interview in Playboy or Esquire or some place. Can't recall his name, probably dead now, he was a longshoreman who wrote sociological books. I but never did get into his essays/books. Been too hassled.

And so. Yas, yas, I am a renown warrior, needs to fight, crazy and if from a different place, amid waves in space. But you forgot I am angry about racism and this abuse of children and the unfortunates. EGIL is about an armed and experienced culture in robbery. It may be said TALES FROM THE TEXAS GANG is too. But TG is more, mostly its lovers are literate types too, not really necessarily enchanted of blood lust - the literate reader understands TG discusses this besides much else. I am literate and get nothing of my language from EGIL. You may love EGIL but it is not my cup of tea. I read it twice, that is plenty for me.

Good you finally found a means of getting respect in the schizoid nation, bike repair. I hope you have not been in another crash. Biking in large cities is crazy.

Much going down today. You did show me a decent site for alternate or truer information, yet what I have had does it better for me, Kessler and clan and lately Debbie Lusignan. I am busy over a decade. Ever stranger, I can show people I care for where to find working information, and usually they cannot well hear me.

I knew TG was radical and I enabled getting it printed in summer of 1978 just when Reagan got in and got war on drugs hotter. Gunman on horses who eat peyote and talk about matters was too early.

Yas, yas, life is hard but I do have a perfect daughter with children. You should see these kids. Whose parents understand killing. These are free kids, with large minds.

Much going down all the time. Today Jim Kessler's The Raw Deal, one hour shorter than his The Real Deal audio, tells of NYPD and real F.B.I. are furious Hillary is not quite yet caught. You would have to go see, I am not scooping it for you. But though it is throughout Alternate News, today. Latest now, Killary and Bill would often join this convicted pedophile billionaire at his Orgy Island in rape of children. I am telling you.

Wats wi you?

Love,

　　Bill

Steve,

Thanks for art card, a bit of a strange one.

Kelly brought me it today and said this is the perfect job for Kyle.

Rodney must have a decent and affordable connection, if he can afford that, being he long back lost his pharmacy license. He had been afraid of scoring, maybe Mack whom he became friends with

is a help, but still Rodney needs an inheritance like has Mack. But should you see him tell him Bill says hello, please.

This of child rape clubs I have encountered much on the Web. Surprisingly, Kelly, too, who only believes MSM, is now hearing about it frequently. We spoke of it on a dog walk recently. There are well known politicians involved, in Europe as well, we hear. Who knows why politicians this much. It gets worse than mere rape, kids do die. We did not talk long on it on this dog walk. Like he did not want me to get anything new to him, he said. "It is everywhere." There is too much to disbelieve. Books have been written. I read online parts of one that has sold much, maybe it was though audio, I forget. Steve, it is just too much, it really is everywhere. I am not going to give you a scoop.

I had been picking up on the reality, which in the United States had grown from the sixties. Having my own child, I became further alerted. Cynthia and I told Madrea to go for the eyes. Then you can get a break to run. Richard's father, attorney D.H., had some conversation with me in Lyla's house maybe 3 decades back. We were sitting at the bar, nobody else near. Lyla had this gathering, I forget why. He said then, nobody should ever leave a child alone in a playground in even the daytime in Prairie Ridge. He, too, knew it had grown worse. A decade or two before that conversation kids could be left in city playgrounds in the day in Prairie Ridge, but this is no more.

Probably it has not been like that in Mexico. I don't know. Like I say, it became this way on this side of the river since the sixties. I don't know about Canada. But as even Kelly with his fixed news hears it is global, adult clubs for this, all over, what can I say. From where can I begin to tell it 35 years later. I think my kid is turned 32. She is powerful. While, horror is on Earth more now.

Past week I ran into somehow on the net Most Famous Photos of the Old West. It is vast. These are remarkable looking individuals, but also is sprinkled in some few photos of the earlier film actors, and actors from Bill Cody's shows, and the difference is plain. For me the real people look familiar. Even the cowboys, who like to pose with their guns, as did mountain men too naturally, gun, knife with foot long blade. There were very many attractive women who joined gangs and they enjoy posing with these big .45 sixguns. Less frequently, with rifles. A lot of Indians too, deep faces, anger. USA built itself on slavery and more general rapine. So it was, but these photos are of people in struggles, besides the others, pistoleros and so forth.

Where from here.

Far Out,
   Bill

Caryl,

Past couple or so days my laptop is erratic, if it appears to be better in one way it is crazy in a new way. With much work at it, I believe I have mainly seen what you have sent here.

Well, as with 9/11, which began these bombings on non-combatants in seven countries thus far, it astonishes how little USA citizens can see or believe. What you have above posted, is small example of the madness - how can they do all this in public and the Democrats be so not there. Of course MSM shows nobody anything. While incredibly Hillary can freakout in public, scream and throw things at Secret Service people or others with her. She looks horrible in these photos.

All is further weirder this past 15 years. What could Trump do. He will likely not buck Big Oil. I dunno, maybe he has guts enough to stop the drone bombing in 7 nations of goats and kids and dogs? Ah, I doubt it.

I am having especial problem with physically controlling an email - trying to scroll, as in up or down. I must touch it very, very carefully, or, it goes up, it goes down, by itself even sometimes, up, down, up, down.

Love,

Billy

Note from the narrator:

From "The Prince Hope Show" ...

This public service announcement brought to you by Rolaids and the American Spelling Bee Council of Bowling Green.

How do you spell Al Queda?

Your toilet is plugged, and you know who did it.

Al Queda.

You have a flat tire on the freeway.

Yup, Al Queda.

You fall into a giant pothole as you turn off the freeway, disappear for days and who did it?

You got it, Al fucking Queda.

Your burrito is undercooked and you get indigestion.

There ya go. Al Queda strikes again.

They are everywhere.

Sleeper Cells.

Caffeine Cells.

Amoeba Cells.

Al Queda. Bob Queda.

Ninjas. Ghosts. Fairy tale characters.

You have never seen them, but they are everywhere.

This message brought to you by The United States of America Dept. of Homeland Security.

Have a nice day.

It's a very tough pill to swallow for Americans to consider that the media is controlled, that the government is not on our side. Americans believe in democratic elections, and we cherish the idea that we have a free press, and that we have a Democratic government. We're taught since the time that we are kids that we live in the greatest democracy in the world. And when you realize that your elections are controlled, the vote count is fraudulent, that the media is controlled, and that they're doing a 24/7 psy-ops against us day in and day out. Woah. It's too much for most people to handle. And they're not ready to leave those cherished beliefs. So, they would rather say, oh, he's just a conspiracy theorist, everything's fine, don't worry.

— Christopher Bollyn

Those who make peaceful revolution impossible will make violent revolution inevitable.

— John Kennedy

TWENTY-ONE

They gathered around Zima's table inside her tent, large enough for everyone to stand. They leaned in close and all serious, pointing to a map of the area, just like you see in black and white WW II pictures.

Each of their names was written on the map in red with arrows showing the area they would command.

They talked again about lines of supply, communication, initial tactics and fallback scenarios.

"Pilot Mountain," she said, pointing to the spot down the highway, south about fourteen miles. "If we get separated, things go to shit, that's where we meet. It should be on your GPS, we talked about all of this."

"A long time ago," Buster and Ariel droned together, so tired of hearing that.

Even on paper, there were problems. They had talked about all this so long ago, but it still was not settled.

"Oh my," said Ariel, putting one hand to her mouth.

"Now what?" snapped Zima.

"Well, another army comes," said Brandon.

"Ye-es," said Zima, her attention diverted by voices outside.

"Well," said Ariel.

"What if they don't come."

"The other army," said Brandon.

"We attack guerrilla style," said Buster.

"Attack what?" said Brandon.

"Cars going by?" said Joe.

"There's nobody out here."

"Steal the mail?" said Brandon.

"Steal their cats, dogs?"

"We just stay out here," said Zima.

"I think that's what they said."

"What?" said Brandon, turning away.

"The Fuck?" said Ariel.

"Is that?" said Zima as she shoved her way through them to storm outside.

She saw a white Winnebago and another vehicle, a van, or a RAV, some shit. She walked up to the driver's side of the olive green RAV, surprised to find an older man.

"We've got this reserved," said the man.

A lady leaned over from the passenger side to say "the card club, every third Thursdee of this month. We've done it for years, don't you know?"

"I'm afraid you don't," said Zima.

"We were here first."

"I'm afraid that doesn't matter," said the old man.

"You have to get reservations," said the old woman.

"At the city hall," said the old man.

"I was afraid of this," said the old woman.

"Didn't I tell you? I was afraid of this."

The man and the woman from the Winnebago walked up, concern laminated on their faces.

They showed Zima the paper they had received from the city office to make sure they had these camp sites for this weekend.

"You folks will have to leave," said one of the men, moving front and center to take control.

Zima walked away, leaving the four old people to talk about the camouflage uniforms, boots, weapons and Ernest T. Bass and some Lebowski T-shirts with the profanity.

Zima waved her hands to get mosquitoes and Brandon, Ariel and the others away from her as she walked in hurry to be by herself to text Lara. She didn't get an immediate response, so she called.

"Hey," said Zima.

"You don't by chance have reservations for these campsites?"

"Brooke said something about it," said Lara, "that we maybe should do that."

"I thought she took care of it."

"Well, she didn't," said Zima.

"Goooddd-damn it," said Lara.

"Yeah," said Zima.

She looked behind her as more cars began to pull in.

"We have about a hundred old people here saying they have reservations. What do you advise we do?

"I can't hear you!" said Zima, turning away again and walking.

More cars grumbled up over the gravel, pickups, all sorts of vehicles.

The old people crawled out and some other people climbed out of their cars, wanting to know what's the hold up?

They mingled.

"Is this the rebel camp?"

"No, I don't think so. This is card club. We've got our camp-out, the third Thursdee of this month. They pulled out neatly folded mauve calendars, from purses, back pockets, shirt pockets."

"You would not believe how many fucking rivers there are around here," said a young woman in camo, wearing a Lebowski shirt with profanity.

"We were over there, somewhere, no there, for two days, before we decided to move? Is there a Zimma here? Zima? Zim, Zim-somebody."

The grey hair and the white hair melded with the camo and the black T-shirts, against the background of the prescient browns, oranges, reds of the woods.

Zima slumped on a stump by the wooden outhouse talking to Lara in the basement headquarters in Minneapolis, explaining the situation, that the troops had finally arrived, but that they did not have reservations.

"Force them to leave," said Lara.

"This is the revolution."

"Yes, but," said Zima.

"They probably haven't heard, who we are, you know, anything about that, and I don't think they would really care."

"You have to make them care. That's what this is all about."

"That's very fine and dandy of you to say, sitting in your cozy bunker ..."

"You have no idea what I'm going through!" shouted Lara.

"My suggestion," she said.

"You do what you want to do, but my suggestion is that you point some guns, draw some weapons, make it happen. If you have to fire, so be it. We have to start some time. Might as well be now. Are they armed?"

"Some, I suppose. Brandon has a long knife, probly not sharpened. Buster's carrying around his dad's 12-gauge like he's fuckin' Matt Dillon, not the actor."

"I meant the old people," said Lara.

"Send them on their fucking way, take control."

Zima sighed.

She wanted to put this off. It's always happening later, next week, next day. She wasn't really ready, but shit.

She had her AR-15 at her desk in her tent. It probably didn't have to be loaded. Someone was coming with the rest of the weapons, might be in this group that just got here, she thought. But there was no time to discuss anything. It was up to her. She didn't want to ask any-fucking-one's opinion, in fact, she couldn't, and that made it all possible.

Brooke stood in front of city hall with her arm cocked, a brick in her hand.

Inside she saw Bobby at his desk and Karen staring out at her, her hands on her hips, scolding Brooke for something that she couldn't hear what, either that she had done or was about to do. Down the sidewalk came Tim Taylor, walking as fast as he could, one hand raised to get Brooke's attention, and down the street came the four giant, red Suburbans with shady windows.

Maybe Brooke could draw the brick down, set it down, and go in and take her seat at her desk, finish that mailing to the schools about the upcoming sale of Girl Scout Cookies and that a portion of sales would be going to the after-school recreation program. Or, she could put the brick down and be wrestled to the ground by the men in the Suburbans and taken to Sheriff Taylor's jail, for a while, and then somewhere else for a long time.

The glass cracked deliciously as the brick went through the outer pane as well as the inside window, rubbed over Karen's desk, broke her computer screen and flumped to the floor at Karen's feet.

Brooke smiled. She hadn't known if it would break, the window, maybe some of those these days are really thick and don't break.

These did.

She ran.

The four red Suburbans had gone past, finding no parking spots and were now employed in making a giant U-turn, forcing a mini-van to wait.

Sheriff Taylor found himself torn between chasing Brooke, for a few reasons, and going inside the city offices to see who was hurt and also giving Brooke a chance to get away.

He saw her sprinting down the street, stopping, starting, as if to go inside some store or alley, starting again, stumbling.

He heard the music, the bass, rumbling from the red Suburbans as they performed the routine together in the middle of the street, and he sang along, in a low humm.

"Testify."

He removed his cap and turned to go inside the city offices, where he checked the window, the computer, and asked if everyone was okay.

"All right."

Zima strode out of her tent, holding her AR-15 across her chest, looking as stern as she could manage for as scared as she was.

"Hey!" she shouted.

"Hey!"

She pulled the trigger and a few rapid rounds exploded and echoed, and she had held on.

It *was* loaded.

Everyone looked at her.

"All you old people!

"Hey! You!"

She shot again.

"All of you ... all of you who are with the card club ... you will have to come back *next* Thursday!"

A few of the old people started heading toward her, pulling out their calendars and papers.

"No!

"Stay there!"

She aimed the weapon at them.

"Do not *show* me no fucking calendars!" she shouted.

"I have talked to the city office, hall, the town head."

"The city manager?" someone said.

"That guy!" said Zima.

"You are all here on the wrong day!"

She spoke slowly.

"The ... wrong ... fucking ... day!" she said as if trying to make someone of another nationality understand you.

"You are here way ... the fuck ... early, all a you, so go home! Now! Next Thursday, go."

She pointed the gun and walked toward them as the old people backed up, hands raised, some with hands behind their heads.

She pointed the gun, here, there, herding them all into their vehicles, all with the same incredulous look on their face, wondering, no, knowing that they had not gotten the date wrong, it says right here. This is the right date. "Thursdee."

They backed up, turned around, headed out, slowly, all the old people faces staring right at Zima, all with the same hardened glaucoma eyes that said, this is the right ... *fucking* ... date.

These are the trenches of America's battle for world domination in the 21st century.

If not stopped, it will be a short century.

Since 1945, America's Manifest Destiny, posing as the Free World's Crusade against the Red Menace, has claimed twenty to thirty million lives worldwide and bombed one-third of the earth's people.

In the 19th century, America exterminated another kind of "red menace," writing and shredding treaties, stealing lands, massacring, and herding Native populations into concentration camps called "Indian reservations", in the name of civilizing the "savages."

By 1890, with the massacre of Lakota at Wounded Knee, the frontier land grab — internal imperialism — was over.

Now there was a world to conquer, and America trained its exceptionally covetous eye on Cuba and the Philippines.

American external imperialism was born. ...

— Luciane Bohne

TWENTY-TWO

"What're we gettin'?" Korey yelled down the hall.

The basement apartment CRUSHER HQ was not that far from the Green Mill and within reasonable, some thought, fast-walking distance of Divanni's, so the revolution often thrived on meatball subs and Green Mill specialty deep-dish pizza.

Korey went into Lara's office where she and Kaitylyn had Google Earth on their big screen computers showing the campground where Zima's bunch was gathering.

Lara had yellow sticky arrows on her screen to show where the different battalions would deploy.

"Regiments?" she said to Kaitylyn.

"I don't know, divisions maybe?" said Kaitylyn.

"Patrols, units," said Lara.

"Groups?" said Kaitylyn.

"Okay, I'll be back," said Korey.

He grabbed his helmet from his office and dragged his bike up the steps.

"Later," he said.

Lara's Foo Fighters ringtone went off, meaning it was from Hector.

"WTF," Lara said to Kaitylyn as Kaitylyn took a call from Zima.

"What the fuck does WTF even mean?" said Lara.

"WTF what? Not even an exclamation point. Does he not know I will not respond to anything with no exclamation points?"

"Zeem needs coffee," said Kaitylyn.

"Did we not include coffee in the provision drops?" said Lara.

"God-dammit."

"No," said Kaitylyn.

"She says she needs real coffee, from Trader Joe's, and can we bring it?"

155

"Sure," said Lara, "why not."

"What's up from the boys?" said Kaitylyn.

"Hector says WTF/LOL."

"WTF what?"

"I know, right?" said Lara.

"I'm just gonna fuck with him right fucking back."

She texted: *Your mother here. Found magazines. What tell her?*

"What'd he say?" said Kaitylyn.

"WTF," said Lara, "that's' what he always says."

"How they comin"? said Kaitylyn.

"Not bad," said Lara.

"We sent some folks. They're diggin' away like a bunch of beavers."

"I don't ... beavers dig," said Kaitylyn, "but yeah, good, what do I tell Zeem?"

"Tell her to move out," said Lara.

"If she really wants my opinion they need to divide into groups or whatever and spread out, deploy, get fucking started. We can't do anything from here, from these computers. It starts with them. Geezuz-fuck, how many times?"

"Ten-four," said Kaitylyn.

"Will do."

Dodging cars, head down, whisking through leaves, open car door, head up, Korey pounded down Grand, smelling the beginning of school, the sorrowful end of summer, he'd always liked school, not really, he felt out of place there, but the idea of what school was supposed to be like, all goodness and light and everybody happy and the weather, the glorious beginning of school, all the schools of the Twin Cities, pre-schools, elementary schools, middle schools, high schools, colleges, Macalester, St. Thomas, St. Catherine, everybody feeling it, corduroy in the air, the colors, the whole thing a crisp apple, that's what just made him feel happy.

He shot off, veered right to go down Summit, and the state fair and football is starting, oh, man, he loved this town!

And then another block to where the old group home sat, big and musty smelling, with photos inside of some early historical Saint Paul shit on the walls leading up the steep, winding, wooden steps, perhaps to Narnia.

Korey slowed down. He stopped and stood on the sidewalk, watching the people up on the high porch.

Just like they used to.

That could still be them, if ... only, well.

The old group home, where Korey and all the others worked, perched on a kind of a knoll on the corner, commanding the area. It had three stories, quite the edifice. A big old house right in the middle of the city, with a history, liquor, gambling, prostitution, some of the stuff that made those homes on Summit possible, but not quite as far under the table.

And then down the street and over, over, was the workshop, or center, the facility for disabled adults where some of the staff had second jobs and where all of the residents attended Monday through Friday if it didn't blizzard.

Geronimo was everybody's friend, saying hello, kidding with people. He also liked to steal food when he could and he didn't like to cook. At the group home, when it was his turn he had his ways of getting the staff to do most of the work.

At the workshop he worked mostly in the shred room, stuffing paper through the shred machine, and on two days of the week he went with a staff around town to pick up paper from businesses to bring back to the workshop to shred.

He recorded his own songs and had nicknames for everybody. New staff members would only have to wait a couple of days before they got their new name from Geronimo. He didn't really like to shower, but on Saturdays he would lounge in the bathtub in really hot water for an hour. He also liked to draw, and dance, and smoke, but he was trying to quit because of the cost, but sometimes he would sweet talk staff into giving him one.

He had his own flat screen TV in his room, and he had his regular shows, History Channel, Ancient Aliens, Discover, wrestling, and on fall and winter Sundays, football all day long, 24/7.

Geronimo was a 9/11 freak. He saved everything about 9/11 and put it on his walls, in his closet, his desk drawers, flags, ribbons, clippings, magazines.

And on the wall, pinned to his cork bulletin board was what everyone just called The Letter:

I will risk my life for the people and everyone and my girlfriend and do rite. For all time.

It is me who will give everyone their dream and put a fist into fears. And take a stand.

And we have every right to work and live and injoy life and live like we want.

Geronimo will lead Man for their future will turnout.

I am The Crusher.

Ta-daaa!

Lots of people were up there on the porch. They must be home from work. It's wrestling night. They're either going over to some other house or waiting for them to come here. Korey and Geronimo had started wrestling night.

They were gonna name each brigade after a wrestler, then it was super hero, then there were other ideas that got tossed around and all the T-shirt crap.

Korey just stood there on his bike, on the sidewalk, watching the old group home and thinking about how right it felt there, so at home, so comfortable.

Jim was there in the shred room when Geronimo found that airplane ticket.

He would never give up the ticket. The director, program manager, said we had to get it, that it was something they couldn't do, take things out of the shred room. They even said their executive director and board of directors were talking about it and the cops got called in, maybe the DHS, Homeland Security, all that shit. It was bad, no fun. But Geronimo wouldn't give it up. He'd scream and throw things. It was his. Geronimo was a big kid, big man, a giant. He hid it and said he lost it and there wasn't much they could do after that.

Korey thought he liked the color of the ticket and he knew he had something valuable that everyone else wanted. And it had a little airplane graphic on it.

I don't think he'd ever been on a plane, Korey thought, sitting there on the sidewalk and hearing the guys on the porch and almost being able to make out their words, and maybe if he had this he could go on a plane and he'd be flying like a superhero. Geronimo never said this, but that's what Korey thought.

Geronimo was even on the Prince Hope show, that afternoon radio show, it was a big deal. They didn't make it about the ticket he found, but more to talk about Special Olympics, but it really was all about the ticket. Geronimo told Korey that while they were on a break Prince Hope asked him about the ticket, joked a little about was it really real and said something like, hey can I see it? Geronimo said, no way, Jose, and he wasn't joking. And then he died.

He had a heart attack. It was at the workshop, on the porch, in his bedroom, the tub, Korey never really heard.

He just knew it was a big deal and lots of the staff got suspended and because he was also there in the shred room that day, he really got suspended, and they weren't supposed to talk to each other and some of them didn't, and so Korey never really heard what all happened. He didn't even go to the funeral because he was afraid he would get arrested or something.

He did hear that when they cleared out all his stuff, the PD came in with some other big shots and a police officer to look through his belongings.

"I don't think they found what they wanted to find," Jim had told Korey. In fact, Korey knows they didn't.

And then they all got their jobs back, even Korey, because somebody said Geronimo took the blame for it, on his death bed, in the ambulance, while he was lying on the bathroom floor, or in his hospital room, something like that.

Geronimo's funeral was right there in the neighborhood. Korey had watched it from the outside just like now, sitting on his bike. And he had followed the funeral cars and the hearse to the cemetery, over on something-something.

He'd never gone to the grave. He figured they watched it, to capture any CRUSHER rebels who stopped by.

Korey's phone buzzed.

A text from Lara.

"ASLAN."

WTF, he thought. That's not good.

He needed to get back, but he didn't get the food yet. He shoved off and peddled down the sidewalk, past the group home. He looked, stared, at those on the porch. And they stared at him. A couple of the guys waved and yelled hi. Korey waved back but he didn't recognize anyone up there. Nobody.

Korey put his head down, headed to Davanni's. At the intersection the light turned yellow and he plowed right through. He'd text his order, come right back and then hurry to HQ and find out why Lara is making jokes with the bat signal.

First he had to do this.

He knew where the cemetery was because he went by there whenever he got the chance, over on river road.

It was "a well-kept space", that's what it said on the plaque at the gate. Korey coasted in on the dirt lane, around a curve and back again. He stood on one side of the bike on one leg while still moving, then walked over the grass, up the little hill, to the shade tree.

About ten feet away he lay the bicycle down and his helmet.

He folded his hands and walked up the little incline to the headstone laid flat on the ground in the grass.

Geronimo.

I will risk my life for everyone and my girlfriend and do rite.

Korey's phone buzzed, this time a text from Jim asking if he got anything from Lara.

Korey stood over Geronimo's grave, trying to take it all in, the mound outlining the body, the wilted flowers someone had left, the Happy Meal toys, how the grave looks toward the river.

Boomboom. Two car doors slammed.

Korey looked up and saw two men, in sunglasses and suits, headed toward him at a fast walk from the top of the hill where the cemetery path wound.

Korey whipped around, picked up his bike, leaving his helmet, jumped on and sped away. He heard car doors and the rhoom! of an engine.

... Korey put his head down and pumped, through a red light, around cars, to the St. Thomas campus, up the sidewalk, across campus, turned around and came back, across the same light, through an alley, through four alleys, up the hill between Grand and Summit avenues, through the smell of wood smoke into the Macalester neighborhood.

He stopped, stood straddling the bike, watching through the branches and bushes the scene: an ambulance, a fire truck, the street blocked, firemen in yellow directing traffic, shit scattered on the lawn, computers, desks, pillows, papers. Police cars were parked right up on the terrace, like stranded boats, hanging over the curb, lights flashing, sirens said that more vehicles were on the way.

Lara, Kaitylyn? Nowhere to be seen. Korey heard the talking on the police radios and touched the pistol in the sleek black holster inside his pants.

On the radio he heard "CRUSHER," Lara's full name, Kaitylyn something, and then he heard his name, and Jim's.

Korey forced into the hedge, right up to the garage. He unsnapped the holster and kept his hand there as he got to one knee.

School kids with little backpacks walked past slowly on the sidewalk, turning, staring, hurried along by the older ones. Korey cursed and moved to get the stout, sharp hedge branch out of his back.

Korey leaned forward, waiting for Lara and Kaitylyn to be hauled out. For sure, Jim and others were also watching from somewhere close and they would free them right there.

"I know-a."

Kaitylyn worked her phone with both thumbs.

She and Lara sat in the back row of the movie theater, showing who-knows-what-and-don't-really-care, as Lara kept hissing instructions.

"Tell them," she whispered, leaning way over.

She didn't have her phone, couldn't remember if she left it there or what.

"Tell them we're pulling back, Plan B, ASLAN."

Kaitylyn put her nose to her phone and worked.

"Keep digging," said Lara, rubbing her chin.

"Deploy, attack, disperse, diversity."

"Diversify?" said Kaitylyn.

"Yes, yes," said Lara.

She hurried off to get snacks and returned with diet Pepsi's and popcorn.

"They should know. We talked about all this a long time ago.

"Not good for you?" said Lara when Kaitylyn shook her head at the pop.

"How can it not be?"

Marv Sannes, Independent Party Candidate 2014
at US House of Representatives

I just finished Michael Hastings book: "The Operators". No doubt in my mind that he was murdered. 1) He viollated the "con code" of the media-military-industry-war brotherhood. 2) The 3 explosions of his car is so obvious and so quickly covered by the LAPD - part of the brotherhood - it was meant to be an obvious and in-your-face murder. To expect justice for 9/11 or for Hastings' murder is living in the myth. Nobody's going to rise up - the best we get is to find each other and live with the freedom from fear and the knowledge that we are on the right side of THIS myth. Buying Amy Goodman is the same kind of thing, Chomsky and that whole crew of the "compatible left". I'm sure she feels justification: "Look at how many people I'm reaching with these other truths!" Hahahaha I wonder what my price is?

TWENTY-THREE

They each took a certain spot on a certain river, some stream, some fucking shit.

Zima pointed and planned and told them all as clearly as she could as they stood around the table inside her tent and again as they all stood in a circle outside her tent, and again as she walked each vehicle out of the parking lot toward the gravel road and wished them all good luck.

She did not tell them, any of them, about what just happened in Saint Paul. Most of them would not know what "ASLAN" even meant.

Zima turned away from the last car to her own group, her own brigade, smiled, put her head down and walked fast to her tent.

In a rush, she gathered things in her arms, hurried to the door of her tent and set them down on the ground, dashed back inside for more. They had talked about this a long time ago, at this time she must remain calm, think about things not associated with what was happening now, fool her mind and her body into not realizing how fucking big a deal this was right now.

Cigarettes. Where were the cigarettes. They had been here. She saw them, red pack, white pack? She did not really like to smoke, but she might have to.

Oh, this was so much fun, not fun, but exciting, very much exciting, and she was so afraid, terrified, so many things could happen. With both hands she shoved thoughts of her family out of her head.

"Who's riding with who?" someone said to her from outside the tent.

Zima stopped and thought and delivered the answer, then resumed her quest for her other shit.

What the hell happened to Lara and Kaitylyn, she thought and felt sick in her stomach. There were those she did not trust and she could not help not trusting them, even though they had talked about how this would happen.

She had never been shot. That would hurt. She broke a finger once falling face-first from a tree. That hurt. She spotted a half-eaten Snickers on her night table and gulped it, wishing then she had chewed and enjoyed it. She smelled diesel fuel and bug spray. A gunshot barked. She stormed out and stalked right over to the smiling one and berated him about how this was not fun, this was not a fucking game, and hurried back into her tent.

"You just gave away our position!"

She stalked back.

She grabbed away the AR and set it carefully against a tree.

This was all on her. She had to do this on her own. It was big, maybe too big. She liked the big, solid boots she wore. They made a difference. If she were wearing tennis shoes maybe she could not do this. In a flash she thought of all the personal drama happening these last days and right now among the other commanders and the troops, all the little squabbles and troubles, screwups and worries, all the shit they forgot to bring that they just have to have, all the things they did not know, all the stupid things they thought and said, and all the great things they said sometimes.

She smelled the fall, so close-by, maybe heard the river over the insane rustle of everyone hurrying to get ready. If she did not absolutely have to be here, she wouldn't.

"Sir, Zima, Zeem!"

"Yes, what?"

"Do you have the list, what we're supposed to bring?"

She grabbed the folded paper from her back pocket.

Zima looked at her own pile: socks, ammo, grenades, poncho, toothpaste, brush, hairbrush, extra water, batteries, extra coat, pants, underwear, Snickers, chips, two books. All to fit in a hockey-type nylon bag, and then her K-bar knife, her AR-15, handgun on her waist, no helmets, just ball caps, whatever. They talked about helmets before and decided not.

She shouldn't have to carry it far, to the vehicle, whoever still had room for her, then to the deployment by the river. And then the battle comes to her, to them. She didn't think, they weren't supposed to, have to walk really far, not too far.

Her brigade or whatever was staying right on this river, the Ararat, just down farther, to what Zima thought was a better position and out of the way of the old people if they came back.

"Okay!"

Zima stepped out of her tent, raised her hand high.

"Let's move out!"

And she hated how that sounded, but it had to be done.

"C'mon! Let's go! You guys!"

* * *

Max, Ariel, Morgan, Buster, Brandon, and Joe had divided up the troops and taken pretty much an equal number, their own brigade, and already headed out in caravans to the spots assigned to them by Zima.

So Max sat on a stump looking at Stewart's Creek, or Stewards, depending on if you had an old map or what. His rifle lay on the ground. He wore his Battle of Mayberry T-shirt, the Lebowski version — not Ernest T. Bass — which made no sense, and even so, hardly anyone he knew had seen the movie, but someone had, but that had all been discussed and figured out long ago and so now was the time to go with the flow. He got that. But, still.

They had been dropped off and then walked into the woods to the riverside and had made camp.

Max spotted two little trees, tiny, their arms wrapped around each other, leaning toward each other. They would grow up in that pose. For ten years, twenty years, sixty years they would remain. He liked the idea of that, but it seemed so odd, so unreal. That doesn't really happen. But it should.

It should.

Things were happening. Without even looking Max could hear the buzz all around him of the others, the clanking of cooking stuff and weapons, the flapping and billowing of tents, the thunk of axes. Maybe later they would not make a fire, but tonight, what the hell, that's what he had told them.

He talked and texted with the others. Joe thought he was at the wrong river. The map he had said "Fauthners" and the old sign here said Faulkner's Creek. Morgan can't find Seed Cane Creek. Ariel can't find Moore's Fork.

"Just stay put," he told Joe.

"Keep looking, ask Zeem," he said to Ariel.

"You want me to come help?"

"No," said Ariel.

Here there were folks trying to find and declare the designated crapping station, strumming guitars, polishing weapons. Most of them seemed happy. Max wanted to tell them something, but then why take away the last happy day they have, like the second grade girl getting off the bus and spotting her mom on the corner, and the look in her eye as she dashes to the mom to tell her about her day. She is never going to be that happy again. Even as it just begins, it's over.

Something big was about to happen, maybe important, probably loud, Max thought. He pressed his pen into the little notepad on his leg. If you notice at the really big events, how common things are, or the really big celebrities, you get close and the thing you notice is how normal they are, maybe more in control, maybe nicer, maybe some things, well, they have to have something to be that famous.

Soon enough those dancing in the river like this is Woodstock will learn what wounds look like, how it feels to be really scared, to have someone die right next to you, to kill someone.

Fighting is important. He wrote it down. This shit stops here. After battles things change. History is made. History changes. This thing that happens tomorrow could change history, just think of that.

"Things don't happen as they are planned in combat, they happen like a car accident."

He wrote that down and put parenthesis around it. It wasn't his, but he wanted to remember it. Maybe use it as a chapter heading quote or something down the line.

Brooke heard about what happened to Lara and Kaitylyn.

What do I do? she wondered as she sat in a tree in an alley with about six orioles, probly more. She texted Korey back and Jim. She texted Lara, Kaitylyn, Evey, Zima.

"Can't talk," said Zima.

"Shit happnin hope u ok, talk latr."

From her perch Brooke had the perfect view of main street right in front of the city offices. Her tree still had all its leaves and the oranges and reds and now the deep, pure, dark, yellow of her own hair. She moved her butt just a little to try to get comfortable without falling out.

She watched Sheriff Tim Taylor talking to the men in suits, their Suburbans taking up all the parking right in front of the city offices. Karen came out, her arms crossed over her chest.

Taylor pointed down the sidewalk.

One of the men looked up, right at Brooke and Brooke had to tell herself there was no way he could see her in all these fucking leaves and branches and greenery and shit. But then if she gave herself up, they might go easy on her, easier, fewer years. Is the death penalty still a thing? He looked away.

Max heard that Ariel's brigade was stuck in traffic. She reported that it was hard to keep all the vehicles together through each light and sometimes the lead vehicles had to pull over to let the others catch up.

Joe said he didn't fucking care what the name of his fucking creek was, they were staying right there.

"Good," said Max.

Max liked Joe. Joe's brother had been in the Army, deployed. He was supposed to be here. Joe knew a lot about guns and hunting. They needed somebody like him. Max made the sign of the cross on his forehead and asked that Joe not get killed right away.

Max asked, texted Zima, they were supposed to text and only call when absolutely necessary and do neither, if they could manage. None of them could. He asked Zima because he really could not remember what they had decided, do they just start shooting on their own, or is it up to Zima to go first, or does Lara tell us, or just how does this work?

Zima said "go for it."

And Max, thought, so this is the revolution.

Go for it. ... What?

Nobody knows where anybody else is, what they are doing? Even after all those situps and running and Lara screaming at Camp Sweaty and reading all those books on war and training hand to hand and at the rifle range, which did not really work out that great, was just his opinion. Even after all of that, and the boots and camo and T-shirts and food and "logistics" classes in Kaitylyn's apartment, it was like they had done nothing.

The headquarters is sacked, destroyed, Evey went home, won't talk. The whole world hates us, and I'm supposed to just go for it. I'll go for it all right. I'll go for it right back home and have a life and write "Off The Road," that's what I'm gonna do in about two seconds.

He shook his head at the ground. Just start shooting, shoot someone, capture a farm house, push over a contract postal carrier's pickup and set it on fire, take over a Kwik Trip. Actually, that might work.

Max perked his head up.

What was that?

It sounded like gun shots. Probably somebody was practicing for deer season.

Max turned and stood. More shots, rapid shots, different weapons, rapid succession, still quite a ways away. He ran.

Lara sat in the back seat of the F Bus. She had a Flex Ticket just for this occasion, actually. She found her phone. Her phone was dying. She texted frantically after hearing about the shots that Max had heard.

She received texts boom-boom-boom. She looked up and scowled at the bus driver in her big mirror as they hit some bumps. Impossible to work in here.

From Zima: Can't talk.

To Zima: What is happening? Just tell me.

From Max: Shots fired.

From Korey, From Jim, From Kaitylyn, From Evey, From Hector.

Max sprinted to the command vehicle in the high grass, leaned inside, grabbed the map and plopped to his knees to spread it on the ground. Soon he was surrounded by the others, asking him what was going on, asking each other, pushing in on his shoulders to see what he was looking it.

He plopped to his belly and followed his finger around the map.

"It's Joe," he said, and then looked up again to try to place the shots now coming continuously.

"Or Brandon," someone said, poking the map.

"Ariel's here," someone pointed, adding exactly nothing.

What a Muggle, thought Max, pushing himself up to a hop with both hands.

Max stood and stuck his chin into the air, still trying to understand. Now there were sirens, and it seemed as if ...

As if ... this were the revolution ... also the apocalypse, also the end of his life, his complete destruction, humiliation, exposure ... because there were helicopters, tilted, wobbling like landing geese, meaning business, completely serious ... coming over the hillside on the other side of their little river.

Little lights lit up on the bottom of the helicopters, sparks, flashes.

The bodies around Max thumped and jumped back and to the ground and the bodies and voices made clichéd cartoon noises, *oomph,* and *ooh* and *ohhh!* Something plopped onto his hand and Max looked at it and it was blood.

They screamed and cried and shouted and red oozed and flowed and grew on the tiny gravel spot and in the grass around Max.

Max ran to them all at once and knelt over them and touched them and said it would be all right.

Max saw others shouldering their weapons and pointing at the helicopters. He saw one young woman on one knee and her shoulder jerking rapidly from the recoil.

He did the same.

Max made an attempt at looking down the barrel, but mostly he concentrated on his finger on the trigger, how the trigger felt not at all comfortable, and the sharp ridge that hurt and dug into his finger, but he pulled and his shoulder jerked and it was so fucking loud and real and serious, too much so.

He took it away and looked to see the result of what he had done and found none.

He jammed the gun back into his shoulder and now a veteran he knew just what to do and he pulled the trigger back and sprayed out a line of fire at all the helicopters at once. The air around him filled with smoke. He smelled it but that was too much, mostly he heard things, shouting, firing, and now the helicopter blades. They hovered over the river and kept firing, stirring the water into swirls.

And they would sit there forever and kill them all if someone did not make them go away. More bullets thudded into those already lying on the ground and that is what Max could not stand, the sound of the thumps like defenseless melons on the truck gate, just sitting there. And even as he screamed so loud and so silently because he was only one little man with the whole world happening right there, lines, strings dropped out of the helicopters and little ants climbed backwards down the lines, threads, strings, swaying, whipping, back and forth as Max engaged his own line of departure, ran toward them, the river, with his rifle across his chest, into the flying rocks and the water and the dust.

Joe and his men and women were dug into the side of a river, the name now did not seem at all important.

The trees on both sides of the river were thick and hung out over the bank. The water was narrowish, about fifty yards, is what one of the guys had said and added gratuitously, Joe had thought, that he always judged distance by a football field because he used to play football. The river was rocky, you could see the bottom, and not a great barrier, not much protection, Joe thought.

For now it was quiet, but a few minutes ago there had been lots of action. Joe's Brigade had formed a line at the river, of which they were proud, at least Joe was. They had found a fucking river and had all their gear and a spot for the vehicles and then this kind of natural ridge and there was the other side where the other army was supposed to be.

And they had heard shots.

"Shotguns!" someone had said, and for a moment they had all hunkered down, waiting for them to miss or go away. And then more booms, single booms, and then a double boom-boom, and that did it.

Someone on Joe's side fired, either straight into the air by mistake or across into the other trees by high anxiety or on purpose.

And so, most of Joe's line, lying on its stomach, had pulled up their rifles and found a way to fire from there or gotten to one knee or two knees and started firing, out of boredom, maybe disgust with the ways of the world, or fright, or wanting to be a part of a group.

They lay right in the middle of their side of trees, so leaves flew everywhere and they could really only see the water, not the other trees, but they heard the bullets, actually their bullets ripping the other trees, tearing at them, wounding them, breaching them, making a dent, perhaps making a real difference, like a strong letter to the editor in a small town about a non-sanctioned topic.

Joe had smiled.

"Wow," he said.

"Nice."

Which meant they had really done something. Was it too soon for a bump? Some people rolled over on their backs to smoke.

Boom!

Boom!

Boom-boom!

The shotguns on the other side answered, ripping their side, showering them with leaves, big oak, maple leafs, now with holes, with whole sides missing, in little bits, beginning to turn, red, orange, still fully green, now dying, lying silent in the grass on Joe's side.

Now fully out of fear Joe's line turned and opened up, everything they had. They were not going to die here, they were young and did not want to find out what it felt like to be shot, bleeding, screaming with only seconds left to live of a life that was really going to be so full, the most full ever, a super-life, maybe the best ever in history.

Their own leaves showered down and back at them with now a little breeze.

Boom! Boom-boom!

Joe's line flattened, hugged the little ridge, which might have been a stone fence at one time, overgrown with flora after many earth-shaking events of the river leaving its banks, receding, again, again, loving the ground, the rich soil, earth is life, instant hippies.

It went back and forth like that and then Joe waved his arm in the air and shouted for his people to stop.

They heard shouting on the other side and "motherfuckers!" "cocksuckers!"

"What the fuck you doin' over there!"

One engine turned and turned and roared to a start, doors slammed. Another engine and both pickups — someone said they were pickups — spun and roared off away, throwing up mud, then skidding on the gravel road, more shots out the windows and epithets, threats and promises.

"Die motherfuckers!" as they sped away.

"It's hunting season," somebody said.

And Joe, thought, *oh.*

Shit.

Ariel's Brigade had left their vehicles in an abandoned lane, taken time to cover them with branches, grass, old cardboard and an old sign for a gas station, and headed into the woods to find Seed Cane Creek that had to be right over there.

They pushed and pushed, pushing away branches, from their faces, out of their sides, around their ankles, through bushes. They called to each other to keep everyone together.

"Over here!"

"They will hear you!"

"Who?"

Finally someone pushed and pushed and fell through, into the light, onto very, very hard red, jagged rock, piles of it that ran to forever this way and that.

They all came through, one at a time and then all at once.

Ariel climbed up the steep incline, over the red rock that was slippery, up to the railroad tracks. They all followed her, slipping, helping each other. Some balanced on the track, two tried to walk on the tracks in opposite directions using the rifles for balance and that didn't work.

So, yeah. Ariel stood in the middle of the tracks with her hands on her hips, looking down this way, turning to look the other way, up at the bright sky, her hand at her brow like Daniel Boone. They had heard some of the shooting, but they were working so hard in the bush nothing else mattered. But now she wondered where it had come from.

She pointed to where she kind of remembered where Joe's group was supposed to be.

Some people started to wander and some sat down, on the rocks and on the tracks, and some started to point their weapons at birds in the air. One person, and then two, now three, complained there was nothing to eat in their packs.

"Pringles?" someone said.

"Really? Pringles? Not even barbecue."

Max told someone or wrote it in his journal that a lot of it was a lot like what they had read in the books assigned to them by like Lara and Kaitylyn, Jim, Korey, them.

How it would feel in combat, or should or might. And he said sometimes that worried him, that he wouldn't feel like he was supposed to feel. And some of it was just right, he said.

He said he did feel excited when it finally happened, maybe but not really like when you finally start writing after thinking about starting for a long time, or start that long Saturday run after thinking about it all week, or if you get into a fight like in a bar and you didn't plan on that, but while it's happening and right after, it's not that bad, it's more fun than bad, except if you are really getting your ass kicked, he said.

"You're kind of like ... it's a little bit like playing war or army in the neighborhood, running around, hiding, but more than that, actually more fun, if fun, no, fun isn't the right word, but intense, a thrill, a rush.

"Yep, when I, all the time I had been getting, trying to get ready I was nervous, that I would hurt somebody, that I would get hurt, that I would just turn and run. That might be the worse thing, I think.

"And then I saw those guys on the ground, bleeding, screaming, the insides of one girl's head, somebody else shot in the throat. I started to hate right then. I mean I hated before, lots of things. There's a lot of hate that got me into this in the first place, but this was different. It happened right then and that's when I charged those helicopters.

"And just like the books said, I remember it all, probly because I could have died. I wanted to see everything, record everything, feel everything, no matter how bad it was. I don't remember anything at all about the last twenty times I've been to the same grocery store, but these seven minutes, nine, eleven, I don't know how long it was, I can see it all, all at once, everything. No shit. I am not shitting you. Do I look like I'm lying? Well I'm not. Maybe a little. I don't remember how I got to the river. I saw those bloody friends of mine and then I was at the river. I don't remember how I got there."

Max put that AR on his hip and just sprayed those helicopters with the ropes hanging down with the men climbing down like ants. And he actually hit some of the men/ants and he heard some of his bullets thump-thump-thump into the sides of the helicopters. And others joined him and the helicopters veered like bees and pulled away. And the ones they had dropped, well, you could see them plain as day because what they had figured was long grass to hide in was only up to their ankles and even when they went flat to their stomachs you could see them.

And there were only a few, so Max charged into the river. He was going to kill them all himself. He was a hero. He was loving being a hero and he was a hero maybe for Geronimo, maybe for his girlfriend, the one he would have someday who would be his loving, faithful wife for decades and decades and they would tell their children probably every night at bedtime how Max had charged into the river to save the world, and it had actually worked. He had saved the world and now you have this nice house in this nice neighborhood and these nice beds and books and your own drawings from school on the walls and the refrigerator.

Max charged, not knowing how deep the river was, and the others charged with him. Max for one, fell face-first into the water and somehow kept one arm up, his rifle dry because he knew from television shows that he should, that he had to.

He came up with that feeling in his whole head when you swallow water like in a pool, that it goes up your nose and you panic. Max shot up, fought the water, the current that he could now feel but could not see from the shore. He pushed hard with his legs and worked his arms, trying to remember to keep firing. He heard others behind him doing the exact same thing.

They made it to the high grass on the other side and huddled together. They heard the men/ants talking to each other up on the little hill. They sounded worried, scared, wondering where Max and his people were while ducking from fire from the rest of the Max Brigade on the other side, though they would not know that's who it was. They would only think of them as insurgents, criminals, whatever labels Prince Hope had put into their heads.

Max made hand signals, pointed, you two, go there, you there, you with me.

And they fucking charged.

Not right away, first they slipped and fell in the opposite side mud and high grass and sticks and rocks, but after that they charged, shooting from their hips.

Max says that as he was charging and firing and seeing little faces in the grass with eyes looking at him he wondered who they were. He wondered if they would kill him before he killed them. He really wondered that. Because you have more time out there, he said, if it is you. If it is you, you have all the time in the world because each moment, each second is so precious and you make such good use of your time.

You do not waste it wondering what you will do later or worrying over what you did before. You think about now and there is a lot of now, plenty of now, when you think about it. As on stage or on the field, the crowd goes away, there is only you and these few shitheads.

He aimed from his hip as he ran and screamed and he felt the thuds of his bullets, maybe one, two, maybe a half dozen as they went into the body of this one guy who was kneeling in the grass shooting at Max.

Max charged, his face contorted, screaming though no one heard him, and more so as he saw the terror in the man's face, the man that he charged, the one other person in the world, he and Max. The man faltered to a side and put up a hand forcing Max to lean in to smash his face with the butt of his rifle. Max raised the gun and stood over the man, screaming.

"Aaaah! Get up! Get up! Aaaah!"

Max, his face red, spit on his lips and snot filling his nose, sweat covering his forehead, his neck, raged at the man by staring and huffing and taunting then pleading with the man to get up.

The man lay on his side in the grass, his mouth open, a fly already sitting on his lip. Max smashed the man's face to get rid of the hideous fly.

Bullets flew around him, some of his own people were wounded. In a minute or two the rest of the ants in the low grass were killed. One was crying and pleading for his life and those standing over him decided to drag him, walk him down the little hill and through the river back to camp. Max ran at them and screamed they should kill him, but they pushed him away.

Max sat by the man that was his, his kill, and as he had heard it was done he reached for the man's pockets. He touched the man and he was solid, with weight unmoving. Like a large animal that had been alive minutes before but was now dead, no more, because of Max. More than an animal. Quickly he forced himself to dig into the back pocket for the billfold. He had it and kicked back, away.

It was black, not expensive, Walmart, two ragged dollar bills, a little brown folder with a hunting license, a military or law enforcement type identification card and his photo I.D. driver's license, a photo of a small family, another of a red pickup on a car lot.

Max's kill was Thomas, Tom DePaul, of 14271 Locust, Mount Airy, North Carolina, 29.

A young man, though older than Max, a military, police type, athletic, and Max had kicked his ass. Totally defeated him. He was dead. So dead. Right now he was meeting his relatives and God and floating right above them right here and understanding everything.

Max looked around and could not breathe. He raised his head. He jumped to stand to get his head high enough to breathe. He opened his mouth wide. He ran five steps this way, five back. He bent, put his hands on his knees. He raised back up again straight and his head came out of the water at last. He gulped gallons of air and raised his hands above his head in fists.

He staggered away, came back, picked up his rifle, dropped the billfold and tried to stand straight to walk down the little hill to the river.

Unaware, Max slogged through the river. He found someone with cigarettes and held out his hand for one. He sat on the ground. Somewhere someone had put in some music. It played tinny over the camp site, "don't you know I'm talkin' 'bout a revolution."

Max stuffed the cigarette into the ground and ran to vomit in the nearest bush clump. It hurt so bad. And there was no control. It forced him to let it all go. He knelt and threw up everything inside of him that ever was.

They had actually fought them back, the giant mosquito bees with the guns and the man ants descending out of them bent on scurrying toward them and devouring them, which they would have done, but they didn't.

Max stood, careful not to step in his throw up. Like a cat, just as he was walking away he kicked both feet back to try to throw more cover.

They drew together in a clump and talked all at once, pointing, yelling, all at one time. They shot weapons into the air and whooped. Max pointed and threw up a perimeter. More troops slogged across the river and up the little hill to stand with the dead to watch for what was to come. He arranged for burial details and things to be said and crosses of sticks to be constructed.

Max texted and called, trying to reach Lara and also the others around him, close-by to tell them what could not be told.

He and his men and women gathered around a fire in the daylight. They sat on stones and dragged logs over for benches. They talked and smoked.

Zima called and said she was bored. There was nothing happening at her river.

"Why don't you come over?" said Max, "hang out with us."

Zima said she thought she might. She asked directions. Max said he had no idea, but there was a river here and their river might connect with Zima's river if you followed it.

"Or not," said Zima.

They actually fought them back and what a relief and surprise it was and it gave him his motivation to write.

Max wrote this because he was sure, one hundred percent certain, he would be dead by morning.

QUOTE REMOVED BY ORDER OF DHS, UNITED STATES DEPARTMENT OF HOMELAND SECURITY. [DHS US2FA]

TWENTY-FOUR

Caryl,
Am back from HEB experience, more tired than usually.

Well, yes, the professional Democrats are crooks and their voters
are "sheeple." Kind of a funny term these times. And you should know who else is crooks and sheeple. My siblings only accept MSM and if I tell them the Obama administration has continued the W. Bush administration their minds rebel, and vomit actually. The human being during vomit can't hear. Truth is, the Obama administration went worse than the Bushies. It is same shit but larger. Heh, "on steroids" this time around. Perhaps, Berry already knew the score, had no intention of fussing, being raised C.I.A., not a USA native.

I expect when Obama consults with Trump it will be just like when the Bushies consulted with Obama. Obama knew to not be taken out and Trump will too, I expect. USA is a gangster nation, plays for keeps like maniacs.

Perhaps for New World Order Hillary will be tossed. She is unstable. What further use can they have of her.

Always good to hear from you and now you are expanding. Why not. Not to matter we are in our seventies.

Love,
Billy

Note from the narrator:

From "The Prince Hope Show" ...

Nominations are currently being accepted to re-name all the places we have named for horrible people.

... Ronald Reagan National Airport, The 10th Mountain Division Highway, 90TH Infantry Division Highway, 173D Airborne Brigade Memorial Highway, Gerald Ford Memorial Highway, George Bush Intercontinental Airport.

If we are going to name things after famous bad people, then why not ... well ...

How about ... Ted Bundy National Cemetery, John Wayne Gacy International Airport, or Jeffrey Dauhmer Memorial Freeway, the Charles Manson Space Needle.

Rather ... Here's a thought ...

Why not name things for good people rather than terrible people.

Why not Dan and Phil Berrigan International Airport.

Dorothy Day Interstate.

The Emma Goldman Freeway.

Brought to you by Citizens For Naming Things After Good People Rather Than Horrible People.

Richard Dolan: Left Forum, NYC, 5/22/16

The top sixty individuals on planet earth have as much accumulated wealth as the entire bottom half of humanity. ... so when you have a situation like that and these people are ensconced in the transnational corporations that dominate everything ... that's a war. What they don't want us to know is that this whole thing is happening, because then we might have something to do about it. They require compliance. They require distraction and deception."

...One level of control is the pledge of allegiance. It starts the process of working with the system, be a team player.

Another level – cultural distractions, dancing with the stars, sports.

A form of brainwashing and distraction.

...There are always those persons in our society who want to feel like they're being informed and they turn on CNN and which they become, in which they will become permanently distracted and confused, and again this is by design. They are the propaganda department of the state department and the C.I.A., that's what CNN is.

... Above account for ninety-five percent of the mind control in our society, and it works very well. But then you have the occasional necessity ... color revolution, regime change, false flags.

... Let's go back to Seattle in 1999, the WTO protests. When you have a situation where the entire middle class of a nation feels it's being disemboweled, which is really what we've got, when people believe they have rights, they're really not going to take that lying down, they'll protest, as they did in Seattle, when more than 44,000 people shut that city down. This is a totally unmanageable situation to those people at the top of our food chain. This is eighteen, nineteen months before 9/11. So what 9/11 meant is that the hammer came down on us, they beat us over the head with a big national security stick, and away goes this idea of people protesting.

The Boston Marathon Bombing. I think the primary purpose of that was to roll out the ubiquitous police, which is now a fact of American life, in which you have 19,000 police breaking into American's homes of Boston residents as if there's no big deal. Well, we've gone through all that now and that's part of what we are.

TWENTY-FIVE

Max found his notebook and pen and put it on his knee and hunched over it, continuing with what he had been writing before, so intently so that there could be no question he was not to be bothered.

When it got dark he shoved over closer to the fire.

It was his great story that he intended to write, maybe a huge novel of a thousand and more pages. He would take the rest of his life to write it and it would be great, and it would point to his being great and not really all of the dozens of other things he also knew of himself but also vaguely doubted because he favored rather his being great. And as long as he didn't start the novel he could keep inside him the idea of his being a great novelist and working on this great work.

But shit he had to do it now.

He had all these fucking notes, but what did they mean? They were notes made on Walmart receipts and liquor store receipts and the coupons you find in cigarette packages and shit like that.

So Max took these disparate notes, spread them out and began.

The Big Bernays
By Max

When a tourist visits Washington, the capitol, they come up the big white stone steps, past the giant statues of Lincoln, Reagan, Bush, Clinton, Nixon, fifty feet high ... into the The Great Hall of Lenin bin Laden ... big, black and white photos, small photos, giant photos, a few drawings, paintings ... moon landings, 9/11, Oklahoma City, Wellstone, JFK, MLK, RFK.

It went all the way to the end, a big shined floor, about a hundred feet wide, a thirty foot ceiling, and it went a long way.

Toward the end there were big black and white photos and paintings and drawings of Mohammed Atta, James Earl Ray, Sirhan Sirhan, Lee Harvey Oswald, David Lee Chapman.

And at the very end gigantic black and white photos framed in black, of Adolph Hitler, Joseph Stalin and the Big Bad Wolf.

Michael Dumpfy is the guy who cleans The Great Hall of Lenin bin Laden every day. He punches in at 3 p.m. and works to midnight with an unpaid hour off for his lunch. During that hour Michael Dumpfy works on his novel in the broom room on a sawhorse with the door closed and the little bare light on the ceiling all the light he has or needs. He writes about life on the Half Planet Shtup on the other side of the moon, flat as a pancake. Why it was called Shtup nobody ever knew or cared to ask. It's motto? Some planets do have mottos. It's motto is The Children Need To Be Carefully Taught.

On The Half Planet Shtup the only conversation they have are the lines from the movie "The Big Lebowski."

I don't see any connection to Vietnam.

New shit has come to light.

That had not occurred to us.

They have found that is all that is required. They used to say more things, but since the late '90s, trying to be very clever and amusing, over time that is all anyone says anyway, so they made it a rule of sorts, de facto.

Michael Dumpfy the janitor is calling his story "The Big Bernays."

It's about how this one guy, Bernays. His real name is Bernays Bernays, he sort of rules all of Shtup from behind the scenes and he is bored and he likes to see what he can get everyone to do and that amuses him for a while.

Well, he wants to get everyone to believe that this one guy that he doesn't like is a Bampire.

See, Bernays Bernays has a little granddaughter and when she says Vampire it comes out Bampire.

And that's as far as Max got. There was more of the story inside him somewhere.

And when you die, you will finally understand yourself.

That was the last thought that occurred to Max. He wrote it down, raised his head and looked around. *Chirping.* Max rubbed his kneck and heard his stomach growl. Faint light pushed back against the dark, dishes and pots clattered, lighters flicked, boots scuffed over gravel.

Someone softly strummed a guitar and somebody moaned, just waking up in a tent.

Max lit a cigarette and flipped through his thick legal pad, all the yellow pages blank, most. He sighed, breathed deep, signed the top in printed letters and dated.

Without looking he unsnapped the holster at his side. They had really gone all out on these handguns. You get what you paid for someone had said late in the night so long ago, black, sleek, balanced. Max ran his hand over the quality metal, smelled it, shoved it hard into his mouth and jerked the trigger.

It just clicked. He'd used all his bullets to celebrate killing Tom.

With the barrel still pressed against the roof of his mouth Max looked around. He heard something, something faint and growing louder, blaring, like war elephants jogging over gravel to attack a tiny bamboo village, and playing loud music from boomboxes attached to their backs and to their sides. Max imagined the sight, and removing the barrel from his mouth he searched the ground for a scrap of little paper.

In the faint light he saw shadows, images and he walked toward them, moving, both he and the images, parallax, in and out of focus and vision.

He stopped and they stopped.

And he sang along to the sounds coming from the images on the road.

"Fuck you, I won't do what you tell me," he whispered.

"Fuck you, I won't do what you tell me."

TWENTY-SIX

Bix,
Terrible about Jimmy. But strange he fractured a femur. How could he walk? How did they take him to a hospital? With damage of femur bone he would have been unable to get out of bed? How could he have even got in his bed?

The Wilders are the oddest family I have known of. The five males have not been close, and Minnie has looked after them individually better than had Josephine. But Janey tried. Jim was more the intellectual, curious but very timid. He too was freaked by the civilization but had no guff to get him by.

He was making too much noise when I lived there and they gave him more drugs, a lobotomy of "anti psychotics."

At 9/11 I was there yet again, had been to the cabin for Medicine Dog a year or two. Had not enough food quite, had eaten a lot of dog food. Bonnie had insisted in my being legal, so took out for rent. Without paying rent there was enough food for Medicine dog and me too, back when I ate like two heavyweight laborers. But the funny part there of 9/11,Vietnam vets Jim and Bob could not look at their tv. They looked at the floor, I observed. First morning and I had a bicycle I took Medicine for his morning jaunt, trying to not laugh in public. Knowing naught about concrete and steel I assumed planes really had been commandeered by Muslims to wreck two skyscrapers because of all the hell we have given those Islamic nations. A few years then I slowly understood how physically impossible, began talking at family and friends who not knowing and hoping to never know of my information figured Bill is in error. Bill always hated civilization, and so on. So just look at a goddamned floor, rather than aluminum and concrete and steel and atomic mini explosions and several buildings destroyed in the complex and

185

wow did the Brits fuckup, this woman on USA tv telling Building #7 was gone too but she had not been notified it was bold right behind her - she was too early on the date. And so.

It is a strange time to be alive. Well, here goes another Post to my timid friends, fifteen years later.

And so.

Caryl,

Thanks for this batch of this extraordinary intriguing theme of where is humanity in this civilization's sudden avalanche. I had not known of Charles Einstein. Had someone turned you onto him? I wonder whom you talk with these days. I have also this morning read the several - I think it is seven others - he offers from his essay. These are sincere good writers all wondering what next. Too I see you want Mike Blackbird to read these writings.

Next Bix sends two emails and I considered writing all three of you together. Though, with Mike, you can lead him to the river but he won't drink. He labels such as this "political." Saying he is not "political." Oh, he votes, Democrat of course. You have heard me laugh at the matter. For me, these several intellectuals are not writing about politics. I call their works sociological. Present humanity studying their navels wondering where have we gone amiss.

Also have noticed C. Einstein has an amount of these pieces, including one on psychedelics. So I read that one this morning too. Nothing for me to disagree with him about. Oh, I like Putin, he does not, is about it. While, crux of all this, folks ask what next. Why have we so badly misplaced our natural ways.

I believe David can be enjoying these writing from you this morning.

Caryl, tell me more, who has directed you to Charles Einstein? Or are you in a later age epiphany? I do believe Jackle would be interested in this material. He had prejudices but he had great curiosity.

I'll head on, see these two from Bix again right now.

Love,

Billy

Note from the narrator:

From "The Prince Hope Show" ...

" ... we are also sponsored tonight by
Greatest Generation Beer
brewed from the finest something-something.
Look for the long-haired hippie on the red, white and blue can ... because it's not about killing just because somebody tells you to and not being smart enough to think for yourself.
It's all about the courage to fight for what is really right.
Greatest Generation Beer.
... it is actually great.

On February 23, 1943 three courageous German college students at the University of Munich were beheaded by the Gestapo after being arrested five days earlier and convicted of treason earlier in the day.

The group included 22-year-old medical student Christoph Probst, 24-year-old Hans Scholl, also a medical student, and Hans' 21-year-old sister Sophie. They were part of a small group of university students whose code name was the White Rose.

As were many other alert Germans, the White Rose was fully aware of the atrocities that were being committed against certain non-Aryan minorities. They had seen clearly the loss of liberty, the shredding of human rights, and the disturbing reality that the war was probably already lost.

— Gary Kohls

Never doubt that a group of thoughtful, committed citizens can change the world; indeed, it's the only thing that ever has.

— Margaret Mead

You might say that I'm young, you might say I'm unlearned, but there's one thing I know though I'm younger than you ...

— Bob Dylan

In revolution, one wins or dies.

— Che Guevara

TWENTY-SEVEN

"You should pull out and ..."
Zima's phone cut out.

She could guess what Lara was going to tell her.

They should go find someone to help since nothing was happening where they were. She called some others and they went into her tent to look at a map in the light.

Her phone buzzed, she looked at it, just Lara, she already knew what to do, they kept talking, hunched over the map in the low light.

Lara, now in a booth in The Green Mill, sent Zima's voice message: – "Hey, you should pull out and go to Hooterville-Pixly, I think it is. I think we, we think, we have too many units, brigades, troops there. We're gonna find a way to get something going elsewhere. We're getting re-set up here, a room, internet, maps, food, hope you are okay. How far is Hooterville/Pixley from you? Is it in Kentucky? It sounds like Kentucky. We're thinking about that? Or Cicely, Mayfield, something like that. We'll have something for you by morning, love you."

"Thank you," Lara said as their pizza came.

Zima and the others decided they were not that far from Max's camp. They would travel the river.

"It's really just a creek."

And it would take them right to Max's front door.

And they would be there for what would probably be a full-on assault by the government just before dawn.

"That's how we roll."

As she set down one boot into the water right where the moon showed the little ripples and the rock Zima thought about many things.

She heard the rustle of all of their gear, their now many boots in the

189

water, the vehicles being moved away, the smell of the doused campfires, the taste of caramel rolls on her lips. She licked them.

"This is the right thing to do," someone said.

"Thank You!" said Zima.

The boredom sitting there waiting for something to happen, hoping nothing happens and then nothing happening had been really too much. Getting into the river and having to make every step count on the slippery rocks made her feel that she was doing something.

Someone played a flute and Zima stopped herself from saying no. It was so great in the silent night and the water and the moon and the rebellion.

At Camp Sweaty they had been taught not to march close together, but that would have been really no fun and kind of scary. They grouped together in the river in the dark, to talk, for comfort. Nobody was out there anyway to actually shoot them. Zima's Brigade did not yet believe in the reality of the rebellion, she thought. They believed in books and movies and in their phones and in cigarettes. They believed that their weapons were heavy and a nuisance and that their T-shirts were okay, not great, they might have picked another logo and/or color, and one in their right size, but np.

Zima wanted to kill.

She didn't know why and she hadn't told anyone, but the thought had excited her at the first late-night meetings and she knew this was her calling. And she took it as sort of a trick of the gods that on the first real day of battle she is left out. She thought she wanted to kill because of the good it would do to fight the rich and break the oppression, but there were nights when she could not sleep because it was so clear to her that hers was a simple obsession with doing damage and she was broken and weird and the rebellion was just an excuse. But in the morning, so far, those goblins of doubt had fluttered away in the light and she had felt fine.

They walked and walked.

Their legs grew tired and the water deeper.

They no longer lifted their feet out of the creek to step but rather shoved their thighs through the water as it rushed at them.

The flute had long been stashed away. They did not talk. They called out to each other to count off. Each one was now a number and Zima listened to the count to make sure nobody was missing. She watched the time and every half hour she pointed to the shore for rest and smokes.

The river masked their talking. Nobody was going to hear them, not there, whether they lived or died. They might have all died right there from who knows what and much later they are found with their brigade T-shirts and camo and flute and weapons and somebody looks down and says the fuck is this?

What time is it? Are we going the right way? I thought the river flowed with us. Was that a gunshot? I hear lots of guns. That's hunters. At night? Okay, saddle up, let's go, hit the water.

We could walk on the shore, someone said.

Zima had really not even thought about it.

She pondered.

It would be even harder to walk on the shore with its pitch and irregularities and up higher there were trees and brush and in farther are roads and fields and houses.

"Nope!" she shouted.

"In the water!

"Now! On the double!"

Zima was amazed they did it. They splashed into the water, holding their weapons across their chests, pushing into the creek now a river.

On the double?

Had that just come out of her mouth?

The river widened after a long turn that had promised to kill them all with the fast water and the big rocks and the many times hurrying to pick up someone who had fallen.

Zima's Brigade could now pick their collective sodden feet from the water.

The sun threatened to rise from the little hill on their left.

As they pushed on, now slowly, out of the water, not sure they wanted to, toward the shore, a face-down figure, twisting, moved so slowly out to great them.

They smelled gunpowder and heard moaning, ashes skulked past them like Dementors leaving the club in the low light of another beautiful southern morn. Someone played the flute and just as quickly was hushed down by flapping hands.

Zima forced her boots up the shore, into the grass.

She stood in silence fighting to see, to understand.

The sun now perched on the little hillside, something hung in a tree, smoke rose from the fire pit, dark spots filled the camp.

Her troops spread out, heads down, touching the dark spots with the tips of their boots, moving on.

A young woman sat in a tree, talking fast, crying, waving her arms. Zima walked over to her and asked someone to try to talk her down.

"And get that body down," she said, pointing to the young man swinging from the limb.

A large vehicle sped away on the gravel road, skidding, music playing loud.

Zima walked away, alone, toward the road, smelling the smoke from the fleeing truck or whatever still in the air.

Her boot bumped something solid in the grass. She backed up. She forced herself to squat, to get closer.

"Ohhh," she moaned as she saw it was Max.

His eyes were wide, his mouth open, flies on the lips, tasting the sweet caramel of the rolls Zima had handed out to all the commanders.

Max's arms stretched out in a "T." His nose was bloody, caked.

His T-shirt was ripped, cut down the middle, jagged, and pinned to his chest by his own knife was his yellow legal pad with his story.

There were red marks where someone had circled misspellings and quickly scribbled "run-on" in the margin.

Joe dug into his backpack and pulled out the tinfoil goody. He sank his face into the caramel roll.

He walked down the line. His people. Loving them, his troops, hearing them talk, stopping to visit, and thinking how he was so proud, surprised and unlikely to be with such a unique fucking bunch.

Life had divided and now a grand canyon lay between ten minutes ago and now.

He smiled at some of their conversations.

Some cheese, some wine and some rays.

And was frightened by others.

Nothing is worth taking one human life. Stay poor, stay oppressed, stay stupid as fuck, whatever, just don't do it. I'm tellin' ya.

The Battle of Seattle.

No, really, that's what they called it.

Jack Kerouac, mad alive with America and the road. It goes around and around. It don't go nowhere. The highway.

Network! I won't take it anymore.

Is that a group? A book?

Movie.

Never saw it.

Joe chewed on his roll, swiped his face, but it was so sticky.

He dug into his pocket for cigarettes. He was used to wearing shirts with pockets. These T-shirt uniforms weren't good for that. When you put your smokes in your pants pocket they get crushed.

Ariel felt alone out there on the tracks losing control of her troops, pulling her hair back into a makeshift bun. She stuck her nose into the air to try to hear what was happening elsewhere. She flattened her map on the hard red rock and tried to understand where she was and where were the others. She sucked at this shit and she wanted to cry.

She stood and just to do something she practiced moving her right arm up and down while holding her rifle, double pumps they called it, and it meant something, but she was not sure, circle-up, move out, sit down, shut up, she couldn't remember now.

Ariel tried to remember it all, what was a fire team. She shook her head.

Murat walked up to her. That was what they were to call him.

"So," he said and Ariel thought of punching Murat in the face with the end of her gun, the butt. She did not have time for whiners, she was so way past patience and understanding. She looked at him, hoping he would understand her need to kill him if he said one more word.

"What if you knew, I mean *knew* that Hitler was created by American business leaders and sent to fight the Bolsheviks because what they really fear is everyone getting a fair piece of the pie."

Ariel heard Hitler, Bolshevik and because and pie.

"What?" she said, shaking her head, looking away, down the tracks and struggling to be a cool leader.

And so Murat just repeated what he had said and Ariel hated him inside her own head, the kind of person she had found way too often lately, so smart and so wanting to talk for so long.

Ariel sat on the tracks and this time accepted the offer of a cigarette. She stared into the sun and pushed her camo cap up on her forehead, revealing a red line where the cap was too tight.

She couldn't get through to anyone for advice on what she should do.

And then boom, a text from Joe.

We're just over here, not much happening, you could come here.

How about robbing a train? said Murat.

We could do that, yeah.

So Ariel had her people hide in the brush by the tracks. After about fifteen minutes a train whistle blew and Ariel pumped her rifle up and down, which maybe meant here it comes.

The train got closer and Ariel raised her weapon to her chest and came out of her hiding spot, still crouching, making hand signals all around her.

She saw the smoke first as the train rounded the bend. The tracks rumbled and the rock rattled as the train roared.

Here it came and such a mass of metal and movement and Ariel had to duck her face away and drop her rifle to cover her ears and it was right there, right on top of them, for too long, beating the tracks with that rhythmic pounding, and it was gone.

Ariel stood, unsteady in the hard red rock on an incline, watching it go.

She turned, raised one hand up over her head and pointed toward the woods.

And so, they had had their first combat action.

Joe found a tree with his back and slid down to sit, the cigarette in one hand and the remainder of the roll in the other. He thought of where his rifle could be and thought he had remembered when the first rocket plopped into the river, fizzling, smoking.

More bottle rockets rustled the leaves and plunked the trees.

Joe sprinted down the line to get his gun as the others rolled to their stomachs and readied their weapons.

Now, boom, boomboom, came the shotgun blasts through the leaves and boom! something sent water flying. That was an M-80 someone said.

"Return fire!" Joe shouted just as his troops tore up the trees on both sides of the river.

Sheriff Taylor sat at his desk talking on the phone to his brother at the National Guard armory.

"I think we've got to get out there," said Sheriff Taylor.

"They say there are rebel troops over on County 3. It's that CRUSHER thing. No, really, right here."

"The guvner's got to do that, Timmy."

"Bobby Dawson heard at coffee they were fired on while they were huntin' and that ain't right and they're all headin' out there right now to kick some hippie ass," said the sheriff.

"Well, you can't call out the National Guard on that, can you?"

On the curb, around the corner from the sheriff's office, right in front of the Little Bird Diner, sat the four giant Suburbans, red, with grey shaded windows, music pounding from inside.

The music stopped.

Those inside the second Suburban put on black headphones as they sat at desks and technical equipment.

One of the guys in suits nodded to the other and the other returned the nod. They ate butter and sugar sandwiches and listened to Sheriff Taylor and his brother.

For several minutes Joe and his troops lay on their stomachs firing through the trees, and each of them by now had an opening in the leaves to see into the water and across.

Ariel heard the guns. She stopped and decided which way and she charged into the brush.

"Follow me!" she pointed straight ahead, making her own path.

Behind the trees opposite Joe's Brigade a half dozen pickups were parked in odd angles on the dirt road. Men stood in the truck beds, taking cover behind the cabs, getting up now and again to fire into the trees.

"The fuck is that?" said one of the young men, Bo, wearing an unbuttoned flannel shirt over his belly over his jeans.

He looked the other way down the dirt road.

"Shit!"

What he saw were two clouds of dust from opposite ends, both sides of the dirt road behind the trees behind the river, and now they were trapped.

"Hey! Looka here!" he called to his friends.

They stopped shooting and watched as Sheriff Tim Taylor's squad car led one line of National Guard trucks toward them on the right side and another squad car leading another line right up to them on the left side.

"Fuck!" said Bo.

"What's a goin' on here, boys," said Sheriff Taylor as he got out and walked toward them.

"Not much," said one of the young men in the pickups.

"Just out huntin'."

Taylor and the others scrambled and ducked as rifle fire zinged through the trees on their side and pinged into Taylor's car and the sides of the trucks.

Taylor waved to his brother in one of the trucks and his brother waved a hand and two dozen troops climbed down from the trucks.

Ariel pushed through the trees, swiping branches from her face, trying to decide on a maneuver that would help to save Joe and his brigade, hammer and anvil, circle around, uh, god! she bit her tongue as she stumbled, catching herself and moving into a run, extracting her weapon several times from the reaches of the branches and bushes.

Joe yelled up and down the line in a hoarse whisper for everyone to stop firing.

They listened. They heard talking, somebody said they had heard trucks, jeeps, tanks.

"Oh, I doubt that," said Joe, but only to himself.

"Holy shit," he said out loud as he looked through the ripped leaves right in front of him, like a frame in a religious store.

At the same time, as if they had practiced and talked about it all a long time ago, a line of troops, young men in camo uniforms, helmets, boots, pants, all that, emerged from the opposite woods. Every fourthth man was a man in jeans, ballcap and open plaid shirt. They all held weapons across their chests and looked serious as shit.

Joe laid his rifle flat on the ground and put the site right on the belly of a young man, not more than fifty yards away. That man wanted to kill Joe, just look at his mouth, his eyes. He couldn't wait to cross that water if only someone would let him loose. Why did he want to kill Joe? What had Joe done to him? He didn't even know Joe. Joe hated and feared the man at the same time as he tried to understand him.

The National Guard troops and the young hunters looked at each other as if waiting for someone to say go. One of them, an older man standing next to Sheriff Taylor in the line, walked toward the river, poked the stock of his weapon into the water, reached a foot in and stepped back.

The young man across the stream from Joe, with the belly like a catfish seemed to sense that Joe was staring at him. He looked through the leaves and made direct eye contact with Joe and raised his rifle to match Joe's weapon, barrel to barrel.

Sheriff Taylor shoved up into the water up to his knee as a bullet ripped his hat from his head and another tore up his knee. He fell into the water, rippling red.

Joe heard a boom and looked to his left just in time to see a head explode, just like a melon, spraying him with brain and skull and hair and bloody juice like veins and everything all mixed together.

The National Guard commander roared and pointed and charged into the water and the whole line followed him, swirling the river like piranha.

In less than a moment bullets and yelling and booms and smoke filled the air.

Joe pulled down his gun and rolled over as a round tossed up the grass where he'd been.

"Let's go!" he yelled and gestured with an arm.

"Let's get outa here!"

He stood at the end of the line, hollering, spinning his arm like a third base coach trying to get all the runners home.

"C'mon, c'mon!

"Go-go-go!"

A few stayed on their bellies, firing at the troops slogging through water, hitting their targets. The river turned pink.

Joe ran. With wind in his hair he ran, cutting his face on the branches, the sweat stinging his eyes.

He felt others running with him, heard them, saw them beside him. He would not be the last one.

Black boots stomped the dead leaves covering the woods.

Ooof!

Joe fell so hard, so unexpectedly, on his face and chest and his gun did not discharge and he got up, and did not look back. He scrambled and clawed and he got going, stumbling, now up and running full speed.

Ariel stopped for a moment to listen. The others stopped with her. Like a doe at a clearing she sniffed the air and smelled gunpowder. She heard voices in the distance, like children playing, excited, yelling, high-pitched.

Dogs on tight cords now clambered into the river and helicopters sped low over the water, now swerving over the trees, left and right, swooping, searching for prey. Helicopter fire raked the matted spots and corpses of Joe's Brigade's former position, punching holes in the plastic Coke bottles and Twinkies wrappers.

The choppers pulled straight up, high into the air, just before reaching Ariel's Brigade, turning to make another pass.

Ariel heard crashing through brush, got on one knee and waved her arm for the others.

The sounds turned to slow, heavy steps, heavy breathing.

Faces emerged, faces Ariel did not recognize. She raised her weapon and aimed, tried hard to take slow, deep breaths, wrapped her finger around the cold trigger, squinted down the barrel, wiggled her toes and ...

Joe's head popped into her site.

"Joe?"

Joe looked all around in a panic. Ariel stood.

"Joe!"

She waved her arm.

"Joe over here!"

"Ariel!

"Run!"

"What?" she said.

"Run! Just run."

She grabbed him by the shirt.

"No, wait. What's happening?"

"They're coming," he said.

"Who? Who's coming?"

"They. Them. You know! Go! Go, go, go."

Like a wrestler he threw up his arms and ripped free from her grip, disappearing into the woods.

Ariel listened intently. In the distance, though she couldn't see super far, she did see branches moving and the sounds of a large group, yelling, clatter, stomps.

She knelt and slowly put her AR to her shoulder.

She looked around her and saw a whole line doing the same thing, a dozen of her troops on one knee, weapon to shoulder. She heard and then she saw the giant helicopters. They looked like pre-historic birds up through the trees way up there but still so close, closer than you're used to seeing them.

Ariel stared again down the site of her gun, now through the scope.

She saw red plaid flannel, a white belly, like a tail-walking whale humping through the woods. She heard the roar of the approaching horde, like Zulus, chanting as they ran, what her brain told her, like misheard lyrics on the radio, was "YAY! HOO!" "YAY! HOO!" "HOOGA!"

And it was a pack of wolves and Indians running together and that is exactly what she thought at that time.

Ariel stood and looked all around her.

Calmly she waved her arm, and then she ran like hell, and they all ran with her. Into branches and bushes they charged, away from the hooga.

The Ariel Brigade caught up with the Joe Brigade and together they fell through the woods edge, into the hard red rock.

Behind them came the YAY! HOO! and the crashing in the whole woods of a hundred front end loaders.

"Whooo!

"Whooo-whooo whooo!"

The smoke showed at the corner.

Ariel stared into the woods. She looked down the tracks, over the tracks into the next woods. Suggestions, polite and not, about what they should do rained at her from all sides. Joe paced back and forth, stumbling on the sharp rock.

The train drew closer, loud, the cars rattling.

The tracks rumbled.

"Follow me!" said Ariel.

She pointed up and over the tracks and charged up the rocks to the rails, where she stopped and stood on the track, balancing.

Again she hollered, commanded, pointed, admonished, encouraged, again and again and finally Joe and the others began to move up the rocks, following her over the tracks and down the other side, where they turned and stood, facing the train, the tracks, the woods on the other side.

The train blasted again right in front of them. Faces and bodies and bellies pushed out of the woods on the other side as through the pages of a book, white faces, white men, with perhaps some few wolves and Indians in the back rows.

Ariel had the actual thought that you can go through weeks and months with just about nothing at all happening and then sometimes in just, well, boomboomboom, way too much to even follow it all happens.

One of them up front, seeing Ariel and Joe and the others, raised his rifle and fired, and in less than one instant the bullet hit the side of the engine and ricocheted back, through that same man's belly and back, lodging with a solid whump! in the oak behind him.

Ariel saw it. Saw the white belly turn red just as the train cut the armies off, each from the other. The cars whipped between them. Some of the troops out of long habit took to the task of counting the cars. Each army stood there, watching the train, seeing those on the other side through each gap in the cars, their faces flashed and they watched each other, so close, so loud, looking to the end, as people do, to see the caboose, but all the way down, past the turn, it was all stock cars, some closed, some few open.

"Okay," said Ariel to anyone who could hear.

"Let's go."

She turned into the woods, not waiting, as a helicopter swooped down the tracks, over the train, between the two woods.

Joe caught her.

"Whata we gonna do now?"

"Run," said Ariel.

They did.

Note from the narrator:

From "The Prince Hope Show" ...

This PSA message brought to you by the DEA, the prison construction industry, and your local and federal politicians since who knows when.
    Thanks, Jesus.
    Thanks, Buddah.
    Thanks, Allah, thanks Allen The Alien ... for the Drug Wars. ...

QUOTE REMOVED BY ORDER OF DHS, UNITED STATES
DEPARTMENT OF HOMELAND SECURITY. [DHS US2FA]

TWENTY-EIGHT

Caryl,
Glad to hear of your cheer. We'll see from here.

I was quite surprised, had thought Debbie Lusignan was right. She believed "the fix is in," Killary would get it. Looks like the fix was not fixed good enough.

Trump may get shot, or say barely pricked with cancer by somebody hurrying in a crowd is popular these times, maybe a well paid secret service person. Fifty million could do.

I had not been much interested in Trump, don't care about all the silly crap the liberals need to believe of him. All the shit they say he has said, he would be a blithering idiot. What if he is. James Kessler has thought he is not that lame.

I had not cared to be around siblings and esteemed old friends jumping on Trump, as in sport. Aw, common, Bill, be a sport, Trump is no good. Hell no, not when what I have to tell others is classified as Blackbird-taboo-speak. Get real, people, can't you ever.

What Lusignan had said of Trump is any fear of what Trump may do Hillary has done first. OK, liberals do not know much, all they read is pablum. Fixed USA news.

Then, to believe in cosmos of love eternal, Jesus and Buddha and Mohammed love all the ants and men and All. We be God's little critters. I love my late Medicine Dog who is holy. Choyota is holy as well. Kat too, a holy cat. All dogs and cats are holy, spiders too. We are all One. Love is the Way.

The Way, I say. The Way!

Oh well. Either way you like to add it up, very much more is coming this way.

Mas, mucho mas. We are not old ladies, re. Hunter S,

Thompson's classic, FEAR AND LOATHING IN LAS VEGAS - more to come, more to come. Men folks over here, men folks over in here. Minds tough as my daughter's. Down in yere, can we be tough as girl scouts? More coming, more coming.
    Ever Further,
        Billy Frank
            Love,
            Billy

Mike,
    Finally we are getting a steady rain, this afternoon. There has been rains in the area but mostly it missed this property. It was an ax day, 30 minutes much of it sitting in chair at the wood, catching breath, and I have been slipping my schedule in between showers conveniently enough, past days. Understand, I am not a true laborer, but a body builder. Don't know what you might prefer as an approach, if you yet think to get yourself an ax. Do get the fiberglass handle, a world invention, the ax head does not take all the shock, which has caused ax heads for thousands of years to come off the handles. I am a lazy puncher, a body builder sort of lout, thus do my whacking, dig it in via wrists, abdominals, legs, 20 strokes then sit down. I rest from one to almost three minutes, not quite three, to do two sets twenty reps inside a five minutes. Am not hitting altogether fullest force, but work on form, form is most important, torque it in, but hopefully do not embed it, because it takes time and energy getting the blade back out. I guess Abe Lincoln would just be at it doggedly, a lean fellow, but I want to keep my big arms. Well, really, every other day does catch up with me, starts tiring a lout in a few mildly savage days. Like I say. Kelly is happy enough for all these dried oak chunks for fireplace, this winter, measured at about two hand spans, Blackbird long fingers. Yeah my aristocratic hands get a bit tired, fingers tired, particularly right hand which wrist I broke in a fall from galloping horse half century back somewhere. In between days I do ten minutes of deadlifting sets with 200 lbs., therapy for old back injuries, tires the right hand. Very, very slowly healing my damaged left knee dog walking.
    Hope all the above makes some sense. Back in the fifties somewhere I understood something about the ancient Greeks believed in "form." Get the form down first.
    Yeah, it is all interesting. Maybe old guys can outflank time, somewhat.

Hey, USA president getting elected this date. Yaw haw.

Bunch of fuckups anyway, can get us all killed anytime, Packy agrees. I know him. Anyhoo. See nice sentence from Forest today.

Further,

Bill

Jim,

It looks to be so. I had glanced over the "Is Michele Obama a Man"

from you last week or whenever it was. OK, I will again pass this toward 30 restless souls.

It is more of our fantastical and I am bothering with old friends many who find it easier to believe I have lost my senses post 9/11, so I hesitate to hammer their cages more than I already have.

But thanks. It is humorous, and I work to keep up with you. Whew, talk about it. When do the Obamas go on the lam?

America, America the beautiful.

Yours,

Bill

Caryl,

Truman knew they wanted to surrender. Chiefs of Staff knew, all knew. This is known, historical. I am getting a bit tangled while starting the afternoon inebriation. Have an email in from Geoffrey now. He notes you ad I are basically getting along. Now in our seventies. Yeah, we are oldest friends.

I understand this you send on the mindset of Japanese solders yet. I did read in the seventies of this stalwart figure who never surrendered. I have known of all this. I had in our exchange compressed the whole, in sake of my point, my hurry to my point. That people are people.

Comanches could do this. With lance and horse, and perfected horsehide shield to catch a bullet and ricochet it, one expertly goes forward. I be emotional. No turn around and no quarter. Some will do this, anywhere, of a culture.

Anyhoo.

Got a word from Geoffrey, Bonnie's offspring.

It is always good to hear from you.

Love, Billy.

It is also in the interests of a tyrant to keep his people poor, so that they may not be able to afford the cost of protecting themselves by arms and be so occupied with their daily tasks that they have no time for rebellion.

— *Aristotle in Politics*

Why does the guerrilla fighter fight? We must come to the inevitable conclusion that the guerrilla fighter is a social reformer, that he takes up arms responding to the angry protest of the people against their oppressors, and that he fights in order to change the social system that keeps all his unarmed brothers in ignominy and misery.

—Che Guevara

Janey got a gun.   — Aerosmith

One of the deep secrets of life is that all that is really worth doing is what we do for others.

— Lewis Carroll

TWENTY-NINE

The men standing in the red rock on both sides of Sheriff Taylor shot right at the train, not seeming to know it would do not much good and not seeming to remember or notice what had happened to the first guy who tried that.

He slapped at the rifle of the one guy and then the other guy as well.

More rifle shots pinged the train, some bouncing back and thunking the trees.

"Bless your heart," said Sheriff Taylor, watching yet another man raise his gun against the train.

Down the line, at the curve, naturally drawn to such things by nature, those who weren't tending to the man wounded in the belly or taking the time out to go pee or climb trees, stared at a figure sitting on the edge of an open boxcar, legs and feet dangling.

They held their weapons at their chests as the figure approached.

Some waved as she waved, smiling, like the lone person in a parade in the Bavarian hills, like a train headed away from Buchenwald.

"How *you* doin'!" one of the men yelled.

The train clattered along, rolling back and forth and leaping up and down like a young fawn, anxious to see more.

At the road, the four-way intersection to Mount Airy, Flat Rock, Toast, and Bannertown, Brooke waved like a homecoming princess to the four red Suburbans parked in front of one stop sign, one man in the ditch doing his business, looking back over his shoulder.

Note from the narrator:

From "The Prince Hope Show" ...

This message brought to you by your local county jail.
Give us your tired, huddled masses, yearning to be free.
And we'll lock 'em up.

Put them in a small, dirty, old, crowded out-of-the-way county jail.

If they think the Statue of Liberty is holding up a torch and not a middle finger, send them to us. We'll teach them what it's like to be an American.

Why do we need to be pardoned?

What are we to be pardoned for?

For not dying of hunger?

For not accepting humbly the historic burden of disdain and abandonment?

For having risen up in arms after we found all other paths closed?

For not heeding the Chiapas penal code, one of the most absurd and repressive in history? For showing the rest of the country and the whole world that human dignity still exists even among the world's poorest peoples? For having made careful preparations before we began our uprising?

For bringing guns to battle instead of bows and arrows? For being Mexicans? For being mainly indigenous? For calling on the Mexican people to fight by whatever means possible for what belongs to them? For fighting for liberty, democracy and justice?

For not following the example of previous guerrilla armies? For refusing to surrender? For refusing to sell ourselves out? Who should we ask for pardon, and who can grant it? Those who for many years glutted themselves at a table of plenty while we sat with death so often, we finally stopped fearing it? Those who filled our pockets and our souls with empty promises and words? Or should we ask pardon from the dead, our dead, who died "natural" deaths of "natural causes" like measles, whooping cough, break-bone fever, cholera, typhus, mononucleosis, tetanus, pneumonia, malaria and other lovely gastrointestinal and pulmonary diseases?

Our dead, so very dead, so democratically dead from sorrow because no one did anything, because the dead, our dead, went just like that, with no one keeping count with no one saying, "Enough!" which would at least have granted some meaning to their deaths, a meaning no one ever sought for them, the dead of all times, who are now dying once again, but now in order to live?

Should we ask pardon from those who deny us the right and capacity to govern ourselves? From those who don't respect our customs and our culture and who ask us for identification papers and obedience to a law whose existence and moral basis we don't accept? From those who oppress us, torture us, assassinate us, disappear us from the grave "crime" of wanting a piece of land, not too big and not too small, but just a simple piece of land on which we can grow something to fill our stomachs?

Who should ask for pardon, and who can grant it?

— Subcommandante Marcos

THIRTY

"No, it's o-kay.

"Really.

"I wouldn't say so if ...

"If I thought you had ..."

Lara talked to Ariel.

"You did what you had to do. Living is good. Being alive is a good thing."

She and Kaitylyn commanded a table in the back of a simply gigantic Dunn Bros. by the university, all their stuff scattered, computers, notebooks, books, bags. They still hadn't been able to find another apartment, and had been riding the train and bus around town most of the day and night, one keeping watch while the other slept.

Ariel handed the phone to Joe, who was sure he was to be scolded.

"I just couldn't take it," he said.

"No, it's all right, Joe. Yes, we're used to seeing the human body intact, nobody can be ready for that."

Lara said goodbye and stared hard at Kaitylyn as she brought their coffees. She could just tell that Kaitylyn had not tipped the baristas, she never did. She always, always said that's what they are *supposed* to do, get the coffee.

Kaitylyn saw Lara's glare and averted her eyes, finding her spot at the table and preferring to get to work.

People, thought Lara.

"All this fucking shit," she said out loud, but not too loud, as they checked her emails, most of which were who was pissed at whom, who didn't want to be in whose brigade, who was dating whom, who didn't like certain others, who thought they should be patrol or unit or whatever leader or sub-command, who thought they should be paid and maybe we should just start a union.

"Yeah, right?" said Kaitylyn.

And for sure.

Oh, there it was, perfect, the latest from Prince Hope.

Lara opened it.

Lara knew that Kaitylyn was angry with Joe for running. They'd already talked about that. Kaitylyn and Korey had been the ones who had been so big on books and knowing about the history of war, of revolution, battles, strategies, from the Romans to Navy Seal hand to hand tactics. They had gone over and over all that shit during their shifts and overnight at the group home. And then they had practiced and drilled and had classes at Camp Sweaty, but it was never going to be enough. They were never-ever going to be ready. Kaitylyn and Korey knew that and so did Lara. One of these days it was going to come right down to it and it would be like they had done nothing, and that's what happened to Joe. Just lucky Ariel had been there and their brigades were alive and free.

"But the thing is," said Kaitylyn.

And Lara knew, here it comes. She put up one finger to say, just a moment, as she replied to Prince Hope. The finger came down.

"The thing is, you have to fight, that's all there is to it," said Kaitylyn.

"Yeah, I know, I know, but," said Lara quickly.

Kaitylyn was done, done with that. She shoved over some paper, moved her coffee mug, drew some other papers to her.

"We need air support," she said and Lara had coffee coming out her nose.

"Really?" said Lara.

"Mmm, hmm."

Kaitylyn leaned into her computer, her brows narrowed so seriously, as if she could make it happen.

Lara let her be.

What she wanted to do was move Zima over with Joe and Ariel and have them continue the assault of Mayberry, but this time as one combined force. And they had too many brigades there, she'd decided. Buster, Morgan and Brandon would be transferred to new fronts. They also wanted to get an indy guerilla group going. DIY. That was on today's to-do list, too.

She pulled her yellow pad out of one of her bags, not that one, the other, yes.

Her indy group notes:

They would be rogue, not wait for orders, just go out and do it: key cars, disrupt speeches, dirty tricks, put up specially made yellow "Fuck The Troops" ribbons and stickers.

And they needed guerilla, underground radio, especially because of this latest thing. Might as well put that in the pile with air support and a laundry and lunch service.

They heard the news on the TV in the other room. The government was calling The Battle Of Mayberry a conflict zone or something, just a protest, doesn't get more than a minute's time, while at the same time, Lara and Kaitylyn knew that just that morning every one of Prince Hope's subscribers had received the same text, that anyone with knowledge of CRUSHER should report it, must report it, or be considered a terrorist themselves.

That's what Prince Hope had told her yesterday, that it was going to happen. She told herself it was good to know those things, but she also knew that the others were beginning to maybe not trust her because she was kind of friends with Hope. When he was their captive for those three weeks they had talked a lot. She'd played her fiddle for Hope and he said he liked it and maybe he could get her into his stage band, and things like that. Yeah, when he was on television he said things like all CRUSHER rebels should be executed, but Lara thought she knew the real Prince. The one deep inside of him who wanted to do the right thing, not the public fucker.

But then just now, right now, she had received this email:

I read and had some trained psychologists read your emails.

We have all come to the conclusion that your mental illness makes you a threat to yourself and others.

It stands out like dog's balls.

Was he right? About her? About the revolution? Was she crazy?

She sighed.
Oh, man.

Lara got an email from Kaitylyn, whose knee was touching her knee.

It was about how she thought the troops needed some review training on frontal assault, envelopment, searching and traversing fire, "shit like that."

Sure, Lara replied and switched to her phone for a text from Zima.

Zima had read some of Max's stuff.

"Like an auto accident," said Zima.

"That's good," wrote Lara.

"Yes," she wrote back to Zima.

"I know he died, it's just good. I knew that. Don't you think I knew that? Why would you not think I ..."

She hit send and shoved away from the computer, flung a five dollar bill at the barista who struggled to catch it like a fluttering knuckleball and stalked outside to sit on the metal bench and smoke and watch traffic.

Such a beautiful day, sunshine, people laughing. She tried to get into that, but inside her head was a revolution. That's where she was living and it was impossible to get out of there, like prison, being out in the sun with happy people just made it worse. She almost wished she could be out on the front lines with a weapon. This was just too fucking hard. She fired her cigarette at the sidewalk, stalked it where it bounced and stomped it, then stormed back inside. She also had ideas for Korey and for Jim.

"He's old," said Kaitylyn when she got there, not looking, staring straight into her computer.

"Stop," said Lara, sitting down.

"So old."

Note from the narrator:

From "The Prince Hope Show" ...

This message brought to you by The Boogey-Man.

The United States of America has a huge military & hundreds of bases round the world that the people were told for fifty years were needed exclusively to counter one enemy: Communism.

And now there aren't any Communists anymore.

The C.I.A. needed to be so huge to counter the KGB, but there isn't any KGB anymore!

The F.B.I. needed to be so huge because the Reds were everywhere even under our beds, but there aren't any Reds anymore!"

So – we don't need the military and bases and C.I.A. and F.B.I., right?

Yes. Umm-no.

There are terrorists everywhere. They attacked us on 9/11.

And there are Big Bees from Mexico.

And so there you go. We still need almost all of your money.

I was once like you are now
And I know that it's not easy
To be calm when you've found
Something going on
But take your time, think a lot
Think of everything you've got
For you will still be here tomorrow
But your dreams may not

— Cat Stevens

THIRTY-ONE

I was able to actually catch up with Lara and Kaitylyn around that time during one of their Dunn Bros. work sessions. Not the same Dunn Bros., another, this one over on Wabasha in Saint Paul, or another, there are a lot of Dunn Brothers in the Cities.

I asked Kaitylyn about Jim.

Jim, she said.

It's strange, the first time I talked to him. He wasn't the type to work at a group home, that's what I thought. He said it was because he jumped off the porch early, I never asked what that meant. He was a peasant, an unlikely legend.

What is the legend, I asked, but she didn't say.

He is a klutz, stumbler, but he has big ideas. I don't know how he could have robbed all those banks. He was always breaking something or hurting himself, I just don't see how.

Anyway, and I was complaining about something. There were a few of us there in the kitchen. I think he transferred from another house, same company.

I said, something like, I don't know when they expect us to get these in-services, training things done. That's what's on my mind.

And he said, Oh, it'll be all like, it'll be fine.

You're awesome, Jim.

That's just what I said, because it totally calmed me down. I know you don't understand.

Is he robbing banks?

Now? Right now?

We don't know. We think he is, because we see the money.

He shows you the money.

Yes, he shows us the money.

215

* * *

I felt out of place that day talking to them, not at my best, just didn't fit.

I realized it, but there was nothing I could do and maybe it was just as well, but still, uncomfortable, for me. I can't explain it, well, it's like, here, we assume a certain norm, day to day, what we are used to, what is our routine and maybe we come into contact with others, maybe at a reunion or family gathering. We see the others are in a totally different place. Maybe they are all interested in marble vs. granite countertops or white vans, or the Rockies relief pitchers, and you just can't understand it. You long to get back to your own norm. It would probably be like that for someone coming out of jail, or going into jail for that matter. Or, someone without much money and having to join a conversation with people with access to what to him is a lot of money, like that?

I noticed Lara looking toward the door, because she should, but also keeping an eye on Kaitylyn. She seemed to be totally up to both tasks.

They talked, laughed about something they'd heard on the local sports talk radio show that morning, about how someone had played a joke on various hotels, seeing what outlandish requests he could get away with, like wanting to have his room prepared with a photo of a dog dressed as a boat captain waiting on his bed, or a caricature drawing of the hotel staff on his pillow. And I guess he got away with it, got it done.

Anyway, I was feeling like I was wanting to get away myself, but there were still things I should find out if I could.

So, Korey was opening the new Minneapolis-Saint Paul front, the Mary Tyler Moore Brigade they were calling it, and he was not happy about that, but they had a theme to uphold.

Prince Hope had taken to mentioning Lara in his shows and on television and like she was his girl and he was acting all cool about having a young revolutionary girlfriend and I'm not sure how she felt about that.

The TV in the other room blared coverage about The Battle of Mayberry as they were calling it, too, and how there were still some rebel groups in the area that the government thought could be eradicated quickly, and that made Lara and Kaitylyn very nervous, I could see.

I wanted to ask about bombs, and so I did. I actually said the word, bomb.

Do you use them? Are you going to use them?

"No," said Kaitylyn.

I looked to Lara and she was doing something else, letting Kaitylyn take it.

Look at The Weathermen, she said.

And I said, yes, okaaay.

And she explained that when people today talk about them, the '60s radicals, they don't recall what the times were like, what we were doing to the Vietnamese, how people were dying, everywhere, they just see that these people set off bombs and killed people or tried to kill people. It sounds gross these days, hideous, criminal.

"Well," I said.

And I explained to her that that was exactly what they were doing now.

"We are not hiding," she said.

"We are not placing bombs and then running away into the dark.

"That's what's going to make the difference. Our children are going to have to live here and talk about us, what we did. And they will be able to talk about us if we stand toe to toe in the daylight. I don't see that as a problem."

And I said something about how it still might not be taken well and I could see that Lara was trying to get Kaitylyn's attention for something else and that was as far as Kaitylyn was prepared to go, as far as she could go probably. I guess there's only so much that you can have figured out, even with all their overnight jam sessions, as they called them, I guess.

Why did they talk to me?

They trusted me, I guess.

And I probably served a purpose as someone writing it all down, their side of it, because I, well, they told me in various ways that they really didn't expect to have children and grandchildren, you know?

And I was interested. That's kind of a big thing when you think about it. Most people I would suppose wouldn't give a god-damn, even with full-on television coverage and late night talk show revolutionary romance gossip. Even with the revolution right out on the sidewalk it's not what's really on your mind. You still want to preserve your life, your own interests, your own enjoyment, right down to the end, I'm pretty sure that's how it goes, and so if someone really wants to take hours to listen, they realized that wasn't going to happen every day.

And they told me about the things they were working on, full knowing that I could run over to Prince Hope right now and get on national radio and television and spill the beans, or to the police. I knew I wouldn't, not now, but I don't know how they knew. Maybe they were just the trusting type. Or they were willing to take the chance. I think they wanted there to be a really cool account of these times, a real history, the truth, and this was the only way, and if I ran to the authorities, well, when they got out they would just start over.

Anyway, from my notes:

They were going to continue the assault of Mayberry/Mount Airy with the combined Zima, Joe and Ariel Brigades.

Brandon, Buster, Morgan would each take over a new front. Somebody, I forget who, was going to Mayfield. They were sticking with their TV show theme thing, which was supposed to be chilling to America, I guess. They determined that Mayfield was in Ohio. So I guess someone is going to invade Ohio. Morgan will hit Cicely, Alaska, actually Roslyn, Washington.

And I thought this a touch of at least partial genius or not as crazy, they are also going to do fake attacks, just right here from their computers, with press releases and computer games. It's a way for Lara and Kaitylyn to be involved and also to throw off the government and also it makes them seem larger than they are, I suppose.

So, yeah, somehow they are also going to hit, attack, invade, surround, destroy Bedford Falls, Grover's Mills, Raccoon City, South Park, Springfield, Hill Valley, and Genoa City, so they'll be busy. They thought they might be able to farm some of those out. They have lots of techie types in the Twin Cities who might do that for them, if Jim can keep the money flow going. It's ambitious, but hey, we're all gonna die anyway, that's what they said, I think it was actually Lara.

I was going to leave, but I stayed. They moved, to another Dunn Bros. They were on foot so I gave them a ride. We headed to Golden Valley this time. I asked them what's with Dunn Brothers, are they sponsoring you? And they said they just like the coffee and people leave you alone and don't ask questions. Free WIFI, said Lara. They wore disguises, kind of, now, since they were on TV and in the papers. They colored their hair, of course and got all these kind of funky, I would say, clothes from Goodwill and makeup, to make them look older, sometimes really old. Sometimes dead, said Kaitylyn once.

So here we come into Dunn Bros. on Lake. Lara didn't want to go to Golden Valley. Too fucking far, she said, and I guess she had a boyfriend from there once, absolutely did not want to run into him, was NOT going to G-V.

Well, we had an interesting drive over to Lake Street.

"This is crazy," Lara said.

"What were we thinking."

She sat in the front passenger seat. Kaitylyn in back. It's a red RAV 4, not new, but I like it.

"How did you get into journalism?" Kaitylyn asked, maybe not hearing what Lara had said. "Like, who are you?"

I smiled into the rearview mirror at Kaitylyn intensely staring me down.

"Well, I've got a blog," I said.

"Yeah, I've seen that, but," she said.

And then, as Lara started up again I tossed out a few tacks about college and previous non-important work history.

"This will never work."

Lara turned to look at me, then Kaitylyn. She pulled her laptop from her big bag, a kind of Colombian-Lakota-Burnsville hand-made collage of materials and design.

"I'm going to be a fiddler onstage."

Kaitylyn maintained eye contact in the rearview, a bulldog.

While watching me she replied to Lara.

"That's over dear." She stretched to put her hand on Lara's shoulder.

"That woman at the Fourth of July parade, she died.

"He doesn't love you. Using you to get the rest of us, that's what they do. I'm so sorry. He will fuck you and leave you lay.

"And you were saying?" she focused again on me.

"You don't even know my name," I said.

And Lara agreed that was so, just as I said the first thing that popped into my head, Walker, Texas Ranger, and wondered how many weapons the two of them were carrying combined.

"That's hilarious," Kaitylyn said, looking like a bank robber dealing with the comedian teller.

I battled traffic and almost said James, James Bond, and said Harry. Harry Potter."

"Tough room," I said as they just stared.

"Whatever," said Kaitylyn, sliding back into her seat.

"We should have divided into shotgun, rifle, handgun, knives, bow and arrow brigades, that would have been so bad-ass," she said, watching people out her window.

"We still can," said Lara, again reaching for her computer.

"It will be done."

"I don't think that'll work," said Kaitylyn.

"We need a new office."

"HQ," I said, trying to get back into good graces.

"Here we go," said Lara, pointing.

"If I can just find a," I said.

"There," said Kaitylyn, "right there, there, geezuz, you missed it."

"I'll just go around the block," I said in my most smoothing tone.

They gave me a cursory update on Hector and Reuben.

"Digging away," said Kaitylyn.

And also Evangelina.

"Somehow she got Rachel's senior yearbook," said Lara.

"Rachel?"

"The girl she killed," said Lara.

"Oh."

"Yeah. Pretty bad. She's not doing too good and ..."

"She's pregnant," I said.

"Yeah," said Lara.

"It's just one fucking thing after another," Lara added as she opened up her email.

We commanded a window booth overlooking the sidewalk.

After awhile I was feeling I needed to get away to a run-down neighborhood bar.

And so I excused myself, asking would they be able to get along without me.

And so, I took off, confident in finding just the bar I needed and there it was, perfect, wood bar, dark, dart board, just the one TV.

I took out my computer, something new there I imagine, but I wanted to write down more of what I had heard from the two rebel generals over in the Dunn Bros. front window, and these two older gentleman were talking and the lilt, the generous, almost loving tone of their conversation, beneath the TV and the racket elsewhere in the bar and the sidewalk noise and the traffic, that it was so different, I listened. And I shouldn't have, but I took it down, typed it, as close to word for word as I could come.

I'll call one of them Bill and the other Mike. I wrote it out as two letters they might send each other. Maybe one is the brother of the other. I don't know what it adds to our story of the Dunn Bros. Revolution, but it's happening in the same time, it must be a part of the story, wouldn't you say?

They were visiting here from Iowa, not overly impressed with the city, perhaps big Hawkeye fans?

Mike,

You sound sad. Not easy to answer this note. We ought to though get a new line going. Harder to find stuff in these long lines. I am still having odd computer trouble. Did a few minutes ago get a note from Bix, and he did say he had the audio, ALL WARS ARE BANKERS' WARS.

I have not had worries you herein speak of. I have felt memory of other incarnation and have disliked our civilization. I grew up thinking I was not exactly a human. But I felt superior. But the civilization offered me nothing. Boredom has been a problem. Outdoors, I am easy in, too.

There is a point where we who both love outdoors differ, not about the outdoors, we can agree that is sublime, but, I think you have felt you should not get too sour grapes on the foul civilization.... It is only foul because of the people in it, har har....How maimed they be....

Early, I admired Mexico more than USA, for the people are easier going and kind, unlike nervous gringos are more apt to share some food with a hungry stranger. And thery laugh in the street a lot. If, maybe not so much by now, during this power of murderous gangs and their very government of course all who profit from illegality of cocaine, from Columbia. The C.I.A. controls Columbia, and Mexico thus far, and so on. Past few decades I have been too leery to spend more time in Mexico. I get attention. But I love Mexico.

I have felt kinship, tremendous past with New Mexico, much as Mexico or more. But here I am, no rudder on my ship all my hard life. Ah, the Hill Country is ok.

Just 21 and I don't mind dying, said early Bo Diddli. I like that.

Cops can shoot me, but I am neither worried nor making any plans. I doubt in ten years I am going to feel much difference. Very hard to heal a knee injury now. Back injury I have lived with since my twenties.

And I have Madrea and the kids. Yes, I sympathise, you never managed this. I barely did. It is a lot.

Coule days back Kelly and I drove in and I said Madrea is the most sensible adult I know. Kelly: But she is your daughter.

Yeah, a good thing she is.

Well, Mike. We could talk more in these metaphysical areas. Oh, we don't have to use that word. These are reflections. All is reflection, vibration shimmering eternally.

Further,

Yo, Bill:

When I was young, I had various fears: Was I handsome enough to attract interesting women? Was I strong enough, to handle a serious fight? Did I have enough talent, to write anything worthwhile? Is there nothing that really, really attracts me?

Those fears are gone with the wind. Time and, changes. The onlyfear I have left is, how much time have I got?

There are a few things, writing and, some other stuff, I want to finish. I don't know if I'll have the time.

When you die, I think that's it. Nothing is left. You are gone forever. If you guys die first, I will be sad. In a sense, I'll probably be happier, if I go first.

Life is a party. It has dancing, music, hopes and dreams. But, sooner or later, we all leave the party. We have no choice. The party will end. Dust into dust.

I've had a pretty good life. A couple of failures: I have no children. I've always liked kids. Would have been good to have some.

And, my second failure, I should have studied physics and math in a serious manner when I was young, back in high school. At that time, I did not understand how essential math was to understanding everything else.

Probably, the best thing in my life has been spending a lot of time outdoors. That was a very good decision. I've always felt real comfortable outdoors.

Well, take it easy, Bill. I'll catch you later.
Mike

Note from the narrator:

From "The Prince Hope Show" ...

We are proud to be sponsored this week by The Minutemen.

Guarding American's borders from poor people.

Our own great-grandparents were poor and they came here from other places.

Huddled masses, yearning to be free.

We are Fighting for freedom from poor people.

Taking aim at frightened lasses, crouching by a tree.

We urinate on The Statue of Liberty.

We defecate on Ellis Island.

We've got ours, crunched tight in our cold, dead, clammy hands.

In just sixty seconds we are able to desecrate the whole idea of America.

We are The Minutemen.

... It will be done, and nobody will be able to stop it. Because that gangster nature of global Western dictatorship is now so complete, and it is so frightening, that no country on earth would dare to intervene and then have its legs broken, face smashed, or eyes poked out. It is all down to a mafia approach, or inquisition, or the Crusades.

— Andre Vltchek

... But nothing is happening. The majority of Europeans and North Americans appear to be thoroughly apathetic towards the state of the world. They keep stuffing themselves on cheap subsidized food; amusing themselves with the latest gadgets. They keep voting in those right-wing governments and they believe, increasingly and blindly, that their societies are an inspiration to the rest of the world as the sole examples of democracy and freedom. Go to a pub in the UK or Germany, and everybody knows everything. You will hear it repeatedly: politicians are swine, corporations are controlling elections. If you stay long enough, after several pints of beer someone will perhaps slam his fist on the table. "We need revolution!" Then everybody agrees and they all go home ... the next day — nothing.

— again, Vltchek

From the comments section:
You must be a hard core proud "conspiracy theorist" which requires memory skills of previous events, imagining alternative explanations, assume secret police (i.e. cia/mossad/M15/6) involvement and communicate with known and trusted other people.

THIRTY-TWO

And so, yes, I have talked to all of these young people, perhaps once, some many times, and whether these interview notes are in order or not, I don't know, and to tell you the truth I don't really care, that would be for someone else at the time. For me, it is enough to get them down, they existed, they exist.

After he witnessed the trashing of the headquarters from the alley I guess Korey took off. He got on his bike and just rode, all around town, to think. He didn't hear from Jim and it wasn't until the next day that he heard from Lara about what had happened. And then they decided a bit later to ask him to open the local Minneapolis-Saint Paul front, the MTM Brigade or whatever.

And so he began to work on doing that.

Korey, sometimes he goes by Kory, thinks it's more incognito, I don't understand myself. I don't think it is. It's not.

Well, we're still in the fall when all this is happening.

And so, what does this mean, I asked him, setting up a local front, how does that work? Is it like the Guardian Angels in New York? Or The Weathermen? Or what?

And Korey, at least to me, was always kind of hard to talk to. He didn't say much. He just said, come on, and so I followed him. And once we were moving, walking pretty fast, just the two of us, it's like it was easier for him to talk.

"Imagine," he said.

"If I told you right now it was your job in life to start a real war right here. What would you do? You've got people and equipment, food. You've got places for those people to be, but then what do you do? What do you have them do? You go out onto the street and you what?"

I shrugged.

"Exactly," he said.

"So, that's what I'm doing. I have no idea. I'm trying to understand. Lara and Kaitylyn, they don't tell you anything. They can't. They don't know anything."

Korey carried a pistol in a holster under his jacket and a rifle in a guitar case over his back. He wore his brigade T-shirt, the Orange CRUSHER version, under his jacket, with green army type pants, black boots, long black, curly hair under a TWINS cap.

And just walking all over, looking around. He called it night patrol. I called it work. We stopped about, well, it was after midnight. We stopped for a smoke break right on the Stone Arch Bridge. And by then he had it pretty well all figured out, he said.

They would take Fort Snelling, Camp Ripley, take out bridges, The Stone Arch Bridge and the Wabasha Bridge, take down icons, command high ground, media, river, basilica in Saint Paul as base, state capitol, the university. Lots of kidnapping, mayhem.

He had a whole plan in his head and of course I knew he was nuts.

Two guys out in the dark in the middle of a whole big city talking about how they are going to take it over, and I told him so.

"This is nuts," I said.

He leaned on the rail and pulled himself up. Then he jumped, into the dark, toward the river that I could only hear.

I reached for him and called out.

He hit something. I saw him by the cherry of his cigarette and the moon. He was standing on a stone piece of the bridge, a round something. He climbed right back up. He must have been here a hundred times maybe thinking the same thoughts.

"I used to think that," he said.

"I'd go out for these walks all night and get pretty depressed, knowing I couldn't do anything, that things would never change, but then I met Lara, Jim, Buster, Kaitylyn ... Max.

"It all starts like this," he said.

"Like what."

"Like with one person. Nobody has a thought with somebody else, or very rarely, ya know. You have thoughts in your own head, on your own. It's like, I don't know, this is how I think about it, it's like, ya know, you're thinking about how everything should just be overhauled, and if you're crazy, you jump, and you fall, but if there's something good to your thoughts somebody else is going to be there already, probably, and then you go together. Does that make sense?"

I nodded and turned, just to be going. I was getting cold.

Note from the narrator:

From "The Prince Hope Show" ...

And now, for another episode of "The
American Stuck In Traffic."

You never know what you'll do until you do what you do
When you're broke.

— Todd Snider

THIRTY-THREE

JIM.
That's what it said on his coveralls, the orange coveralls he used for robbing banks, his uniform. Underneath he wore his brigade orange T-shirt with the CRUSHER logo.

He did it because he liked doing it, damn it.

Not because they depended on him.

That just ruined it.

He slammed the door shut and again to keep it there. He flung his rifle strap over his shoulder and walked up the little walk, opened the glass door and headed in, pointed the rifle at the teller, then somebody behind him, get them all in the same place, god this was a small bank.

Well, shit.

The reason he robbed banks, was he liked it. It was interesting.

"Yeah, in a bag, yeah, I've got one here if you, okay, thanks."

It was going to the root, not arguing, not voting, just going and taking it, taking it back. He didn't really give a shit where it went, who got it, but Lara and Kaitylyn had begun depending on it, so shit.

"You'll have to get down, there, yeah, just sit for awhile. Don't fuckin' do nothing, just don't, okay? Yeah, good, like that. Yeah, thanks."

It was something nobody else could do. They could, but they wouldn't, a hundo reasons.

It was his zone, for some reason, like being on stage or on the field, the crowd goes away, probably like that.

The Educators!

That's it, that's the movie that Jim was trying to remember.

Yeah, and that closing scene, nice, with that song.

That was his getaway song.

He sang it in his head when he left a bank, whenever he remembered.

This other guy.

Think of him like something like the guy who chased Dillinger practically everywhere or Bonnie and Clyde or that posse in the movie that keeps coming after Butch and Sundance. Who are those guys? Those guys. He sat right in front of the desk staring straight ahead until Prince Hope came in and sat on the other side of the desk. Hope leaned back in the old wooden swivel chair, plopping his red tennis shoes onto the desk, looking back over his shoulder for a moment at a sound on the street coming through the open window. ... *Javert.*

The man was probably even taller than Hope and skinny.

He longed to be down on the street with the rest, but his family needed ballgame tickets and so here he was, once again. And he had a rather large family. He had slipped into the red tie on the way up the squeaky wooden steps.

"You've got your own car, vehicle?" said Hope.

He nodded.

"Insurance?"

"Yes, of course."

"Twizzler?"

He sat up to shove over the open pack of red Twizzlers.

The man took one.

The man bit and chewed the Twizzler, staring at Prince Hope, Hope staring back, also chewing, like two guys across a poker table or maybe the produce stand at Super One, trying to figure the other guy out, just chewing.

The man thought of Hope as an asshole, basically somebody with enough pull and money to make other people do things, but there was also a subtext, maybe, of someone like him, who gets him, like nobody else did, a novelist who wrote this book to you, who sees you are sensitive, fun-loving, brave, imperfect, and who knows, and not that many do, that going to the root, the real meaning, scrubbing in the corners, sometimes means shooting some fucker in the temple or under the left nipple. It must be done. It should be done, probably a lot more times than it does, too, to be perfectly truthful.

"Come over here," said Prince Hope, once more extending the Twizzlers pack.

The man took one and Hope put the whole pack on the window sill.

Hope twirled his chair around and the man knelt on one knee. They stared at people on the street to see if they could get them to look up.

And if they do, you look right at them.

It freaks them out.

And that's kind of cool.

"I don't know if you know who I am."

Hope hummed and sang low.

The man sang the rest in his own head and waited. Hope bobbed his head, got his hands poised ....

... Hope did the drum riff in a circle on an invisible clock in front of his face.

They pushed their faces into the screen, pointing lasers into the backs and heads.

This time, nobody looked.

I think some times people looked.

Hugo Chavez, Lumumba, Arbenz, Romero, Allende, others – from Blum ... Evo Morales. You can read it in Vltchek, too. Actually, Kennedy, King, Wellstone, too. Really. You need to read.
— Kaitylyn conducting an overnight study session at the group home during the time of planning

However, if we are ignorant to our own functionalities and internal processes, someone who does understand the human psyche and emotional centers can have a field day preying upon us, which is the reality we occupy currently.
— *Methods of Mind Control,* nomasternoslave.com

Craig McKee: McGowan explains in Part One why people are so hostile to the idea that Apollo was not what we were told: "... it is not the lie itself that scares people; it is what that lie says about the world around us and how it really functions. For if NASA was able to pull off such an outrageous hoax before the entire world, and then keep that lie in place for four decades, what does that say about the control of the information we receive? What does that say about the media, and the scientific community, and the educational community, and all the other institutions we depend on to tell us the truth? What does that say about the very nature of the world we live in?"

Craig McKee: This is why the term "conspiracy theorist" has been cultivated and baked into our culture - to defend those in power from having the big lies challenged.

THIRTY-FOUR

Jim slammed his door, again, again, thought of Max, how he would have thought about things.

Max, Jim told me later, when he was talking about this robbery, wondered what kinds of thoughts the clients were having as they worked at the shred machines. There was no way of knowing, not unless they were talking out loud, which some might have been. But it might be fascinating, or it could just be one long run-on sentence like the rest of us. Of course I don't fuckin' know, Jim said.

Jim, some called him Panda, had a sort of self-deprecatory, fuck-you mien about him, a sort of perfect personality, the sort that some writer described as young boys assured of their dinner. He appeared to not give a shit, and I suppose that's half the war right there.

And when he talked, or after you talked that is, he didn't answer right away and the urge was to rush in another something to explain, but it was just like it took awhile, like, have you seen the animated movie, umm, *Zootopia*, the sloths in the Department of Motor Vehicles? Like that.

He also wanted to be a part of the Indy Group, throw blood and ketchup around, vandalism, disruption, and then getting away with it.

But, as he said … he was kind of … committed … to this bank robbing gig. Which in his mind wasn't that bad.

"Weekends off," he said.

"I take weekends off. Not like at the group home.

"Weekends off, holidays, all that shit."

And he said he missed the others.

"That's why I even got into this fucking shit," he said.

"I, it was cool being a part of the group, them, sitting up late, talking, getting excited, friends, ya know? And now I don't see nobody."

And he talked about Hector and Reuben.

233

* * *

It had been awhile.

I hadn't asked for permission or made notice to Lara that I was going up to the Iron Range. Better to apologize. I know, right?

And there they were, as I had left them how long ago, burrowing into the side of a hill, tools everywhere, laughing, throwing things at each other.

They weren't alone any longer, but they still worked side by side.

By now the whole underground project was more like Underground and heading for UNDERGROUND, not really a joke anymore. Anyway, I didn't laugh.

Except to hear them having this kind of fun right in the middle of the revolution with texts going out to every phone in the country that you were crazy and dangerous.

I asked them about that, right off.

They stopped, which I hadn't expected, rolled right over to sit, pull their knees up and gulp that flavored water.

"You think the world is on your shoulders," said Reuben and Hector nodded like I could tell they had already talked this to death.

"You see this girl. This really happened. Yeah, to me. She's in a car with her mom, yeah, dad, whatever. In any case ... she is being taken to school by someone we assume is a parent or at least a relative or an abductor who has certain standards. But the look on her face. Woah. You have been thinking the world is on your shoulders, when actually it is on hers. What does this do to you or for you?"

"I don't know," I said.

"C'mon!" he said.

"What does it do! Tell us."

"Uh, I don't know. What does it do?"

"Oh, geez!" he said, taking another swig.

"How you doin'?"

Fine, I said.

They asked about Lara, the others, but of course they were right up to the minute with whatever news there was.

I said it was too bad about Max.

"Do you ever appreciate something really beautiful as fully as you think you should?" said Hector.

"I guess he wrote that. Zima said."

"Yep," I said.

"Yep, you do, or?"

"Yep, he wrote it, not that I ..."

"Yep."

"Well," I said, and that was enough to get them up and moving. They took me on a tour. There was a door right in the hill that I for sure couldn't see before we went in. There was some little lighting, cords, steps, steps straight, up and down. I don't think I needed to duck, but I was hunched and ducking the whole time, like when they get into helicopters on *MASH*?

I was way in back and up front Hector and Reuben were talking constantly to each other about how this all got made, how they have had some great volunteers and designers.

"Engineers, actually."

Reuben stopped to say that so we all stood there to let his comment have its moment.

"Students," said Hector.

And then I heard them talking about Geronimo, somehow they got on that. I think it was about his intensity, his love for wrestling on TV.

"He knew all the stats."

This time we stopped because Hector stopped.

"History, all that shit," Reuben added.

Thousand-one, thousand-two.

And we're walking.

We go around and around and now we have come to a mud wall and we have to go back. I'm in front, but I don't want to be. I let them go ahead.

And they're talking non-stop. It's cold and wet.

I ask them about the whole underground phase of the revolution.

How's that supposed to work?

You are underground, right here, but there's a big country out there.

They both stop and say at the same time, "We'll get there, patience ..."

Grasshopper I mumble just as they both say it at the same time and just laugh and laugh.

We stop for a rest and I'm pretty tired of being underground.

"You put a lot of work into this," I said, finding a mud ledge to park my butt.

"Yes, but it's good to be busy," said Hector.

They both started to smoke and I reached out a hand to say, maybe not such a good idea, but they were pros at this I guess, so I accepted one and we sat, perched on the wall like underground goats.

They talked about everyone and everybody. They liked to gossip.

"Remember Korey?" said Reuben.

"Yes, I was just," I began.

And Reuben looked at Hector and Hector shook his head at his own ragged tennis shoes.

"He was like," said Reuben and he stopped like he'd dropped the football.

Hector picked it up.

"Walking around, everywhere, all angry and shit. That's when I first met him. It was like he had some deep thoughts in there because it was like we were all out walking on a nice fucking day and he's all grumpy and sour."

"Profound," said Reuben.

"Yeah," said Hector, almost connoting air quotes.

"But, maybe, I think he was just mad."

"Yeah, could be," I said.

"His tennis shoes were his superpowers," said Reuben.

"Gerry," he said.

"Tennis shoes," I said.

"Yep," said Hector.

"He liked 'em," said Reuben.

"Yep," said Hector.

"He liked DC Comics," said Hector.

"Whaaaa?" said Reuben.

"You silenced the room with that one, bro."

"Oh yeah," said Hector.

"Marvel. Marvel. Marvel, Marvel."

"Not DC," said Reuben.

"Nope," said Hector.

Reuben winked at me to say, what a stupid shit my brother Hector is to say DC not Marvel, oh, man.

Note from the narrator:

From "The Prince Hope Show" ...

Coming soon to your county fair, the traveling display:
THE United States of America Hall of Shame
These are your lone nuts, the wackos, the criminals, the terrorists, the long-haired wierdos in the greasy raincoats in the subway at midnight.

America, where we produce monsters who appear as anyone, and yet through their actions and inactions kill the prophets, keep the poor in the gutter, and still continue to live out their lives in peace, in America ... and long later, die, on television, with full honors ... and still we say nothing about their crimes ... but go home after the parade, shaking our heads, at least, finally ... rid of them.

Please come out to your local county fair to see the traveling display, photos, memorabilia of The Bush Administration, Ronald Reagan, The Warren Commission, The 911 Commission, Paul Tibbets, Harry Truman, George Bush Sr., Bill Clinton, Janet Reno, Lon Horiuchi, the F.B.I. sniper who shot and killed Vicki Weaver while she was holding her 10-month-old child behind the door of the family home at Ruby Ridge.

You can also see historical Hall of Shame displays of the medical examiner at Sandy Hook, and a real-life display of the desk of reporter Bob Woodward who supposedly uncovered Watergate, but was actually a C.I.A. agent who did not let it get out that the break-in was really all about the JFK murder.

Come on out, to your county fair.

It's pretty much all there.

Every director of the Bureau of Prisons, Every director of the INS, the IRS and the F.B.I.

Step right up, throw a tomato, hit Clinton in the nose and win a stuffed animal for your sweetie-pie. Fulfill that recurring dream you have of punching George W. Bush smack in the face.

These are your lone nuts, the wackos, the criminals, the terrorists, the long-haired wierdos in the greasy raincoats in the subway at midnight. America, where we produce monsters who appear as anyone, and yet through their actions and inactions kill the prophets, keep the poor in the gutter, and still continue to live out their lives in peace, in America ... and long later, die, on television, with full honors ... and still we say nothing about their crimes ... but go home after the parade, shaking our heads, at least, finally ... rid of them.

THIRTY-FIVE

Bix,
  Not much here either. I think Kelly returns from Vermont tomorrow. Madrea and her mom and kids are expected tomorrow. I don't know about Bonnie. Nor does Mike know. We do the dog walk - he is taking care of Kelly's dogs, cats, longhorns, one horse now. He does talk on and on, nervously, not much content. I wonder why he does this. Both he and Kelly can be slow to hear a sentence from me. Past couple of years I am trying to heal a knee, maybe I am, but some days are worse or better. I primarily do the walk for Choyota, though like to keep up with the river, see the water fowl too. Am of late too asthmatic again, popping decongestants, which work synergistic with alcohol, so get back to here and short workout and study of End Times.

  Well, hell, were I to try telling Richard what I know of Obama and Hillary and others he would call me a conspiracy theorist again. But Trump ain't shit. What if Trump does try stopping the 9/11 Wars that bleed the nation. He is a businessman. What if he does try talking to Putin. Putin is smart and strong. Oh, I read not MSM.

  Ah, was listening to some Jesse Ventura videos this early morning. What a smart man, funny too. He has another book out.
  Further,
    Bill

Morning, Bill,
  No news here. Did have breakfast with Richard Wednesday.

239

He's fine as his family is.They are having a big gathering last night. I didn't go, was invited. All his sons are married and working.

Richard was a bit worked up over Trump, angry. Trump is not a likable man, a man, who if he was not born rich would be selling bad drugs on the sidewalk.

Great weather here. All the Blackbirds there? Bonnie make it in? My greetings to all the Blackbirds.

This morning, as per email, my cousins Louan, and Robert, whom you met in San Marcos, will be calling me

Robert lives in New York. He wakes -- retired -- and walks interesting long walks in New York he writes. He is a reader.

Take care, Bill.

Bix

Geoffrey,

Yeah, homo sapiens, and probably some other types, not Bigfoot, around a campfire is ancient, togetherness, unto telepathic.

I do wonder do any Bigfoots have canine friends. They may. We link with canine.

I do not dismiss "Muslim agend." Can't tell, this appears absurd. But it as well is looking like Obama's parents (one white) were Muslim and abroad he had been born Muslim. Besides C.I.A. - his parents were, probably. He was raised C.I.A., probably....Hum....

I had liked him before all the Drone Program. Alright, possibly he is a slick liar, a figurehead without power. I don't care. What he and Biden and Hillary and gang have been doing is complicit in 9/11, denying reality of 9/11 but terrorizing third world countries to take their resources, in 9/11 Wars. Revenge. Conquer and loot. But it is going badly now.

What you say on being a white fellow in Japan is interesting. I had not known this, quite. Why do you scare some people. Maybe we can put that together. Imagine being black in USA, where murderous cops favor whites. Hate myth of black fellows have bigger dicks, hate some have become celebrated athletes, who have white glamor girls. Anyhoo, am surprised there is some fear like this for whites in Japan. I had not considered this.

Love,

Bill

PS Geoffrey, I am sorry, and feel I am not political. Do not politics need two or more sides. Do not two or more sides agree children should not be blown apart. In Schizoid Nation they blow kids into pieces. Perhaps were Barry living next door to Caryl he could charm her into thinking he is a nice guy. Yeah.

Hey Bill,

You know I do hate to get into political conversation. It upsets me, and as I've said to you many times, it seems pointless now that there can be no agreement on what news is real. To me, this "news" about Obama trying to spread a Muslim agenda in the U.S. is clearly not real news, but Caryl and you would say that all this news I get from NPR is fake, so there is no way forward. On a personal level, Caryll's point about my living in safe Japan and not being exposed to the problems caused by immigrants is well taken. Of course, here I am the immigrant, and I have seen many gaijin acting badly, being drunk and not respecting the culture. The Americans seem to be the loudest. And, I feel judged being an American. I feel the looks of distrust, the stares from old Japanese men on the subway, even though I try hard to be respectful and cause nobody to feel uncomfortable. It can be tiring, this feeling of always being judged. Though it is no real correlate, I can intuit that being black in the U.S., and always feeling suspicion and loathing wherever one went would be tiring, and one could easily develop a complex and start to behave the way one is expected to bahave, because fuck it. Like here, when I am walking at night, trying to give people space when I pass them from behind, and not alarm them, yet still get the looks of fear, a little part of me wants to howl at the moon or something, just to confirm their suspicions, though I never do. Of course, I also meet Japanese people, often older folks in the country, who worry not at all about my being a foreigner, beyond maybe slight amusement, and who treat me neither as special (that also gets tiring) nor threatening, and for them I feel such great appreciation. I am against almost all the tenets of radical Islam, but living in L.A. originally, where I went to school with Muslims and people from all sorts of cultures and religions, to me they were just regular folks. I guess part of the divide in thinking in the U.S. comes from geography and demographics. Most of the people I know who come from the big cities (New York, L.A.) and are around immigrants all the time, seem more accepting than the people who are probably less exposed to them, and somehow feel more threatened. I do have a couple foreign friends who live in Europe, and they have talked about problems caused by the large groups of immigrants there. I accept that unrestricted immigration can cause a lot of problems, and is no simple matter. I just also feel so priveleged to be born a white American. The plight of the poor Syrians, just to take one example, is so sad. These are just poor families with kids, living with such horror. I realize the U.S. cannot take them all, but they deserve compassion.

Anyway, I am not going to quote people, or look up "facts" to share or any of that. It's pretty pointless. I'm sure that were Caryl and I to sit and have a conversation we would get on fine. Actually, I think that if Caryl were to sit and have a conversation with Obama that did not involve politics, they would probably get on fine, too. He would be less easy to demonize. But, I will spend no more time on this. It leads nowhere.

I am glad that Madrea, Cynthia and the kids will visit, Bill. Please send them all my love. Maybe you can all build a fire and sit around the fire and look at the stars. Sitting around a fire is an experience beyond all borders and beliefs.

Love, Geof

Bix,

Seems like I said, Janet Phelan is spoken well of by her friend Susan Lindauer, and is a nearly murdered journalist, with her own book out, EXILE. Names of these two famous active ladies are easy to google. Both have been interviewed on Jim Kessler's The Real Deal, and many other places on the web too, past several years. Both have survived what most men would not.

During these post 9/11 years, alternate news grew up. During Susan Lindauer's fantastic ordeal, while locked up, her boyfriend kept working to help, and found blogs he could tell all this to. That snowballed, went on into radical radio stations, much went back and forth, and the non-political actual news came together.

By now, corporate news is much worse stupid. I wonder, such saps paid so well have no sense of what is up. They are not taking their money and getting away.

I am lately a big Julian Assange fan. He is having more fun. You know, he had made use of Brady Manning's bold material, the machine gunning from helicopter this group of guys standing and talking, vehicle drives up to pick up a crawling guy, gets machine gunned, couple kids in the vehicle. Brady or Chelsie Manning broke no law by man but he is doing 35 years. Would you agree with me, or not, our friends who have already forgotten Brady Manning are a wee fucked up?

"Fucked up." Functioning poorly biologically: spiritually or regarding food.

Since 9/11, USA journalists are getting murdered more frequently. We know it. Aside of Main Stream Shit, much today on Net of list of Killary's killed, keeps getting bigger. Meantime, all this of her desperate physical condition. Sounding like she can flop over dead any time now. Or this zombie might not finish her speech at her inauguration. Either way you look at it, her handlers for her inauguration will be wired poor devils.

Besides this is fakery. She is seriously unpopular. Way more unpopular than Trump or Bernie in this possibly least ever before popular USA presidential election, where this time the entire thing is rigged.

Bix,

The whole picture is too huge and shaken up. Spy vs. Spy. A box of nuts shaken up. Certainly we have the kernel of ruling billionaires, here in the West. They live insanity besides they can pay well for mad creativity. They want spy vs. spy because they want the unwashed to always be shocked/confused, certainly unfocused. You know, we carry on, like in the famous jazz song, Masquerade.

Citizens believe their USA has the biggest weapons and it is not so. Competition ongoing in our military industry has too much blinding glut, too, too, many hogs at trough, so many best airplanes and submarines are flawed. Have you read, I hope you have. At this time Putin appears noble. Seems to not lie. Maybe he does, but the USA lies very much more than anybody. Delusional maniacs like Hillary think USA is King. Fucking nuts. Well, she is very ill, propped up, maybe so badly this of her health cannot keep covered up.

Hopefully she can be exposed before she is Pres and rushes to nuke cooler Russia.

Further Out, Bill

Far Out,
Bill

Steve,

Kelly picked this one up yesterday. Maybe I should look at this Art Card while stoned this afternoon. I may not have correctly copied your start of AC. "Top Bill?" Vintage Bill?

Gee, Geoffrey, Mike Blackbird, now you, and the scorpion story was tossed that date into a note to Mike Novak who sends me these radical works. Ah, glad you read my stuff with Novak or even bits with Kessler, but enough Bill got stung by a scorpion. Bill is telling sleepy heads about USA War is Peace, dogs, goats, children are daily dismembered, gathering enemies of USA stupefied children. Uh, can the stupefied children maybe read TG or EP or the sort?

I have not read yet any Franz Kafka, and "Kafkaesque" is in the dictionary on my desk. He seems to have written all about schizoid nation. Fascism is schizoid, a nation with guns/money to ignore or make use of the less well heeled. Schizoid is what cannot work. War is Peace.

Without my ever yet reading Kafka, EXTREME PREJUDICE by Susan Lindauer, THE TERRIFYING STORY OF THE PATRIOT ACT AND THE COVERUPS of 9/11 AND IRAQ, sounds very Kafkaesque. The Patriot Act is fascist, renders our constitution useless.

When the Judge in his retirement visited Kelly and me briefly - maybe Janus was gone - and he and Kelly and I took a short walk to the river and back, he kept dodging conversation with Bill. At a point, I tried. Richard, what do you know about our Constitution these days?

More than you do, was this ignorant retort from the Judge.

Bill: Well, Richard, I don't know....

He and Kelly were shuffling along well ahead of me, I had the sore knee that date.

All he wanted was retirement, property, respect. I do not know is he still taking medicine for high blood pressure.

On seeing Bill's old trailer house, he had remarked on his surprise seeing "how much room Bill has."

How interesting is that.

Beside Bill can still scare anybody he cares to, on a sore knee day or either way.

Well, hell, he got me this SSI. Whether I deserved it or not. Like the Frenchman said, in THE EMERYVILLE WAR: So what you are lazy. You are a human being. Any human being should have food and shelter.

Well, this is very funny, in USA. Maybe not so funny in Europe. Judge R.D. Hatch III is a USA case.

Hatch was 76 past Nov. Bill will be 76 Sept. 17. I remain dangerous, glamourous. We made choices.

Further Out,

Bill

Mike,

"Starched flag" is a joke I used with Geoffrey, who has I think seen pictures of the flag, as well as read arguments about the flag on the fake Moon. Joke being: Do we pretend there is air on Moon to flap our flag - being USA citizens are ignorant as telephone posts.

It is meantime not a tin flag used. It has different ruffles in different pictures. I just then looked at 3 different photos of breezy flag in Hollywood studio, in my copy of AND I SUPPOSE WE DIDN'T GO TO THE MOON. EITHER?

Hey, you or Geoffrey can mess around about the flag. I had said to Geoffrey he will have no "intuition" that we "probably" did land guys on the Moon, if he spends a minute looking, at for example the fluttering flag. And so, Geoffrey as ever said he read how they excused their fluttering flag, and their account is worthy of hearing, or to such effect. Thus Bill made his insider joke, or made insider joke to Bill the insider....THAT, if USA jerks are so BLOODY IGNORANT they need to see the fucker flutter on a Hollywood Moon, we are surely doomed.

Please, spare me my deeper wit, doomed or not yet doomed.

What my family cannot look in the eye is my work, study, years. Past couple days I listened to James Kessler/Dennis Cimino talk about the Moon Crap for two hours. Have you guys forgotten? It DOES NOT HAVE TO DO WITH THE FAKE LITTLE PISSANT FLAG ONLY. Sorry I get surly. 2 fucking hours then, all this, TECHNOLOGICAL, AND SLOPPY HOLLYWOOD, fake lights, fake shadows, a BLACK SKY, when that sky from the Moon is blazing, diamond studded.

If you don't want to know, you need not. Yet, you want to waste my time. Pretend I am a sloppy mind. They told Lyla he could be a great scientist so you prefer to believe those guys, psychologists, in Houston in 1957, were ill educated.

Would you not hear me say I care not if the psychologists in Houston in 1957 were stupid?

I don't get self doubt. Never did. Never mind, not for Mike. Tomorrow night Kelly and Janus have their old friends to visit, Gary and Vivian, Debbie and Mike, they will make fun of Trump and believe Killary is a nice lady. I have told Kelly I am too angry to be around it.

Did you see Obama shed tears over Sandy Hook, couple years after Sandy Hook, but he did so all the same. Slice in half one onion and rub finger tips into it and on stage wipe tears.

What, no tears every day for Middle Eastern kids, North African kids.

I am too angry to be around it. Try to remember I have killer impulse.

Oh, not for you to remember.

Not for you to know what I know. Too late.

Many years I have presented proof 9/11 is inside and these are 9/11 Wars, worst period in USA fake history. Forget it. Not for you to know.

Far Out,

Bill

Yo, Bill:

With regards to the flag on the moon, please pay better attention.

You did not read my my last note correctly. They didn't bring a starched, cloth flag to the moon. They used a metal flag. Probably, made from aluminum.

I know, I know, all of us have bad memories now days and, have troubleconcentrating but, you gotta pay better attention. Don't drink so much when you are writing emails. You gotta keep the brain working.

Anyway. This is what I know, from reading about the Apollo missions. They used a metal flag. Probably, aluminum. See, first, you make a waving aluminum flag and then you paint the U.S. flag features on the aluminum model.

Go back and read about the original Apollo missions. I might be wrong, they might have made the flag out of iron but, my guess, it was aluminum. That would have been lighter and, easier to handle.

I don't know where you got the idea that the flag was starched. In my last letter, I told you that I figured the flag was made of aluminum.

There is no atmosphere or wind on the moon. Obviously, if you want a waving flag, where you can read/tell what nation is on the moon, then, you do not bring a normal, cloth flag. You bring a painted, metal one.

Bill, I make an effort, and try to write letters that are clear and not garbled at all. I always look for mistakes, and I correct my letters before I send them. You should extend me the same courtesy.

Read what I write, before you comment on my letter. It is better to check twice, make sure everything is right. Being sloppy has a certain style but, it's pretty useless, when you are trying to figure stuff out.

Your brother,
                    Mike

This nation must have a revolution every twenty years in order to cleanse it from the control of the special interests who will inevitably exercise power beyond their numbers.

— Thomas Jefferson

I have squandered my resistance for a pocketful of mumbles, such are promises, all lies and jest, still a man hears what he wants to hear and disregards the rest.

— "The Boxer," Simon & Garfunkel

What I want is for every greasy grimy tramp to arm himself with a knife or a gun and stationing himself at the doorways of the rich shoot or stab them as they come out.

— Lucy Parsons

Custer died for your sins.   — Vine Deloria

I John Brown am now quite certain that the crimes of this guilty land will never be purged away but with Blood. I had as I now think, vainly flattered myself that without very much bloodshed it might be done.

— John Brown was hanged on December 2, 1859. Before he died, Brown issued these words in a note he handed to his jailer.

THIRTY-SIX

What about Evey? I asked Hector and Reuben.

They said they had taken a break from the digging one day to go to see.

We stayed in the weeds, said Hector.

To watch, said Reuben.

Why? I asked.

Why didn't you talk to her, to your parents?

That is over, said Reuben.

It would make it harder, said Hector.

They both turned quickly away, but came back to tell me what they had seen, and what they had imagined.

They're both about half crazy. Right here, that's what I wrote in my notes.

Evangelina sat outside on the metal bench, cold, breeze, leaves, apples covering the ground, holes from skunks, the garden, her father already on the ladder tacking plastic outside the windows and so Evey lamented the fact that she would not be able to sleep with her face in the open screen in the fresh breeze, listening for the sounds of the woods. The yearbook sits in her lap. Evey had borrowed it from Abby Inquvist, that's another whole story right there. It was there one morning, covered in dew. Saying on cover, color of cover – school saying, motto, sports, logo, with a yellow sticky note on the page where she could find Rachel's senior photo.

"Evangelina! Lunch! The baby!"

Yes, mom, yes, she knew she had to eat for the baby, too, what the fuck. She picked the book out of her lap and rested it on the table of her belly to be closer. She had pretty much memorized the book the morning it had arrived so now she knew right where to go to inject the quickest, most deadly shot of hurt into herself. Not the class photo, but the laughing shot of the choir club, and then the volleyball and then the back pages with all the signatures and notes and the "wishes" where Rachel had written in her own hand what she would do with her life.

"Your mama has lunch for you. It's on the table."

"Yes."

Evey kept paging.

Her father finished and hauled the ladder to the garage, did not glance at her as he went in the back door. Her mother looked out at her from the front porch, then later around the corner by the back door. A bit later her face appeared in the kitchen window. Then both the mother and father looked out the back window, their faces enveloped by the red and white curtains.

The little breeze slunk away. The mail car stopped at their box on the road. The yellow school bus let out the children across the road and for a moment Evey heard the laughing children on the bus, that is if she even noticed. No one knows.

The sun went down, one coyote and then a few yipped for a brief moment. One owl hooted.

Her parents wrapped her food and put it away. They closed the front and back doors, not all the way.

Note from the narrator:

From "The Prince Hope Show" ...

Now please join us as we look in on the new CBS Reality TV Show:

"One Day in the Life of an American Solzhenitsyn, an American Mandela, an American Thomas Jefferson — an American Prisoner."

Therefore, even when the likelihood of success is against us, we must not think of our undertaking as unreasonable or impossible; for it is always reasonable, if we do not know of anything better to do, and if we make the best use of the few means at our disposal.

We must never lack calmness and firmness, which are so hard to preserve in time of war. Without them the most brilliant qualities of mind are wasted. We must therefore familiarize ourselves with the thought of an honorable defeat. We must always nourish this thought within ourselves, and we must get completely used to it. Be convinced, Most Gracious Master, that without this firm resolution no great results can be achieved in the most successful war, let alone in the most unsuccessful.

... For great aims we must dare great things.

— Carl von Clausewitz, *The Principles of War*

THIRTY-SEVEN

"This was Ruth Anne's store."

Morgan whispered to the person beside her as they smoothed over the wood floor.

"My parents watched it Monday nights while we did our homework."

The store smelled of pine. There were neat piles of new T-shirts, many colors, set in smooth blonde wood, and sayings, tourist cards, caps, almost like the general store it was in the TV show. There were jeans for sale and whiskey down another aisle, cans of Dinty Moore, Skoal, *The New York Times*, even shelves of books for check-out. You made out your own library card and left it in the recipe tin.

Two older women stood by the front window, apparently discussing the line of orange CRUSHER T-shirts.

Morgan made her way to stand close enough to hear and nodded and smiled when one of the women looked back, not sure if what she had said would be accepted or possibly enough to get her arrested.

"Don't vorry, I'm with you," Morgan nudged in and whispered in her best French resistance voice.

"What a Muggle," Morgan heard the old woman say to her yet older friend.

Morgan slapped her hand over her mouth with wide, excited, incredulous, happy eyes to hear that and she and Sandara hustled out of the store before they burst out laughing.

They walked down the sidewalk arm in arm, almost skipping.

"Megalomania," said Morgan.

"I think I've got it, you might catch it, watch out."

Sandara smiled and turned her skip into a jack-boot march.

"No, really, it's like ... I do everything for show, and it's got to be a big deal, will I get famous for this. I was thinking the other day and it scared the shit out of me, I could trace it, events, things, all the way back as far as I can remember."

They split up to walk across the street. They peeked in the office of Dr. Joel Fleishman and asked someone to take their picture in front of the Roslyn mural, Morgan searching for a moose.

"I read on Facebook that the Indians recognized six shades of gender," said Sandara.

"The mask you live in," Morgan said.

"Yeah," said Sandara.

"You think it's your fault, but it's not. It's the limits of the culture, you transcend it, but it's powerful, pulls you down, makes you feel guilty."

"I know, right," said Morgan.

"You're from Iowa?" she asked Sandara.

"Yep, Keokuk."

They headed toward the bar.

"Wait, KBHR," said Sandara, pulling Morgan into the middle of the street to walk crossways. "You said you wanted to see it, I think there it is."

"Wow," said Morgan, her nose pressed into the glass of the old radio station.

"This is it, exactly it, wow."

They checked it all out, the microphone, desk, chair, old albums, notes on the wall.

"This is where Chris in the Morning sat, wow," said Morgan.

"I never saw it," said Sandara, still pressing her face into the glass with her hands as a frame. "57 AM," she read.

"The Brick," said Morgan.

"Bar?" said Sandara.

"Yes. The bar."

They walked in and grabbed a booth.

"This is different," said Morgan, "but part of it looks familiar."

"Anyway," said Sandara.

"Back to the war."

"Yeah," said Morgan, still looking around in wonder, "wow."

"We need to get air cover," said Morgan, looking around, at the walls, the tables, the bar, the people.

"Hey," said Sandara.

She snapped her fingers in front of Morgan's face.

Morgan looked straight at her.

"Okay, I'm back," she said.

"I'm here."

"You said air cover," said Sandara.

"Yep. Air cover.

"That's from ...

"Thank you."

They moved their hands back to accept the water from the waitress.

"That's from Lara. She said we're getting killed without air support."

Sandara smiled sardonically.

"That is just like them."

"Yeah, right?" said Morgan.

"Like we're supposed to steal a plane and then, what, who can fly it, put guns on it, drop bombs from the cockpit."

"I can fly," said Sandara. "They teach it in high school in Iowa, there are no cars just kidding. No, my dad ..."

"Really! You can?"

"Yeah."

"Wow.

"Now all we need is an airplane."

They got their beer, in frosted mugs, waved to other troops who came in but didn't sit by them. They were still supposed to be incognito at this point, that was Morgan's idea. They were camped all around the town, in town in the parks, out of town. It was sort of past tourist season, but still nice out, in fact, the best time — but tourists missed it.

Morgan was nervous about making a big stink, standing out and attracting attention, somebody calling the cops. Nobody was supposed to know yet that CRUSHER was out here. Give them some time to enjoy this. And besides, it was hard to pull the trigger, to take that step up onto the stage from the crowd and interrupt the play, so much easier to sit quietly in the dark. But that T-shirt at Ruth Anne's. Were they a thing already?

Sandara had been in Morgan's brigade in North Carolina, but they hadn't known each other. When the brigade got transferred out to Washington by Lara, Morgan had to find ways for everyone to get out there, basically on her own. CRUSHER had some money to give and some transportation, but a lot of that had to go to transferring the basic necessities across the country and not much was left for the actual people.

Morgan had complained and Kaitylyn had said she understood and was working on it, and Morgan said like how and Kaitylyn said nothing in response and Morgan said to herself that's how people communicate these days, a negative response is just no response.

Morgan thought Sandara already showed some signs of combat fatigue. She'd seen it in others. But actually, they had not even been in battle. They had just waited by their creek or river, probably the wrong one, heard all that noise from the other spots, didn't know how to get there. It was actually one long week or so of hell. She could see why Sandara was wiped out already.

She stared at Sandara through her mug as she drank her beer. How did she get here? What had she gone through to be sitting here. Wow. To be able to pull out from whatever life she'd been living, whatever life she'd planned and was already plugged into up to her neck. And how had she even heard about them? Did they have internet and all that in Iowa. Probably. Yeah, of course.

A bunch of guys walked into the bar, in camo pants, hats, big guys.

The boys got to play at war. That's what they do when they hunt. The animals can't shoot back, but these girls can.

That's what ran through Morgan's brain, involuntarily, she didn't ask it to, it just did.

She hated these guys and she could kill them all now.

The good Morgan, the not crazy Morgan sat on her other shoulder now and told her — yelling with hands by mouth because it was getting loud in there — that everybody's intelligent, everybody's dumb, everybody's bumbling, everybody's skilled, just at different times.

Sandara started to talk about flying and Morgan stared over Sandara's right shoulder as Sandara talked and drank. Morgan thought about how much freedom the quote generals had in this army. Lara just sent you out and it was up to you to make it happen. Kind of cool, kind of not, scary.

"So, what I thought," Sandara was saying as Morgan was thinking about how she would walk right up to those guys, stab them all, shoot the others and this bar would be quiet, for a while.

"And I thought," said Sandara, "we have nothing to talk about. Your country is not my country, I'm outa here. But where could I go?

"You know?

"Heyyy ... he-llloooo?"

The WAP-WAP-WAP of a helicopter drowned out everything in the bar, flying low, humming loud, right over the building.

Morgan sprang, pulled her sidearm and ran outside, the weapon in both hands.

She knelt on the corner, aiming the Glock at the copter as it swerved away, out of town. Sandara stood beside her, her weapon also pulled, aiming into the sky.

The noise of the helicopter slowly flapped away, leaving the diorama of Morgan and Sandara aiming their guns, frozen. They moved their eyes, not turning their heads, to see the cement steps and doorway filled with large men in beards and camo, staring at them with wide eyes and open mouths.

Morgan and Sandara hustled into camp, excited, in a hurry.
Morgan had an idea.
She ran from group to group, tent to tent, campfire to campfire.
"Have you seen Actually?"
"He's over there?"

"Where?"

Actually was a guy from somewhere in California. His name was not Actually. Morgan didn't really know what it was, but they called him Actually because that's what he was always saying.

She remembered him talking about how his grandmother had went to a couple of the Northern Exposure fan get togethers here in Roslyn. And something about the airplane that Maggie the pilot actually flew in the show.

She found him squatting by a stream washing little stones.

"Yeah," he said.

"Actually, it's not that far. My grandmother will be here soon. They're having another reunion. I'm not sure of the date, I'll check."

"No," said Morgan, "just where is it, the airfield?"

Actually stood to look around and try to remember. He walked off one way and then another. He took them down a gravel road and across the fairway of what could have been an old golf course, then to a large open field.

On the far end sat a white plane with a propeller. They ran to it.

Do we have plane gas?

Is that a real thing?

Bombs? Guns?

Yep. How many fit.

Two, three maybe, four could squeeze, maybe.

I wonder if it still runs.

Sandara sat in the pilot's seat, Morgan next to her, Actually in the back. The engine sputtered, then roared. They bounced high in their seats, coming down hard as they picked up speed over the field that looked smooth but was not.

"Oh god, oh god," said Actually.

"We're gonna hit that tree!"

At the last moment the wheels left the earth, kicked off like a giant bird. Sandara pulled back, they lifted almost elevator straight and shot up, pinned back in their seats like astronauts.

"Wow," said Morgan as they leveled out.

"Man, how cool."

They balanced submachine guns on their laps as they scanned for the helicopter.

They seemed to just sit in the sky as they passed over endless trees, a river, another river.

"Look," said Sandara, nodding.

"That's our camp!" said Morgan.

They went low. Sandara wagged the wings and they waved with both hands.

The plane hummed and people on main street waved and smiled.

"Can you land this?" said Morgan.

"On that rough field? No way," said Sandara.

"Way," said Actually.

"Well, do the best you can," said Morgan.

"I need to piss."

Note from the narrator:

From "The Prince Hope Show" ...

And now for another episode of Mark, The Most Dangerous Blogger on Earth, in his parents basement working on his blog: Cheetos Dust & Moon Dust Are Both Orange.

Those protests are totally useless.
The rebellion is difficult now.
Before, all it took was dope and long hair.
And the establishment was automatically against you.
What was considered subversive then you can buy in shops today.
Che Guevara T-shirts or anarchy stickers.
That's why there aren't any more youth movements.
Everyone has the feeling it's all been done before.
Others tried and failed.
Why should it work for us?

For all revolutions one thing is clear ...
Even if some didn't work, the most important thing is ...
that the best ideas survived.
The same goes for personal revolts
What turns out good, what survives in you,
that makes you stronger.

What do you think?
How many people down there are thinking about a revolution.
In this moment, not many.
At 10:45 they're watching TV.

Not being a part of all that is not the problem.
The problem is finding something I really believe in.
Got any ideas for me?
Follow me.

— The Edukators

THIRTY-EIGHT

"This ain't workin'," said Morgan.
"There's nothing to attack. These people are too nice."
"So, what do we do?" somebody said.

Those sitting in chairs on the sidewalk in front of Ruth Anne's store had a wonderful view of the woods and hills to the east of town.

"Looka that," somebody said, pointing to the things coming down the hill, black things, maybe green, maybe lots of different colors, tromping down through the brush toward the east edge of town, the city shed and the industrial park that didn't have anything yet, but there was some talk a couple of years ago about a pine cone business, making something out of pine cones.

"Elk, now?"

"Yep, coming down. It's that time of year."

"They should be going up, not down. Those are deer, cows. What, who has that many cows?"

"They are turkeys."

"Nope. See how they kind of clump together as they walk and then all spread out and then come together again?"

"Yep."

"Well, what does that?"

"Beats me."

Morgan led her troops down the hillside, walking through low grass, rifles slung over shoulders, carried at the side.

"Well, I heard there was a secret cord," Morgan sang.

"That David played and it pleased the Lord," Sandara sang.

Then they sang together.

"But you don't really care for music, do ya?"

The rest of those walking near them sang along.

"It goes like this, the fourth, the fifth."

Those others walking came close to be able to hear, then they joined along, as they all neared the town: "I know this room, I've walked this floor. I used to live alone before I knew ya."

With heads down they shuffled through the grass.

The first ones hit the streets and their boots rubbed over pavement. They quieted while the others still in the grass sang yet louder.

"I've seen your flag on the marble arch. Love is not a victory march," they sang loud, like an approaching choir.

"It's a cold and it's a broken ..."

Morgan raised a clenched fist, waved it back and forth and all was silent.

She waited at the road for everyone to get there.

They formed into groups and headed out across town. Some went to Ruth Anne's store to shop, some went to the bar, some pulled up chairs to sit with the old men on the sidewalk. Some formed into two's and walked around town, talking to people raking their lawns, played with children playing ball.

Morgan and Sandara walked to the radio station and not knowing how to get in or if they should try, sat on the concrete ledge below the big front window, their boots dangling. Morgan tipped her cap back and lifted her head to squint into the sun.

A Native man in his twenties wearing a blue plaid shirt walked over to them jingling a big ring of keys.

He smiled and said one of the other troops had said something about them wanting to get people to come to a meeting.

"Why don't you ask them?" he smiled.

"How?" said Morgan.

"On the air," he said.

"The air?" said Sandara.

"The radio," he said.

He asked if they would like to tour the radio station.

They said yeah, sure and hopped down off the ledge.

Morgan sat in the chair. Does this work? Yep it works. You might want to start with some music. You don't want to scare anybody by just talking. They haven't heard it for a while and they will wonder who's in their house, but they will get used to you.

Like this? Try this, he said ... He flicked some switches, turned a knob, swiveled the microphone closer to Morgan, wiped some dust off the console.

It played in the room.

"It's going out?"

"There's your red light. Yep."

Some people on the street looked up at them and smiled and gave the thumbs-up.

"Umm, hello. This is Morg in the ... what time is it.?"

"About noon."

"This is Morgan at about noon."

Well, how do I say it.

And she explained to them who they were, exactly who they were, they were CRUSHER and they had been camped outside on the hill for a little over a week now, "and we are here to change things, not really here.

"Well, we would like to have a meeting, if you want, somewhere where we could talk to you all, if you want.

"How's that?"

She looked up at Sandara.

Morgan stood on the gym floor facing the bleachers, her boots felt solid on the wood. Her rifle leaned against the podium. The sounds of people gathering echoed on the walls filled with the high school sports logos: Home of the Warriors.

She stood aside, touching the podium with the tips of her fingers, waiting for people to get seated, to greet each other, for folks to stop coming in through the two doors leading to the school cafeteria.

She moved behind the podium.

She talked loud. There was no microphone.

"Hello!"

Hello they said back to her.

Morgan saw her troops mixed with the town people, old people, young, babies. A klatch of middle schoolers huddled on the first bleacher row, involved in their own thoughts and schemes.

"Thank you for being here. I suppose you wonder who we are."

"We know," said someone from town.

"Oh, okay, well, yes, we are CRUSHER ... as you already know."

She watched a woman doing needle work, crochet maybe, in the middle section, with a dog at her feet, a shotgun in her lap that Morgan just now noticed. A quick glance showed others from town had also brought guns.

"We're supposed to take over the town," said Morgan, moving around to the front of the podium, careful not to knock over her gun.

"Buuttt, I don't know ..."

She looked to find Sandara for some eye contact validation, finding none.

"We know," said someone else from town.

"We know why."

A tall, broad Native man stood in the bleachers.

A white man stood.

A white woman, others.

"It's okay."

One said and others nodded.

"It's okay?" said Morgan.

"Really?"

Morgan shuffled closer and those in the bleachers scooted toward the middle and they talked.

The town people asked if the soldiers were going to walk back up to the camp. Morgan said, no, the plan was to stay down here in town, somewhere.

"We'll figure it out," she said.

"You will stay with me."

The woman with the needle work and the shotgun in her lap looked up and straight at Morgan.

The town people, one by one, offered their homes, their cars, their trailers, their campers, their teepees, the fire station, their cabins, to the CRUSHER troops.

The young people of the CRUSHER Morgan Brigade left the gymnasium in ones, twos, threes with the town people.

They talked, cooked, and in at least a couple of instances, slept with the town people.

Morgan stayed with the woman with the felt boots and the Cubs cap, the shotgun and the brown dog, the Goldwater button on her black leather jacket.

They stayed in her camper parked on the edge of town.

Her name was Mollie.

Mollie suggested they go to the hillside and sit.

"That's what I do," she said.

"Really?" said Morgan.

They walked over the gravel lot and down the hard dirt road.

"And fish, and go to the bar, and freeze my ass off for eight months. It's not all you think it is, living in this famous town."

"No, I wouldn't think," said Morgan.

Mollie stepped right on Morgan's line.

"It's just regular. But we have an NX Club. We go to The Brick and watch videos. We're all big fans. That's fun. That's probably the most fun about being here is knowing those people. I'll probably leave pretty soon."

Morgan followed Mollie into the grass ditch and up into a field.

"Where?"

"I don't know, maybe the real Cicely, but that's Talkeetna. I don't think you can ever get to the real Cicely, but it's fun trying."

"You could take your grandson with you, if you want. I mean he's great and all."

"He's here?" she said.

"Actually?"

"I thought I was right! That's exactly what we call him!" said Morgan.

"I didn't see him," said Mollie.

"Well, actually," said Morgan, "he was doing war training, computer stuff, with helmets and goggles and all that shit, kinda Star Wars, very much Star Wars."

"Simulator," said Mollie.

"Yeah, exactly, that's it."

"How did you?"

"How did I know that big word?" said Mollie.

"No, I ..."

"Before I came here I worked for a big think tank. You might have heard about it, the Aspen Institute and before that the Ra ..."

"Really?" said Morgan, as she spread out the blanket for them to sit on after Mollie nodded that this was the place.

"I'll bet you wish you were back ..."

"Sometimes. Sometimes I sure fucking do. Sometimes not so much."

"What happened?" said Morgan as she sat and crossed her legs, put her rifle across her lap just like Mollie. The brown dog sniffed around the area then trotted back to sit. Morgan smelled wood smoke and pine and heard the highway hum. She untied her boots, grunted to pry toe to heel.

"Oh," said Mollie.

"You're looking for the big moment, the catastrophe, the thing that happened one day at work that changed my life forever, that made me go home and puke into the garbage can in the kitchen."

"Yes," said Morgan, not looking, reaching for the Doritos in her bag.

"Well, you're right. That's exactly how it was.

"I was a project manager and I had been through one thousand trainings, seminars, workshops, but one day I said no.

"They told me we were going to do this one thing for team building, some fucking game that you are supposed to submit to, laugh, forced fun, and write a report later about how it was beneficial.

"And I said, we're not doing that shit. And that was that."

"Woah," said Morgan, crunching her chips and passing the bag.

"That is a big deal, huge."

"Yes. It is. It's huge. And it destroyed my life. And so I was looking for big things to fill my life because I was depressed, hike the Appalachian Trail, bike across Europe, take nine cruises, shit like that. And then I came here, to enjoy the good life, the fantasy, and I did not want to leave, could not leave."

She bowed while sitting and softly mumbled, ta-daa.

"Why are you here?"

"I just think it's the right thing to do."

"Bullshit."

Mollie pulled out her cigarettes.

"You have no fucking idea what you are doing, and that's a fact."

"Yes I do."

"No. You do not.

"But that's okay. A person has to do something.

"But then again you'll ruin your life."

"No, I won't."

"When you are old it will bite you, this."

"Don't you wish you would have done something?" said Morgan.

"Like this?"

Mollie smoked and leaned back on one hand to look at the town down there, the few people walking, a dog.

"You have an old spirit," she said.

"I have no idea what that means," said Mollie. "I've just heard people say it."

"A lot of us do, I think," said Morgan.

"Already old and gonna die soon," she tried to make it sound breezy.

Morgan laughed then smiled. She swiped hair from her eye and sucked down the wood smoke.

Sans ado, while the warm-up band played something jazzy, Prince Hope ambled onto the wood stage in Saint Paul, carrying his golf club, wearing his red tennis shoes, white suit, long black curly hair, wire rim glasses, a big straw hat. He had shaved his beard.

The crowd applauded, smiled, poked each other.

"That's him!"

Hope sat at the piano, setting the golf club on the floor.

He played along with the band.

Lara sat in one of the metal folding chairs, working her violin, in a red dress, red shoes, red bow in her hair, red lipstick, nail polish, the works.

Prince Hope rose as the number ended, walked to the microphone and introduced the show, welcoming the radio audience.

He told a joke about airplane food, one about golf and one making a dig at the current local politicians. He swung the golf club as the show went to commercial and followed-through with his swing to walk to the wings, where he conferred with others about the script.

The show included a ventriloquist, a gospel singer, a folk band and a famous local poet from the inner city, Minneapolis. Coming out of the final break Prince Hope walked from the wings with his familiar wooden chair, which he brought to the middle of the stage. He sat backward and faced his audience. A stagehand brought him a hand-held microphone.

"Well," said Hope, "it's been another long week in my home town," and the people cheered and stood, then sat obediently, hushed, nudged each other and settled in, fists supporting chins on narrow armrests.

"CRUSHER," said Hope.

"The name personifies something in America, something we can't quite understand, hold in our hands."

He held out a hand and turned it into an upside down fist, brought it down, the other hand signifying a flower.

"We see so many of our young people joining CRUSHER, leaving home, radicalized by the internet, for what?"

And then he told, reporting accurately of Morgan in Roslyn, the ongoing battle of Mayberry, the sneaking suspicion that something was happening in Ohio, Jim's bank robberies, a search for Mayfield, the now growing rumor of the indy groups.

And then he went into a story of a young person who had left home to join CRUSHER.

"South Saint Paul," said Hope.

The audience sat entranced by Hope's deep, skilled voice, red tie against all that white background, the high-top red Keds, the intelligent prose and nose.

"He was a peasant, Bob of Saint Paul, and he wanted to find himself, and he decided to find himself in the revolution. Why did he join the rebels, CRUSHER? Well, there was a girl, of course, and in part he followed her, and in part he was getting away from some things, and in another part he was going to be a hero. He would have been an unlikely legend, but he always had big ideas. He liked to draw.

The girl gave him a white rose one wonderful afternoon and said, "be the white rose," and he thought about it, and then forgot it. But he didn't forget her.

And when you die, you will finally understand yourself, she had told him.

And so, he had that going for him, he figured, which is nice.

And he had also received an email in his spam folder, which he checked regularly.

It said terrible things about our country and how CRUSHER was going to make it better.

He deleted it, logged out, erased that day's history and his internet history for the past year, and he ran. He went out running and did not ever want to come back, but he came back. He was hungry. He ate a ham sandwich in the shower and wondered what to do.

And now, months later, if you were to see Bobby you might not recognize him if you were in his graduating class, with his combat fatigue, so deep, his face gone camo, so unrecognizable to one who hasn't been there, as they say. They do say that. But he has been there, into the soprano pitch of human conflict, the experience of killing, of seeing death and wounds, loss.

Bobby got a tattoo before he left, a CRUSHER tattoo, the wrestler, on the inner left forearm. He wasn't supposed to. Those were only for the leaders, the ones who had formed CRUSHER how many long months ago, in the deep nights of a Saint Paul summer on the front and back porch of a group home.

Bobby was here, in town, just the other day, in fact, he might still be here. He might be here tonight. I talked to him. I asked how it was going. He said they tried. I said, who? Who tried? He said, the Berrigans, Abbie Hoffman, Fred Hampton, but you know how it goes.

We sat on a bench and watched traffic. I think he was on leave. He told me about our family traditions of war and that this was not much different. He said he enjoyed the camaraderie of the revolution, of combat.

I asked him what he had learned. He said, how to take a hill by frontal assault or envelopment, how to deliver searching and traversing fire, how to kill by punching one finger to the throat, and he said he felt good, still, even after all he'd been through, that something big was happening and he was a part of it, something big was still coming. He told me about how he had liked playing war in the neighborhood, and Risk, Stratego, firecrackers, bottle rockets.

I asked him if he remembered seeing the movie *Red Dawn* and he said, no, he hadn't heard of it.

Hope's voice had lost a bit of its smirk, depth and superiority. He let the microphone dangle and not all of his voice was making it out to the crowd. Only those in the first rows could really hear.   ...

And that's why I helped them to kidnap you, Dad. You did? Yes. Why? Why! Because it seemed like the right thing to do. I was mad at you, at the time. You needed to be taught a lesson.

... And that's the news from my home town, where all the police and soldiers are thugs, all the Democrats and journalists are cowards and all the Homeland Security lone gunmen ... are about average.

Now was Lara's big part.

She put her fiddle to her chin and sawed away the intro to the closing song as Prince Hope rose from his chair with the microphone and did the voice-over for the last commercial. ... Minnesota Ice ... It's Cold.

The people stood to make their way to the aisles, probably asking each other if the story about the young man on the bench was real or just made up, as they did every week.

"It sounded so real."

"Yeah."

Mollie and Morgan gathered up their things and descended from the hillside, Mollie to go back to the trailer and Morgan to check on the person she had asked to man the radio station, making sure all the announcements were getting out about the concert and barbecue.

"Love will prevail!" Prince Hope shouted from the stage.

"Goodnight everybody."

He then stalked off stage left, right up the aisle toward the back.

"That's him!"

People pointed as Hope walked amongst them joining the throng making their way to the sunny Saint Paul sidewalk.

Outside he stood and eventually there were those who approached him to mingle and take photographs.

That night Morgan sat by herself in the back row of metal folding chairs watching the band, a mixture of troops and town people calling themselves "Coup d'etat." She smelled the barbecue and heard the howl of winter in the distant dark. She wondered about her sentries, a little, there wasn't much for them to do and so she had said if it was quiet come on down for some chow.

Lights had been strung up and down main street and a stage pounded together right in front of The Brick.

Sandara sat next to Morgan.

"Nice night," she said.

"Yep," said Morgan.

"So many stars," Morgan said, leaning back.

"Not like in town."

"Nope," said Sandara.

"And the full moon. Wow. What would it like to be up there?" said Morgan.

"You know, just buzzin' around. I've always loved astronomy, stars, UFOs, all that stuff. It's just fascinating, and then you think about how big …"

"Let's go."

Sandara got up, grabbed Morgan's arm and tugged her along.

"Where we goin'?"

"You'll see."

Sandara led Morgan to the softball field.

"Look," she said.

They saw by the moonlight the plane parked at home plate and pointed toward center field.

"What the?" said Morgan.

Sandara explained it was set up for the game tomorrow between the troops and the town. She'd been asked to take off on the field to make a big deal out of the game.

"Let's go," she grabbed Morgan's hand and crawled through the busted down backstop fence.

They scrambled onto the field like high school kids not wanting to go home yet after a party. They heard the music, smelled popcorn and Sandara pointed out geese flying across the moon, honking.

"That's where we're gonna be in about a minute," she said.

"What are you doing?" said Morgan.

"We're going. Up there."

Sandara pointed again at the giant moon.

"Really? This thing has lights?"

"Kind of."

"Kind of?

"That's enough?"

"Yep, kinda.

"And it's practically daytime."

"Not really," said Morgan.

They climbed in. Sandara gave Morgan a boost up and then pulled herself in.

Morgan found a coat on the floor and put it on, drew it close around her, found another and handed it to Sandara.

Sandara gave the thumbs up and held it until Morgan returned it.

Morgan smelled gas and smoke.

Sandara was smoking, biting the cigarette between her teeth, squinting against the fumes, messing with buttons and knobs, her ball cap now on backwards.

They slid off home plate, bumped over the mound, tore up second base, and there was no way they would make it.

They bounced over the outfield, and shot right through the hole in center field, into the gravel parking lot, headed toward a dark area that Morgan was pretty sure was the woods.

They pushed off like a fat goose, now almost straight up, leaning way back in their seats to miss the trees and up, toward the moon like Santa's sleigh in a hundred movies that Morgan couldn't remember right now, to join the birds.

Mollie looked back from her seat at the concert and saw them crossing the moon. She turned back, smiling, and wrapped her coarse blanket tight around her shoulders.

They swooped back over the concert, waving.

"Look!" shouted Sandara and Morgan leaned over the side to see the lights and the people and the dogs.

"Wow."

They flew out over a glittering river, followed it for a while, then Sandara swerved and plunged them into piney darkness.

Morgan looked for the headlights, seeing none. She could totally not see. She felt the cold air and her hair stretching straight back and felt like she did when she sometimes turned off the lights of her car to scare herself to see what it was like.

Something ahead was darker than the rest of the dark.

Mountains, thought Morgan as Sandara gently pulled them up and back.

Morgan heard barking. She looked up.

Geese! They honked and worked, their eyes wide, heading somewhere extremely important.

Sandara let the geese just go.

"Which way is back!" Morgan shouted.

"I don't know!" said Sandara.

"Oh," said Morgan.

"Maybe this way!" said Sandara as she took them in a leftish arc.

Morgan leaned over the side, searching for the little lights on main street, the lanterns that people had gathered, and the flashlights and Christmas lights and lamps from home.

"There!"

She pointed and leaned over to point across Sandara's body.

"There! Down there!"

Sandara guided them down, way down, toward a line of lights, a long line, too long for main street, more like a city.

"If that's the highway!" said Sandara.

"I know how to get back!"

Morgan nodded, not knowing what Sandara had said.

They went low, too low, thought Morgan. Look out for phone wires and stuff, she mumbled.

They flew over jeeps and green truck after green truck.

And tanks.

The long line was stopped.

Sandara flew over and over more vehicles, with flags fluttering, to the front of the line.

Morgan hung out her side as far as she could.

"Woah!" she said as they flew right over a big pile of blood and guts and legs and fur, where the front truck had hit something.

"A Bigfoot!" shouted Morgan. "I heard about those out here!"

"Wow, ohmy god!"

"Moose," said Sandara.

"Moose!"

They went on, over the empty road, hearing the hum of the plane and then one shot.

"We have to get back!" Morgan shouted.

"Yup," said Sandara.

* * *

Morgan asked Sandara if she could land in the dark.

"It's not dark!" Sandara shouted to convince herself perhaps.

"Moonlight!"

"Yep, you're right," said Morgan, gripping whatever handles and straps she could find in the dark plane, feeling so much of nothing below them, seeing the tops of trees whipping past, feeling the cutting cold on her neck.

It hurts so bad to care.

She somehow thought of the words of her grandfather sitting in his big chair in front of his TV with his beer in a box at his feet. You should just take care of your family. That's all that matters.

She thought of how bad it would hurt when they crashed. Do you feel it? Or is it like getting a shot and it's just all numb?

Probly not, she thought as she grabbed the dash with both hands as Sandara whipped them around to head down to the ball field. As they dropped down in sections like stopping at each floor on an elevator a few deer trotted away to the edges to the outfield foul lines.

"We need to get ready!"

Morgan stood straight on the stage at the microphone.

She pointed and she implored.

"Secure the perimeter," she said, and then told them how they would do that.

"Get on the radio," she pointed at someone and that person skidded off in the gravel toward the radio station.

"Get your guns. Lock your doors. Get up on your roofs, if you can, or in your deer stands."

Morgan laid out a plan already in her head about where they would put sniper teams in the woods, how they would block the road heading into town with trailers and boats on trailers and RVs.

"We can do this," she said.

"Okay, town dismissed," she said.

They worked through the remainder of the night, hauling junk cars up by the freeway entrance, four sets of road blocks with snipers at each one.

Pete from Kansas and Nick from Arvada manned a machine gun nest right behind the "Welcome To Roslyn" sign.

A production line was set up in Ruth Anne's store preparing molotov cocktails and sandwiches. Mortar teams perched on the roofs of the machine shop, the gas station and the bakery.

The old cannon from the city park was pulled up close to the entrance at the top of the hill for show, along with the fire truck with its lights flashing and siren running, hooked up to a generator to preserve the battery in case they really needed it.

Morgan kept her troops separate from the town people doing their own thing with their rifles and shotguns poking out living room and garage windows.

She expected it all to come at them from the entrance off the freeway, the other sides protected by the mountains, river and woods.

Morgan caught her head bobbing as she sat with her rifle across her lap on a metal folding chair in a sandbag bunker on the hillside where she and Mollie had rested peacefully. She kept watch with John and Teresa. She texted back and forth with Sandara, guarding the plane and outfitting it with explosives.

The red sun climbed the mountain.

Morgan took a deep breath.

The morning lay tense and dry and crisp, everyone watching toward the rise in main street as it headed up toward the highway and farther down the freeway ramp, listening for fighter jets and bombs and the sighs of wounded horses.

An eagle glided in big arcs above the town and a dog yipped playfully as every day, playing with the men sitting in wooden chairs in front of the hardware store.

At about noon, some of the town women began to worry.

We can't go on this way forever, they said. Everyone is nervous. The children are scared, they're not playing.

While the men talked in the chairs and climbed the trees and deer stands with weapons, the women organized a basketball tournament for the kids, at three different sites around town to make it a big deal. And they cooked. They set up long tables right down main street and filled them with watermelons, sloppy joe's, potato chips, cherry Kool-Aid and baked beans, big trays of it all.

Ty from Queens stood at the top of the hill, leaning against the cannon under the "Welcome to Roslyn" sign, texting Morgan whenever he had something.

The afternoon dragged out. The ladies from the Moose Auxiliary put wax paper around the trays and waited to see that everyone was full before putting it all away. Mollie's friend's grandson was on the second place team in the two on two tournament, and people began to think about dinner.

Some kids, they weren't supposed to, took horses and rode the back way by the river path to check out the freeway and didn't see anything.

The crisp afternoon turned into magnificent night, with sounds of a dog somewhere and people talking on a porch, somewhere a TV on with an open window. Now and again a saw fired up and buzzed, stopped, started again. An impish breeze opened and closed a squeaky door. Those with radios listened to the static of KBHR, waiting for something to talk about.

The smell of wood smoke found Morgan, who sat on her camp chair using the light from her phone to read a topo map. If they attacked during the night she wondered what she could do. She begged a cigarette from John and stared hard into the dark, seeing nothing, listening and hearing everything.

She looked up and saw the fucking hu—GEEZUZ—mongous sky, star-lit, twinkling, with airliners moving here and there, the giant moon making them all an easy target.

Morgan passed the word that everyone was to put on face paint and someone was sent to find that shit in the supplies trailer.

An actual rooster or something, maybe a prairie chicken, crowed as the sun stood up slowly behind the mountains, head high, showing the world in such a different light, of hope and a future, thought Morgan as she watched from her hillside, knowing it would be a long day because she was already so tired.

Ty stood at his post by the welcome sign, talking to the guys in the machine gun nest, smoking, drinking coffee brought to them in Styrofoam cups from the diner by runners.

"Wow, great service," said Ty, raising his cup to Pete and Nick.

Nick nodded solemnly over Ty's right shoulder toward the road. Ty turned and saw someone coming. He walked to the barricade and stood behind the snowmobiles tossed onto the pile, a '70 Artic Cat Puma, a '66 Panther, a '66 140D, already all talked over and discussed by Pete and Nick.

Ty walked out around the barricade to face the newcomers, two men walking slowly down the middle of the tar road. The sun lit them like the stars of the community play, a guy in button-down cowboy pearl collared shirt and jeans, with sidearm and blue windbreaker, carrying a walkie talkie, and the other playing the part of the sheriff.

Ty waited as they approached, feeling others join him.

Ty talked briefly to Morgan on his phone, then moved a step to assure the two men he was blocking their way.

"Morning," said windbreaker man.

"Hello," said Ty.

"This must be Roslyn."

"Yep."

"I recognize it, from the show."

Ty looked back over his shoulder, seeing Nick and the others, more behind the barricade.

"Yup. I never really."

"Good show. Didn't have all those sleds, those are worth money."

"You'll have to move those," said the sheriff-type guy, stepping up.

"Yeah, can't really do that."

"You know who we are," said windbreaker guy.

"Yep."

"So, you took over the town. What do you want?" said the windbreaker guy.

"Yeah, it's a revolution, so," said Ty.

"Yeah, we heard, what do you want?"

Somebody from the back said something good in response.

"How about you take this down and we talk about that," said sheriff guy.

"That's a good idea," said windbreaker guy.

"Are you in charge?"

Ty shook his head.

"She's on the way."

"Oh, okay," said windbreaker guy, exchanging looks with sheriff guy.

Windbreaker took Ty off to the side. Sheriff guy talked to the others, posing some questions about hunting, fishing.

"See, what we really need is the ticket. You can have the damn TV town," said windbreaker guy.

"Ticket?"

"Yeah," said windbreaker guy. "You might not be the one to talk to. How soon will ..."

"Morgan."

"Morgan, be here?"

"She's on her way. We sent the wheeler."

"What ticket?"

They looked up toward the sound of the motor, puttering up the little rise in the road. Morgan got off behind the barricade and walked around everyone, stopping at the sheriff, who nodded toward Ty and the windbreaker guy. She walked over.

"Something about the ticket," said Ty, flashing quick subliminal air quotes.

"You're Morgan?"

Windbreaker guy reached out and Morgan shook his hand.

"Mike Braxton. Nice to meet you."

"You, too."

"Ticket?" said Morgan.

"Oh, you might not be the one to talk to? Is there someone else."

"Yeah, Lara," said Ty.

Morgan looked at him hard.

"Lara?"

"We don't have the ticket, of course," said Morgan, landing hard on the word.

"This is the revolution. You will have to leave."

Braxton and Sheriff exchanged smirks.

"Is that right?" said Braxton.

"And we are fighting for our rights. You should join us. The people have no choice in anything, this is the only way."

"People will get killed. You could get killed. I could get killed. You want that?" said Braxton.

"Might be some good comes of that," she said.

"Listen, young woman, this doesn't need to happen," said Braxton. "Is there a coffee shop in there, there must be? The Brick is that still there, was that really there?"

Morgan nodded and said, no.

"No. That's it?" said Braxton.

"That is right," said Morgan.

The sheriff and Nick and the others, out of things to talk about, just stood there, each looking around.

"All right, have it your way," said Braxton, waving and nodding to the sheriff-type guy.

They walked away up the road to the crest as the sun showed them out.

"We better get ready," said Morgan.

"Yu-up," said Ty.

Note from the narrator:

From "The Prince Hope Show" ...

And now, get ready ... to be released for the Summer
Movie Season ....
My Big Fat American Auschwitz.
Muslims and Terrorists and Commies, Oh My!
Towel-heads and Negroes and Homos and
Liberals and Tin-foils and Wet-backs ...
Poor people and you people and they people ...
Oh MY. ...
Eagles and Beagles and Edelveiss. ...
Saurkraut and six-packs.
My Big Fat American Auschwitz.

Coming Soon.

The narratives expose the anxiety that we will die and never be recognized or acclaimed, that we will never be wealthy, that we are not among the chosen but remain part of the vast, anonymous masses. ... The wrestlers like all celebrities, become our vicarious selves. They do what we cannot. They rise up from humble origins into a supernatural world of tyrants, divas and fierce opponents who are huge and rippling with muscles — mythic in their size and power. They face momentous battles and epic struggles. They win great victories. And then return to befriend and confer some of their supernatural power to us. "For the truth is," wrote Jose Ortega y Gasset, "that life on the face of it is chaos in which one finds oneself lost. The individual suspects as much but is terrified to encounter this frightening reality face to face, so attempts to conceal it by drawing a curtain of fantasy over it, behind which he can make believe that everything is clear. ..."

— Chris Hedges

THIRTY-NINE

Morgan had returned to her chair to sit and found Mollie there. Morgan told her about the scene at the barricade. Mollie asked Morgan if she didn't think maybe she should try some kind of negotiation? "You work in social services, hon', said Mollie. "You know what CYA means, right?"

Special agent Braxton and the sheriff in the big cowboy hat sat at a table in The Brick, looking around like tourists, across the table from Morgan and two of her lieutenants.

"So, as you said," said Braxton.

"This is the revolution."

"Yes," said Morgan.

"Didn't they try that in the '60s?" said the sheriff, accepting his water from the waiter.

"I guess," said Morgan, "thanks," she said to the waiter.

Morgan jiggled her leg up and down. She practiced slow, deep breaths.

Behind her she felt more rebels. Over Braxton's shoulder she saw her troops standing in a line, holding rifles, handguns, wearing the various T-shirts, many having served in other brigades before coming to Oregon: Nothing Is Fucked, Darth Vader, Santa: He Knows, CRUSHER.

She heard a helicopter overhead and smelled cigarettes, fried onions.

She was meeting with the F.B.I. and she was the leader of an army, with guns.

She breathed in, out, looked straight into Braxton's eyes.

Braxton smiled and scooted up closer to the table. He reached across with his water glass in both hands to get close to Morgan.

He whispered.

"Nobody reads news anymore. Do you? Do you subscribe? Of course not. And you know why. And I know why. Because every November they will start talking about Lee Harvey Oswald killing John Kennedy. They are still perpetuating that myth. It is truly amazing. When practically the whole population knows that is false. Think about it. They don't know what else to do. The knowledge of the people has progressed to the point where we actually know what happened, but the government or the New York Times has never made the big pronouncement, though they have known the truth all along. It's truly comical."

He leaned back, took a breath, sipped his water, accepted more from the waiter.

"That's good," he said.

He leaned again over the table.

"It's similar to global warming, nobody ever really says it out loud, but everyone knows it's there. Picture a gathering of Russians on the sidewalk, dressed warm, in Red Square reading the latest news in Pravda. They take those papers home to line their litter boxes. It's the same here. And if they are forced to tell the truth about Oswald then they are going to have to tell the truth about 9/11, Oklahoma City, Waco, San Bernardino, Aurora, Orlando, Sandy Hook, Boston. Where would it end? The truth about everything? Oh no, we can't have that.

"And so ... we commemorate each year around Thanksgiving the day shots rang out in Dallas, the shooting of President John F. Kennedy by Lee Harvey Oswald, on Nov. 22, 1963, on a Friday, at about 12:30 in the afternoon."

He moved even closer, sticking his head almost on Morgan's side.

"That's what you are up against, Morgan.

"You can't do this," he added as he sat up straight.

After a few more minutes of small talk Braxton and the sheriff got up to leave, walking through the gauntlet of guns and T-shirts to the cement steps outside. They walked down the middle of main street the length of town, out to the barricades.

Morgan was greeted with cheers and high-fives, a shot of something strong and songs on the jukebox blared because she had told the United States to suck it.

She gulped down the whiskey and felt the knot in her stomach growl.

Note from the narrator:

From "The Prince Hope Show" ...

And now from the Actual American History Channel ....
Tonight we will hear an excerpt from the book "Disturbing
The Peace."
.... sponsored by Powder Milk Democrat Gonads.
"Heavens, they're pasty."
"Voice For The Voiceless"
... Fort Benning, Georgia. August 9, 1983. The summer
sun was finally setting. It was time to act. Time to engage
the Salvadoran troops.
Roy Bourgeois was ready, but he was not so sure that
Larry Rosebaugh could penetrate base security.
Rosebaugh, a gentle Oblate priest who had worked with
street people in Brazil, reminded Bourgeois of St. Francis.

And if there is any question what it's an allegory for I will tell you. It's the powers that be in the United States of America. It's profiteers. War is for profit. It's not to save the world for democracy ... no, bullshit, it's for the top ten percent. And the young people who see this must recognize that blind faith in your leaders will get you dead.
— Donald Sutherland, speaking about
The Hunger Games

FORTY

A t about noon they heard a helicopter and then saw it coming into view headed south, then turning toward them. The sound became more insistent, louder, like a giant flying unbalanced dryer headed right for them it came, swooping low, right over main street ... right over Morgan's hillside bunker just like it knew she was there. She saw the pilot and co-pilot. She felt she could have reached out and touched them. The co-pilot, or man in the co-pilot seat, flipped Morgan the bird. Morgan watched it buzz overhead and back toward the mountain.

Through the afternoon more helicopters buzzed the town and small airplanes droned overhead, back and forth. They heard more machines moving somewhere and big booms occasionally, like cannon fire.

Through the day the rebels broadcast from KBHR, jazz mostly, and every fifteen minutes or so an announcement that "this is the revolution, we are CRUSHER, we are not terrorists, we are here to fight the empire, please join us, we are doing this for you, tonight's special at The Brick is cheeseburgers and large Freedom Fries."

At 4 p.m. Morgan walked down from the hillside and ordered the long buffet table in the middle of main street taken down and asked everyone to get off the streets and go to their homes. She walked up to see how Ty and Pete and Nick and the others were doing then said she would spend the night on the hillside where she could see more.

At 5:37 p.m. KBHR went down, losing all power.

At 7 p.m. scouts reported to Morgan and Morgan reported back to Lara and Kaitylyn troop truck movement from the interstate to the off-ramp.

At 10:14 Morgan, sitting on a folded blanket on her metal folding chair behind a short wall of sandbags, reported to Lara, "Toby Keith blaring from the woods," and that she would like to be cremated if they found her body. At midnight she saw someone walking up the hillside and said "hey,

283

lady," to Mollie. They sat for a while and smoked and ate fresh apple pie and drank coffee. At 1 a.m. they listened to dogs barking.

At 2:15 a.m. Mollie stood and Morgan stood with her and Mollie hugged Morgan around the shoulders then turned to walk back down the hill.

At 4 a.m. all was quiet as a spotlight parted the sky like a kid trying to find the Christmas presents in the basement.

At 5 a.m. it began with one boom.

"This is it," Morgan texted to Lara.

She turned to the others in her bunker and asked for a report from the scouts and sniper teams in the woods. She called Ty at the front snowmobile barricade and asked if he had anything yet.

The music stopped and a steady pounding of boots on the tar entrance road filled the valley.

"You hear that?"

Morgan texted Sandara, still keeping watch over their air force in the ball field.

"Orcs," Sandara texted back.

"Don't say that," said Morgan.

"It's getting louder, get ready."

"Just say the word," said Sandara.

The marching grew lusty, accompanied by singing, sing-song, deep chanting.

It stopped.

Morgan felt the cold on her nose and stuck her head forward to try to hear and to see.

The dark began to lighten as the diva sun finally arrived, paused, poised for its entrance.

A scream erupted at the front gate.

A rebel yell, thought Morgan, how clever.

Sparks flashed in the dawning light, single shots, then bursts.

The scouts and snipers reported "shitload movement."

Morgan directed her mortar teams to the tar entrance road beyond the snowmobile barricade. She heard Pete and Nick's machine gun nest let loose. Ty called and screamed something that Morgan could not hear.

Morgan ducked as three fighter jets streaked over her from behind at tree-top level, lighting up the town with their machine guns and dropping their bombs in the downtown area, then swooping back for another run.

"Hey!" came the text from Sandara.

"Yes!" said Morgan.

"Go."

Morgan's HQ team got flooded texts and voice messages from all over town, the west side where town people fired from their houses, keeping off the government troops, for now. Someone heard bulldozers and tanks plowing up the woods off the power line passageway.

Sandara whooshed over Morgan's head toward the front gate, with someone hanging out the side with her AR-15 slung around her arm, Sandara holding a cigarette in her teeth and a Molotov cocktail in her left hand. Her radio blared. Morgan smiled and hummed a low, *Hal-ay-lu-u-u-ya* prayer.

Fire fingers flicked up and down back in the woods and Morgan thought how fitting. With Mollie and a couple of other locals they had just read Sun-Tzu, chaos is your friend.

Sandara disappeared over the crest, in the Orcs now.

Ty crouched behind the front barricade, rising now and then to fire over the top, as Pete and Nick let go again from the machine gun nest. Actually sat in the command tent at his computer switching from outpost camera to camera trying to follow the battle.

Sandara's plane wobbled back, low, engine sputtering, a body hanging limp out the side, smoke trailing, going down. She waved with a wrapped hand as she went right over the bunker. Morgan jerked and jumped when she heard the crash landing behind her.

She stood and watched and watched, switching back to the front, searching behind her, until she saw Sandara climbing, crawling up the little hill toward Morgan's bunker.

Morgan called Ty and got nothing.

A beautiful sunrise rained a spotlight down onto the town.

The fire behind the west side roared and took out the first trailers and shacks.

Lara texted Morgan with exclamation marks and Morgan did what she could to relay the news.

Mollie crawled up the far side of the hill on her stomach, dragging her shotgun behind her.

"Where's Bow?" said Morgan.

Bow was Mollie's dog, a Christmas present from a few years back.

"He's here," said Mollie, "right behind me."

"I don't see him," said Morgan.

Mollie looked and could not spot the big dog either, and there he came.

Mollie climbed inside the bunker and sat to light cigarettes for Morgan and her. Together they smoked once more.

Kaitylyn tried calling Morgan. Morgan didn't pick up, but rather stood and laid down a line of fire sending the government troops to their stomachs as they began their assault of the final hill.

Actually leaped into the bunker just as they all ducked a helicopter diving low and raking them with machine gun rounds.

A garage next to The Brick exploded straight up, a volcano eruption, raining bits of chairs and tables and molten metal around the town and halfway up the hillside, smoldering red hot.

"The good stuff," said Mollie.

"Long story," she said in answer to Morgan's eyebrow query.

"You're gonna have to get outa here," said Mollie to Morgan matter of factly.

"That ain't happenin'," said Morgan as she stood again to fire.

"Down!" Mollie pulled on her arm.

Sandara hurled a Molotov in the general direction of the advancing line, falling far short, having to duck back down to escape the blowback.

In Minneapolis, in the new CRUSHER headquarters, Lara and Kaitylyn worked their setup, thanks to a donor, computers, phones, wall charts, TVs, projector screens and a big battle table in the middle where they had displayed the Battle of Cicely from what they had learned from Morgan, Actually, and Google Earth.

Kaitylyn chatted with Brooke on Facebook. Brooke was in a public library, wouldn't say where. Kaitylyn asked what was she going to do? She suggested, Mayfield?

Lara worked the battle table and tried to talk to Morgan in the bunker. She moved the toy army men into the town and up the little hill toward the last stand bunker, as Morgan and Sandara had been calling it.

Someone else talked to Korey in downtown Minneapolis, someone to Zima, chest deep in some creek still slogging toward Mayberry. Jim had called and left a message.

"You need to get out of here now," Morgan said to Mollie.

"The captain goes down with the ship."

"No," said Mollie.

"This captain survives to fight another day."

She nodded to Sandara to convey an already decided upon notion as Actually jumped up to take the front of the bunker.

"That is not how it goes! Let me go!" said Morgan, realizing they were up to something.

She fought them, slapping, punching, kicking, spitting.

"Spit?" said Mollie.

"Seriously?

"They need you," said Sandara, tying Morgan's hands behind her back with a rope.

"You are tattooed, one of the circle, you must survive. That's the word I got."

"Bullshi ... !" shouted Morgan just as Mollie wrapped a rag around her head and into her mouth that Bow had just brought with him up the slope in his mouth.

* * *

The line of government troops stood as one to continue their trek up the hill.

Pop! Pop!

Two of them plopped, nose-first, into the hillside as CRUSHER snipers high in the trees on the other side of town, fire snapping at their feet, found the backs of the government troops with their scopes.

Mollie and Sandara and the others wrapped Morgan tight with ropes and blankets and straps onto the sled. Mollie and Bow gripped the slobbered rope. Mollie saluted Sandara then turned and pulled the sled and Morgan down the other side of the hill.

Sandara, Actually, and the others climbed over the sandbags, lifted their heads, threw out a rebel yell and charged the waiting line of government troops, just as the bombs in Ruth Anne's store and Joel Fleishman's office exploded.

"Anything?" Kaitylyn asked.

"Nothing," said Lara, looking at her phone.

Lara walked to the battle table and reverently removed Morgan, Sandara and the bunker from the little hill crest.

Mollie and Bow huffed, puffed and grunted, hauling the sled through the damp bog at the edge of the river. Mollie untied the waiting canoe, pulled it closer, securing it by a stump to be able to get one end of the sled up onto the edge of the canoe and then throw the ass end in too. She worked, hardly aware that the silent Morgan was a living thing, not just a bag of apples, and then she caught a glimpse of Morgan's wide, scared eyes in the midst of all the rags and towels and ropes around her head and shoulders.

Mollie got down close and whispered.

"It's okay. It's okay."

Mollie looked back over her shoulder at the crack of a rifle. She saw figures standing on top of the little hill. She coaxed the dog to hop into the canoe. She got one foot inside and pushed off with the other. She picked up the waiting oar and shoved off into the little stream, ducking low, letting the trees hide them and the little current slowly take them away.

Kaitylyn received a text from Morgan's phone.

"Hey!" she said to Lara and they both looked at the message.

"This is special agent Braxton," it said.

"Oh, they've got her phone," said Lara.

"Who am I speaking too," said Braxton's text.

"It's over," said Lara to Kaitylyn and Kaitylyn shut it down.

Now action must be taken
We don't need the key
We'll break in
I've got no patience now
So sick of complacence now
I've got no patience now
Sick of sick of sick of sick of you
Time has come to pay
Know your enemy!
Come on!
Yes I know my enemies
They're the teachers who taught me to fight me
Compromise, conformity, assimilation, submission
Ignorance, hypocrisy, brutality, the elite
All of which are American dreams

— Rage Against The Machine

FORTY-ONE

"Courtesy of Actually."

Kaitylyn plopped a packet on Lara's keyboard.

Lara stood over by the copier, papers in her hands.

"Korey?" said Lara, not looking up.

"Holding tight," said Kaitylyn sarcastically.

"Not to be seen."

Lara held up a crumpled inside page of the morning newspaper with a news story circled.

"This Korey?" she said.

Kaitylyn shrugged her shoulders.

"Dunno."

Kaitylyn moseyed across the room.

She talked over the copier.

"You gonna be in the band again? That was creepy."

"What? I don't know. He asked me. He doesn't ask about anything else."

The copier finished but Kaitylyn still talked loud.

"What do you talk about?"

"Things, what we believe."

"He wants us all dead," said Kaitylyn.

"Yeah," said Lara. "Not me."

"He could have you picked up by the special unit," said Kaitylyn, using air quotes.

"They were in Mayberry."

"You know that I know that," said Lara.

"He hasn't though. I don't know why. Of course I don't why."

They sat at the round table for the meeting.

"I wish there were windows," said Lara.

"I know, right?" said Kaitylyn.

A few others joined them, coming in one at a time from the other offices on their floor, the entire wing of a local college dormitory having been turned over to CRUSHER, courtesy of someone somewhere.

Kaitylyn and Lara had agendas, the others didn't.

"Okay," Kaitylyn looked up.

"I'll start."

"Morgan, where is she?"

The others shrugged or shook their heads.

"I dunno," said Lara.

"She wanted, they wanted the ticket, what ticket?" said Kaitylyn.

"It's that shred ticket, the airplane ticket," said one of the others at the table.

"Who has that?" said Lara.

"I dunno," said someone.

"It's weird," said Lara.

"Yes, it is," said Kaitylyn.

"Is anybody doing anything with these?"

Lara opened up the packet from Actually.

"Do you guys know about these?"

The others shook their heads as Lara passed around the papers that Actually had prepared before he died, while in the "Cyber Warfare Tent" at The Battle of Cicely, air quotes, depending.

Kaitylyn smiled as she looked at the piece of paper she was given.

"Very cool, actually," she said.

The others smiled, too.

Lara was not. She read intently.

"What is this!

"We can't do this."

"I think we already are," said Kaitylyn, pushing her paper over to Lara.

The documents showed where Actually and his team had planned fake battlegrounds, by attacking, through cyberspace, and employing bots to engage in cyber warfare, and also on other fronts, the towns of Raccoon City, South Park, Springfield, Genoa City, 17230 Valley Spring Road in the San Fernando Valley of Los Angeles, Hill Valley, Dogpatch, Eastwick, Elwood City, Fife, Alabama, Frostbite Falls, Jericho, and Millennium City, with CRUSHER ships leaving the New York Harbor to attack Muggleton and The Emerald City.

"This is ridiculous," said Lara.

"17230 Valley Spring Road in the San Fernando Valley of Los Angeles?"

"Mr. Ed," said Kaitylyn.

"Ohmygod! We'll look like fools. They won't take us seriously."

"Seriously?" said Kaitylyn. "Really?

"Are you actually saying that?"

"Just stop," said Lara.

"There is no Muggleton. Do your research."

"It will get attention," said someone.

"Exactly," said Kaitylyn, pointing.

"We need some recruits."

"And ... it will occupy their minds for a while. It might confuse them."

"It is ridiculous," said Lara, still fuming.

She read from one of the documents: This is Actually. If you are reading this, I am a dead sucker. [*Lara shook her head and kept reading.*] Long live the revolution. [*Lara mouthed "oh, brother" and kept going.*] You should know that right now CRUSHER troops are headed toward these cities. Citizens should prepare to either join the revolution or defend yourselves. We Are CRUSHER.

Lara took a deep breath.

"And so, these have gone out to the news media?"

"I assume so," said Kaitylyn.

"Not yet," someone else said.

"Make certain they do not," said Lara.

"And when we announce we are going to be attacking Mayfield, they are not going to believe us."

"Read your Sun-Tzu, my dear," said Kaitylyn.

"I have!" said Lara.

She collected the documents from the others, stuffed them into the manila envelope and pushed it aside.

"Let's move on," she said, working to calm herself.

She actually put her hands into a yoga-type pose and took a deep breath with closed eyes while Kaitylyn and the others watched.

"Continue?"

Kaitylyn looked at Lara.

Lara nodded.

They talked about what was happening at Mayberry with Zima, Joe and Ariel.

"They need bullhorns," said Kaitylyn, finding a note she had made to herself.

Responding to the look on Lara's face, Kaitylyn tried to explain.

"They have an idea that they are going to circle the town and shout to the people inside and tell them about the revolution, why we are doing this."

"And then the government troops will know right where they are and go kill them."

"Yeah, that could happen," said Kaitylyn.

Lara took another deep breath and asked if anyone would like to try to find bullhorns and ship them to North Carolina.

A young woman in red braids and a nose ring raised her hand.

"Thank you," said Lara.

"And Miss Brooke," said Lara.

"Any news?"

Kaitylyn searched her pages of notes.

"Yep," she said, putting a finger in the air to call for time.

"Anyone seen any good movies?"

Lara asked the others. They all shook their heads.

"Okay, here," said Kaitylyn.

"Brooke ...",

She searched the narrative.

"Here. ... Would like to go to Mayfield."

Kaitylyn nodded and looked at Lara because that was something they had also discussed.

"Or to Queens."

Kaitylyn read from Brooke's text.

"Where the Archie Bunker show was, right?"

Kaitylyn scrolled with her finger and read.

"Yes, that's it. I want to go to New York. Please arrange it."

"Sesame Street," someone said.

"That's where it was."

"Is," said someone else.

"Is," said the first someone.

And then the others at the table began firing off shows they remembered watching with their parents or grandparents.

"Dick Van Dyke."

"Cheers."

"Yeah, Cheers."

"Sopranos."

"Yeah."

"Seinfeld!" two people said at once.

Everyone was laughing and talking, repeating lines from the shows.

Lara waited and then said:

"Now might be a good time for a review.

"Why are we doing this?"

"To save the world," said someone.

"No," said Lara, "the other thing, the towns, the TV shows.

"Kaitylyn?" said Lara.

Kaitylyn repeated from memory:

"It's because these TV shows are what our parents and some of us grew up on and it means a lot to them and we hit them right in the gut, where it hurts."

"Also?" said Lara.

Kaitylyn looked up for the answer.

"And because these towns are not real. We live in fantasy. Our whole world is fantasy, news is fantasy, history is fantasy, fantasy is ..."

"Okay," said Lara, putting up a hand with a pen in it.

"Nobody gets it," said someone.

"So, where should Brooke go?" said Lara.

"Will she go where we send her? Does it matter what we say? What is our opinion, assuming we have a say in the matter?"

Nobody said a damn thing and Lara moved on to the next item on the agenda list.

"What else ya got?" said Lara.

"Indy groups," said Kaitylyn, running her pen down her pad.

"Underground.

"Evey ... and back to Morgan and ...

"Mollie, I think," said Lara.

"Mollie," said Kaitylyn.

"Morgan and Mollie," said Lara.

"And Jim," said Kaitylyn.

"And Jim," said Lara.

QUOTE REMOVED BY ORDER OF DHS, UNITED STATES DEPARTMENT OF HOMELAND SECURITY. [DHS US2FA]

FORTY-TWO

B ix,
It is not the Republicans. Nor Democrats. The Killarycrats do the rigging this time and she and Obama are Neocons. Today is spy versus spy. The Constitution is not there now. Cops can take away your car, slap your wife, beat on you without true excuse. You are no better than Brady Manning. Obama administration imprisons whistleblowers like never before.

Today I did not think to get the name of this guy whom your email showed doing this article on the Republicans doing the rigging. You see what I mean now. This time the Democrats did the rigging. Keep an eye on this guy, Bix. He is a double agent. This time the Democrats did the rigging.

Democrats/Republicans are exactly equally involved in Big Oil and War. They have no reason to worry who votes how, they own it all. Debbie Lusignan says get you bodies on the street. We have not recourse, says she.

I love her but she may be incorrect. What has always worked with people on the street is kill them.

9/11 Truth is too slow in fifteen years. Only via rush of 9/11 Truth meantime can there be too many people to kill. Kill half the military. Kill anybody in Congress. Many are killed in fifteen years. Very many killed since Kennedy, MLK. Ram in the Truth. Then might they try to kill half the military. It has been absurd. Ugly diseased puke. Fucking open up 9/11 is one goddamned chance. Absurd, this day. Pitiful. Weak, pitiful. My sister might weep in anger. It has got to be done. Kick open 9/11.

Packy,

Today I speak of importance. Yesterday I was drunk.

Sad you will not correspond. I have needed your help. Fifteen years ago America was nuked. (Mini-nukes, see Iraq, other scenes.) I am obsessive and have kept up with what the Truther Community learns. James Kessler who is our age and knows as much as anyone is my main source. He is a dynamo, spends he says his last years doing this. I don't know how much you know. I don't know if you are interested. If you pull out yesterday's Posting to Bix, 9/11 Anniversary, you could locate where Kessler sent me materials. Were you at your pleasure in the brilliance of James Kessler to check out these three places he gives, abruptly you would know more than ninety percent of the Truthers. Ninety-five percent, mebbe 96. Ah, .98.

How I need your help is I have had nobody to talk to. Bix is sort of a closet Truther but he is not intrigued, besides wishes to not upset Bonnie, his good friend. My siblngs....I worry about Mind Control....Yes.... Past decade is my greratest shock.... I kept following my correspondents and learning, as they also were learning, but my siblings cannot bear my subject. I don't know can you imagine. Probably you need to be there. Blackbird-Taboo-speak.

Look, come on out. I will not pick on Packy, though he likes to dish it out. Excuse me, I am your oldest friend, I am serious. LET ME TELL YOU WHAT I DO KNOW.

Everybody has flaw but what Packy does have is curiosity. LET ME TELL YOU WHAT I DO KNOW. If YOU WILL NOT TELL ME ALL ABOUT IT. Right now Madrea and kids are not here till maybe Thanksgiving and I have two spare beds, a big foldup Madrea uses with her and Xyza, there is besides that the kids' room normally closed off.

Possibly you have been interested or somewhat, and know some things. Understand again: I cannot utter Taboo-Speak to mine sibliings. BUT COME OVER IN HERE AND LET ME TELL YOU WHAT I DO KNOW and you can drink all my wine you can not barf. Barfing is no fair, waste. I AM RECEPTIVE TO WHAT YOU DO KNOW. Please leave out sports and pussy and personal injury.

We are in fascism, you know it. May we talk.

Love,

        Bill

Bix,

I now be hearing too about Homeland Security. I lack perspective, details like Patriot Act kills the Constitution what the hell is Homeland Security for? Heh, I guess this is how my siblings believe I am simple. But we must do what we can.

Or, maybe neither do my siblings understand Patriot Act or Homeland Security. We have not been long civilized and Bill is last. Bill will not abide

Blackbird-Taboo-Speech.   Respect no authority.   No reservation forever.

Bix, I understand Killarly is possibly least popular person who has run for USA President. She gets few votes. Of course Trump is way ahead. But Killarly has a bigger organization, and Trump can be outed, anytime, maybe best before Killarly faints from bowel obstruction in public.

Please tell Richard I hope next time I see him he has read the Patriot Act and has more to tell me regarding the Constitution. If he takes seriously his job as my lawyer (paid for in blood past life) who got me SSI maybe he can tell me all about Homeland Security while he is at it.

Love,

        Bill

Afternoon, Bill,

Many like Trump. This is Trump territory here, signs on the cars, stuck in the front yards. I see few Hillary signs. No, this not like Hippie times. Who would have believed something like the Patriot Act could have blossomed in this country, or Homeland Security.

Richard has not come back to A.P. So have had little social interaction, except for exercise classes.

Richard and I have talked about coming your way in October. I believe Bonnie and Mike might be there.

    Take care, Bill

    Bix

Philip,

Hello. My siblings are unable to look at 9/11 and the 9/11 Wars. We don't need to talk about my siblings. I would not mind, but perhaps you prefer talking about the larger situation.

I took a year or three to start identifying as a Truther. I have no idea how long have you looked into it.

Truthers are getting together more than ever. Needs to happen. Too damned many closet Truthers. 9/11 Wars feed the billionaires and bleeds USA commoners ever poorer. The people are fearful of authority worse each year. The Patriot Act renders the Constitution dead.

The main stream press is lies, including anything on NPR or PBS to do with grand USA now. USA is the most ignorant nation regarding 9/11. As said many USA Truthers have not come out.

It surely does not take long to just look at it. Fifteen years back already, mostly USA shocked commoners have never peeped. I think....

Philip. I am on this family property in the Iowa Hill Country on the Raccoon River, in a trailer with dog and cat. I am a novelist. Now what I do is these "Postings," drink and carry on with any who may may care to join in. Ah, I smoke some pot too. One must rest.

There is much Alternate News on the Web - I think my siblings do not know this - while mainly I follow JamesKessler. blogspot.com. There are others whom I like via Web and have not met personally. Kessler does very much audios, he is a retired Philosophy of Science Professor,

has well diagrammed the JFK Assassination, and now 9/11. Here is a same cabal, next generations. Jim Kessler will get it all, if maybe he hasn't this moment....Seems to me he has....

He and friends produce books, Moon Shadow Books. Latest is AMERICA NUKED ON 9/11!

is probably the title without my stopping this to check it. These mini-nukes is how molten lava of concrete and steel was some months lava, molten, in the ground of the Trade Center former complex. Much of the Trade center vaporized, blew over Manhattan, distributed cancer, I and family lost a best friend.

Here I am. If you care to carry on, I can do this.

Yours,

Bill

Barron,

Probably, Packy's excuse in never answering BlBlackbird's masturbatory Postings is not now Barron has broken his back. You and he have chemical restiveness, slightly different between the two of you but very much different chemically are you two from other people. Of course, everybody is very different to start. Eat more meat. It is fortunate for all that neither of you are vegetarians. B-12 lack would rattle your grey matter, put you insane, B-12 is this necessary.

I can't recall how far back already it was Michele spoke at me, saying she dug TG and wanted to get these Postings, nice to start her day like that. I presume you two are doing the fits and starts routine. Try to think maturity. What your father should have done.

Probably, any of you, Packy too, would enjoy this Sane Progressive woman, Debbie Lusignan. A woman of power. You have to see it to know.

Primarily before her I got information from James Kessler and friends. Yes, you had introduced me to a decent source, and I see nothing to compare with either Kessler or Lusignan -they are BUSY. Busy. Sincere, with terrible passion.

Whew, oh yeah, listening to Charles Mingus. We are what we are. Do not fool with me.

Ah, lately past Hillary Clinton's being the least popular presidential candidate in history with the richest backing and rigged voting machines, the Web has become a blast of her "illness," and is she using doubles for fake appearances in public.

I brought it up at Kelly this morning walking dogs. He knew nothing, could hardly follow, said: The Earth is flat.

What? What do you mean?

There is still a Flat Earth Movement, some people think the Earth is flat.

As I said yesterday, my siblings do not know of Alternate News. I cannot tell them, because they think main stream news is real.

USA Today of course is main stream yet speaks of Hillary's doubles. Has some photographs. Either way you want to look at it, it is bizarre, and some suspect Killary is dead right now.

Imagine.

Suddenly I am notified Mike Blackbird has emailed.

Further,

　　　Bill

Caryl,

Much thanks, you are well at this time.

Yes, Killary is a phenomenon. All this throughout the web about her, however necessarily real. Besides her health trauma, and will doubles be used for her before she dies in public somewhere.

It is true she said after destruction of Libya and the popular ruler Omar Khadafy: We came, we saw, he died. I had heard this, then I saw it, on the Web. He was trying to surrender, yet an example of torture was made of him. Libya has petroleum. Khadafy was giving newlyweds money, was turning desert into oasis - he was decent.

She is unusually unpopular - the voting is rigged - yet my siblings know nothing real about her, will vote for her. They see no Alternate News, have zero conception of Alternate News, I cannot communicate that little bit to them.

Let's talk about it all. Please be in immediate touch.

Love,

Billy

Caryl,

This presented is interesting material and the Allies won the war. Their history is here now. It is easy to get accounts, pay the tellers of the desired accounts, those accounts not of threat to the arranged bullshit history. It continues, thousands...of puny years.

USA is not special. Get over it. USA is a plunderer of nations, and now USA time is done..

I have seen enough this day. Can my siblings be mind controlled

Good I have pot. Besides I am powerful from chopping dry oak. I consider I have extraterrestrial girlfriends. Wish I could recall. We will see. What comes down the road.

Yours,

Billy

Caryl,

Thanks. Saw just then her video. Primarily she is correct. She is in her eighties and looks like a cigarette smoker. I like her on the gun bit.

Love,

Billy

Mike,

Simply that you got my note to Philip as requested is the whole of my wonderment. Thank you for that.

You have been talking at me too strangely, too robotic. Strangely, too strangely.

Bill

Yo, Bill:

I sent your email address to Philip. I did not send his email address to you.

It is the polite way to do these things. I forwarded your note to him. I assume he got it. Which means, he's got your email address.

He may be busy, I don't know. If you don't hear from him in a few days, let me know. I'll phone, see what's happening.

Mike

Mike,

Never got it.

Bill

As noted earlier, I sent your note several days ago.

Mike

Mike,

Must I ask you each day to get a single answer? Have you passed my note to Sokol?

If you cannot do this could you get me his email? Truthers must talk.

Reality,

Bill

Mike,

Glad to hear you passed my note to Sokol. Got no note from you about it. Hell no. Will await his reply....

Mike, try to get it, I have known you. You will fake it when you are out of reality. You ought to know me.

Here we are: In your above you say it is normal in demolition for floors to fall upon floors.

I really do not feel like putting up with your crap. Yas, yas, floors fall upon floors, going down.

THEY DO NOT GAIN MOMENTUM.

You waste my time.

Bill

Yo, Bill:

If you are demolishing a modern building with explosions, floors often fall, one by one, on top of each other. Go read about demolition. It is a well-known process.

You gotta answer arguments with proof, not, just derision. Saying "bullshit!" is not an argument. It says you disagree, nothing more than that. Fine. Say it, and then, go on from there. You got to show proof. Good proof. That's the only thing that matters.

Mike

see you later

Mike

CoJonesGrandes October 6, 2016 at 4:43 pm

Someone showed up in the Chani project forum on 16 Sept 2011 with the handle 'ashamed' and posted a few msgs:

"Just for the record. There were 5 planes on 9-11 not 4. When we gathered, some forcibly, at THE air force base, there were 58 converted passengers from a 5th small commercial airliner."

"I Intend to share everything, one step at a time.

I was fortunate in the sense that I had an immediate family ten years ago. This spared my immediate termination. Those that had no immediate family, which they could use as leverage, were taken away, still immobilized and terminated.

Because I had an immediate family, my conversion ratio was deemed at 80%"

"There are about 300 of us living on or in a place called K.I.R.A."

• *CoJonesGrandes* October 6, 2016 at 4:47 pm

More msgs from 'ashamed':

"Shortly after our arrival on K.I.R.A, in February of this year, we noticed building contractors, coming in and going out of restricted areas. We assumed that they were building new housing modules for us. We are treated very well but our living spaces are very cramped. Last night, after dinner, there was an announcement that we should all watch our cable TV at 21h. The usual voice came on saying that we should all prepare for the new arrival of 600 more converted "friends". Most of us were angered by this news and them calling the new arrivals "friends". This will triple our population from 300 to 900. This concludes me to think, that whatever they are planning, will be bigger than 9-11."

"We lost internet access a few weeks ago. We were told it was due to two satellites malfunctioning. We back online again and everyone on K.I.R.A has access. Most of us here are treated very nicely within limits. They are very kind to us given our circumstances. Our Hall moderator knows I posted here on the 16th. When I told him last night that I was going to post again he just said it's ok and that I'm wasting my time."

I got kicked out of that forum so I haven't checked out if there have been any more msgs from the guy. I'm inclined to believe he was genuine but people tell me I'm gullible......

FORTY-THREE

Brooke rolled into town, her head bouncing on the window as the bus bopped the speed bump in front of the nursing home, swung around the corner before wheezing to a halt at the truck stop café.

She recalled her dream:

She's sitting at the café in Mayberry and her landlady is pouring her coffee. Barney is sitting next to her and Aunt Bea next to her on the other side. They are all having apple pie, but Aunt Bea doesn't think it's as good as hers.

"The crust isn't flakey," she says.

Barney is talking to Brooke. It turns out he is a serious, thoughtful, intelligent man, not the one portrayed on the show.

Who knew? Brooke asks herself in the dream.

"Anytime we try to be someone other than who we really are it makes it more stressful in our life," he says and then sips his coffee, puts up a hand to the landlady waitress for more coffee for everyone over here please.

"Oh, yeah," says Brooke.

"As a secretary, I ..."

"No," says Barney and Aunt Bea nods in agreement with a forkful of pie headed for her mouth.

"As a rebel," says Barney.

"A spy," says Aunt Bea through a mouth full of pie.

"What do you mean?" says Brooke

"I think you know," says Barney.

"Thank you," he says as the new pot arrives.

"No," argues Brooke.

"No, you don't under ..."

"Seneca Falls," said the driver glumly as she lumbered down the steps to head inside for her break.

Brooke had intended to go to New York.

She asked how close she was and found out not close.

Wow, what now? She had coffee at the window and saw no red SUVs. She asked for a sweet roll. She checked her messages, lots from Kaitylyn, one from Korey.

What's up? She texted Korey.

Korey is in a tavern in downtown Minneapolis, alone, sitting at the bar. He asks Brooke if she has any money.

Yes, but, she responds.

I need to make some money, he says.

Aren't you supposed to be fighting? You know, the Mary Tyler Moore Brigade, all that?

That's a fucked-up name, he says.

Yeah, but, she says.

I think Prince Hope would pay for the intel on CRUSHER, he says.

Don't do that.

Why.

Just don't. Why would you? Are you drinking?

He calls her and she answers and goes outside to sit on a big rock to talk to Korey. The wind whistling makes it hard to hear and sometimes people are walking past and it's getting chilly, but Brooke works hard to listen to what Korey is going through.

They're rippin' us off, he says.

Money, from CRUSHER, and they go out every night. It's a big game for them.

Brooke tried to tell Korey about Lara's family and her life and Kaitylyn and how she didn't think it was so bad, whatever they were doing. She tried to say all that, but she didn't really get started, Korey wasn't listening. He just wanted to talk.

All Evey does is sit home, that's what I heard, said Korey. I thought she was this big rebel, and her fucking brothers, what the fuck are they doing up there anyway? They shouldn't even be here, they're illegal.

"You hear about Morgan?" he asked.

"Yes."

"What was Mayberry like?" he said.

She told him.

"Who's still there," he said.

She told him what she knew, which wasn't everything.

Then she heard Korey ask the bartender for another beer and waited, because she knew it was coming, for Korey to complain about his father and his brother and tie it all together with Lara and Kaitylyn and then return to the question of whether to tell Prince Hope all about CRUSHER.

He already knows, thought Brooke.

Brooke listened and said "okay" about a dozen times.

Korey stopped talking. She pressed the phone into her ear. She heard him breathing. She heard somebody come into the bar. Then scuffling, walking on wood. She thought she knew the bar now. A door squeaked open. She heard water, a flush. She jerked the phone away from her ear, held it close enough to hear the door again and stomping on wood.

"Brooke? You there?" he said.

"Yes. I'm here. Of course."

"What about you?" he said.

"Me? Well, they want me to go to Mayfield, is that Ohio?"

She waited for him to respond then kept going.

"I don't know, I just don't know. NYC would be so cool, don't you think?"

She paused again.

"Plays, the subway, people."

"Blowing people up, shooting people," he said.

"That's what you're supposed to be doing."

"Yeah that.

"Not sure if I want to bring all that there."

"It's already there."

"Yeah, but. Yeah."

"You are a spy."

"Yeah."

"The spy, Stratego. There's only one and the only one who can kill the general."

"Yep."

"That's cool."

"Yeah.

"What if a spy, the spy doesn't want to kill the general. Maybe she thinks the general is hot."

"Yeah, I guess."

"You guess?"

"I don't know, yeah, I guess."

She told him about her dream.

"Yeah, I been havin' some crazy dreams too," he said.

"The other ni ..."

"This isn't about you, she said. "Not all of it. Some of it's about me ... god ... damn ... it," she growled.

"The answer," he said.

"Be careful," she said.

"Brooke wants to be soccer mom, kids, home, PTA, all of that, don't need revolution, don't want it, everything is fine as it is. You see a hundred, a thousand, a hundred thousand mini-vans on the highway, all the same color, and you like it. You can't find your mauve mini van because every other vehicle in the Walmart parking lot is the same, and you like it.

"And you are trying to be a rebel.

"And one day, you're gonna blow."

The wind whined in the phone.

"What're you gonna do then?" he said.

"I don't fucking know. What can I do, what should I do? I could get a job and infiltrate the city government in ... Seneca Falls, or maybe a bank, yeah, I'll do that and relay all this info back to L&K.

"You there?"

"Like what?" he said.

"Like what what?"

"What info?"

"I don't know. I'll be underground, that's what I'm sposed to be. Just fit in and be against all of it, send info somewhere and then blow it all up, or somebody else does, maybe you."

"Yeah, maybe," he said.

"With all that intel, yeah, I guess."

"Well," said Brooke.

"Yeah, me too," he said. "I gotta to go. You take care."

"K."

"Seeya."

"Yep."

Brooke hurried inside and asked for the restroom.

According to other diners in the restaurant at the time, "a lot of red Winnebagos" rolled up and men in suits got out and took over the restaurant. They didn't show their guns but you could tell they had guns. The pretty young woman in the long hair with the shoulder bag came out of the bathroom and they surrounded her and walked her to the door and into one of the Winnebagos. After she came out of the bathroom you couldn't see her anymore because they were just all around her. She might have been saying something, but there was so much commotion and talking you couldn't really tell.

That testimony is right there in the police report.

I guess somebody called the cops.

Note from the narrator:

From "The Prince Hope Show" ...

... Join us now as we join, in progress, the next installment of ...

"Nebraska Ink: Amelia Earhart, Tattoo Artist Of The Heartland."

The locals know her as Babs.

Her shop is on main street, between the barber shop and the cafe — with a picture of a floundering big plane atop the front door.

She got off course, or she's hiding out, waiting for her chance to do what she was intended to do so long ago by FDR.

Or, maybe there was no spy mission for FDR, just a desire to fly around the world.

She doesn't seem to care anymore. She just wants to be free to live out her days in Nebraska, doing what she loves — talking about the Cornhuskers and making tattoos.

QUOTE REMOVED BY ORDER OF DHS, UNITED STATES DEPARTMENT OF HOMELAND SECURITY. [DHS US2FA]

FORTY-FOUR

Caryl,
   Good morning, nice to be hearing from you again. Well, Mike Blackbird lives in Boulder, a university town, He moved there many years ago, left Berkeley for Boulder for the mountain climbing. But Mike seems to be setting on moving out here. He feels to be "too old" for the serious mountain climbing. He does enjoy fossil hunting out here, finds these ancient rocks with fossils. Then he goes into books to understand what he has. He still wants to be famous probably. He has bought a load of his rocks to Boulder, via his car I think, a little sports car, I guess this was piece meal, and now he is going to have all of it shipped back to here, where they came from. I forget what the large box of it all weighs. Return rocks to the land of rocks - this is very rocky Earth - rocks everywhere. He will build his big pile of rocks ever bigger, fossils. He is a bit mad, Caryl, cheerfully so.
   There is more disagreement going on in the USA, probably Europe too, about the Nazi Germany/Hitler history. There is plenty propaganda pro and con. Nations lie and the victors of war lie the most. One thing I have come to be more informed of, via James Kessler and friends, is that Hitler did not gas anyone. That is physically proven. Of course this statement upsets many who grew up believing Hitler had millions of Jews gassed. But these were workcamps, for Germany's war effort. They had a soccer team, even a brothel, all kinds of stuff, to keep them healthy and willing to work hard. What did kill them was the Allied saturation bombing, a horrific war crime, destroyed the railroads, everything. People starved then, beside malnutrition brings in disease. But that is those

piles of wasted corpses in these well used photographs. I am not certain about Hitler's evil, exactly. He liked animals and children, and he was talented as a painter. Germany had been ganged up on and misused from the first world war, which Germany did not start. Even Mike Blackbird agrees Germany did not start the first world war.

There is a very much larger history in the above. I still do not know a lot, do understand there is physical proof there were no gas chambers.

I understand by now you are concerned about Muslims. I'm not, don't care there. I care about fascism in the USA presently. USA citizens fear being called "conspiracy theorists" and the 9/11 Wars blow up so many, non-combatents and children, USA citizens have come to not speak of that now either. Trump, at least, has spoken of this folly. The billionaires of oil and war grow into multi-billionaires and the USA population is poorer. I am curious and concerned how the Zionists, who had a hand with the C.I.A. in 9/11, have this fantastical amount of influence in the USA government.

Understand, there are Hebrews and there are Zionists of Mossad. I don't care about normal Jews or normal Muslims.

I am for Vladimir Putin. Whatever his imperfections, and he gets very poor press from the main stream USA, indeed lies, USA is all lies about itself in the main stream now, Putin is keeping Syria and Iran upright. NATO slowly loses ground. Hillary has wanted to nuke Russia,, Syria, Iran.

Caryl, what I am finding some fascination in is the Hillary Clinton biography. She appears to certainly have doubles, see USA Today. There is rumor she is dead. She has been secretly very ill, for sure. The voting has been rigged and she is unpopular while the C.I.A. act desperate to right now just get her in as the figurehead, dead or alive. Strange stuff.

Take care of yourself and always be welcome to visit out here anytime.

Love,
Billy

Note from the narrator:

From "The Prince Hope Show" ...

... Stay tuned for next week's episode of "Edward Snowden, Jedi Warrior," when we will see the brave Jedi disclose the really good shit he's been saving and not just the stuff everybody already knew.

He will tell us once and for all who did 9/11, Oklahoma City, and who killed Senator Paul Wellstone — and who killed John F. Kennedy, Robert F. Kennedy and Martin Luther King Jr. — and why are the murderers still running around like they were born to rule the world instead of showering once a week in the super-max federal prison in Florence, Colorado — the stuff we really want to know — not just the shit everybody already knows already.

"Edward Snowden — Jedi Warrior."

But Americans will have to do more than wake up, as they cannot rescue themselves via the voting booth. In my opinion, the American people will remain serfs until they wake up to Revolution.

Today Americans exist as a conquered people. They have lost the Bill of Rights, the amendments to the Constitution that protect their liberty.

— Paul Craig Roberts

He who marches out of step hears another drum.

— Ken Kesey

FORTY-FIVE

He sat in his car, which wasn't much of a car, but it was a car, on the street, north-south, on the curb, in the front seat now, not that back seat where he had spent the night watching across the big fucking wide main street to where Jim boy had been in his car over there on the side street going east and west by the bank. Right by the bank.

He got through the night without killing himself. That's always a good thing, and usually easier than the daytime.

His name?

It depends. Who wants to know?

Just call him Sniper for now and we'll see how things go. He's the guy who answered Prince Hope's Craigslist ad for a "private investigator."

He watched Jim in his car over there with binoculars. He didn't give a shit whether anyone saw him on this small town main street sitting in his car all day and night using binoculars.

He had one ear bud in an ear and an iPod on low battery.

"Oh, I must have gone crazy out there," he invented his version of the Jerry Jeff song.

Wolf eyes.

That's what he thought about last night and some of the thought was still there.

He thought about what they had told him about Jim and about CRUSHER, the Hoffer quote that he already knew and they didn't know he knew and he didn't fucking tell them: all mass movements generate in their adherents a readiness to die ... *breed fanaticism, enthusiasm, fervent hope, hatred, intolerance. ... draw from the same types of humanity, appeal to the same types of mind* ... blah, blah blah, blah, blah, blah, blah.

Yeah, so what. You gotta believe in something in your life, gotta do something. Fuck.

315

Wolf eyes.

Wolfs were fanatics.

Have you ever, out by yourself in the woods, come across a wolf, and it looks at you, makes direct eye contact?

They do not give one shit. They look right at you, head kind of down.

Those eyes. What to say about those eyes. They don't hate. They think, a lot. They are different than anything you can see anywhere else. They know you.

They don't give a fuck. It's on, or it's not, they don't give a fuck.

Are they dead eyes, seen too much? It'd be impossible to explain unless you had already been there and then it would not be necessary to explain. Well, that wolf would tear you apart, maybe, or just watch you. Lets say he is unimpressed by you, nonplussed. That's definitely part of it. And, they don't give a fuck.

Definitely.

The rest of the night thought was gone and a song on the radio was invading The Sniper's thoughts and passing cars were getting in the way of his binoculars.

It's all about me.

The Sniper realized that. When someone talks about an event, a crisis, even something funny, he has to always talk about something in his own experience to bring it around to him. He shouldn't do that. He was going to do better.

The Sniper wore a green hoodie, faded green.

He watched the old whatever it was clunker that Jim boy drove, he never was good at cars. No movement. The bank workers were beginning to pull up in their regular parking spots and walking in, one by one, never together. It was a red brick building on the corner. Old. It was like one of those buildings that's now Goodwill or an alcoholics meeting group and you see that it used to be a bank.

This Jim guy had been in one of The Sniper's groups, back in Minneapolis. That's crazy. You probably weren't supposed to kill someone in your own group.

He watched the people downtown, going to their jobs, their coffee. He ripped open a bag of Tostitos with his teeth, a small bag. He thought of his days in the military and compared it to theirs. They had lives. He was sitting in his car with a rifle waiting to kill someone. But he was getting paid, same as them. He thought of some photos of vets back from deployment, in some magazine article, some eyes show life, some show displacement, they are gone, because they have to be, they can't be here. Dead. He looked into the rearview mirror at his own eyes, as he had done a hundred times.

Under his hoodie he wore an orange CRUSHER T-shirt he found at Goodwill.

After this he was just going to go sit in a bar and relax, forget about shit.

He heard a lot about these CRUSHER fuckers in group, from Jim.

They all have distinct personalities, fears, passions, and insecurities, that's what the group leader had said to kind of comment on what Jim was always sayin' 'bout them, but you weren't s'pose to comment, just listen, but this fucker always thought he had something big to say.

Fear of abandonment, chaos, darkness, predators.

The four primordial fears.

Do not look at your subject. Subject will sense being stared at and they will turn around and look right at you. Fucking try it at Walmart once and you'll fuckin' see.

He remembered kneeling at the one fucking window with that fucking Hope.

A tall man walked toward the bank with a leather bag clutched to his chest with both hands. Nothing like being obvious.

The Sniper thought again, as he did every day, about his high school classmates, the ones who had the guts to go to the reunions. They're not really heroes, nor do they want to be, not really my kind of people.

He dug into the pocket of his sweatshirt for the note. He'd scribbled it to remember it after reading it some fucking where.

... the interests of a tyrant to keep his people poor ... and be so occupied ... daily tasks ... no time for rebellion.

Aristotle. My man.

Fuck!

Somebody is pulled up right next to Jim's car. Don't wake him, thought The Sniper, perhaps even saying it out loud. He needs his rest.

The cops. It's a cop car.

Fu-uck.

The Sniper reached over the seat into the back and hauled up his scope, just the scope.. ... He set it on the window ledge of the driver's side window and watched the one male police officer looking into the front window, tapping on the window.

Now you see Jim sitting up, rolling down the window and talking to the one police officer while another police car pulls up behind the other one, this second one with lights flashing.

What the fuck now! thought The Sniper.

The tall, skinny guy holding the leather bag tight to his chest with both hands has stopped to watch the police. Some workers on their way inside the bank have paused on the cement steps to lean over the railing to see around the corner to watch what's going on, just for a moment because it looks like it's hard to hold that pose for very long, and they have to get inside, on time.

The Sniper individually cusses out the cars going past in front of him. *You* stupid fuck. *You* cocksucker. *You* motherfucker.

He reaches for gum in his front pocket. Gum that he only hopes is there. He's not sure. He pulls out a swatch of paper with another scribbled note, this one in pencil.

Failure is everywhere. Failure is imminent.

He presses his eyes against the scope to catch the latest and has to agree that is probably true, but one has to keep going. What other choice is there. In fact, it is kind of reassuring, the failure thing. Who needs more pressure. Right? In fact, the added pressure does no good. The odds are too great. Settle into the inevitable like a big chair in front of the fire with a drink in your hand. Pull that handle and put your feet up.

Ahhh.

Now the police had Jim outside of his car and both officers were talking to him.

He's pointing to the bank, to the backseat, to the ground, to the sky.

One of the officers gets into his car and leaves, now the other one is going. The Sniper ducks down and at the last moment yanks the scope from the window.

The Sniper sat up after the cops had gone. He watched Jim now sitting in the front seat of his own car, maybe drinking coffee from a Thermos, maybe staring right at The Sniper. The Sniper began to get a crink in his neck. He was parked sort of in front of Jim and to watch Jim and the bank he had to torque his neck and shoulders and body back and to the left. The clock on the street on the bank showed that it was almost opening time. Jim screwed on the top of his Thermos, began collecting stuff from the seat next to him and reaching into the back.

He got out of the car, locked it, pulled on his blaze orange ball cap, carried his gun like a lunch bucket and a sack over his shoulder and walked up to the cement front steps. He let an older woman go ahead of him and then shuffled up the few steps, held the door for her and they went inside.

About twenty minutes later — The Sniper had *heard* these robberies take for fucking ever — Jim burst out the front door and leaped the steps, ran to his car, unlocked the door, jumped in, fired it up and roared off.

The Sniper had his rifle, with scope attached, perched in the back window.

He sat in the back with newspapers Scotch-taped to the sidewalk windows.

"That's me in the corner," he hummed as he aimed. "Me in the spot ... light ... losing my ..."

He fired just as Jim rolled through the stop sign, the bullet going over the car's roof and nicking the red brick bank.

Jim turned left and roared away right past The Sniper's position, smoke rolling out the muffler like a mosquito fogger and money streaming out an open window, swirling around main street.

The Sniper, well, here's my thought on that. In fact, he's got nothin' else goin' on. Might as well take his time. He's got a job. The worst thing in the world is filling out applications, trying to make it all fit, trying to find a job, a place to fit in, that good feeling.

The money is trailing from Jim's vehicle, floating around, caught by cars going by.

Somebody comes to stand in the bank front door as the two police cars pull up again, this time in front.

As The Sniper is standing over his open trunk, a guy comes up to him with a fistful of money, asking if it's his.

The Sniper wraps the scope in a soft cloth, saying, "No, I don't care about the money. I do and I don't."

"Gotcha," the guys says, looking at the scope, the trunk, the newspaper in the windows, turning and stuffing the money into his front pocket and walking on.

The Sniper.

Okay, his name is Danny. Daniel Dragone in school, Big Dan he was in county, Little Dan to his brothers, Dan the Man on his ball team, Danny Danger that's what they called him in his unit. The Red Dragon.

The Red Dragon makes notes while he's waiting for Jim to rob his banks and take his one shot, and he picks up a paper here and there, just to take a look around, ya know?

Well, he sees nothing in the papers about the robbings, nothing about the revolution.

He hears from Prince Hope, how's it going? Oh, fine. Yep, okay. Need anything? Nope. I'm good. Called in on pay phone. There's one in St. Joe. Drives forever to get there, trailing Jim and sees it on the corner waiting for Jim to come out of a bank maybe he's checking out for later, who knows?

The poor, the people, one guy just sitting there, on front cement stoop talking on phone, the anguished, distorted look on the man's face, in sweatpants, smoking a cigarette at one thirty in the afternoon. Talk about a bomb ready to explode, and terror, my fucking Christ.

Danny Dragone, The Red-Headed Dragon, he thinks that would be a good name for a super hero and he doodles a little on his notepad. It's actually a Big Chief that he found in a Dollar Store somewhere. He didn't know they still made those. He never had one. It was soft, with lots of room, felt good, nice to write on, no wonder the kids liked them.

He's sitting there, stretched out in the back seat, somewhere, newspapers on the windows. When, not if, the cops come, he just tells them he's waiting for his wife in the store or he's in town for some event that he saw advertised somewhere on the way in, the gun show, the garage sales, something.

Well, he's wondering what it would be like, ya know, to meet one of these "Japanese Soldiers," that show up every now and then, ya know, who has been hiding all these years and doesn't know the war's over. He's got on this old helmet and the same clothes and he's got vines all over him, wire rim glasses, a long knife in his belt, shit like that, right?

Well, what if there was a guy from the Sixties, maybe one of the Weathermen, who emerged like that, in the United States, who has been underground, hasn't seen TV or read newspapers or talked to anyone for all this time. He's been, umm, in the mountains, living off the land, after they bombed something and they all said they were going to the mountains and maybe he's the only one who did.

Somehow, or for some reason, he comes out, maybe he needs a mint, or he's walking around his mountain and he goes too far one day in a new direction and he comes out in somebody's backyard while they're having a Sunday Football Day Barbecue or some shit, some kid's fucking birthday party of something and he climbs over the fence and he falls onto the thick, soft lawn and there he is and everyone stops talking and looks at him.

Danny wrote out that story, how they would all circle him and creep closer and lean in low and see what he was and what it would mean.

Danny looked up and saw Jim firing up his car and getting ready to turn left and roar away past him.

And that was the way it went, as I heard it, through what was left of that fall, through the winter. Jim kept going and going, never getting caught, getting the money and sending it back to Lara and Kaitylyn and The CRUSHER Rebellion or whatever it was called by that time. It wasn't called much as almost not anyone ever heard of it. But it was a big deal in certain circles that liked to think they were on the edge.

And so, what I did during that winter was hibernate, not that you're interested, but I'd always wanted to kind of do that, but you can't because you have to go to work, but I had this reporting gig and they were paying me and I didn't have to go out, just keep tabs on the revolution, which I could do without really going out, sometimes I did, but I didn't really have to.

Anyway, hibernating, it's not fun. You, at least I, get depressed, need to be around people, have people notice me, talk to me, give me some validation. It's weird, but it's me, maybe it's you, too. The cold and the snow kind of have a way of changing things, things go on, but different. It's good, in a way, in a way it's not. It's hard to explain. If you know, you know what I'm talking about.

Anyway, yeah, Jim kept going I guess because he was liking it and he wasn't dead or in jail yet. He ate good, kept gas in his car, was seeing some places and Danny the sniper just kept following him around, taking pot shots every now and then. I guess. My dog died. Yeah. I can't really talk about that. You can't really bury a dog where I live in winter, so, yeah, anyway. And Lara & Kaitylyn, L&K, the Bobsy Twins, well, I didn't really hear too much from them or about them, and then Morgan and Mollie were still loose, maybe lost, trying to get back in touch with the revolution. I guess they talked about trying to retake Cicely, but the government troops kind of killed mostly everyone they finally found out, so, yeah. And Zima and Joe ... and ... yeah Ariel were still encircling Mayberry-Mount Airy, but some of their troops went home to do other stuff and they did get some new recruits because, I guess, Lara and Kaitylyn got this new hot shot recruiter somehow ... anyway. My dad, when he was in the nursing home, used to watch *Bonanza* as much as they would let him. And Prince Hope was still having Lara on his show now and again and when he was on TV talk shows he was still talking about CRUSHER and that was kind of the only way anyone ever heard about the rebellion. He wanted to kill them all, still, I guess. Not all, but some of them, is what I heard. I dropped my land line phone and thinking about getting rid of my TV, but I still like to watch football. I don't know. Not totally decided yet. I like coffee, sitting in a coffee shop, and the feel of cold on your face, and walking around in a city, the crunch of packed snow if you are wearing warm socks and good boots, and walking past people who are all happy and shit, kind of, in a way anyway, being a part of it, especially if they smelled like cigars or perfume and you kind of took that smell with you for a few steps. If I was a bear I could hibernate, not give *a fuck* about anything. My dad never watched *Bonanza*, probably as a kid, but never when I knew him. In fact, he hated it, thought it was mundane. But in the nursing home, I think he even told me this, he said it felt like it was real, it took him back, and that's where he wanted to be. I don't know, I don't understand. I probly will some day. Not looking forward to it. And, let's see, just going over my notes ... umm, "Underground," yep those guys were still working, but the ground is hard in the winter, that's what I've got written here, and Evey, I would guess she's still home. When I was young I used to love cars, now I don't even have one, again. I know what it was now. I thought the perfect car could define me, probly make me into something, more than I am, was, motorcycles too. Yep, that was definitely it. Korey hasn't, well, at least I haven't seen him. There's the indies out there, I assume, and the Battle For Mayfield is supposed to still be in the works, but I couldn't say for sure and somebody said that someone is trying to find out where Mayfield is, not sure. When I was married I didn't really want to go anywhere, everywhere was boring, because it wasn't "too the point," as I so often remarked. It wasn't what I wanted to be doing, which was writing. Nothing was more fun, more timely, more relevant, more exciting than my own thoughts. I actually said pretty much that quite a few times, I'm sure. The fake battles that Actually got going, hmm, I have to check on that. But today is my off day. I give myself a free day every week, no writing, no calling, no nothing. I am going for a long walk to a coffee shop, and then a movie. Maybe I'll find some good smelling folks.

Spring bloomed.

But not for everybody.

In the north, in Minnesota, where many of the existing CRUSHERs still hid out, spring comes falsely, with hope for change that is not to be trusted, leading everyone through two and three months of false promises, fog, clouds, continuing dark, until some day in June the sun begins to boil. It is October that is the true wonder of Minnesota, but anyway.

Spring. Blooming. All that shit.

Danny Dragone sat in his car, cold, running the heater just every now and then to save gas. Where they were I don't think either he or Jim even knew.

And then when he went to restart the car it wound and wound and ground and buzzed, nothing.

Danny fetched his scope from the trunk, his rifle in the backseat and his Doritos and his coffee and walked off across the wide, wide main street toward Jim's car. Danny got in on the passenger side. He waited. He got bored and looked around at all the junk and crap and comic books in the fucking car. He reached a long way to grab the movie on the back floor, "Miracle," about the United States hockey team that Jim had watched at least fifty times.

He watched as Jim ran past on the sidewalk.

He almost always did that, in the big hurry forgetting where he had parked, then his pistol and bags in his hands, he has to set everything down on the street to unlock the door. He jumped in.

"What the fuck you doin' here,' man!" said Jim.

"I'm outa gas, man," said Danny.

"I'm cold."

Jim worked to start the car.

"Fuck!"

It wouldn't start.

"Pump it," said Danny as he rolled down his window and stuck the rifle out, aimed at one of the bank guys peeking around the corner.

Jim got the car going, revved it, sending up the cloud of smoke that had become his signature, sped off, through the stop sign with Danny pointing the rifle at the bank people crowded into the door. They swerved big at the turn, also one of Jim's features, and flew past Danny's dead car. Danny thought of three things he wished he had not forgotten in the car and offered the Doritos to Jim. Jim shook his head, irritated.

"What's wrong?" said Danny.

Things had not gone perfectly well in the bank.

"They don't shut up sometimes!" Jim said, swerving to miss too-slow vehicles, taking a sharp corner, now another one.

"I say, please be quiet, they don't shut up."

"Yeah, some people just gotta jabber," said Danny, hoping to calm Jim, who was going to crash for sure.

"Yes, thank you!" said Jim.

"And! And!"

"Hey," said Danny, hoping Jim heard him.

Jim slammed on the brakes to miss a mom and her kid in the crosswalk, then smoked the tires to go, then slammed on the brakes again at the next crosswalk for the red light, just like in that one movie. Danny smiled and looked at Jim to ask him what movie, but didn't because he was pressed back into his seat as Jim took off again.

They hit the edge of town and kept going as Jim told about how the people in the bank hadn't behaved very well and there wasn't as much money as he thought. His pants were getting tight, and just a hundred things that were beginning to bug him about robbing banks. Same ol' same' ol'.

"I'm sposed to kill you," said Danny.

"You're doin' a piss-poor job, I'd say."

"Yeah, I know. I know. Fuck off.

"You only lock the driver's side. You always do that, it drives me crazy, man."

"Yeah, whatever. Really? Well, you always park in the same spot. I always wonder when you're gonna shoot me for real."

"I do shoot for real."

"You always miss. It's like you don't want to hit me."

Danny looked out his window for a while.

Jim offered a few more of his own critiques of Danny.

Fuck you, man, said Danny.

Fuck *you*, said Jim.

They didn't talk for about ten miles, each lost in his own thoughts, dreams.

Jim asked Danny if he wanted to join him, join the revolution.

"I'm sure Prince Hope's fuckin' figured out you're not doin' your job by now."

A white man can't fight a guerilla warfare.

Guerilla action takes heart, takes nerve, and he doesn't have that.

He's brave when he's got tanks. He's brave when he's got planes.

He's brave when he's got bombs. He's brave when he got a whole lot of company along with him, but you take that little man from Africa and Asia, turn him loose in the woods with a blade, with a blade — that's all he needs, all he needs is a blade — and when the sun goes down and it's dark, it's even-steven.

— Malcolm X

Enjolras, pierced by eight bullets, remained backed up against the wall as if the bullets had nailed him there. Except that his head was tilted.

Grantaire, struck down, collapsed at his feet.

— Victor Hugo, *Les Misérables*

I have always thought that in revolutions, especially democratic revolutions, madmen, not those so called by courtesy, but genuine madmen, have played a very considerable political part. One thing is certain, and that is that a condition of semi-madness is not unbecoming at such times, and often even leads to success.

— Alexis de Tocqueville,
Recollections on the French Revolution

Revolution does have to be violent precisely because the Pharaoh won't let you go. If the Pharaoh would let you go, the revolution won't have to be violent.

— Michael Hardt

FORTY-SIX

She was a double-looker. The woman you look at twice as you move toward her. The first time you notice her and you realize you want to see her again and you time your look. But this one you didn't want to see because she was beautiful, but rather because she was interesting. She wasn't these other women, that's for sure.

She sat against the wall, in the big half moon booth in the corner where she could face everyone and everyone could see her.

Next to her sat Rick, too handsome with his curly black hair for a fat woman, but Skylar Brown wasn't just any fat woman. She demanded to be noticed, feared.

They sat holding court in the Awesome Sauce restaurant, food all around, breakfast, pots of coffee. The place was packed, people coming by, bumping close while Skylar talked to those crammed into the orange booth about the revolution.

She wore her hair long and thick and sported one wrestler earring.

A stack of books rose next to Skylar on one side, a few more on the table next to her long yellow legal pads.

"It's all about Mexico and it's not," she said, holding up *Rebellion of the Hanged.*

"Get outa here kid, ya bother me," she did W.C. Fields to chase a young boy standing at the table watching her.

"He's from the cast of Les Mis. He really is. Are you seeing this?"

But the boy was gone, disappearing into the legs of the adults.

"The man, the myth, the legend," she pretty much shouted as the waiter brought more coffee. The waiter smiled weakly and asked if there was anything else, then scurried away.

Every once in a while she gave a slight head bob to punctuate a sentence or meme, just perfect to be hip and edgy, new, but familiar.

"We don't want to be this."

She poked the Mexico book.

"This cannot be us."

She poked it again.

"Just sayin'."

"We need to *win*," she said just as the cash register rang out again.

Her fingernails were purple, not mauve, purple. You could tell that she had one tattoo somewhere.

Skylar Brown and Rick were meeting with the inner circle of the CRUSHER administration, headquarters, the suits as it were, to discuss what to do, what should be done now that Lara and Kaitylyn were no longer in the picture.

"As it were," said Skylar Brown, making air quotes while holding toast.

She ran the toast around the booth to include everyone and exclude the founders of CRUSHER, those with the CRUSHER tattoo, those who had worked at the group home and talked through the night, attended the first trainings at Camp Sweaty.

"There never was a time when animals could talk," said Rick, reaching to the middle of the table for a jelly packet.

Skylar Brown had already introduced herself, announced that Rick and she were a pair, a couple.

One morning they had appeared at CRUSHER HQ and announced they were the new management team and invited everyone to breakfast the next morning, attendance mandatory.

She said she could not say anything about Lara and Kaitylyn, that it was confidential, pointing out HIPAA regs.

"We are at a critical stage," she said, slicing into her blueberry pancakes, waving excitedly for someone who had just come through the front door to join them.

Rick grabbed a laptop from the floor, set it up and got it arranged so that everyone if they scrunched could see. They paid no worry to anyone in the hyper Saturday mid-morning crowd over-hearing or giving a shit.

Rick showed a PowerPoint presentation outlining the relatively short history of CRUSHER, the various events, operations, concluding with an outline of where he and Skylar thought they should be heading. He folded the computer and set it somewhere below the table.

Someone asked yet again about Lara and Kaitylyn, earning a stern look from Rick and an admonishment from Skylar.

She leaned across the table, looking straight on to the culprit.

"We need to move on," she hissed.

"Do I need to be any more clear? Are you getting this?"

Then Skylar straightened up, smiling, joking, like Santa Claus with her elves celebrating another great year. She talked about being in the military, almost. She had been a local high school basketball star and was offered a scholarship to the U, didn't take it, and decided not to join the service.

She and Rick began to gossip about some of the members of CRUSHER, saying he or she is too religious, not religious at all, from a good family, not so good.

"Takes a while to register, right?" she said to someone not quite getting it apparently.

"Anyway," she said.

"All good people.

"So, we need to know about this plane ticket," she said, looking around the booth, getting no response.

"Geronimo," said Rick.

"Found it, shred room, 9/11?"

"Okay, we'll get to that later," said Skylar.

She saw someone go past wearing an L.A. Dodgers T-shirt and said something to the person about Irvine Meadows, and how it closed or was closing. The person did not stop, but smiled and moved on, into the next dining area.

Skylar began to talk about Los Angeles.

Someone at the table took an interest and made a comment about how she watched *The Big Lebowski,* how it was filmed in L.A. and made her kind of want to live there.

"It's gone," said Skylar.

"That L.A. is gone. Me, too, I totally missed it."

"Maybe we live multiple lives," someone said.

"Do this one first," said Skylar very seriously.

Sic Semper Tyrannis

Here is the Ace Baker video, "9-11 Psy-Opera", that is a perfect primer for your friends and family members who are still 9/11/01 LIARS drinking the Kool-Aid – the same sort of fools who probably still believe in the Magic Bullet, the assassination of OBL, the Sandy Hook Hoax, the Easter Bunny, the Tooth Fairy, and Santa Claus. All you have to do is show them the 2hr:13 minute mark in this 3-hour video and then watch their mouths drop to the ground as they are shocked to the core. I have shown this to my college class, and I have a T-shirt and bumper sticker with the snapshot of the frame at the 2hr:13 min mark of this video. Everybody who sees it has no choice but to FACE THE TRUTH that they have been lied to by psychopaths in their own horribly evil government and the US State Propaganda Ministry...

FORTY-SEVEN

"Yes, I heard about her pretty much right away."
I had taken to visiting Evey fairly regularly and once the winter broke I got up there as fast as I could. I met her at the door, meaning I was not to go inside. The little one hid behind her legs with gramma right behind. Evey peeled herself away and closed the door behind her, fairly gently.

We walked down their little dirt driveway. We walked past the little metal bench where she had read the school yearbook for so long at times in the past. There were cigarette butts scattered. I asked her if she had taken up smoking.

"I did," she said.

"I'm quitting." She lifted her sleeve to show me the patch.

I said I could imagine how her parents felt about that.

She explained that her father was in the nursing home now, it was just her mother. She looked away sadly, anxious to change the subject.

We walked in silence for a while to give respect to the subject of her father and mother. At the mailbox and the dirt road we stopped. I waited for her to take the lead, to return to the house, send me politely on my way as she sometimes did, or ...

She turned left down the road. She walked next to the ditch, allowing me to walk on the outside, where the man was supposed to walk.

Evey said she had heard about Skylar.

"And Rick."

"And Rick."

A prairie chicken roared up and away, scaring the shit out of me.

"What happened to Lara? Kaitylyn?" she interviewed herself.

"Nobody knew."

"Do they know now?"

"I don't know," she said.

"It just happened."

"A hostile takeover," I offered.

"Maybe," she said.

"We don't know where they are. Maybe they arranged this with Skylar and Rick. Maybe it was Prince Hope. Maybe Lara and Kaitylyn wanted a way out, maybe they were killed."

We walked quite a long way before she spoke again, over a little wooden bridge. We stopped to look at the water and where it went, into a swamp and woods, then she moved on.

She stopped with a skid, throwing up smoke, and looked up at me.

"Definitely got things moving."

"Yep," I agreed.

"You need to meet her," said Evey.

I knew I did, but I didn't really want to.

Not really.

Note from the narrator:

The following is drawn, paraphrased, somewhat redacted, from the essays of Max, Kaitylyn's journal and Brooke's as yet unpublished account, The Pothole Diaries.

For what it's worth:

... We have taken over the airwaves.

We have dumped the tea into the harbor, stormed the Bastille, we are eating jelly doughnuts without a napkin in the West Room.

We are shitting in the Rose Garden and telling fart jokes from the microphone at the front railing of the House of Representatives.

Mount Rushmore has fresh egg on its faces, and the Pentagon has been ransacked by welfare moms and rednecks, redecorated and turned into a free daycare center for Northwest D.C. families.

Outside the C.I.A. building and the J. Edgar Hoover F.B.I. headquarters building, the sidewalks are littered with broken chairs, busted desks and dented badges.

The overhead highway copter cam shows George Bush Senior being shoved unceremoniously into the backseat of a sheriff's car outside the Midland Country Club.

There is a low-speed chase taking place outside Dallas with George W. Bush in the backseat of a white Bronco threatening to hold his breath.

The Obama Family is attempting to take off by helicopter from the White House lawn, but there are fifty people hanging onto the landing skids and the copter cannot take off.

Hillary and Bill Clinton have been captured in clown disguise, sitting in the Dairy Queen on 2nd Street in Little Rock .

Karl Rove is in protective custody in the D.C. city jail.

And Sologdin knew equally well that "the people" is an overall term for a totality of slight interest, gray, crude, preoccupied in their unenlightened way with daily existence. Their multitudes do not constitute the foundation of the colossus of the human spirit. Only unique personalities, shining and separate, like singing stars strewn through the dark heaven of existence, carry within them supreme understanding.

— Alexander Solzhenitsyn, *The First Circle*

FORTY-EIGHT

The bus stopped right by the dorm. I went to the front door, area, asked at the desk for Skylar Brown.

A young woman appeared and said, no, she wasn't Skylar, but she could take me to her. I got a plastic lanyard from the front desk: VISITOR.

We entered at a door marked: ENTER and walked down a narrow hall with thin carpeting, open rooms labeled with hand-made signs and slogans, photos, just like a college dorm. I looked as we passed and saw young women and men in cramped spaces, desks, computers, cork boards. I heard a copier working, and voices. We walked past a lunch-type meeting room and stopped at the end at a closed door, simply labeled by plastic number two on a tiny nail.

"Come in," said the voice inside after my escort knocked. She opened the door, announced my name and pushed the door for me to go on in.

I recognized her from descriptions.

She sat at a cheap, college dorm-type desk. The room was bigger than the others, with bulletin boards, posters and photos on the walls, along with samples of the various CRUSHER brigade T-shirts, hanging by a single pin or nail.

She finished what she was doing, got up and walked around the desk to greet me.

She shook my hand.

"Skylar Brown. Nice to meet you."

She stepped back to allow us both to view the room.

"We are going to the mountains, where we should be. This is ridiculous. A copy machine. I know, right? But for now, here we are. It's what the board wants. If it were up to me ..."

She motioned for me to sit and grabbed another chair and pulled it up.

"Coffee?" I asked.

I was so freaking tired, could not go through the propriety of waiting to be asked.

She looked around the room and said, fresh out.

She smelled like strawberry. I no doubt reeked of cigarettes.

There were books at her feet, on the desk, and in various places around the room.

"So," she said.

"You are a reporter? For whom?" ...

"It's complicated," I said.

"I understand you're working for Prince Hope," she said.

"Sometimes I wonder," I mumbled.

"How does that work?"

I said, sometimes not very well, trying to make a little joke.

"I suppose so, sounds like it. Have you published anything yet? About this?"

Not yet, I said, now making eye contact, the kind meant to fend off.

She saw me looking at the books at her feet. She picked up a few. It got noisy in the hall, some people arriving, laughing. She got up and pushed the door to almost closed. She wore a large, comfortable looking dress, sandals, camo socks to her calf, and her hair in a braid with a big, I won't say fat, golden accouterment.

She showed me the covers of the books, *Sun Tzu, The Face of War, WAR,* another one. She described each one briefly and let them sit in her lap as I paid cursory attention.

I waited for her to talk, thinking it might be the best tactic. She waited with me, messing with something about the dress.

"So," I said. "How's it going so far?"

"You want to know about Lara and Kaitylyn."

That's what she said.

"I can't tell you."

"Why is that?" I said.

"It's not what you think."

"You know what I think?"

"No, tell me."

"I meant how do you know what I think."

Smell of rolls, giggling, someone brings in a tray with coffee. Oh, you didn't need ... both of us grab one, set the coffee tray on the desk, smile, hurry out ... Well, I guess we have coffee.

How I did not see it before I do not know, but now I see a camouflaged handgun on her side in a holster, matching apparently pretty well with the print of her dress, not camo.

And now I see a new rifle sitting on the floor leaning against a wall.

"I am having some problems with," she begins as she walks to take another attempt at closing the door halfway.

"With the staff."

"Yeah," I said. "I wanted to ask you about ..."

She chewed quickly with a finger raised to cut off my sentence because she had something more to say.

And she went on about how the "staff" didn't seem to understand the transition and were not wholly "on board," in her opinion.

She intimated that some had already been eliminated, and I do not think she meant killed, that's not what it sounded like to me.

And no, I didn't fucking ask more about that, which I suppose I should have, but there is something to say here. Sometimes later you have to trust what the you in that earlier situation decided was the right course of action, even though later it is not possible to remember how you felt or what were all the little fucking nuances and shit. You just remember the "macro situation." So.

We moved from the two stand-alone chairs by the door over to her desk. She assumed her spot behind and I slid over a waiting chair behind on the other side.

She began to lecture. I took notes and listened. She was not half bad. I was waiting for her to start pacing back and forth while she talked. I hate that. I've had teachers like that.

"Victories are important," she began.

She listed Persians, Marathon, Greeks, North vs. South, United States cavalry vs. Indians, Hitler, Eisenhower, etc.

I threw in Yankees, Red Sox and she did not even slow down a step.

"They determine people's lives, for a long time."

I nodded, noted and noticed the fucking Samurai sword on the wall behind her and how it did not appear to be supported by anything, no nails, just there.

She quoted Eric Hoffer, about the personality traits of the enthusiast ... or fanatic.

I now saw a nice plaque, the kind you might find at a nice plaque store by a lake: We Are Here To Kill V.C.

I was making on again, off again eye contact in order to keep looking around the room. She was now actually pacing back and forth behind her desk, not a leisurely stroll, but more like in a carnival if you are a yellow duck and you're trying to not get shot.

"We are not the militia."

She stopped.

"That is not us."

I nodded to I guess say, okay.

"The cops are an occupying army," she said.

"The Black Panthers were right about that."

And then she threw in something I'd heard somewhere before about the four primordial fears and I don't know where that fit in, but I now saw all kinds of weird and cool shit on her desk, military type shit and like hippie shit and micro-management corporate shit, just little shit, all thrown together on that desk, and she kept talking.

She talked about Rand, and other think tanks, about what do they do anyway, and all that money and it comes down to us anyway, with no money, to do something.

And she talked more about Bernays and how propaganda got started in the United States with Wilson and that war and some other stuff about that.

"Secrecy is the enemy of truth," she said as she sat.

I nodded, trying to not let my eyes close.

"If they told us the truth there wouldn't be any conspiracy theories. "Right?"

"Yep," I said as I looked down to my pad and wrote "Yep."

Later I saw my other notes from that little short course:

Nobody wants to fight their own kind.

You need to fight the numbness. You can't fall in love with power and destruction and you can't be numb to the horror. You have to be open to it all, and a lot of it is pain. America cannot rescue itself by the voting booth.

[Yep, there's that.]

"The sales effort was unparalleled in its scale and sophistication," I think referring again to Bernays and Wilson.

"So," she said, making a move to again open the door. The hall and the rest of the offices were silent. I wondered how fucking long we'd been there.

"WWE is fake and the rest of it even moreso."

I scribbled it down, most of that, trying to understand where she had gone to as I wrote.

"Oh, wrestling," I said.

"You're talking about wrestling."

"Yes, of course," she said, stretching, looking out her window, her back to me.

"This plane ticket. I just can't figure it out. What's up with that. You know anything about that?"

She said all that facing the window then turned to me.

Columbo, I thought. Officer Columbo. She has watched that show. I almost smiled.

I said, I don't know, I'd heard something about that before, but at that point I still didn't think it was very important.

"You put up a good front," I said.

"Or, you are just as you seem."

How so? What do you mean? she said as the look on her face said I will kill you, too, just as I have those skinny little buggers, and you should know that.

"Why haven't we heard about you before?" I said, not looking at her as I began shutting down my shit.

"Well, I don't know, I wonder why?

"Why do *you* think that is?"

I said it was probably time for me to go.

Without comment she sat and began working at her desk.

I started to close the door then pushed it silently wide open.

Well, I had nothing better to do than go right back to the bench and wait for the bus. I had a sandwich and I'm sure that's why Korey sat down next to me. He came out of nowhere, drawn to that Subway bread. It was already cut in half and I forked it over.

He chewed for a long time before either of us said anything. The bus came and went, another. It was a nice day, why not sit? And watch things, hear things, feel the sun. And that bread, wow god.

"She's okay, kinda different," he said.

I knew who, but I said, "Who?"

"Her."

He nodded behind us, into the building.

"She said I could do whatever I wanted," he said.

I waited, watched the people all around us board the next bus. It roared away.

"What do you want to do?" I said.

"Not sure."

"Where's Lara? Kaitylyn."

He wiped his mouth with the bag and looked at me then away. He crunched the wrapper into a ball and tossed it neatly left-handed into the wire bin. He pulled his jacket tight around him and crouched over his knees and shivered, patting the concrete with his tennis shoes.

He shrugged his shoulders with his fists shoved hard inside the little jacket pockets then looked out at traffic. The sun hurt his eyes. He smelled. I wanted to offer him a comb. I didn't have one.

Korey sat up straight and put his arms back over the bench, stretched out his legs, crossed them at the ankles and began to talk.

I couldn't hear him because of all the city noise, just stuff.

I scooted over closer, fumbled with my recorder, got it to where I thought it was on, facing toward him, inside my jacket pocket, then not wanting to chance it, just took it out and rested it on my leg. He saw it, just kept talking.

He talked about his plans for The Stupid Mary Tyler Moore Brigade. He had a talk lined up tonight in the back room of some bar in Dinkytown, another tomorrow. He had his supplies organized and stored, away but close-by, T-shirts, some food. He had maps and plans for taking over the downtown first. He'd been practicing rappelling on his own at night on the bridge. He said sometimes he let himself down into the water and held onto the rope and just sat there in that water and he thought that was great, being so close to disaster.

"Where's Lara?" I said.

"She's around," he said.

"Around?

"What the hell happened?"

"I don't know, man," he said as he got up and walked away, his fists shoved hard into his pockets.

"The real damage is done by those millions who want to 'survive.' The honest men who just want to be left in peace. Those who don't want their little lives disturbed by anything bigger than themselves. Those with no sides and no causes. Those who won't take measure of their own strength, for fear of antagonizing their own weakness. Those who don't like to make waves—or enemies. Those for whom freedom, honour, truth, and principles are only literature. Those who live small, mate small, die small. It's the reductionist approach to life: if you keep it small, you'll keep it under control. If you don't make any noise, the bogeyman won't find you. But it's all an illusion, because they die too, those people who roll up their spirits into tiny little balls so as to be safe. Safe?! From what? Life is always on the edge of death; narrow streets lead to the same place as wide avenues, and a little candle burns itself out just like a flaming torch does. I choose my own way to burn."
— Sophie Scholl

"How can we expect righteousness to prevail when there is hardly anyone willing to give himself up individually to a righteous cause? Such a fine, sunny day, and I have to go, but what does my death matter, if through us, thousands of people are awakened and stirred to action?"
— Sophie Scholl

"Fantasy. Lunacy.
All revolutions are, until they happen, then they are historical inevitabilities."
— David Mitchell, *Cloud Atlas*

FORTY-NINE

Hello, she said as I sat down.
She was already there.
Kaitylyn?
She's okay.
Okay.
How about you?
She shrugged.
So, yeah, what happened?
She was kidnapped.
They had been planning this all along.
She agreed to step down and be silent.
She's not going to be silent.
She's in contact with some of the others to stop this and do it the right way.
She has given up because of what happened.
She had given up before and Prince Hope arranged for a way for it all to continue ... because he believes in it ...
... because it is good for him to have something to fight against, or seem to fight against.
She's in prison. She's at home. She's in hiding. She's being held somewhere.
Kaitylyn? Kaitylyn is good, but hurt. No. Prince Hope didn't have anything to do with this ... he's old ... this is something else. Yes, she's a plant, but by who? *Whom?* I swear I will slap you if you do that again.
I imagined the conversation as I rode the bus around town, looking for Lara and Kaitylyn. I stared out the window knowing it was useless, but I had to be doing something. And there they are, on a bus bench, talking. And there's Brooke walking up to them, talking about Narnia, like three friends walking home from school on a bright fall day, so engrossed

in their conversations, so happy. How could anyone ever understand how they felt at that time. It's not them. The bus stops and goes again. Whoever that's supposed to be don't even notice the rest of us.

The bus passed up Summit Avenue, such beautiful homes and lawns and fantasies. I allow myself to see myself and my family in those cozy mansions on warm summer evenings and a frigid January night. We go up and over the hill and down into Saint Paul. We stop at a corner right in front of a family run funeral home. There is a little marquee in the front door with names. I don't imagine my own name. I imagine the names of the CRUSHERs, Lara, Kaitylyn, Zima, Korey, Jim, and then we wheez, squeak and pull away.

The bus smells, exhaust, it's bumpy, stop and go. My stomach is urpy my grandmother used to say. She's not here, but she is. I often imagine her looking over my shoulder, walking beside me, in the same room. Maybe she is, maybe not. I hope someday we get some answers. I'd stayed in contact with Skylar Brown. She often referred me to Rick, nerdy, handsome, hairy, dark, wears black like Johnny Cash, always on the move, always on the phone. They're still going to the mountains. Okay, I say. Most of what I get these days is about Korey, and it's not good.

I read about him, Korey, sometimes in the papers, on page six, at least I think it's about him, and The Mary Tyler Moore Brigade. They talk about the T-shirts.

Rick says Korey's willing to talk to me. I said I already talked to Korey not that long ago and he didn't have much to say. He says he doesn't know anything about that, but that now Korey is willing to do an interview. I say, fine, I'll see when I have some time. Then he says Korey wants to talk to me, and then he arranges a meeting and I go to it. Korey is not there.

Again, something is arranged.

We meet at a bench by the river. He loves that fuckin' river. He says we must meet out in the public, around people. Maybe he thinks I'm going to try to have him killed. I ask him if he's ever seen *The French Connection*. He says with Adam Sandler? I say, no.

He's changed because of Skylar and Rick, he says, but mostly Rick.

I said, "oh, really."

I offer him a smoke. He doesn't smoke anymore.

He says he used to be one of the guys, or at least he tried very hard to be one of the guys, though he knew he wasn't and the guys all knew it, but they tolerated him because they liked him, this was when he was in high school, all his football, hunting, drinking friends, riding around town. But now Korey has gone against them. I say what is his hometown. He points north. He says that's what was bothering him. He felt like a failure to them. He was spending too much time on Facebook, he said. I said that sounds fairly familiar. He asked if I meant his situation or Facebook.

I said Facebook, then both. Now, he said, he knows who his real friends are. I said, who. He said, Skylar and Rick.

Korey said he wants to be like Geronimo. I wouldn't even mind being retarded, he said. He was a hero, said Korey.

"He did it. He went all the way. That's why we're here. That is why we are here."

I tried, but I couldn't put myself in that mind. I still didn't really understand what these young people who once worked together at the same group home and got to know this big young man named Geronimo ... how that inspired them to try to take over the country with guns.

To me, I don't know, I think I'd just try to make a life for me that I liked and call that good.

I asked him who he thought Geronimo was trying to be and he just shook his head then looked away.

And then, there they are: Lara and Kaitylyn, sitting on a bench, forlorn, now laughing, slapping at each other, now — no, again it's not them. Goddamn it.

The ticket, the big ticket Geronimo supposedly found while working in the shredding room at the Friendly Face facility. Who had that ticket? Did they use it? How did it get into the shred room? This is intriguing. I've read about Operation Northwoods. I would like to know more about this. Where will I eat tonight? At home alone or out somewhere alone? Should I go to a movie? Will I ever want to get off of this bus? Who is that? What is that happy family right there really like?

I ride the bus around Minneapolis-Saint Paul looking for Lara and Kaitylyn because I don't want to be sitting in my apartment alone. I probably should be reporting a little more intensely and in person at some of the sites of the CRUSHER rebellion, but I don't feel like it today. I decide what I will do. I will ride this bus until I see a friendly looking down home bar, get off, have some beer and some food and then get back on the bus and go home and be able to sleep. A happy feeling floods my body as I begin to look.

There's one.

When I was at Harvard College, I was in Gov 182, that was taught by Henry Kissinger, and Henry Kissinger started the class right out ... Kissinger just announced right at the beginning with all the men in the class there who were waiting to run the world, telling us, "look if you think that our government doesn't have the right to lie, steal, cheat and to kill in order to forward the best interests of the country itself in the world then you shouldn't be in this course."

— Danny Sheehan, on Gary Null radio show,
May 20, 2016

And Jesus entered the temple and drove out all those who were buying and selling in the temple, and overturned the tables of the money changers and the seats of those who were selling doves.

— Matthew

FIFTY

Rick had begun making speeches around town, they said to make money for the revolution. He was really into it. I saw him advertised on the side of buses even and posters in the windows of restaurants and cafes. I saw him speak at a church a block off Lake Street one night. He was good. It was all about war and how you have to wage war in your personal life to have victory. It was pretty much all plagiarized from one of the books Skylar had encouraged me to look at while I waited, it seemed, for hours in her office. Not fucking Clausewitz or, or Keegan or O'Brien, one of the others. But the people seemed to like it. And then I got a buzz on my phone. I was set for these news alerts. They were usually nothing. This one was definitely not nothing. I looked around to plan how I would get out of the packed little church, then made my way to the side door. I splurged for a cab and got out in a hurry right at the river walk, where a crowd had already gathered.

"What's going on?" I asked.

"It's CRUSHER, up on the fucking bridge," someone pointed.

"Who's CRUSHER?"

"The singer!"

"No, *idiot*, the group, that thing."

I didn't know how anyone could tell. It was already dark.

There are lights up on the bridge, old antique-looking, and right now a dark figure could be seen running down the bridge and reaching up and smashing them with something. Once in a while there came a flash then the pop of a gun.

It appeared to me that Korey and his brigade were engaged in full-scale battle with the police and national guard.

Helicopters buzzed and shined spotlights onto the scenic bridge. It was actually beautiful, the flares arcing into the sky, showing the downtown, the big buildings, the crowds gathered on the other side of the river, like a Fourth of July palooza, the flares shimmering in the wide river.

Automatic small arms fire rat-a-tat-tatted, burped, roared and echoed in the river, downtown canyon. You could tell who was doing the shooting by the light of the barrels, either up on the high bridge or down on the road.

Someone tried to make a point on a megaphone.

Now someone had opened up with music, loud.

"Someone likes crap," someone with a suburban liberal sound said.

I thought of how the police could have just let them be. How long could they stay there? Not forever. But they couldn't do that for some reason. They had to shoot and get them off of there now. Tennis shoes padded as the brigade spread out along the bridge span.

I perched for a short while down below, standing on a bench, not sure what vantage that extra twelve inches gave me, but there I was. I felt a certain insider cachet and should be allowed closer, so I moved, past my little group, goodbye, and some sort of person directing traffic but watching only the bridge, kept going, and then I was blocked, all kinds of police and flashing lights and police car radios squawking.

He was going to be a hero. I remembered that and it scared the shit out of me as to how that was going to happen in the next few minutes. Sacrifice himself for his brothers and sisters, that's what he had said.

I went downhill, a few steps at first to see who, whom, was watching. Nobody I guess. I sidestepped on the grass, through some bushes until I came to the fucking river. I was all of a sudden right there. The best, I mean the absolute best seat in the house and all you had to do was look a little.

Anyway, I was still getting those news feeds on my phone.

I guess they had dragged the Mary Tyler Moore statue from Nicollet Avenue in the bed of pickup or a flatbed or five big guys, but somehow they got it down Portland to the Bridge and there it was, I can see it.

I can hear everything from down here.

I hear some couple reciting the words on a plaque talking about the bridge. Apparently they are that couple.

"This is the one that collapsed a few years ago," the man said.

I said no, to myself.

The wife said no, that's not the one.

I mumbled, good girl.

I found this out later, not that it matters. Well, it matters.

The Stone Arch Bridge is the only bridge of its kind over the Mississippi River. It is made of native granite and limestone, and measures 2100-feet long by 28-feet wide. The bridge consists of 23 arches, and spans the river below St. Anthony Falls in Minneapolis, MN.

Stone Arch Bridge History:

Built by railroad baron James J. Hill in 1883, the bridge allowed for increased movement of people and goods across the river. It served as a working railroad bridge until 1965 but is still seen as a symbol of the railroad age.

So, there you have it.

Like a wife used to going fishing with her husband all day long in the cold and sitting there, waiting, and not making a peep, I settled in. I found grass away from the mud to sit on and bushes to guard me from prying eyes above. I had my binoculars, not really. I had my phone and you can take a photo and then use the zoom to zoom the photo. It takes time, but anyway.

I was so close I could hear the rebels talking up on the bridge. I heard the police talking behind me. When the flares went off I saw the crowd on the other side and hear their "oooh." It was getting so big you could say "crowds." There was rumbling, definitely lots of rumbling, big things over cement and lots of commands, yelling.

I didn't want to think it, but I did and I was stuck with the thought. It was that I was either entitled by my position or trapped. If they blew up the bridge, I was toast. If they attacked from behind me for some reason, same result. If they bombed the bridge, strafed the bridge, if they spread gasoline over the river to torch the bridge, nobody would ever know my name, I would not even be a footnote, a trivia question, nothing. Not a thing. So that is what I was thinking of when I heard someone talking right beside me.

"Can you hear me?"

I said nothing, but yes, I could hear him, and already he was pissing me off. I've been jumpy lately.

I didn't get up, but I stomped the grass where I heard the voice coming from and I found that the rebels, I guess them, had put a microphone there, not just there, probly everywhere. And it did echo, that voice. It sounded big and everywhere. I put my hand over my microphone and yes, I heard it behind me and across the river.

That voice, not a great voice, Korey's voice, kind of a normal, self conscious voice, but not as bad as I'm making it sound.

I smiled.

They had put some work into this and I was proud of Korey.

I thought to myself, okay now, shut up, just shut the heck up before you embarrass yourself. You did whatever and now let somebody who knows what the hell they are saying have the microphone. Somebody with the bass to boom out the revolutionary lingo.

I took my phone and aimed it up at the place where it looked like the CRUSHERs were gathering and then I zoomed the photo and I saw nothing, just a bunch of people with their hands stuffed into their pockets and it looked like they were shivering, watching the river, the crowds, some had rifles.

Then I spotted one guy sitting on a ledge under the bridge, squatting, on an outcrop. I took a photo, did the zoom thing and it was Korey, sitting on the ledge, his feet dangling a hundred feet over the river, cops and people and helicopters all over, fighter jets once in a while, with a microphone to his mouth and I'm hearing him right here like he's talking to just me.

"Can you hear me?"

And I wanted to say, yes, I can hear you, stop saying that, just talk!

"Yes!"

The shout went up from both sides of the river, like Scots on the field of The Battle of Stirling Bridge. (I did spend some time in the main library this winter with the homeless, for company.)

"Okay," said Korey.

"Cool.

"Is everybody having a good time?"

"Yes!"

Some shots popped out from the police side. I hoped they did not see where Korey was sitting. The rebels were scattered along the bridge with armed barricades on both ends. They held the Mary Tyler Moore statue in the middle like a college football trophy. Where they hunched in bunches they were behind vehicles, at least as far as I could see. Whatever they were doing it was apparently enough to keep the police from bombing them or storming their position.

"We are CRUSHER," said Korey.

And I think he was probably amazed and excited that people cheered when he said that. I know I was. I got goosebumps.

Korey, and I have to say he really did a nice job, went into the whole history of CRUSHER, from Geronimo and the group home. He named names, told about everybody. Why? Because he could for one thing. He had the whole city right there and he was sitting on his favorite bridge, his feet dangling and I would have to say that if anyone was ever in their zone, this was it.

He called out a name I didn't recognize and said "Fuck you, man." And for me that added nothing though it probably was cathartic for Korey.

It was just amazing, I have to tell you. I actually wished I had popcorn. It was the best show, the best thing ever. Ever. And I'm not even from around here.

"Nine-eleven was an inside job," said Korey.

He did not shout it, just said it, but even then I thought now it's over. People are going to go home. Nobody wants to hear that shit.

"I know it, you all know it."

He waited. I'm sure he was listening. He could probly hear everyone breathing on both sides of the river. I'm sure he heard not a few weapons cock. He waited until a helicopter left after buzzing down and being shot at, the rounds pinging off the side.

The people cheered the helicopter leaving.

Simply fucking amazing.

Korey went all down the list: Oklahoma City, Waco, Aurora, San Bernardino, Orlando, all of them.

"Paul Wellstone was murdered," Korey said.

He sounded sad, so sad. Nobody said a thing. They were listening. It was his show.

Just wow, I thought.

Oh, well, as Kaitylyn might say, might as well be hanged for a dragon as for an egg.

And he told them about how the wars in Iraq and Afghanistan were all based on the lie of 9/11, and that the government people all knew that.

"But they think you don't know it or you don't care," said Korey.

And he stopped.

And it was silent, on the bridge, on the river sides, even in the city, I would imagine.

People waited for more, but that was it.

I found out later he'd been hit and that during his speech he was bleeding. It was his shoulder and they wrapped it, but the wrap was soaked.

No matter. He could still do this.

And he did.

I sat there on watch, along with some of the crowd, a lot of the police, into the night. It got cold. I shivered and stared into the water, trying not to fall in. The hours wore on and it really is a different world at three in the morning than it will be during the day, totally different. It's the time of Bigfoot and UFOs, worries and wild thoughts.

I huddled my knees up and my arms around my knees and got as close in to myself as I could. My plan was to make it to morning so I didn't get shot walking away now.

I thought and I dreamed, a little, not much, my head dropped every time and woke me up.

I heard a splash, a tiny water plop and I shot my head up. I stared into the dark, across the water and saw shadows. I had to stare hard to see anything. They had planned pretty well, no moon. There were shadows sitting on the water and moving shadows coming down from the bridge. It took me a long time to understand what I was looking at.

The rebels were coming down off the bridge, by a rope and they were dropping into canoes or kayaks out there and then just gliding away, one by one, with the current downstream.

I was watching history, like Paul Revere through the countryside or Martin King at one of his speeches. I really was, this was so cool, I thought. I thought of taking a picture but it was dark and the flash would ruin everything. I just watched with my eyes wide open trying to see everything, record it all.

The last thing I saw was the rope gently swinging and down comes what looks to me like Korey. He let himself down into the canoe and off they went, hunkered down, someone putting a blanket over his shoulders.

I let my head drop and I tried to sleep and maybe I did.

My eyes opened and I jumped. Where was I?

A McDonald's cup floated in the water.

Police and National Guard troops were shouting and running up the bridge from both sides. Two helicopters hovered. Police boats made waves hurrying from the shore toward the rope that hung still.

I stood and stretched and really felt it in my knees and thighs, what a night.

It was glorious is what it was. I turned around, looked around, walked carefully up the slick grass, feeling so great, like history had been reverted and the people running up the Grassy Knoll had run right over the fake policeman there and caught the shooter, like we got a re-do on all of that. I smiled so wide I was self conscious about it. I had to try to keep it down, the smile, because probably it looked weird. I wanted to be with people and walked to where I knew there was this great small-town type café and I sat in the booth that I had hoped would be open and I ordered eggs, hash browns, toast, oatmeal with blueberries, a pot of coffee, everything I could think of. And there were people coming in, together, smiling, talking about the bridge battle, and they were happy and it was so goddamn great. I'm not shitting. You had to be there, but that's all I can tell you is how it felt. There was even a smell of gunpowder in the air, like lilacs.

Note from the narrator:

From The Prince Hope Show ...

And now ...Tonight's Dick Tracy Crime Stopper's Bulletin;
When You See Something Say Something.

Because of the recent murder of investigative reporter Michael Hastings in a fiery car crash in Los Angeles, a special bulletin has been released.

Be on the look-out for F.B.I. license plates in your neighborhood.

When you see something, say something.

Because of the murder of men, women and children in Waco Texas, be on the look-out for F.B.I. license plates in your neighborhood.

When you see something, say something.

Because of the false flag attacks designed to put the public in a state of panic, in, Tucson, Aurora, Sandy Hook, Boston, and elsewhere around the country and globe, citizens are asked to be on the look-out for F.B.I. license plates in your neighborhood, as well as a long, black limousine with tiny American flags fluttering from the quarter panels.

The persons inside the limousine are to be considered liars and murderers.

This has been your weekly Dick Tracy Crime Stoppers Bulletin.

When you see something, say something.

QUOTE REMOVED BY ORDER OF DHS, UNITED STATES DEPARTMENT OF HOMELAND SECURITY. [DHS US2FA]

FIFTY-ONE

Bix,
Had today encountered this two hour video on Edward Snowden, so sat for it. Nobody in the video says it, but we are in fascism. It is shown, in the video. Interesting video. Snowden of course is unique. A supremely nice person, very mature while young, intelligent.

Bonnie called, to wish me Happy Birthday. I thought to wish her yesterday birthday but she said yesterday was my birthday, she tried to call me last evening but could get no answer. Indeed, Madrea had called me yesterday. Bonnie sounded ok, was being nice, asking about my health etcetera. Bonnie had other calls to make, including Madrea. She continues working on getting her affairs together, glad she finally has decent renters in Lyla's house. Was hoping to this date finally get back to her workout gym. Lately, she had been back to her Oregon cabin, since 2 years, saw some friends of hers there.

So maybe she and Mike will be here same time in Oct. She spoke of its being convenient we have this property to gather at, and I said it could become more valuable to us than we yet know.

The Killary stuff is bizarre enough already. Many believe her dead. Not in main stream. But even USA Today shows pictures of her double, or two doubles. These do not resemble her much.

It is wonderfully mad, The C.I.A. want her as president, dead or alive. I guess once she is in, she can officially die of cancer, and USA can bravely carry out her "policies." She has wanted to nuke Iran, Russia. Probably the C.I.A. is not that illogical yet.

Further,
Bill

Strike out in new directions, even if they involve risk, don't get caught up fighting the last war.

Try to recover the fluidity of mind of your youth. When you find yourself obsessed, your thoughts revolving around a particular subject or resentment, move past it.

War is progressive.

Your mind is weaker than your emotions. Unintimidate yourself.

Your days are numbered. Will you pass them half-hearted and half awake or with a sense of urgency. Enter new waters. Stake everything on a single throw. Act before you are ready. Transform your war into a crusade. Create a threatening presence.

Occupy the moral high ground. Penetrate their minds. Destroy from within.

— *The 33 Strategies of War*, Robert Greene

I wanted you to understand what happens to the mind when the suspicion levels are allowed to evaporate. Americans know nothing. And there's a reason for that. Our media. As a friend of mine notes: "The ghosts of Hearst and Pulitzer must be banging their heads against the spectral bars of their infernal cages at the terminal stupidity of their modern counterparts. Assuming they get 24/7 CNN in hell. Which is a fair assumption, since no greater torture could be imagined. Anyone delayed in Atlanta Airport can attest to this.

— Lionel/Michael Lebron

FIFTY-TWO

So, yeah, I'm sitting in a café, doesn't matter which one or where, there are dozens and dozens of these things all over town, somehow, how they get the money or the energy, I don't know, and suddenly Buster and Brandon sit down, looking like ... very serious park chess players with concealed carry bulges in their jeans. I know because mine is also making it just a little bit difficult for me to enjoy my coffee.

I'd met them before, but they were definitely uninvited here, during my breakfast, sitting very close, in my personal space, during me-time.

I let them know it.

So, how's Korey? I said.

"He's fine," said Brandon, a skinny black kid, from Minneapolis, I think.

"This is about someone else," said Buster, the one Asian CRUSHER rebel I knew of.

"Lara," said Brandon.

"Kaitylyn," said Buster.

I put my newspaper down, put up a finger to ask the waitress for two more coffee cups.

Buster said no thanks.

Yes, please, said Brandon.

So we talked.

It was noisy and busy in there, pretty much my favorite place for a Saturday morning treat, for myself.

"Okay," I said, taking out my note pad.

Buster put his hand on the pad.

"Don't do that," he said.

I thought again and agreed, put the paper and pen away, folded my hands around my coffee mug and prepared myself for bad news, took a deep breath. The paper and pen was my comfort zone, my blanky, to tell

355

you the truth. I needed them. Without them I was out in the open, just this person.

Now Brandon gets up out of their side of the booth and sits on my side, I infer that I should move over. He sits down, very close, leans over closer. Geezuz fuck, I push back with my butt, my shoulder, as firmly subtle as I could.

Brandon begins as Buster leans over his side of the booth and they are both leaning in and I'm leaning away like an artist's conception of a man in a rowboat being sold life jackets by professionals.

"They just came into the office one day," Brandon begins and we shoved on, away from the safety of the dock, out into open water, completing each others sentences, stepping on each others lines, "with all these guys in suits and took them away, that's all we know." How do I know you're telling the truth? You really don't. What about Prince Hope. You know all about him. I doubt that I do.

He's really on the side of CRUSHER. He is? But he can't show it, they'd kill him. Who? You know who. What about The Special Unit, The Red Unit? We don't know. We think they're working for Prince Hope. Sometimes I wonder, what about the massacre at Mayberry? Mount Airy? That was somebody else. Sure looked like The Special Unit from what I've heard. Anyway, Prince Hope, he just wanted to keep Lara out of this and Kaitylyn too. But they don't want this. They're coming back and we are going to be strong as shit. Really? Really, man.

What if I don't believe you? You don't really have any choice. I would have thought Hope would have let you know. Maybe he doesn't trust you. Why would he not trust *you,* man?"

And then I realized it.

Skylar and Rick were the ones who Kennedy or Blake or Ben had told me about, who didn't want to be in the rebellion. They were with the group that quit way back when.

Note from the narrator:

The following is drawn, paraphrased, somewhat redacted, from the essays of Max, Kaitylyn's journal and Brooke's as yet unpublished account, The Pothole Diaries.
For what it's worth:

For decades, centuries, America and the world has been protected by those strong enough, smart enough to hear the voice of honor calling to their hearts.
Those brave warriors to whom we owe our freedom.
Who can forget Dorothy Day, Emma Goldman, Eugene Debs, George McGovern, Peter Maurin, Ammon Hennacy, Lucy Parsons, Big Bill Haywood.
And today we salute those who continue to answer the call.

— The few, the proud, The Women From Code Pink
— Food Not Bombs, A Global Force For Good
— Be All You Can Be ...
— Join We Are Change or your local 9/11 Truth Group today
— Aim High, with The National War Tax Resistance Coordinating Committee
— An Army Of One or Two or Three at four in the morning, underwater through the swamp with a hammer in their teeth, over the fence, through the fence, into the building to hammer on United States Military killing machines and destroy them
— The Plowshares Movement, defending freedom and humanity since September 1980
— We're Looking For A Few Good Women In Black
— Be Part Of The Action, The World Can't Wait
— Veterans For Peace: It's Not Just A Job, It's An Adventure
— Peace Is Our Profession: Join the Occupy Movement
— There's Strong and There's Catholic Worker Strong

Semper Fi
Ooo-rah

FIFTY-THREE

Mike,
  To remind you, please pass my note to Sokol. Good old Sokol. Odd last name, Japanese?

Wondering if you know anything about Killary is dead. Perhaps she is not yet. There are a couple of doubles for her, re. USA TODAY, mainstream. One of the doubles is slick, youthful, verbal.

C.I.A. chose Hillary, madly have 2 or 3 doubles and all technology to date to use on screen to present anything. Replace parts, do anything for to be seen by the unwashed. Our Other Side have creativity, yet their main ants got no sense.

Mike, it is interesting, most strange shit. You could forget pledging allegiance. Remember, Lyla had you and me able to pledge allegiance to the USA flag. Before Kelly was born. Bonnie was an infant.

Forget pledging our allegiance might you not mind noticing my example. For me if not possibly you too all this with Hillary must be USA president or her corpse is a tad fascinating.

Can you imagine?

It pleases Putin. He has not cared to strike first. Too bad he gets USA dishonest press. He is a good guy. Heh, another rumor is Putin poisoned Killary. Well, whatever, poisoning Killary is reasonable. She is a rabid bitch. Worse than poor Trump.

But don't neglect passing my hello to Sokol.

Love,
    Bill

We have to create culture, don't watch TV, don't read magazines, don't even listen to NPR. Create your own roadshow. ... (we are told) Get a degree, get a job, get a this, get a that.' And then you're a player, you don't want to even play in that game. You want to reclaim your mind and get it out of the hands of the cultural engineers who want to turn you into a half-baked moron consuming all this trash that's being manufactured out of the bones of a dying world.

Nature loves courage. You make the commitment and nature will respond to that commitment by removing impossible obstacles. Dream the impossible dream and the world will not grind you under, it will lift you up. This is the trick. This is what all these teachers and philosophers who really counted, who really touched the alchemical gold, this is what they understood. This is the shamanic dance in the waterfall. This is how magic is done. By hurling yourself into the abyss and discovering it's a feather bed.

... I had a price on my head by then, I was running out of money, I was at the end of my rope. And then they recruited me and said, "you know, with a mouth like yours there's a place for you in our organization". And I've worked in deep background positions about which the less said the better. And then about fifteen years ago they shifted me into public relations and I've been there to the present.

— Terence McKenna

FIFTY-FOUR

They rushed toward a fork in the river.

Mollie sat in the back of the canoe, Bow in the middle looking around, and Morgan in the front.

"So," said Mollie.

Morgan pointed right, then left, then turned around and said shit I don't know.

Like Bizzarro Lewis and Clark they meandered backwards maybe along the same path, headed from the smoking Cicely battleground to the CRUSHER Headquarters, the window booth at the Saint Paul Domino's on Snelling Avenue.

With no phone they had no way to connect to the rest of their group. Morgan scanned the sky looking for Sandara to buzz over searching for them.

"Our whole history — including Germany, World War II — all fake. They don't let you know who Hitler really was!"

Mollie shouted as the river got loud with a few rapids.

"That's fucking ridiculous!" Morgan yelled back over her shoulder, keeping one eye on the rocks and also pointing.

They went on in silence, for a while, then Morgan said, over her shoulder, that in her school they once had a speaker, about something, she couldn't really remember what, but that, as she sat in the back row, she smiled, and it made her happy, like that speaker was there for her.

"What?" shouted Mollie.

"And I watched that woman leave and she looked kind of sad, not a lot, because the other students were laughing and didn't seem to like what she said. I wanted to go tell her thanks for coming and let her know somebody really, really liked her, but I was just a kid."

"What!"

And they went on like that, for a while, around at least one more bend, with Mollie telling her version of American History, that Morgan could not hear, as Morgan hummed to herself.

"Hallelujah, hallelujah."

The river got even louder and Mollie gave up her disquisition and sought her mind for a song.

"Winter 1963, it felt like the world would freeze, with John F. Kennedy, and the Beatles."

Morgan looked around smiling big and singing.

"Hey ma, ma, ma!"

"Hey, ma, ma, ma," they sang together, then Mollie nodded sternly at some rocks headed their way. Morgan turned back and resumed her duties, listening to Mollie's gentle, steady nudging of the water. She leaned her head back, held up her arms in what looked like a yoga pose maybe to Mollie.

"Can you believe it!" shouted Morgan.

"What we are doing?"

Mollie smiled.

Morgan raised her hands into the air again and screamed.

"How great is this?"

They both jumped and looked as someone on shore banged on a pipe and they saw people scurrying in the brush, now some old cars, a roof.

"Hey, Mollie! How old are you, anyway?"

"Nunya-eight," said Mollie.

At the next island Mollie headed for a beach, smacking it hard. They scrambled, getting their feet and most everything else wet to secure their lifecraft. Bow ran to explore the new world.

For a while they sat on rocks and looked around.

Mollie dug into her giant Colombian bag and pulled out a whisky bottle.

"Hey!" said Morgan.

"Wow, that was luck."

"Yeah," said Mollie, "I know, right?"

They chugged and passed it back and forth

"Well," said Mollie.

"That's a deep subject," said Morgan.

"You know the water is freezing, but finally you jump. Why?" said Mollie.

"Why do you eventually jump?"

"Because you have to?" said Morgan.

"You could turn away," said Mollie.

"Yeah," said Morgan. "I guess."

"I had an uncle," said Mollie and Morgan slid off her rock converting it from a stool to a backrest. She shoved her hands into the sand and watched all around, and all around them the woods stood stoic with the excited, manic stream rushing in between, telling wild stories.

Mollie said something else about the uncle who was a bit different.

"Yeah?" said Morgan vaguely, staring up into the sun and clouds.

"Yeah," said Mollie and then she stopped, just watched the water.

Then she started again, telling her story as Morgan closed her eyes and rested her head on her rock.

"My father said that, about my uncle. I think he was proud of him, but you couldn't really tell."

"Yeah," said Morgan, her eyes fighting to stay open.

"It took him his whole life, I've finally realized it this moment," said Mollie, "to tell me anything about all of this. Just that little bit squeaked through, and that was something."

"A crack in the clouds," said Morgan, eyes closed.

"So," said Mollie.

"You've read your Sun Tzu?"

"Yup," said Morgan.

"Everything in war is the art of deception," said Mollie.

"Something like that," said Morgan.

She yawned and rolled over, curling herself up in a ball on the warm sand.

Mollie said something else.

"Yu-up," said Morgan, drifting off.

They got up, got moving, pushed out again into the water. They passed people on the shore who waved, some did not. Morgan said she thought probly the people had heard of "The Battle of Cicely" and that they were heroes. Bow lay asleep in the middle of the canoe.

Mollie wondered about food and where to sleep, where this river went to. They entered a darkened canyon, high hills and trees on both sides. The river narrowed and the water grew fierce, angry. Crows cawed and they didn't hear them.

Mollie pointed at a moose with water and vines dripping from his mouth and antlers. She looked back at Mollie and saw a serious face, then ahead at the rapids. Mollie made it through, but they were soaked.

They emerged to a wider spot, peaceful, with calm water. Mollie smiled and pulled the paddle from the water. Morgan waved to some kids on the bank and Bow's tail wapped them both and they laughed.

Mollie's head exploded and showered Morgan and Bow with sticky red goop. Morgan screamed and reached for Mollie's slumped body.

Her head leaked, turning the water scarlet. Morgan reached for a sudden sharp pain in her shoulder and looked up, into the woods. Something thumped into her back and her head dipped into the water. She pulled herself out and turned again toward the sounds in the woods.

She moaned and clutched her chest and smashed onto her face, causing Bow to jump out of the way into the water.

He barked and stayed by the boat as it drifted downstream, swaying gently this way and that, the red slick widening. Shots zipped in around him. The children on the shore screamed and shouted not to shoot the dog. Please! He fell behind the boat and yelped when he was hit, in the back, below the waterline. He fought to catch the boat and more bullets popped in around him.

The last one thumped the temple and he floated, front paws stretched out, back legs dangling, swaying this way and that, along with the boat, sinking lower in the water, as the children on the shore rushed along, trying to find a place to catch them before they were lost, as Mollie's finger dragged a line in the water.

Up on the hill, in the woods, above the water, Special Agent Braxton and Sheriff Cranston looked down from their perch in the fire spotter tower. Their rifles smoked out the barrels. Cranston reached to return his cowboy hat to his head. They watched the children, the canoe, the dog, floating down the river until they disappeared behind the trees. They began to put away their equipment. Braxton talked to the agents on the ground and vehicles moved.

He hummed softly to himself as he broke down his rifle and knelt over his gun case: Brought to you courtesy of the red, white and blue, he sang.

"I'm headed down," said Cranston.

"Mollie too? Hmm," he said, stopping at the steps.

"Yu-up. I'll be right there," said Braxton.

Note from the narrator:

The following is drawn, paraphrased, somewhat redacted, from the essays of Max, Kaitylyn's journal and Brooke's as yet unpublished account, The Pothole Diaries.
For what it's worth:

... The kind of people we have running our government ... if we really knew the truth, I believe we would be astonished.
Forget about George Washington and the Cherry Tree. Ronald Reagan making America strong again. The George Bushes riding into the baseball game on national TV to throw out the first ball, then sitting in the front row. Forget about Bill Clinton or Barack Obama the new liberal Democrats who care about you ... Sponge Bob, The Simpsons and South Park, Calvin and Hobbes, Snoopy have more to tell us than those guys. ...
... If you really want to be a true American, you need to know what the C.I.A. has done in other countries supposedly in our names, and make sure to read your William Blum
... you need to know what happened to Gary Webb after he wrote a story about C.I.A. drug running in Los Angeles, a story that ran in the San Jose Mercury News when the web was first getting going in the early '90s. I remember reading that when we first got America Online and I thought, wow, here we go, this is gonna be a ride – and then that was it, now the main media is worse than an underground junior high newsletter.
There is more than enough reason to wonder if we really went to the moon and that the government has been withholding information about UFOs.
At least in the Soviet Union, when they saw nonsense and lies printed in Pravda and Tass, at least they knew they were lies. We are still at the infancy stage in our development ... of not questioning the lies.

And, BTW, Bigfoot is real. I guarantee it.

Bigfoot is real and each one of the millions of high school history books in the bottom of millions of hall lockers are make-believe.

That is really where we are.

That is really who we are.

And so the next time there is a bombing or a threat of a bombing or a bunch of blue backpacks found in Bemidji – the healthy American, the true American, the real American – thinks "C.I.A., F.B.I., the police"

– the real patriot refuses to stand for the national anthem, and rather than another knee-jerk reciting of the pledge of allegiance he says – not until I get some questions answered, because ...

This is important stuff.

FIFTY-FIVE

Caryl,
I had a neat note to you this morning, said I am not doing tit for tat with you, or Mike Blackbird, or anyone. But as I reread my note, was about to mail it, it vanished, and I could not find it.

You must be careful what you read, I repeat. Chaos is a weapon of the fascist, I repeat.

I had been in a hurry to listen to a 22 minute video at Debbie Lusignan's Sane Progressive. In fact, this one is "Clinton racks up neo-conservative endorsements." You would enjoy Debbie. You need to see this one. Indeed it is to do with fascism's chaos-theory. Just Google it, or Sane Progressive, or the mere title of this one of 9/24/16, "Clinton Racks up Neo-conservative Endorsements."

I have not heard her go into much more than present voting scandal.

I have not heard her say "9/11." I have heard her bewail all this USA bombing of children. But she does clearly understand what is up.

She is periodically amusing or furious, and has a sense of her showmanship - like unselfconsciously she wears these low cut blouses - nice skin, like she does pushups - probably does, has nice arms. Geoffrey had told me he read her age somewhere, early fifties or something I forget, maybe "51" is in my head.

To say, she could be show business but she is other. Brilliant, a humanitarian and naturally combative. I doubt she can offend you. In today's 22 minute video she tells the world USA Democrats and Republicans are in cahoots. The neocons are endorsing Hillary. Bush, Cheney, Rumsfield etc. They rigged up Trump as boogyman, hoping he will be more unpopular than Hillary, and of course it will all be rigged for Hillary: MORE WAR. Bomb the kiddies.

She does tell us stuff hither thither, besides as said voting fraud. As to voting, she is behind Jill Stein, the Green Party candidate. Jill Stein seems ok to me. Though I am an anarchist, subjectively, maladjusted in present civilization.

I could see police state in my twenties. Well before Obama, whom I had liked, before any 9/11. Then, I figured Obama would clear up who the culprits. It surprised me how the Obama administration took up the Bush administration work without missing a step. My siblings have yet to see. They be blind the 9/11 Wars expanded. USA middle class shrank as banker billionaires, oil billionaires, war billionaires collected uncounted more billions. The Patriot Act has broken our Constitution at the knees.

There are a few heroes. Brady (Chelsie) Manning, Snowden, Assange, others not quick enough who are locked up.....It is so that the Obama Administration locked up the most whistle blowers for no crime. A cop may stop you and look for dirty underwear and lock you up in zero charge. Box you a bit if he likes. Do you know it?

Obama and all this flapdoodle about who is Muslim is nonsense, for muddy water of chaos. Chances be it Obama is not religious. He is a good actor. Ah, he was pathetic recently, about kids killed (none) at Sandy Hook, and he dabbed finger tips of onion juice at his eyes. As Kessler put it, why had he not wept months earlier on television. For kids he knew never died. Ah, but theater picks its moment.

Then, mine and Debbie's point is (has long been) the USA Democrats and Republicans are a team. About 20 years ago a late beloved cousin of mine was talking about it, and hell, I knew it way before then somewhere in the decades since the sixties.

Am still findng difficulty with the laptop. Just go see Debbie Lusignan.

Chances are you can hear what she says and not be in disagreement.

She is fun.

Love,

     Billy

Note from the narrator:

From The Prince Hope Show ...

And now for a word from National Public Radio, Good ol' Reverend Bob, Miss Thompson Your 5th Grade Teacher, The Police, The Tired Old Editor Strolling Down The Street After A Long Day At The Office, The Democratic Party, The American Legion, The Boy Scouts and Mom & Dad
            — all the people you trust to tell you the truth.

"If a plane would have hit the Pentagon, we would have seen that short film one thousand times by now on Chevrolet commercials and Miller Beer commercials and on commercials somehow juxtaposing the Pentagon, puppy pellets, the Pittsburgh Pirates and the Pope-Mobile.
     So. No plane hit the Pentagon. And because we know that from the lack of Pope-Mobile prevarications, we can be sure that Bush, Rove, Rumsfeld, et. al are liars and murderers. And we can include a bunch more folks in there as well. Bill Clinton, Hillary Clinton. The nice Obama family across the street. They all know the truth and refuse.
     Refuse.
     To tell us.
     And that's the truth and I don't care what happens to me, it's just important that you know.

This has been a word from National Public Radio, Good ol' Reverend Bob, Miss Thompson Your 5th Grade Teacher, The Tired Old Editor Strolling Down The Street After A Long Day At The Office, The Police, The Democratic Party, The American Legion, The Boy Scouts and Mom & Dad
            — all the people you trust to tell you the truth.

The young generation don't want to hear anything about the odds are against us. What do we care about odds? ...

When this country here was first being founded there were thirteen colonies. The whites were colonized. They were fed up with this taxation without representation, so some of them stood up and said "liberty or death." Though I went to a white school over here in Mason, Michigan, the white man made the mistake of letting me read his history books. He made the mistake of teaching me that Patrick Henry was a patriot, and George Washington, wasn't nothing non-violent about old Pat or George Washington.

— Malcolm X

FIFTY-SIX

"**M**ajor! Pick the hill you want to die on."
"Fucking funny."
"No, I'm goddamn serious. We've got to move out. Go! Now!"

Zima shouted at Joe in all caps.

Joe was "Major," Ariel was "Captain," and Zima was "General." They had decided to get fucking serious. And now, after all this planning to maneuver and get in place to attack Mayberry on three sides, now fucking this.

His brigade was trapped in a canyon south of Mayberry and he needed to get out of there or die.

There were plenty other hills around there and Joe had picked the wrong one. Zima shouted into her phone asking Ariel how it was going now in the north and it was worse there.

Zima decided to move her brigade to support Ariel. She waved her hand over her head and her people pushed up wearily and again waded silently into the river.

Ariel got a text from Joe.
Zima said we're going to die.
Ariel called Zima:
Zima, what the fuck?
Zima replied:
Ariel.
Joe hunkered alone in some bushes, shivering in the twilight, others around him, he can hear them, can't see them. He is giving the word around him what everyone should do by texting what they should do – move up the hill. It's almost straight up and slippery in the rain. People are screaming and crying and yelling. The rain picks up.

It's not raining here, said Zima, are you sure.

Am I sure it's fucking raining! Are you kidding me!

Yes, it's raining here too, said Ariel by text, trying to display calm by not using any exclamation marks.

While she is talking, to Zima and Joe by group text, Ariel, or Captain, is binding her own wound and the wound of another and trying to keep moving, trying to comfort Joe, and in so doing perhaps calm herself, even just a little.

"Do you remember ... in grade school."

"We didn't go to school together," Joe fired back.

"Call me," said Ariel.

Joe called immediately.

"Yes, we did," said Ariel, stumbling on steep slope.

"It's all one big school, actually."

"That's what Actually would have said, or Max," said Joe.

"Yes, exactly. And it was cold out and dark, but bright and cheery inside and it smelled like butter? What did the butter smell come from?

"I don't know," said Joe.

"Think about it," said Ariel.

Back in Minneapolis, Rick and Skylar monitored the battle in North Carolina.

Rick sat at the computer. Skylar looked out the window.

"Somebody's tracking their communications," Rick said.

"It's not good."

Skylar wrapped her arms behind her back and continued to watch out the window.

They listened in silence to the audio of the raging battle as Joe seemed to be making progress up his hill.

"Turn it up," said Skylar, "please."

At just about the same time as this was happening, I later learned, I, and this was genius I have to admit, I just went and asked Prince Hope where the hell were Lara and Kaitlyn.

I sat in a metal folding chair opposite Hope with his messy desk in between us.

"They wanted to take a break. They said they had someone who could fill in while they did that. They "actually" are not taking a break, they are very busy. They think that the internet and their phones are being monitored by the government. They needed to find another way to communicate.

"And they said this young man, who they called "Actually", who is now dead I understand, actually put together a system ... who anticipated they might need this ... and they are now in an undisclosed location learning how to put his work to use ... along with a few other things that they believe will help their cause. I have to go now. I have a show to get ready for, is there anything else?"

Okay, I suppose it's time for some disclosure.

You might wonder who am I? How did I come to be writing this? Who is paying for it? Is it Prince Hope? Is he an evil force or a force for good? What is the Special Unit, the Red Unit, and maybe also ... oh, that's enough, and now I've lost interest in telling you. I really need to find Lara and Kaitylyn, don't you think?

"Zima is asking, telling them to send out fire teams," said Rick.

"I can hear," said Skylar.

"I hope they know what a fire team is, there's not time to explain," said Rick.

"Obviously," said Skylar, now walking over across the room to stand by Rick at the computer table.

Joe did begin to make some progress up his steep hill, but it was dark by now. He texted everyone and told them to hunker in place for the night.

He texted Ariel.

"What's a fire team?"

She told him it was a small unit sent out either on scouting patrol or ambush.

"Might not be a bad idea," she said, "tonight, see what's out there in front of you, just sayin'."

"Not sure if I can," he lied.

Rather he stuck, right where he was, and dozed, and awakened, off and on for hours, sometimes hearing things, rustling, owls, everything amplified to distortion by the dark.

Meanwhile, Ariel went ahead and formed fire teams, groups of three to go out into the night and report back to her.

She thought to text Joe to nag him, but did not. Joe had earlier, when they were together, shared something so personal with her, and she just sat there, her head between her knees, and thought of him, alone on a hill nearby, and just cherished every moment, of that bond, that thing you have with someone that makes you feel special because they have taken a risk to tell you something, something that you could use to hurt them, but you don't.

Over the course of an hour or so her teams came back and said there was somebody up there, movement.

At dawn Zima slogged out of the river onto the bank and up a hill she could only hope was the right one.

Joe was now able to stand, look around, wave to his people and they proceeded to march up the hill.

Ariel did the same.

Zima was also engaged in climbing a hill, all miraculously in the same area, headed toward the town, toward their objective, on the revolution road to victory.

"It looks pretty clear," said Joe to Ariel and Zima.

"I think we're gonna make it, boy last night was bad though, you wouldn't bel ..."

"Ooomph!"

"Aaaa!

"Goddamn *shit*."

Ariel and Zima both stopped in their tracks.

"What was that!" said Ariel.

"Joe!"

They heard rustling and static and gunshots and shouting. They heard Joe talking into his phone, but all they could tell was something was happening and it didn't sound good.

Rick and Skylar listened from Minneapolis, connected by their computer to the communication equipment carried by all their brigade leaders, whether the phones were connected or not.

Ariel called her brigade leader cadre quickly to her and planned how they would move to Joe's position to assist.

Zima continued leaning into their hill, crawling by hands and knees, scrambling through wire brush and brambles to get to the top where they might be able to see something.

Joe didn't want to move ... and yet he felt ... like ... oh, god, it's crazy ... like ... it was almost like the feeling you get when you want to say hello to everybody, like at a party and you have just had your first two beers. He wanted to hug the world, not die, not now, now is not a good time for me, there is so much more in me than this, I am not done.

And then he realized, this is how a coward feels.

He didn't want to be that. He fought it. He fought the urge to live, to survive, to get back home, to be comfortable, relaxed, happy.

He saw himself in his head, as a little kid playing in the backyard, a puppy, flashes of football, classroom, and a family Christmas.

"Aaaaa!"

Joe pushed up and charged, up the hill, his rifle across his chest, tears in his eyes, the world was so fuzzy, but still he could see.

"Joe. Joe."

Ariel said into her phone sternly as if during an intervention.

"We're coming. Joe.

"Let's go, let's go," she said to her lieutenants, rushing through them.

Zima found level, a wide open space, but not a vantage to see below. She had to get to the edge. She ran.

"There must be a dozen parties beside us listening in," Rick said to Skylar.

"What the fuck?"

Skylar breathed deep and paced, her hands folded behind her back, a plus-size Lincoln.

"Launch the drones," she said. "We should have already done that."

"I did," said Rick.

"Here, take a look."

Zima found the edge she needed.

Below her in the scrub brush she saw movement, both sides. She found herself looking down toward a ridge that divided the brigades of Ariel and Joe, and for once she was so thankful for the stupid T-shirts. She knew exactly who was who.

She waved her arm to call up her archers, actual god-damn archers, who had actually been recruited, trained at Camp Sweaty by Skylar herself, and sent on a bus to the battle zone in North Carolina, what the fuck, thought Zima to herself, now or never.

Zima heard what she thought was Joe's voice on her phone.

Usually it wasn't she who made the jokes, but she thought she might be able to comfort Joe. She had no idea what he was going through, but what the fuck. It was her own joke, that she had made up during her wild thoughts while walking all night in the river.

"What's a scary cow say?"

"What?" said Ariel.

"This is Ariel, what!"

"I said, what does a scary cow say?"

"Goddamn it! I don't know what?" said Ariel.

"Moo!" said Zima as someone died in the background and her archers shuffled up, running through the thick leaves, lined up on both sides of her, on one knee, getting ready.

A round smacked Joe in the knee, knocking his leg out from under him and he hit the ground with his face, and he cried out and he crawled. Explosions tore up the ground around him, still he saw nobody, just heard the bullets ripping through the brush and his own men falling.

He felt alone, like it was him fighting this battle, alone. He crawled to a young guy sprawled on his back, squirming like a wounded animal, screaming. Joe ripped open the man's shirt and was not surprised to find the hole in his chest. He tore off his own jacket and shoved it into the wound. Soon the rag and his own hands were soaked.

Something like a punch but harder than that smacked Joe in the back and he fell face-first into the bloody rag and the dying young man. Joe rolled off, away, his face streaked red. He squirmed, trying to reach the awful stinging in his back with both hands, but he could not.

He saw someone above him, a smiling face.

No, Max, said Joe. I'm not ready. I've got so much I have to do. No, please go away. But still the smiling face came closer, the Cheshire Cat but not like that, friendly, loving. Joe put up his hands to push it away.

Sweat filling her eyes, her chest thumping, her arms and thighs aching, Ariel fought the earth to get to Joe and ran thud into something, knocking her down. Her nose pounded and she was angry. The pain in her nose pissed her off and she looked for whatever tree it was she hit because she was going to hurt the tree bad.

A young man got up out of the brush, looking flushed, dazed, embarrassed and angry perhaps at having been laid low by a girl. Ariel flashed a quick look and saw the others fighting hand to hand, punching, jabbing and getting punched and jabbed.

The young man opposite her in the helmet sported a bayonet on his rifle. She had none. Keeping her eyes on him she dug for her handgun, patted her belt, her back pockets, felt for her rifle in her hands, finding nada, nothing, shit, the fuck, she growled and she charged.

The young man in the helmet stood his ground, looked for a moment surprised, then in a determined, practiced, patriotic way he lowered his rifle with the razor sharp pointed knife on the end, pulled it back like a batter getting his rhythm going and rammed the knife into Ariel's stomach, pulled it back and stabbed her again in the shoulder before she hit the ground, then stabbed her again in the back where the heart would be, stomped on her arm to retrieve the bayonet, turned, did a jubilant war whoop and was pounded in the mouth by an arrow that pierced his neck, threw him backward and pinned him to the ground, where he squirmed, and passed to some other side.

Zima somersaulted into the air, a rag doll, and then, in slow motion she saw herself spinning, saw everything, the archers ripped apart by metal shards, clumps of earth flung into the air, trees cracked, knocked to the ground. She hit a rock with the space on her back between her shoulders and fought to breathe.

Constant booms echoed in the broad valley like the Fourth of July fireworks finale.

Rick and Skylar watched on their screen as a drone whirred and swooped and glided, showing a beautiful HD picture of the North Carolina hillsides, the golds, reds, from high up, like an IMAX movie.

It swooped down and followed the ground and then showed bodies and some things close up that it was hard to tell what it was. It pulled up, away, then down again, at scattered bodies, some figures still moving, others walking, approaching. It zoomed down and hovered over Zima like a hummingbird, arms outstretched, head to the side, the big rock in the middle of her back.

The drone again pulled away and you can see angry looks on the live soldiers, some shouldering weapons. The drone heads down the ridge and there are bodies and more movement on the ridge and on both sides, leading down to two separate streams. The drone buzzes like a bee from body to body as if looking for something, swatted at with hands and sticks and rifle butts, cursed, still flickering, flitting from corpse to corpse, and then it makes a straight line, a beeline to one particular soul, and there it stays for a moment to record the death of Joe, his eyes open, his arms frozen. The drone recorded a wisp of something, smoke probably, near Joe, and then it was gone.

The drone moved off and searched, dying person here, dead body there, more troops, some stopping to smoke.

It hesitated, seeing what it did not wish to see, from afar, and then it came a little closer and then a little more. It shot up to tree-top height to escape an onrush of soldiers. Using its zoom the drone showed a body, with an arrow in the mouth, and next to it a woman, in CRUSHER brigade T-shirt, bloody blonde hair.

A soldier came up and using his boot he scooped the body and turned it over, showing on Skylar and Rick's computer screen the face of Ariel.

The stunned drone stayed too long. The soldier turned and raised his weapon and fired, again and again.

Someone sent an anonymous email to Rick.

"What's a scary cow say?"

FIFTY-SEVEN

Caryl,
Be careful of what you read.

USA is racist and cops here kill more innocent people than in any other developed nation.

More blacks get beaten, shot, arrested, not necessarily in that order. USA blacks get the harder sentences for same crimes. Blacks here have less income, education, safety. More anger and fear. USA cops know they will normally get off for beating or shooting a black adult or child, easier than killing a white guy or white kid. The lone excuse Harvard could have for claiming black folks have it as easy as white folks have it is had it been proven black and white people get same treatment from USA cops.... Harvard will not run off a cliff. They are in business.

USA is racist.

All babies are the same. Skin and hair and facial do not relate to genetic intelligence in the homo sapiens. Do you know white infants have as much rhythm as black infants? I know you know I believe all this, all my life. I hope you have understood it is long, long ago proven, besides.

You have heard me tell that homo sapiens is at minimum 200,000 years old. That is far, far older than Caucasian or African or Asian races, of ancient homo sapiens.

If you argue Obama is Muslim and not Christian, this I don't know. It is appearing he was not born American, but was brought up to be C.I.A..

I do not understand what I am hearing of Muslim refugees flooding Europe and America and that many are dangerous. Will have to see better what is developing there, A factor is the

379

wide 9/11 Wars are wrecking nations, people do flee, praying to their maker to allow them and their children to enter countries that are not being bombed. You should not resent terrified non-combatants fleeing for their lives. But, another factor, a theory in fascism, is chaos makes humans easier to rule, in particular this should be the "useless eaters."

It all gets stranger.

Love,

Billy

Note from the narrator:

From The Prince Hope Show ...

A Salute To Veterans and Veterans Day.

Thank you, for all you do, for killing Six million American Indians.

For killing three thousand citizens of Panama in December 1989.

For murdering thousands, millions of people in Iraq. And Afghanistan, Yugoslavia, Hiroshima, Nagasaki, Vietnam.

You are American heroes.

You are not insane, psychotic killers who will do whatever anyone tells you to do.

You are Americans, through and through.

Thank you for all you have done and continue to do.

This Bud's for you.

Because revolution is evolution at its boiling point you cannot 'make' a real revolution any more than you can hasten the boiling of a tea kettle," Berkman wrote. "It is the fire underneath that makes it boil: how quickly it will come to the boiling point will depend on how strong the fire is."

Revolutions, when they erupt, appear to the elites and the establishment to be sudden and unexpected. This is because the real work of revolutionary ferment and consciousness is unseen by the mainstream society, noticed only after it has largely been completed.

Throughout history, those who have sought radical change have always had to first discredit the ideas used to prop up ruling elites and construct alternative ideas for society, ideas often embodied in a utopian revolutionary myth.

Once ideas shift for a large portion of a population, once the vision of a new society grips the popular imagination, the old regime is finished.

An uprising that is devoid of ideas and vision is never a threat to ruling elites.

By the time ruling elites are openly defied, there has already been a nearly total loss of faith in the ideas — in our case free market capitalism and globalization — that sustain the structures of the ruling elites. And once enough people get it, a process that can take years, "the slow, quiet, and peaceful social evolution becomes quick, militant, and violent," as Berkman wrote. "Evolution becomes revolution."

— Chris Hedges

FIFTY-EIGHT

Skylar and Rick sat at the coffee shop around the corner after watching the drone pictures.

"We knew this was going to happen," said Skylar.

"It's time."

Rick had been waiting a long time for her to say that. He made the call.

"We're going wireless," he said to the person answering the phone.

"As much as we can. It will take some time."

"Okay, sounds good.

"Thank you."

Lara set her phone on the table and smiled up at the waitress bringing their drinks.

She sat with Kaitylyn and Sara at The Green Mill in Saint Paul, about two, three blocks from Skylar and Rick. Remember Sara? From The Battle of Lake Wobegon? Other stuff, anyway Lara and Kaitylyn had been taking a working vacation, not much more drama than that, to get away, a stay-cation you could say, I wouldn't, to get a break, and to work on some of the things that Actually had sent them before he died in Oregon. It was all about Morse Code and Ham Radio because Actually figured, he knew, just like everyone else knew, that the government was listening to practically everything they said. He also showed them something else, and this is where Sara and a few others came in. They had set up a pretty cool computer room in the basement of a safe house and they had been planning something.

They finished their drinks and their pizza, so good, crunchy, and the tomatoes and green peppers and cheese, woah.

And so, they went to the basement, got set up, with their headsets, their diet Cokes, cigarettes. There were four of them on four computers at four desks, all set to go. Actually had showed them how to hack into the training programs for Air Force fighter programs at Fort Huachuca. All they had to do was wait for Kaitylyn to shut off the lights and ... *there you go.*

Sara dialed in, clicked, called it up, and there they were, all four of them, flying in formation, headed over the Arizona desert, Cochise County.

"Stay in form," said Sara.

"Put your lid down."

"We've got boogies."

"Bogies I think."

Sara felt her comrades on her wings and glared ahead at four looming buzzard-like aircraft.

She told John, Tim, and Mary to "disperse" high and low.

At Fort Hickman, in the training room, dark and the walls and floor and ceiling outfitted with dark sky or daytime for whatever conditions, the four trainees in the modules called out to each other.

"Who is that?"

"Is this real world or exercise."

"Are you friendlies?" one of the trainees asked.

"No, man," said Tim as he fired his canons.

"I'm hit, I'm hit," shouted one of the Air Force trainees.

"Good kill, great kid, don't get cocky," said Sara.

"He's on my six," said a CRUSHER rebel.

"Enemy lock, flares, out."

"We just lost Tucker."

"Copy that."

"I'm engaging," said Sara.

"Bandits, bandits," said John.

"We just lost Mary!" shouted Sara.

Sara bowed her head and reached out to hold Tim's hand. Tim squeezed.

"God-damn-it!" said Sara.

"Follow me!"

Sara shot out ahead of the others, straight through the enemy formation. She dived low, skimming the ground, then rising almost straight up to follow the lay of the land. She saw ahead of her a valley and buildings.

Sara saw other CRUSHERs at three o'clock and nine.

"Identify yourself," Sara heard in her headset.

"This is Sara. We are CRUSHER."

"Fucking douchebag," the trainee said.

"You're just gonna die. Go back where you came from."

"You goddamn idiot," said Sara, gritting her teeth and licking a sweat drop that had found its way to her mouth. She swerved left, then right, then shot up over a cactus-pocked mountainside.

She swooped out to take a wide angle, then turned back to face the Fort. She fired her rockets and watched their trail as they hit and exploded in the middle of the compound. The others in the group launched, destroying the Fort complex, the landing strips, the planes, trucks, soldiers scrambling, tanks, outer buildings and headquarters in the middle of a convex ring of buildings.

Sara shouted for joy and raised her fists into the air, then quickly grabbed her controls again.

"Hey."

Tim touched her arm. He pointed to Mary sitting two chairs down. Mary waved and smiled to Sara.

Sara smiled wide and ran over to hug Mary before scrambling back to her bird.

Bombing of ROTC buildings, Selective Service offices, and induction centers had been escalating for at least two years, and targets of political violence now included corporate giants most clearly identified with U.S. aggression and expansion: Bank of America, United Fruit, Chase Manhattan Bank, IBM, Standard Oil, Anaconda, GM. From early 1969 until the spring of 1970 there were over 40,000 threats or attempts and 5,000 actual bombings against government and corporate targets in the U.S., an average of six bombings a day. All but two or three of this orgy of explosions were aimed at property and not people; to me they were entirely restrained. Five thousand bombings, about six a day, and the Weather Underground had claimed six, total. It makes you wonder.

— Bill Ayers, *Fugitive Days*

FIFTY-NINE

Buster, Brandon, Jack, Jane, Bumper, Nick, Tayla were the Indy Group Brigade, wearing the Indy Brigade Special T-shirts: The Many faces of Darth Vader: Happy, Sad, Angry, Confused, Besmirched, Excited, Hyper, Nervous, Worried, Bored, Annoyed, Tired, Calm, with camo pants or shorts, camo socks, camo caps, orange tennis shoes.

It was their charge to spread a feeling of chaos and disorder among the population, to make people feel ill at ease, as if they were threatened, to oppose in any way they could, to spread the CRUSHER meme, and not get caught.

They ran in a pack on skateboards, on the train, the bus. They rented bicycles and rode them all over town, snaking this way and that, in sync, like a flock of blackbirds.

They followed people and traded off and traded back and sat by them at work and eating fast food and in the park, fishing, at church, trying to make everyone feel uncomfortable.

They keyed cars, poured paint, burned flags, tore down flags, did graffiti, murals, got up to speak at church without being asked, in movies, in cafes, and got away.

"Why not bombs, plant them and get away," said Brandon one day to Buster.

"We decided a long time ago we're not gonna do bombs," said Buster.

"Why?"

"We're just not."

They sat in a coffee shop, somewhere, anywhere, just not Dunn Bros., anything but Dunn Bros., which was over-running with undercover cops dressed as students these days. That was the word from Rick.

Buster showed Brandon the text he'd received:

"I read and had some trained psychologists read your emails and texts.

We have all come to the conclusion that your mental illness makes you a threat to yourself and others. You stand out like dog's balls. Kill yourself."

"Yeah, and so?" said Brandon.

"The point being?"

"The point being!" said Buster.

"Whatdyou mean? What is it? What the fuck is it?"

"It's probly just from a bank or something," said Brandon.

"Telemarketers, trying to get you to buy something. It's nothing."

"Are you fucking crazy? Did you even read what I showed you?" said Buster.

He showed the text again to Brandon.

Brandon appeared to read.

"Yeah, I read it," said Brandon.

"It's the death penalty," said Buster.

"And it's nothing?"

"I've heard of it," said Brandon.

"It's a meme, a thing, everybody's getting them."

"What?" said Buster.

"Really?"

"Yeah."

"You get one?" said Buster.

"No," said Brandon.

Buster left to get them both refills.

Brandon wasn't at their table. Buster looked around and found Brandon at a table two rows over.

"What's this?" said Buster.

"I just felt we should move," said Brandon, working his phone.

They sat in silence, each staring at their phones, both hands on the phones, at times sipping their coffee.

They sent texts back and forth to each other.

"It's not what I SHOULD do now," said Brandon, "with thoughts of reward, but what I would like to do, given it will make NO difference. I'm talking about the after-life."

"Yep," said Buster.

"Facebook is so fucked," said Brandon.

"It gets me down.

"What you don't see is the ninety-five percent of their lives that are boring and ordinary. The long days at work, the hours watching TV, the family quarrels," said Buster.

"Yep," texted Brandon.

Buster sent Brandon a link to an article on Living in the Now.

"Mindfulness," Buster said and turned to Brandon.

Brandon rolled his eyes. He hadn't received the text yet.

"Oh," he said. "Cool."

Brandon sent Buster a link showing the faces of soldiers, before and after, before they were in the military and after they came back from deployment.

"While there was likely intense suffering during those months, the images show that some made it out with that feeling of relief, and knowing they are still human. Others appear to be fully broken; they are displaced."

"That's gonna be us," said Buster.

"I know, right," said Brandon, actually anticipating the coming action and excitement.

"Hey, let's get outa here, huh?"

The space had quickly filled up with F.B.I. agents dressed as college students all listening to what Buster and Brandon were saying.

Buster and Brandon waited on the corner to see who would follow them out.

It was a girl who looked to be in junior high, wearing a robins-egg blue backpack. They sat on the bench, letting the bus go by as the girl got on.

Buster and Brandon had the idea that the others would go their own way today. They wanted to try their idea alone. In their backpacks and the gym bag that Buster carried were yard signs and plaques saying "Fuck The Police."

They took the bus to a nice, very nice part of the city. They meant to put up the signs but these houses were obviously watched constantly.

Rather, they walked over to the practically exact middle of the downtown where they put on their yellow vests and yellow hardhats, pulled from the gym bag, along with the hand tools they would need. They walked to the side of the bank on the corner, in the middle of the city. They set out one orange traffic cone. They tapped with the little hammer and screwed and even took a five-minute smoke break right there, until finally they had the plaque, very nice, actually, that said "Fuck The Police."

They waited in a coffee shop, texting until night to wait to return to the nice neighborhood and put up the yard signs.

Then they took out their spray paint and wrote on the side of a hip café the acronyms they had invented in order to confuse the police and the straight world about the new CRUSHER lingo: LLL, LoooLO, LMYTRYYY, ADHD, RALPH, etc.

Buster and Brandon were now exhausted, back in the coffee shop sitting silently together at a wooden table, cold coffee next to them, along with closed laptops, pens, paper wads, loose cigarettes and barbecue Fritos.

They sat in the middle of the room between a stately old brick wall and the glass front counter. Traffic passed all around them, people chatting, smiling, busy city people doing whatever it is they do.

Buster sent a group text to the other Indy group members.

"Nobody reads those," said Brandon.

"How ...?" said Buster's eyes.

"You sent to me, too," said Brandon.

"I'm not opening that."

The table behind Brandon emptied when the handsome grey haired couple got up and left, not tipping the barista, making sure to slide their shoes quickly on the mat on the way out, for what reason nobody will ever know.

Two men in suits took the empty table.

Buster got up and nodded to one of the tall men because he had smiled.

Brandon, his back to the men in suits, opened his laptop as Buster returned with a refill for himself only. Brandon didn't appear to mind or even notice.

The stately grey haired couple returned and marched straight to the front counter.

"This isn't right!" said the man, holding up the receipt as the woman stood right close by.

A helicopter hovered above, wap-wapping kind of loud, not as loud as you might think, maybe headed to a traffic accident.

The young woman at the counter studied the receipt.

"Yes, it is," she said, then repeated herself to be heard.

"It is not!" said the older woman, snatching the receipt out of the younger woman's hands as the older man pushed something on the counter that crashed on the floor, shattering.

Everyone in the café watched as they texted to friends and flashes went off from raised phones as the struggle at the counter escalated to shoving and throwing and grabbing, sliding on the slick floor and falling, then scrambling to get up, threats, promises, admonitions, corrections.

The older couple turned to leave, stopping at the door to let the two tall men in suits go first as the café crowd collected themselves, turned back to what they had been doing, calmed down as the excitement passed like an afternoon summer storm.

A pair of young women, headed up to pay, passed Buster and Brandon's table.

"Oh my God," one of the young women stopped.

She squatted to look at Buster — staring straight at Brandon as Brandon stared back — both of their mouths open, Buster's hands on his keyboard, Brandon's still holding his phone on the tabletop with both hands.

The young woman then so carefully reached to touch Buster's face with just her fingertips.

Then she saw the thin wire around Buster's neck, mostly hidden by the flesh, a uniform red cushion beginning to form all around the wire circle.

The young woman dropped to the floor like she'd been shot as her friend's hands leaped out toward Brandon as she noticed in his lap a little sign that said "Fuck The Police."

We call upon all the conscientious citizens of America to assist us in putting an end to the situation which threatens the lives of not only us, but every one of you.
— L.D. Barkley, a leader of the Attica rebellion, killed when guards and police stormed the prison yard, Sept. 13, 1971, 9:46 a.m.

SIXTY

"We need to engage them on the water, in the seas, on land, that's what she says."

As Buster and Brandon slumped in a coffee shop somewhere in Saint Paul, Rick was already talking as he squeezed uncomfortably into a booth in a coffee shop across town to meet with Lara and Kaitylyn.

He looked at Lara and Kaitylyn.

"What?" said Kaitylyn.

"Nothing. Just *damn*."

Lara and Kaitylyn were dressed in costumes.

Lara was the Pilgrim and Kaitylyn the Indian.

Rick was the turkey.

Their shit flowed way into the aisle and over into the space of those around them.

Kaitylyn was showing them on her phone the WANTED poster of she and Lara that had appeared on the front page of the newspaper back then and had been the reason for Skylar and Rick to take their places while they went underground — even though at first Skylar and Rick had been part of the group that had opposed the CRUSHER rebellion, saying there was no fucking way they were going to shoot a gun or try to kill someone.

Why did they come back?

I don't know. If I had to say I would say it was mostly because of their friendship with the CRUSHER people, probably that was the biggest part of it, not wanting to leave their friends out in the cold, so to speak, though they probly wouldn't put it that way, I will.

They got their stuff at Savers.

Lara and Kaitylyn hadn't been out in public that much since the front page publicity photo shoot.

393

And even if it wasn't exactly Thanksgiving time, it was close enough, the same century, Uptown, and that should be good.

But still, Kaitylyn and Lara argued because one of them felt people staring at them.

It's not Halloween. It's close enough. No it's not. Yes, but it is, you're highly emotional. What a loser. Bite me. You'd like that.

I thought you two got along?

We do.

That's stupid.

The water thing.

What water.

Umm, the world is like ninety percent water.

More like eighty.

"Yeah, okay, what water."

Lara looked out at the busy street.

"Houseboats," Skylar said.

"She suggests houseboats. It's the same as your whole hit 'em where they live attack the TV shows horsecrap ... I guess. Her words, not mine."

"Hey," said Lara, looking straight-on at Rick.

"It's great and all that you guys did this, but we are the ones really in charge."

"Uh-huh," said Kaitylyn.

"Well," said Rick.

"Actually not really."

"Kinda-sorta-maybe ... I think so! He-lloooo!" said Kaitylyn.

"Can't we all just get along?" said Rick, half sarcastically, the other not.

"Just think. It might be fun."

"Fun?" said Lara.

"Yeah, fucking fun," said Kaitylyn, looking away, looking anywhere but right here.

"We need to take the battle to all venues, and that means we need to have a navy, fight them on the water," Rick repeated Skylar's most recent mantra.

"Fight them on the water," said Lara.

"Hmmm," buzzed Kaitylyn, making fun by putting a finger to her temple, not catching that Lara had moved on and was now seriously considering the idea.

"What about Waldo?" asked Lara.

"That could work," said Rick.

"Who is Waldo?" said Kaitylyn.

"Wa ..." began Lara.

"Waldo is an enigma," said Rick.

"He is, what is he?"

Rick looked at Lara.

Lara fiddled with the gold square on her hat that just was not quite right.

Rick threw his wattle over his shoulder, scratched his armpit under his wing.

"He's been doing some *special* work for us," said Lara, using air quotes.

"He just might be interested in something like this," said Lara.

"Who is Waldo," said Kaitylyn.

"Waldo is an older gentleman who does repair work for CRUSHER. He was also the fix-it man at the group home, and he sat in on a lot of their planning meetings. He got fired for drinking. We pay him cash. So it doesn't screw up his Social Security," said Rick.

"I know him!" shouted Kaitylyn.

"His name's not Waldo. I can't think of it."

She scratched her headdress.

"Better that you didn't," said Rick.

"Prince is trying to get everyone in the world on his Twitter," said Lara.

Kaitylyn just shook her head.

"He's been working on that for a while," said Rick.

"We've received some of his emails, they're horrendous. He's losing it. I wonder if he's looked into assisted living."

"Yep," said Lara.

"Once he gets everyone, we're skee-rewed," said Kaitylyn.

Rick and Lara just stared at Kaitylyn.

"What?" said Kaitylyn.

"Nothing," said Lara.

"We've been skee-rewed for a long time," said Rick.

"Oh," said Kaitylyn.

I know, Ma. I'm a-tryin'. But them deputies. Did you ever see a deputy that didn't have a fat ass? An' they waggle their ass an' flop their gun aroun'. Ma, he said, if it was the law they was workin' with, why we could take it. But it ain't the law. They're a-working away at our spirits. They're a-tryin' to make us cringe an' crawl like a whipped bitch. They're tryin' to break us. Why, Jesus Christ, Ma, they comes a time when the on'y way a fella can keep his decency is by takin' a sock at a cop. They're working on our decency.

— John Steinbeck, *The Grapes of Wrath*

SIXTY-ONE

A tall, college student type man sat in Dunn Bros. in the university area, someone who must not have gotten the memo about the F.B.I. and others staking out all the Dunn Bros. and that they were off limits for CRUSHER by order of Rick.

He wore a blaze orange T-shirt with a Che image of Alfred P. Newman saying, "What, Me Worry?"

He sat at an old wooden table in the enormous back area, working on his computer, his back to most of the room, mostly empty.

The tall, young man wore a patch over one eye, walked with a limp when he went to get refills, hummed a song to himself, always, always, something, and every minute or so seemed to stop breathing, then miraculously or so it seemed, kept going. He had a mole on one cheek that if it were somewhere else would be perfect, you do not even notice the eye patch, but it was not, perfect, the mole, and it made you want to just scootch it just one-eighteenth of an inch, but you couldn't and so the young man drove everyone that he knew pretty much stark raving mad, so he sat alone with his back to the crowd in the back room at Dunn Bros. wearing a bright orange T-shirt with his jeans and tennis shoes.

The tall, thin young man worked at his computer, humming while behind him the room filled in, all the tables, most of the chairs at all of the tables, regular type people is what they were.

He got up to leave, take a whiz, get coffee, something, and left his computer on, facing the room.

After he was gone just a little while, one person walked by his computer quite randomly and not on purpose and paused to look at the computer screen. The tall, thin young man was taking awhile. Two more people pushed away from their tables to go stand and look at his computer screen, bend low, squat, look closer, pull out pads and write something.

When the young man returned he saw a group standing by his

computer studying his screen. The young man paused and turned away, walked to the counter to order an entirely different sort of coffee than he had been drinking previously or even ever before.

When he returned to his computer and his chair and table he sat, while those in the seats and at the tables behind him continued with their regular conversations.

He hummed a song, quite possibly whatever had been playing out in the other room as he got his new coffee. He worked at his screen, adjusting commas here and there, but it was mostly good and done.

His screen showed, inside sort of an orange border with an official looking CRUSHER letterhead, dated for the following day, and proclaiming "TOP SECRET: LLL/RALPH ... FOR EYES ONLY."

From Commander Actually, Supreme Adjutant of the Large Force
To all CRUSHER Brigades:

They kill the leaders of other countries, they lie to us, take our money, kill the leaders of our country, make us pay taxes for the military to go kill other people and no-body fights them? Nobody? How is that?

And so we fight.

And today we take the fight to these United States towns and cities, that they might feel the wrath of the world they have bombed and murdered.

CRUSHER troops will this morning attack with prejudice:

Raccoon City, South Park, Springfield, Genoa City, Hill Valley, 17230 Valley Spring Road in the San Fernando Valley of Los Angeles.

CONTINUED:

Dogpatch, Eastwick, Elwood City, Fife, Alabama, Frostbite Falls, Grover's Corners, Mudville, Okefenokee, Springfield, USA, Genoa City, Jericho, Millennium City, and overseas, Surrey, Emerald City.

Right now CRUSHER troops are headed toward these locations.

Citizens should prepare to either join the revolution or defend yourselves.

We Are CRUSHER.

Commander Actually

The tall young man, having finished his work, closed his computer, packed it away, tossed his coffee cup, and walked out, as a giant squeak rang out in the big room as all the people pushed back their chairs to stand, to shout, to talk, to call, to hurry out the door and rush into waiting cars, to be hit by oncoming traffic.

Note from the narrator:

From The Prince Hope Show ...

And now for another episode of "The Lives Of The Cowboys."

We see Duke and Bubba Carl sitting in the squad car on the curb, staring straight ahead.
Bubba Carl can sleep with his eyes open.
"Like a fish," says Duke.
Duke can eat two packs of Strawberry Twizzlers in ten minutes.
"Without opening the plastic," says Bubba Carl.
Duke and Bubba Carl came on duty at 730 am.
Throughout the morning they saw a banker walk past and smile carrying a bushel basket of folding money.
They saw George Bush steal two elections and watched The Dancing Israelis as the towers came down. They watched the Sandy Hook Show and the Boston Bombing hoax.
And in the afternoon, after lunch and lunch nap, they stormed out of the squad car to tackle a guy running down the street with a loaf of bread.

... The basic tool for the manipulation of reality is the manipulation of words. If you can control the meaning of words, you can control the people who must use the words.

... Strange how paranoia can link up with reality now and then.

... We live in a society in which spurious realities are manufactured by the media, by governments, by big corporations, by religious groups, political groups. I ask, in my writing, 'What is real?' Because unceasingly we are bombarded with pseudo realities manufactured by very sophisticated people using very sophisticated electronic mechanisms.

... The trouble with being educated is that it takes a long time; it uses up the better part of your life and when you are finished what you know is that you would have benefited more by going into banking.

... It is sometimes an appropriate response to reality to go insane.

... The Martians are always coming.

... Reality is that which, when you stop believing in it, doesn't go away.

... This, to me, is the ultimately heroic trait of ordinary people; they say no to the tyrant and they calmly take the consequences of this resistance.

... The core of my writing is not art but truth.

— Philip K. Dick

SIXTY-TWO

Rick, Lara, and Kaitylyn sat in the headquarters, now Skylar's office. "So, yeah, who is the boss?" said Kaitylyn.

"We are," said Lara.

"What? *You* are?" said Skylar as she entered the room carrying a tray of coffees.

"Of course," said Lara.

Skylar sat the tray down without speaking.

Rick got up to pass out the steaming cups, all white with orange CRUSHER logo.

Rick then worked to set up his laptop, connected with the screen on the wall. He shut out the lights and they watched as he showed them how the Fake Venue project was working.

"See here," he said.

He showed mainstream news reports of suspected violence around the country, "domestic terrorism by people radicalized on the internet."

He showed video from CRUSHER scouts of long lines of military vehicles on the freeways.

"They're trying to find Dogpatch and Frostbite Falls," said Kaitylyn.

"Wow," said Lara.

"Amazing," said Skylar.

"Actually, actually lives," said Rick.

"So, where's Waldo?" said Lara.

"Nobody knows," said Skylar.

"Nobody?"

"Nobody."

I guess I want to insert something here about our CRUSHER rebels. Just totally my opinion, but I have always wondered about their motivation. How could they feel so devoted to this big idea. Is it because they met this disabled guy a long time ago and he inspired them? Yes, that's part of it. And he must have touched something that was already deep inside of them. And he was killed. They want to avenge his death or make it be for something. I wonder if it isn't also something more weird than that, because that's all pretty normal stuff, not really enough, in my opinion, to allow you to risk your life and the big one, to kill someone else. Still not enough. Maybe they thought they were super heroes, with their T-shirts, dressed up like the make-believe TV wrestlers. Maybe they bought into all that more than they thought, or that I thought before. Maybe they were all crazy and coincidentally came to this one place to work and found each other and voila group lunacy. Who knows? I guess everyone, disabled and not, has fantasies. Hmm. But in the end we are just us, which is normal, which is fine. I wonder if it's a good thing to realize that, or not.

Anyway, where's Waldo.

Well. I know something about that.

The tires of Waldo's old pickup, kind of a green, kind of not, rumbled over the rocks of the little road that ran behind the docks where the people in town parked their boats. Right here was the houseboat section. He got two wheels over in the grass. He pulled his lunchbox with him and grabbed his toolbox and shotgun out of the box, so he walked toward the boat with his hands full and his 12-gauge under one arm.

He wore a new CRUSHER T-shirt and new CRUSHER ball cap and camo pants that Skylar had suggested he purchase.

Waldo walked right to where he needed to go, down the line of boats to the one with the wooden sailfish on the hull and under that: Home Free.

He set all of his stuff down on the old wood to get to one knee and reach for the key on the underside of the dock. There it was, right there.

Well, that was something, he thought. He liked most of the kids he'd met at the group home, but he didn't really trust these CRUSHER types to know what they were doing. They didn't know how to fix anything.

The one they were calling Waldo Waterman made the little hop from the dock to the boat, got settled in, opened up the house, checked out the controls, the motor, the lights. Everything seemed to be okay, not great. He'd never really been in a houseboat. This one seemed very homemade, but with all you need, even chairs and a sofa, a radio, some dishes. These folks were smokers. He went around collecting the ashtrays and put them in a plastic bag he found under a cabinet. He took down the American flag hanging wet and droopy on the little pole and strung up his own Chicago Bears flag.

He fired it up, gave it the gas and roared away from the dock, making a lot of noise for so little motion, so much smoke.

He got going, in neutral, the motor and paddles working hard, like a big, fat dog to save his life, gave the plastic bag with the ashtrays a heave, and set the shotgun up on a counter by the helm where he could find it.

Waldo settled in, feet up at the wheel, opened his lunch, ate the baloney sandwich, saved the chips for a snack, had coffee, waved at some people he was supposed to know by being in this boat apparently. The scene was just as you would imagine, water, shoreline, perfectly nice sunset. It takes some concentration, some awareness, a bit of work to appreciate when things are that perfect and I'm not entirely sure if Waldo was into that.

Then he shut it down.

It had been his plan to spend the night right there at the dock and he kept to the plan. For as long as he could stand it he sat out on his deck perhaps admiring the moon, the stars sitting flat on the water. He might have fished.

Waldo started very early in the morning, got coffee going, maybe some toast, fired up the motor, let it idle while he checked his ropes, that sort of thing.

When it was time he gunned it, then backed off, found a steady pace where he was comfortable. He jerry-rigged a way to steer with the mop bucket and mop, the handle, then climbed up top where he already had things ready, a place to stand, his shotgun, binoculars, metal coffee pot from the kitchen.

There was some fog, not much, and there it was, another houseboat, his rival on the high seas.

Steady as she goes, he said out loud to himself, pulled the shotgun to his chest, held it under his arm and began to wave like the star of the parade in response to the ten and more people waving from over there.

Waldo studied the other boat, very much factory made with all the bourgeoisie accouterments, the diving board, outdoor bar, barbecue, the padded deck chairs, the jet skis, the tanned people, as compared to his water-logged trailer park.

Waldo let his mop handle first mate keep the steady course headed straight for the fancy boat. He saw the name on the side: The Mothership, and apparently many or all the bosses and landlords he's ever had.

The people waving with one hand and in the other hand holding a drink began waving with both hands over their heads. Their captain gunned it and began to pull away from Waldo's head-on collision course as Waldo commenced firing, even though he was still too far away for a shotgun. What a full, hardy, serious sound it made.

He fired and pumped the gun and reloaded and drew closer by the minute. The other boat, the motor straining, smoking, throwing up an aft Niagara Falls, edged out of the way as the Home Free just skimmed past, Waldo now hanging over the railing, firing point-blank twelve-gauge blasts, one in particular directed at a young man with red swimming trunks and black hair and now a fist-sized hole in the middle of his back, his mouth and eyes so wide.

The deck of the The Mothership ran a watery red, sloshing back and forth with the waves.

The people screamed and cursed and threw chairs at Waldo.

He kept re-loading and firing as he pulled away. The barbecue had spilled and the boat was now on fire. Some of the people had jumped into the water, some were swimming away and some were hanging over the side, arms stretched toward the water, deceased.

Waldo reached for his binocs and spotted a flotilla of more houseboats in the distance.

He climbed down to adjust his mop to full speed and headed right to them, went to the bathroom to take a dump, turned up the radio in there to country, got his chips and bounced lightly straight to his perch.

Note from the narrator:

From The Prince Hope Show ...

And once again, we hear from Randall in Stevens Point:
"I'm really not talking to any a you, 'cause you know why.

I can't get onto that health insurance website. I can't wait three hours on hold. Who can do that? I'm an action-type guy.

There's just no point in even havin' a job now.

I got my gun, my dog Bubba Tom, my truck.

I told you I'm heading for the woods, then up the mountain.

And that's where I am – right now. I can see y'all from right here, through my scope.

Don't worry, I got the safety on. ... Ok, it's on now.

Tell Bubba Jean I always loved her.

Don't follow me. I got on my camo jeans. You'd never find me.

When you hear about the big shoot-out and all that, then that'll probly be me.

The United States is the greatest threat mankind has ever experienced on the planet.

Just sayin'.

SIXTY-THREE

Mike,
Kelly and I have been doing morning dog walks together, as his new big puppy has big needs. Kelly yet has old Bo, very old, who comes. This morning round normal time to begin the walk Kelly called, from the nearest trailer and property for poor renters that he and Bonnie have had. I think, Kelly/Bonnie want to sell all of Bonnie's cheap rentals. Maybe you know, more in the loop. Past couple or more years Kelly talks in fragmented sketching. Muttering and oaths. Hard for me to follow, and he is irritable, thinks I should know exactly where this place is, being I and my then 2 dogs lived a short period there, overseeing. 2 or 3 decades back. I was today curious, what was he doing there, where exactly is it. He said it is an hour away, he told me the name, always I forget the name of this settlement or township, though I and dogs lived there briefly over 25 years ago. Right now, "with a tarp," this problem renter, who is broke but on property, "with 'some' other homeless people," is burdensome. I said, OK, OK, Kelly, I am just curious. We can talk about it later. Two days ago I have been asking is this guy and homeless friends on top of the tarp or under it. I had heard of the situation condensed, did not then or now find is the guy and homeless amigos under the tarp or atop it. Just curious, Kelly. Bill, this is no fun! Alright, alright, we will talk later! Yeah, later!

"The President has his war, nobody knows what it's for."

Wrong. The Rulers know.

Since that rock'n roll song - ah, jazz. Think it is AS COMPARED TO WHAT? Fabulous licks, and I forget the musicians' names, famous. You may know. You remember the names better. When here you spoke of this guy's name last year on the TV jazz, old guy, unfamiliar to me that day, later I remembered his name, great guy. Ah, Art Farmer? Anyhoo, when AS COMPARED TO WHAT was cashing in, I was with 2 dogs in car at Venice Beach. I tell of it in THE EMERYVILLE WAR. Homeless folks living in cars as I was were abundant and I spoke of what when they have no cash to get the vehicle fixed a little. In that little novel I mention dodging cops, locking car to be sleeping in weeds and dog snuggle, getting to THE EMERYVILLE WAR. Clearly homelessness was increased. Now it is quite increased. War works for the miniscule few. Not even USA infra-structure, construction jobs these days. The rest is brain wash. Bridges, tunnels, highways and dams. I knew it in the nineties. Way, way before I heard of Mike Novak, Jim Kessler, Susan Lindaeur, Mae Brussell. 2 or 3 decades earlier, hell, all of the seventies, eighties, nineties, get used to it. If you tell Caryl Jones that Bill only listens to Kessler, what if she thinks you know what you say?

I start to drink, Bill is crazy. Either way you like it. I figure this week Mike Blackbird has not dementia, exactly. It was/is a bad connection.....Heh, our friends who have no clue think you are functional and well and Bill is.... some kind of other...uh...different....

Or see Bill's record.

Or who cares.

ONWARD THROUGH THE BOILING FROGS,
     Bill

Good morning or could it be middlin' fair. I suddenly see your last note to me, inside this long train of stuff - Caryl's stuff - wonder why I cannot find yours separate somewhere. Well, in order to respond to it, I'll do so here where I saw it, others can see your latest, if they find it interesting. After this one though, I hope to start fresh.

Hum, just drinking coffee, maybe I had seen this later one from you yesterday. I am tired of this.

You go round and round. Maybe this last bunch of silly shit you had brought up 9/11 or related - Caryl says maybe Mike is tired of 9/11.

A thing you repeat, and I often ignore it when you repeat it, is your asking me for proof in these things, telling me that I never offer proof.

We have not enabled do that, Mike. Oh, like we did the mini video, 9/11 TRUTH IN 9 MINUTES, years ago, and you could not understand anything, said the Muslims did it.

I can say, were you to hear what I try to relate in a quickie soundbite, and I am honest and versed, well over a decade for me already, then you would be hearing a detail for your first time.

Possibly you vaguely recall my complaining you do not hear....

We are not truly debating, because you muddy waters and blow up tree stumps and toss in smoke grenades. You truly have no courage in the subject matter, and you know nothing of these matters.

It never registers with you I am only sincere, of course intensely, am who I am.

I am interested in no game. For you it is a game. And yet, you cannot hear. Yet, you never care to know that after all these years I must know things....

....Last night in bed I had to squirt a mosquito or two a few times, lay wondering was I just being mean, upsetting people using this word "dementia." How demented is Mike? I will this morning take that word back, or for a few years, but incredibly you offer argument when you have not made a logical connection. You prefer no substance, blow up another old stump. Yesterday or was it a day before yesterday, you proffered this treatise on the demolition of modern skyscrapers. I went indignant, impatient, bored with it. Amazed you imagine in these years Truthers do not discuss it all. But they surely do. They go far past that bit, Mike. Years now, Truthers are looking closely at all of it, up and down and all around, lava still ran in the ground months later, it became realized mini-nukes were used.

Planes were registered, were not there, only holograms. See the hologram enter the building as if the building is a bank of fog. See, now you go blank.

You don't want the information. You do not know what I am doing, why am I obsessive, how can I say we are in fascism, 9/11 Wars are wrecking nations, bleeding this nation. But please do not toss in flapdoodle. I don't want to wreck your little world, but do not toss in flapdoodle. Flapdoodle is a type of disrespect. Just because I let a lot of flapdoodle go unanswered does not mean you got any points. I am not in the game.

Love,

Bill

Geoffrey,

The Mexican black bean I like much, the kidney (red) bean, the pinto bean, are of a group, similar to other red bean types in Mexico, as must be the expensive bean you can purchase in Japan.

Mike and I are not angry, if annoyed. We never avoid one another. He's tough enough. I do not care to rattle my siblings, will tolerate their mindlessness and Taboo-Speak, but while I write my general police state observations in the Postings, sometimes Mike will remark. It is insulting to me my siblings who know quite zero about 9/11 want to assume I am a fool following fools. Neither has even taken a 9/11 look, Geoffrey. It offends me they know me this poorly. How many years now. How many. And I learn more, be learning more.

Once we were hippies. I wondered then, looking at my roped in parents, how ever can a generation gap like this be. Well, sir. Here we are again. My siblings are roped in exactly as were our parents. Not sure about you, but you need to watch yourself.

The Obama administration my siblings admire and they think themselves Democrats and the Obama administration has continued the Bush administration agenda except even worse. Probably you know Obama imprisons more Whistleblowers who have not broken USA laws, far more than any administration before his. The Patriot Act is purely fascist. Homeland Security.

The official USA account of 9/11 is pitiful, physical impossibility.   But its agenda is conquer these ragged Muslim nations. These years, look at it.   Murder of noncombatants. Perhaps my siblings who believe their leaders, believe as they are told this is War against Terror. I surely fucking hope they do not think this. Of course I cannot talk to them on these matters. So what the fuck do they think?   Geoffrey, I think they can't think. Can Geoffrey think?

CAN'T THINK. My father and I were riding along to some destination and he was thinking (before he changed) we were having to stop the commies in Vietnam or they would continue the "domino effect," take countries on Earth one by one.   We will stop them in Vietnam before they get to the Americas.

Billy Frank: How would they get here?

My irritated father had no answer.

My siblings have no answer. Last time Kelly and I on dog walk had raised voice I asked what did he think, about these 9/11 Wars, killing kids in several nations at once, naturally kill more kids than adults because there are more kids than adults. Kelly at that point was angry, gone blank, quite possibly he could not hear what I said. Next day or so I apologized to Kelly for getting loud, and we get along but I think he has not ever wondered about Obama's wars. Kids. Uh, collateral damage.

Geoffrey. This is sick. 9/11 Wars.

You and others may say you hope to live in peace, not deal with all this. Then let us push human dignity to a side. The Masters of War, Oil Men, Military Industrial and all, already were rich.

They alone profit. You and my siblings get poorer. When do Mike B. and I get severed from social security. Wha? Fucking anytime now I presume.

Hokay, Bill laughs. I was ever so. Any demon any time I look into its eyes. Har hardehar har.

Come on then.

Whee, OK. Guess my letter is ended.

Oh. I have seen Hillary has a couple of doubles. Younger, thinner. Not certain as to the one who debated Trump, yet. Can't get there yet on low energy except before 8 A.M...till the 14th etc.

One thing Kessler did was pull up that Paul McCartney of the Beetles died and this other guy took over, did very well, name of Faul, means fake Paul. Faul is several inches taller, different teeth, ears and so on. It has been done, will be done, the ants are stupid. Stupid has meant "happy," but this will shift.

PAST THE FROGS,

Bill

Bix,

Thanks for word. People are dying. I think I never met Sonny.

Am up early, a bit blank. We were rained in yesterday, but sun later came out and Kelly and I will probably make it in for groceries, after dog walk today. Then I'll fix new wine and maybe trim some bud I had to pull because of a porcupine's daily damage. Have some vodka then and maybe find more to say.

I did yesterday listen again to this year old The Real Deal, #103.   Who Was Responsible and Why....#103, with Dennis Cimino, is thorough. The entire truth from one year ago.... As well, Bix, #103 is captivating. But Kessler's audios are captivating for me.

Meantime the USA economy has bled much, for the Bankers, Oil Men, Military Industrial. The billionaires have done badly, conquering the Middle East and North Africa, maybe they can never fix USA Infrastructure.

I wonder what this means. Our fascists continue with the False Flag efforts. What can they be thinking.

Further,

Bill

Bill:

I think I read some stuff written by James Kessler couple years back.

But, right now, I'm pretty busy.

I'd appreciate it if you pass this on: This is a bad time for me. I'm leaving Colorado, probably, by late October. It is not easy. The Colorado mountains are my home much more than Texas or, California.

But, I'm old and not a good mountaineer any more. And, besides, Kelly could use a hand, mending fence and doing chores on the Blackbird ranch. I like the Bandera area. It's ok. It's where I'll spend the rest of my life.

I have never been interested in conspiracy theories. In general, what I see there is the making of assumptions from inadequate evidence. Lots of people do this, not just conspiracy guys. It is a national failing.

I have very little interest in politics, local, state or, world-wide. I have never spent much time thinking on that subject. Science is a lot more interesting than politics.

There is much to do. I have old friends to say goodby to, affairs to manage, things to end. Plus, I'm trying to get rid of most of my possessions. Moving to Texas, I need to travel light.

Tell your friends that I appreciate their offer. It is polite to invite me into the conversation. However, I have no interest. I am leaving Colorado, a place that I love. Saying goodby is hard.

I have to concentrate on this, right now.
            Mike Blackbird

Steve,

Just tthen I said to Mike Blackbird in his pretense James Kessler had not spoken to him, maybe Griggs or Vaughn could bother to see this of nearly two hours showing it is not Truthers who are delusional. This material is sound. I guess this is the problem. The Real Deal #103. A year back.

Perhaps I should not have started a note to you. Too disgusted.

Am asthmatic, got buds, booze, need both badly, we have been rained in today.

Had you noticed, Kessler has asked Mike B. to join him and Denis Cimino on Web radio? I was surprised, glad to hear. Second time Kessler a dynamic busy hero shows interest in Mike Blackbird. Feh.

If we can maybe get into HEB tomorrow I will also get vodka.

Yas, I am aware, gringos to look at 9/11 risk their thin shelled egg of chicken. Fugit. All they knew is not real.

B.E Blackbird suffered this, changed his mind about Vietnam and joined his kids. Said to me: Son, it was hard for me to come around to this.

I had no sympathy, no understanding of my poor father. In Vietnam his USA lost. They poisoned the environment best they could. And lost. Billy Frank has no sympathy for inhumane mistakes from family or anyone else.

Once we were hippies. I wonder what we are now.

Further Out, I Must Smoke Pot,

    Bill

Geoffrey,

Always follow your zest.

I guess we are still having the drone program. Lately in Syria it happened NATO took an advantage of forty something of the Syrian government troops in a place and killed them. Past couple days Syrian government had thirty or so NATO troops in a place and killed them. I hear there were Israelis and some USA special troops then taken out. For we who are less subjective, facts run in a river. But at this date on the Web is plenty freak out.

Inclusive of we have this USA segment hollering to hit them, and I have read Hillary says this. I never thought taking to the street is much help. We do have other selections. We have the Net.

I am no guide. I never liked being here.

Be conscious. Awake.

Love,

    Bill

OK, Bill, noted.

I keep all you say in my head, allow it to congeal. So, it is there, even if I don't feel the urgency in my gut as strongly as you. The pieces are there, and I can amass them if the need to take action infects me. I have always said that I agree with you that the drone program is a disturbing path to go down, and I don't give Obama a pass on that one. He does have the blood of many innocents on his hands from that. I hope Hillary would not think that nuking would be an option. If nuking around the world were to begin, I suppose Japan would not be spared.

But, my daily reality needs my attention now. I know you speak always with sincerity, so I do appreciated your efforts, as frustrating as it must all be for you.

Love, Geof

Geoffrey,

Telling you of "US Redux in Syria," I had been up early and taken a chill, before sun came out, and in the above note about Debbie Lusignan I misprinted "You" for "She" in "She gets riled in this one."

Quite the chill I took, I found out, walking Choyota in the sun. Should have put on my down jacket in order to do the email. Kelly missed this one because his big pup would not let him peacefully drink coffee first, says he has to figure how to work this routine better. Janus did go with them in the instance.

Welp, since here I am again, I'll do the 30 minutes of ax time to warm up in the sun, see about adding any thought. I have been wishing to applaud your interest in photography, keep forgetting to say I do hear you there.

Lyla all my life told me I am "one track minded." We are what we are.

Steve says he is a painter. Yes, he is. I am not saying anybody needs to go to rallies, marches, go public. I do not go public. Hell no, scared a shitass cop might act bold for his others.

I can, in my solitude, find the visionaries, Novak, Kessler, Lusignan, these who expose our fascist government for confused USA citizens. Inspire dialogue. Without brainwash, 9/11 Wars would not exist. Fellow citizens of shitland need not mimic Billy Frank and quit Sunday School and High School and the USA Navy (one month, asthma solved my problem) and college, one month, Pan America if I remember. Edinburg, Texas, my father footed that bill. Long stories.

Why I am very angry is as I quote Jesse Ventura: WHY CAN'T WE TALK ABOUT IT?

Wha! We can't talk about it? What the fuck is this? A police state?

Yeh. So, who do you kill?

Just pull in sunshine. SUNSHINE. Dry up the maggots. DRY THEM UP.

Aw. We can't just speak of pleasantries?

You got it, MAGGOT HEAD. You want maggots of the mind forever? SO WHAT MAGGOTS EAT GERMS. I refer to maggots of the mind, the human spirit. GET REAL. My grandchildren will not respect authority. Who ever did say heroes are not born, I can say heroes are born, easy to say, but, I am not talking about heroes, feh. I am saying my grandkids will not get ruled. Whether my siblings stay ruled.

Breaking my chill this date has been slow. Breeze is down and sun is out. Guess we had a little norther. Finishing up bottle of SKYY- only lasts 3 days at this point. Oh, two and a half.

We are what we are. When I was 13 I quit Christianity and Sunday School. I had slow physical development but age 14 in high school I would shake up the B-Team, younger footballers going to their games, profess atheism, subject them to naught ever told them before.

I have said, I did have other consideration than the Sunday School. Spirit is larger than religion from puny man. Sure, the A string jackoffs well knew me. They would do this or that.

The B-String coach had maggots of the mind. He would not start me and I quit. Then I did high school Golden Gloves and could have whipped anybody at APHS, I have spoken of this. By time I weighed 150.

Now I have siblings who have forgotten who I am. Kind of tragic, a good story. Give me a drink. I have grandkids, other work.
    Love,
        Bill

They're worse than the brownshirts and the communist element and also the nightriders and the vigilantes. They're the worst type of people we harbor in America. I think we are up against the strongest, well-trained, militant, revolutionary group in America.

— James Rhodes, Governor of Ohio, 1970

Having found the atomic bomb, we have used it. It is an awful responsibility that has come to us. We thank God that it has come to us and not to our enemies. And we pray that he may guide us to use it in His ways and for His purposes.

— Harry S. Truman, President of the United States

SIXTY-FOUR

Jim and Danny sat in a small café in a small town in a fairly large state. It was morning, not early, but not nearly noon.

Jim read out loud the text he'd just received from Kaitylyn telling what she knew about what Waldo had done on the lake.

"Sea battle. Geezuz. I heard they was talkin' 'bout somethin' like this. Fuck."

"He's wearing a CRUSHER T-shirt?" said Danny.

"I guess."

A moment passed as Jim decided how much to tell Danny.

They drank coffee, tried and tried not to hear the conversations around them.

"What was that?"

Jim asked Danny about some people talking over closer to him that Jim could not quite hear.

"Oh. They're talking about Waldo, everybody is. They say he's a son-of-a-bitch who deserved to die.

"I'm translating of course," said Danny.

"That's fucked-up," said Jim.

Prince Hope sat on a sofa drinking coffee with the hosts on a morning talk show on the TV high on the wall.

Jim and Danny had found out that, because of the Waldo incident, Rick and Skylar had gone away, probably to her parents' lake cabin, and Lara and Kaitylyn had returned to hiding.

"Look."

Jim showed Danny his phone, on it a selfie of a dejected homemade Eyore and Winnie the Pooh having coffee.

"That's them," said Jim as Danny handed back the phone.

"That's creepin' me out. It's pretty much fuckin' fallin' apart," said Jim.

"Ah'm fuckin' scared," Jim growled, staring over the top of his cup at nothing.

"Fuck it," said Danny.

"Yeah, fuck it," said Jim.

"We should do something," said Danny.

"Yeah, fuck," said Jim.

"No, we fuckin' should," said Danny.

Jim craned his neck to try to see out onto main street and wherever the bank was.

"Not that," Danny grabbed Jim's arm.

"Remember all your shit," said Danny, "Wild West, Bonnie and Clyde, Dillinger, George Washington, Che Guevara, Malcolm X, all that shit.

"Now is the time. Now is your time. You are in it, right now," said Danny.

"And you have to focus. You can get scared, but don't run, stay put and focus."

"Awright," said Jim, gripping his coffee mug with both hands.

"Perfect," said Danny. "Hey."

"When I was in college, I sat at the little table in the kitchen of the trailer house me and this other guy were renting. I was drinkin' and had my hands on the keys and I was saying I was gonna write the truth about the JFK thing. How did I even know there was somethin' else? I don't know, maybe I saw the Zapruder on TV or somethin' 'cause there wasn't nothin' nowhere else, nothin'."

"What'd you do?" said Jim.

"Nothin', said Danny, "nothin', but that night I remember I was really gonna."

"Yeah, and?" said Jim.

"And that was my time and I let it go past, whoosh!"

Danny ran an airplane hand close over his head.

"Don't do that, man."

"Yeah, okay," said Jim.

"Ya gotta think of somethin', man," said Danny.

They sat and watched traffic out the window, got more coffee, listened to the clatter in the kitchen, the talk of the people around them and once in a while the laughter of the people on the TV high on the wall. They smelled sausage, mmm.

"I'm not nice, I never was. I get sick of that," said Jim.

"Oh, I don't think that's ..." said Danny.

"It's how people fucking see me, I guess. I'm just afraid. When I stop being afraid, that's when I always get into trouble. I'm not careful, I say things," said Jim.

Danny sipped his coffee and looked around.

"That's pretty deep, man," said Danny.

"Yeah, buddy," said Jim.

"Hey," Danny smiled as he began.

"How about this for the opening line of a book, huh?

"When I understood, I am an alien. Huh? What the fuck? Would you read that book?"

"Fuck yeah, I guess," said Jim.

They sat for a while more, then Danny produced a weathered paperback from somewhere, went to where he had the page folded over and began to recite.

"The people are the key base to be secured and defended."

"Hey!"

Jim reached across and Danny pulled the book out of his reach.

"Not here, man," Jim hissed.

Holding the book out of Jim's reach, Danny continued to read, now louder.

"... rather than territory won or enemy bodies counted."

He looked at Jim for a sign of understanding.

"Hey! Dude. Che lost in Bolivia because the people didn't give a fuck. That's the same as here."

"So?" said Jim.

"Well?" said Danny

"Yeah," said Jim.

Danny got up, walked away and returned with a newspaper. He unfolded it, paged through it, recited some sports scores out loud. He offered part of the paper to Jim.

Jim shook his head and got up to piss.

When he returned Danny was poking the paper with a finger like a penurious serial killer and trying to show him before Jim even got sat down.

"Here, here, look, look here," said Danny.

"Ahh, nah," said Jim, "let's just get outa here, c'mon, let's go."

"You gotta see this, no really," said Danny.

"Yeah, what," said Jim, spinning the paper around toward him.

He read.Seemingly with his nose he read about a story about a local man who had written a letter to the editor of this same little paper.

"... we spend the money on this monument rather than on our schools so that we might further tell lies to our children? Bush, no WMD, attacked Iraq and Afghanistan based on lies, and the lies continue, daily. The Bush government itself did 9/11. The troops went to Iraq for no reason whatsoever except to steal oil and conquer. It was not to protect freedom. It was not heroic. We put up monuments to fools and murderers. ... Just make sure to leave room for the next one."

"Woah," said Jim.

"Yeah woah," said Danny.

"What's his name?"

Danny searched the story.

He found the name with his finger.

"Bill," he said.

"He's in the mental hospital," said Danny.

"Right here."

"Where we at?" said Jim.

Danny shrugged.

"Mmm, mmm. Bumfuck, Egypt, I guess."

Jim looked behind him, all around, and spotted a sports banner behind the counter.

Just as Danny read the town name in the newspaper and began to say it, Jim spoke up.

"Bumfuck, Iowa," said Jim.

"We're gonna get him out," he said.

"Who?" Jim asked again.

"Bill," said Danny.

"Bill," said Jim.

Note from the narrator:

The following is drawn, paraphrased, somewhat redacted, from the essays of Max, Kaitylyn's journal and Brooke's as yet unpublished account, The Pothole Diaries.
For what it's worth:

Do we believe what we believe because we have studied, held them in our hands, rolled them around, and decided.
Or, was it because we heard it on the TV from
some person being paid to deliver the message. ...
... It's been a long road.

From a stolen election, to a government-planned attack on Sept. 11, 2001, to two invasions based on lies, based on power, on money.
To a murdered Senator, the one standing in their way, who would not be moved.
We didn't want it to come. We marched. We e-mailed, we sang, we wrote, we got arrested.
But it came anyway.
And it is still here.

We were determined to burn our bridges so we couldn't go back. ...

If the people of the world, in Algeria, Vietnam, and Cuba had to fight to win freedom, why should we white people be exempt? How could we alone have the privilege of winning freedom, an end to our complicity with US war crimes for instance, without fighting.

I didn't think about the fact that the nails might actually kill people. Of course it took quit a bit of denial to not think about it, but denial is essential for warfare. Like soldiers in most armies, I focused on the theoretical goals of the war, on defeating the enemy. The individual lives of those who were part of the enemy effort were an abstraction. If one empathized with the enemy it would be impossible to kill or maim.

... I also began to read and study simple manuals that explained electricity — the difference between voltage and current, what a circuit was.
— Catherine Wilkerson, *Flying Close To The Sun*

SIXTY-FIVE

Yes, that much I do know, positive to positive, negative to ... yeah.
Hello again. I'm out in the cold trying to jump start my car, had to borrow some cables from this guy over here.

Yes, I got a car.

There it goes!

Thank you.

I'm going to sit in my car while we both warm up and just visit with you, whoever you are, for just a moment.

Well, [I think] we're getting pretty near the end, the denouement ... I, for one, will miss them.

I've come to know them. I love how they all have such distinct personalities, fears, passions, and insecurities, with humans there's always going to be a soap opera, super religious, not at all, rich, struggling day to day. There's one I'm thinking of, I won't say his name, he often twirls his beard ... to the others he is SO annoying. And then there's another, when you talk to her, you think she might not hear or understand, but if you wait, she definitely gets it. They have their own nicknames for each other: Panda, Roo, Big Man, others not so nice, and they decided together, somehow that the only way they could change things was by force, the same way their government did things all around the world.

The Special Unit, they are with Brooke, you probably got that. Yeah.

Prince Hope is working to get everyone in the world on his Twitter, he has been for some time, and then send out one of his giant mailings. Not sure how that's gonna turn out, but I've got an idea.

You might not be interested, but did you know that blood was found in Dealey Plaza, not Kennedy's, but up around the Grassy Knoll, up there? Yep. Somebody took pictures. They turned them over to the F.B.I. and of course never got them back, just like the photos of the RFK murder, this one young guy, from behind, a bunch of photos, and then the steel at Ground Zero gets whisked away before they study it, but it's a crime scene. I mean, what? The blood thing, I don't know, but I was wondering if that might have been shooters shooting each other, somebody trying to stop the murder, I don't know.

Well, anyway.

There's some more.

... At eleven, Aaron pulled on plastic gloves and taped a statement about the impending attack beneath a tray in a phone booth across from *The Washington Post* offices. He then moved across town, and at eleven thirty called the Pentagon emergency number. In twenty-five minutes a bomb will explode in the air force section of the Pentagon, he said calmly. I'm calling from the Weather Underground, and believe me this is no prank. Clear the area! Get everyone out! You have twenty-five minutes. Viet Nam will win! ... Although the bomb that rocked the Pentagon was itsy-bitsy — weighing close to two pounds — it caused 'tens of thousands of dollars' of damage. The operation cost just under five hundred dollars, and no one was killed or even hurt. In that same time the Pentagon spent tens of millions of dollars and dropped tens of thousands of pounds of explosives on Viet Nam, killing or wounding thousands of human beings, causing hundreds of millions of dollars of damage. ... The president said our action was the work of cowardly terrorists.

— Bill Ayers, *Fugitive Days*

Blood from the body of a baby bombed to death in Baghdad, blood by the pint, running onto the street as fast as a swift river, has magic in its pure infant cells. Of course you cannot scrub the street clean because the blood from the baby already has covered the street and is in the air.

As they get off at Camp David, Bush's hand brushed against baby blood on the plane, as does his wife's.

At this hour in London, Blair arises in the middle of his long night and goes to the bathroom to try and wash this blood off. He couldn't do it before he went to bed.

In Washington, Rumsfeld stares at the red splotches on both his hands and Colin Powell calls out that there must be something wrong with the soap because it does not get the blood off his hands.

At Camp David, Bush notices blood on his right hand and he goes to the bathroom to wash it off and he holds his hands under the water and rubs them with a bar of soap and then puts them under the water and he takes them out and holds them out to dry with a towel. He glances at his hands and sees the blood of the dead baby is bright on his fingers. He mutters and washes the hands again.

He will do it again. Again this year and next year and through all the years because the blood remains forever on the hands.

— Jimmy Breslin, *Newsday*

SIXTY-SIX

"Benjamin Franklin painted the Sistine Chapel, man, of course he did."

"I know that."

I heard talking and because I am stupid AF kept moving toward it.

I found Hector and Reuben sitting in their cave, having coffee, listening to fuzzy sports talk radio.

"Anybody else here?" I asked.

"Just us," said Hector.

"How are you, man?"

"Long day, tired," I said.

I sat for a while, just sat, I was tired. We listened to the radio. They kept talking in Spanish and English. I might even have nodded off a little.

When I woke up they were talking about Geronimo, then they stopped when they saw my eyes were open.

Rueben said they were expecting an inspection from "the higher ups."

"Maybe today," said Hector, "maybe not."

"You must be busy, getting ready," I said.

Hector kind of looked around at the ground around where he was sitting on a flat rock, like yeah I guess not really.

"So, how's the underground city coming?" I said.

They both looked around.

"Pretty good," said Hector.

He flicked his cigarette butt for distance.

"We're all just such a jumbled mess," I said, forgetting where I was. They looked at me like I had forgotten where I was. I am also writing a novel and going back and forth between worlds sometimes I am not completely here or there, like the Star Trek transporter, you know? Whatever.

I stood and stretched and decided to get to it. I wanted to find out what the fuck was up with this whole underground thing. I really didn't want to come back here again.

So I said:

The idea was to go under the whole United States, to fight yes, but to create an alternative if this revolution thing didn't work out, that's how I understood it, to at least be able to escape, to get away.

They pulled out more cigarettes, handed back and forth matches and sat there like chollos and me the, I don't know what, but out of place, that's what I felt.

They talked back and forth in Spanish.

"Yes," said Hector.

"But," said Reuben, "there's also this treasure, senor Boop."

"Boop?"

He aimed a deadly nod at my chest and I looked down at my Betty Boop pin I got from Kaitylyn a few days ago that I didn't realize I'd been wearing. She got it at some bar, I guess. You buy a pin for a certain amount and you can drink the whole night.

"Treasure?" I said.

"Yes," said Hector.

"We just want the fucking money," said Reuben.

What money, of course I said, with my mind setting off on a fantasy trip of Jesse James and D.B. Cooper.

They left together and I knew I was either a dead man or lost forever.

I heard scuffling and minor arguing.

Reuben swiped some dust off a nearby flat rock.

Hector produced out of his torn, dirty jeans the old map and showed me what they were up to. It was from the Civil War, the Knights of the Silver Service, I think hiding money around the country to serve a further rebellion if the current one didn't work out. Well, that fits, I guess, I said, wondering what cereal box this came from.

No, Hector and Reuben explained to me in not so many words, this was for them, they did the work.

Reuben added that the "pinche putas" from the revolution had stayed just a short time and left. The work was too hard.

"Did you find it?" I said, putting up a hand to squelch a yawn from my too-short nap.

"No, but we are close," said Hector, with eye contact that said they were nowhere close.

"Why would there be Civil War abandoned treasure in northern Minnesota?"

I went ahead and asked the question.

They both explained very quickly and simultaneously that it was because it would not be expected up here.

I said no shit and noticed that even though they said they were working only for themselves they still wore the battered old orange CRUSHER T-shirts.

They talked in Spanish and I heard *chinga* nine times in thirty seconds and I knew it was not good.

Hector got up and put his arm around my shoulders to walk me away from Reuben.

He explained to me that I was in mortal danger because they had slipped up by telling me about the treasure and that it would be better if I had not come.

"But I did come," I said.

"Yes," said Hector, looking me over like a tired judge looking down at the man he must now sentence.

He turned me around just with a slight nuanced touch of my shoulder.

Hector laughed loud as if I had just said the world-record funniest thing and slapped me, hard, on the back. He talked Spanish to Reuben. Reuben scowled back.

"The fuck you talkin' 'bout pendejo?"

Reuben got up quickly and threw up his arms.

He kicked at the ground, throwing up dust and rocks, one hit me in the balls and I dropped to my knees groaning.

"You fucking idiot!" Hector roared.

I felt both their hands on my back. I put one knee on the ground and we all waited in the knowing silence until I could breathe deep and start to get up.

They helped me.

They sat me on a rock and got me a cigarette.

Reuben apologized in English and we talked about sports, women, then sat in silence, listening to the sounds of the underground, including rumbling from a truck somewhere up there that made me feel like I wanted to be out of there.

I got a little lost in my reverie and lovingly clutching my nuts like my lone Christmas present. They were off again in conversation, no wonder this underground town hadn't reached New Jersey yet, I thought.

"But even if we get all this stuff, the treasure or the revolution, we'll still be us and not satisfied and find things to be worried about and complain about!" hissed Hector.

"Well, yeah," said Reuben as I got up to leave.

They were going to walk with me, but I said, no, no way.

Do we talk about the Founding Fathers slurping the same bile from our chin as when we mention The Weathermen? Do we say that they hid behind trees and rocks in order to kill actual human beings with jobs and families and then feel sick in our stomachs? What if The Weathermen had won? What if they had succeeded in overthrowing the United States government?

— Kaitylyn during late night study session

SIXTY-SEVEN

I knew Geronimo, too, not really, people like him ...
All through this, all these many months over all the miles, I've asked every chance I could, about Geronimo, who he was, why he meant so much to these people that they would give up their lives for him, or what he stood for.

It *actually* doesn't make sense, does it? I mean, the guy wasn't right. He was about half there if you get right to it. He's not some big college or ancient state philosopher or religious guy. People who end up being rich, leading big things, having big parts in life are smart. You don't get dummies normally as heads of things. Maybe in the news when they do something very bad, or when they die, or when one of them jumps into a river to rescue a beaver wearing a Cubs hat, but that's about it.

But this Geronimo, Gerry has all these disciples.

I didn't get it for the longest time and it made me think these people are not right either.

I found out in addition to calling themselves CRUSHER, after Gerry's persona, they also had this "The Justice Team" thing. Just something they joked about, I guess, maybe passed the time during the long hours in the group home with high stress work with low pay, high stress lives trying to survive with low pay and no benefits. It helps when you can have something to talk about, maybe fantasize about a little and so they all made up their own superhero to be and together they were The Justice Team.

Get it?

Justice. Just us.

I think it was Evey who explained it to me though I wasn't really that interested.

Gerry and his peers, they liked, no, loved pro wrestling on TV, for some reason they just did. Gerry could rattle off stats, wins, losses, whatever,

433

for his favorite wrestlers, and he called himself The CRUSHER or just CRUSHER.

The workers at the group home talked about that in their staff meetings, whether this was healthy and whether to promote it, and they decided the guys had a right to love wrestling if they wanted to.

"We all do it," said Evey to me.

"Just think of your own day. Don't we all have dreams, perhaps unlikely, that we harbor just to keep ourselves going? And maybe when you are shaving you see buildings that are too big and you have to imagine yourself flying over them, or you could not make yourself go out the door.

"And at the end of the day you come home, and it's just you. Just us. And that's cool, that's normal."

And then she talked about the '60s activist Mark Rudd, who said that like the Christian wants to emulate Christ, he wanted to, desired to, had to try to be like Che, a revolutionary.

"Who are Gerry and his friends supposed to take on as their hero to be like?" Evey asked me.

"Jesus Christ? Yeah, I guess, maybe, but just because their parents or grandparents do, and certainly not Che Guevara.

"But how about Locomotive or The Hulk or Captain America? Now we're talkin'."

It was Wrestlemania, or maybe Go Crazy, or No Mercy, one of those big wrestling extravaganzas they have about every month, and somehow Geronimo figured out it was fake.

"It's all fake," he said to Evey.

"What?" she said.

"Everything," Geronimo said.

And he meant everything.

Evey said she just had to stare at him. He's disabled, not supposed to be able to think like we can, but here he watches some wrestling on television and listens to the group home staff talk among themselves in the kitchen, in the living room, then watches some news in his room, and he's got it figured out?

That can't be right. An autistic savant? And his specialty is "the truth."

Personally I doubt it, but that's what she was feeling as she stared at him as he played his game on his little computer.

"... and frankly despising all falsehood, simple, very human, with the innocence of a genius."

"Solzhenitsyn," I said with wide eyes amazed someone — *like her* — would know that.

"Yup," she said.

That was Geronimo, who didn't know enough to do nuance or lies or schemes, except maybe when it came to getting extra cigarettes or staying up late.

Someone who sees the forest despite all the houses and boats.

Geronimo would begin his most profound statements with "even I know," and Evey remembered when they went to the big haunted ship in the harbor, an old freighter that became an attraction during the Halloween season. Well, this time the theme was, "What the Government Won't Tell You." (Really, seriously, I don't know why. I think this "truth" thing is getting too big, IMO.)

Venture deep into the government's deepest secrets, but be aware, once you learn the truth there may be no return. Many who know the truth now reside in government-based asylums, where they await medical experimentation. If you escape, you may find yourself in a prison cell, and the only exit is the tunnel of death.

Geronimo couldn't wait to go.

But when he returned from the outing, the haunted ship and pizza, he said it wasn't bad, "but even I know there's more than that."

When he was there he had handed his own airplane ticket from Sept. 11, 2001 to the person taking tickets and offered them to use it. The person just looked at it, handed it back and asked them to keep moving along, "there's people behind you."

What else can I say about Geronimo?

I wish I knew him.

Oh, here's something more, he liked to record his own songs. One of the staffs knew how to do that on a computer and they matched some of Geronimo's own lyrics with like rap rhythms. Once he farted during the recording and you can hear it in the song, they just kept it. That's the kind of man I want to be.

He wanted to be the first Down's Syndrome President. He wasn't even Down's, but he thought that would get him votes. They all lie, he said. He had everything planned out, his whole life, almost day for day.

He wanted to get a tattoo of himself as CRUSHER the wrestler, but the group home manager and his case manager were against it. He kept pushing for it, kept getting denied.

He said his tennis shoes were his super-powers. Not x-ray vision or flames coming from his fingertips, but tennis shoes. I thought that was interesting.

"Brock Lesner is tougher, that's why."

That's what Gerry said the last time Evey saw him.

As she was checking out, leaving the house at the end of her shift, just ready to close the door behind her, she heard Gerry arguing with another client about a recent wrestling match, going back and forth about who was a better fighter.

In the final analysis, poverty means death: lack of food and housing, the inability to attend properly to health and education needs, the exploitation of workers, permanent unemployment, the lack of respect for one's human dignity, and unjust limitations placed on personal freedom in the areas of self-expression, politics, and religion.
— Gustavo Gutierrez, *A Theology of Liberation*

All you have to be is acquainted with yourself and you know the whole world.
— Eric Hoffer

SIXTY-EIGHT

The people talked excitedly as they hurried in out of the cold air on the sidewalk and the slush, greeted by a friendly face and voice handing them a program. They smiled at each other to say after all that, and finding parking, we are here!

They smelled the popcorn and the wine, surrounded by the buzz of a big-time city event, quality. They stood for a moment trying to take it in and blocked the way for people behind them, unaware, then moved on, holding tickets high to prove their worthiness and to find their seats.

The crowd filled in, talking loud, then settled like a flock on the water.

The lights dimmed and Prince Hope came out, like Moses or a retired basketball player, tall, in his white suit, red tennis shoes, grayish black hair combed straight back, with the gray-black beard thick and full, the black rimmed glasses, the slow, slightly hunched relaxed pace that he took to reach the not quite middle of the old stage.

The curtain remained closed.

It was just him and the people in this private audience.

Since his closing show he had made numerous come-backs and this was billed as his absolute final show. He was leaving the country in fact, for the Himalayas, where he would be silent for a full year, only whispering if absolutely necessary, maybe years, but would surely never return here again.

That was the story laid out in tonight's program, but nobody believed it, as the newspaper had also run a story just that morning about Prince Hope buying a new home on the hill next to the Cathedral and that he planned to run sheep in a wire-fenced yard and the city council wasn't so sure about it.

Hope told some golf jokes and airplane food jokes, sang with the crowd a few Christmas hymns, then returned from where he had come, off-stage, then stopped.

He turned and walked back to the almost center of the stage and stared out into the crowd.

"Today is the anniversary of the death of President John F. Kennedy," he said.

"And also my father."

He turned and walked back and stopped again, and came back for the third round.

This time he stopped after just a few steps and said that his father loved John Kennedy.

"He thought about John Kennedy more than he thought about any of us, I'm sure. That day was the biggest day in the history of the world as far as my father was concerned. This day."

He turned around and made it the three steps to the side just as the curtain rose, displaying the band and the set and the microphones and little town and the sign that said, "Bumfuck, Iowa."

Everyone laughed and applauded and nudged each other and smiled and were so happy for each other and for their lives.

The show consisted of skits and music and special musical guests and more skits and fake commercials, then an intermission where everyone hurried out to pee and grab some wine and some popcorn, then hurried back, almost not making it!

The troupe went through a regular skit, then a musical guest, a fake commercial for "Left Behind Adult Briefs, for the conservative Christian who misses the rapture," and then the lights dimmed. The big full moon over Bumfuck, Iowa shined bright and Prince Hope made his way to the microphone, not that one, the stage hand waved him toward another, but Prince Hope went right for any damn microphone he pleased. The stage hand got the wooden stool down just before it would have been too late.

"Well, it's been a long week in ... Bumfuck, Iowa, my hometown, at the end of the empire," said Prince Hope and everyone smiled at each other and clapped, a few whistles, then nothing.

"My son is marching off to war," he said.

"He's not marching far."

The theater grew even more silent. People relaxed even more deeply, becoming one with their seats and their armrests and their backrests and their neighbor's foot in their back.

"It makes me think of father and son, shooting baskets, talking non-stop, coming back into the house, not talking.

"My Dad. Would he have let me go off to war, to the revolution? I dare say not. Would I have gone anyway? ... I don't know. Of course I don't know. You cannot.

"My Dad.

"He was headed out that day to take the poodle to get his hair cut. He drove his 1964 Rambler Classic, teal green, white stripe down the sides, white roof, shiny. So proud of that poodle.

"After he dropped John, named after his uncle, at the hair cutter, he headed on back, beautiful fall day, the smell of leaves and wood smoke in the air.

"The account came from a woman who had seen it happen.

"She said she saw my father's car coming up the road erratically, and something seemed to be wrong with the driver.

"She watched and she watched my father, Ken, Kenneth Hope, go right through the stop sign and get T-boned at sixty-five by a Chrysler headed south for skim milk on Highway 5.

"We later learned from the coroner that Kenneth didn't break a bone in his body.

"He was already dead from a massive heart attack and was limp as a noodle when the crash occurred. The woman who saw it all happen said she went over to the Rambler and saw that he was already gone, the car crushed to half its size by the giant impact. The other driver was basically unhurt.

"I was living with some friends in town at the time.

"We were sitting in the living room watching TV and saw a police car pull up.

"My friend went to the door and asked what he could do for the two cops.

"They apparently didn't know my friend had roommates.

"I'm sorry to tell you this," one of them said, removing his hat. "But, your father was just killed in an automobile accident.'

"Well, my friend went to his knees and began sobbing.

"I just saw him," he cried. "He was fine.

"His father lived just two doors down. This was their house and we were renting.

"The policeman looked confused and asked if he was the only one here.

"You are Prince? Prince Hope?"

"I was sitting on the sofa behind the door, hearing it all. I couldn't believe it was happening.

"Everything slowed to a crawl. The words of the policeman sounded like we were underwater. It took five minutes for my friend to come out from behind the door and ten minutes for the policemen to enter the house and tell me what had happened and ask if they could give me a ride.

"They took me to see my father. My mother and brother and sister were already there. We hugged and cried and what I noticed was the sort of relaxed look on my father's face, that I didn't recall ever seeing before.

And he had the little bit of toilet paper still on his neck where he had nicked himself shaving, still wearing his hat, his coat.

"That night my sister couldn't sleep.

"It was late, maybe one, two in the morning.

"She knew she shouldn't do it, but she felt that she had to go out to the crash site, a couple of miles from town.

"When she got there, of course it was pitch dark.

"She saw another car parked there and she parked her car, not knowing what she should do. She sat, thinking about the day.

"The person in the other car got out and began to walk toward her.

"Of course she was scared, but she stayed.

"The other person, a woman, walked up to her window, her shoes sliding over the highway pavement.

"She leaned into the window.

"There was a crash here today," she said.

"A man died.

"Yes, my father," said my sister.

"The other woman said she had been home and just felt she had to come out here, something was calling her. My sister told her about having the same feeling.

"I just have to tell you," said the other woman, Judith.

"When you got to the car he was already gone.

"Not quite," said Judith.

"He was sitting upright, with such a calm, relaxed, almost joyful look on his face, I can't describe it. His arm was still in the window. The radio played, country music I think."

"Yes."

"I just felt that someone should be with him, to tell him it's okay. I touched his hair, stroked it, such soft, white hair.

"His lips moved and he smiled.

"I perhaps shouldn't have, but I stuck my head inside the car and my ear to his mouth.

"Do you know what he said?

"No."

"He said, Mr. President.

"Mr. President.

"And then he was gone.

"I thought that was so strange. "But I thought you should know.

"And that's the news from Bumfuck, Iowa, my hometown, where all the police and soldiers are thugs, all the Democrats and journalists are cowards, and where all the Homeland Security, COINTELPRO lone gunmen, are about average."

Note from the narrator:

From The Prince Hope Show ...

... Funding for tonight's program is provided in part by GoBarbaraBush.com

As well as ...
The United States Navy, A Global Force For Good
The United States Army, Be All You Can Be
The United States, Air Force, Peace is Our Profession
And The United States Marines The Few, The Proud, The Brave
Because ... We could never sell you the truth.
... And by your local, down-home just like you we're all in this together for Mom, For Pie, For Baseball and For Chevrolet – military recruiter. Stop on in now and talk about who you want to kill most of all and we'll sign some papers and get you started on your programming, turning you from who you are now into a real American who can kill.
... And by the good folks at Shop N' Plop indoor port-a-potties for the busy Christmas shopper.
We know soon you'll be on the run all day long, round and round, buying stuff to keep your favorite Americans happy ... but sooner or later yer gonna need a pit stop.
Why not Shop N' Plop?
Shop. And Plop.

I fight authority, authority always wins.

— John Mellencamp

SIXTY-NINE

"I'm such a blonde sometimes!" Skylar remarked as she ran-waddled back into the house to get something.

She and Rick were piling everything into the RAV, headed to pick up Kaitylyn and Lara, bound for Bumfuck. Korey planned to get there himself.

Rick drove them out of town, south on 35, as they gabbed and fidgeted like they were headed to a wedding or a day trip to the Apple River.

Kaitylyn and Lara worked their phones, coordinating the various groups headed to Bumfuck, Iowa for the battle.

Skylar turned in her seat, her back to her door, her legs up, to talk to them all.

"If we can win this one, I think we win."

"What about Mayfield?" said Lara.

"We still doing that?"

Skylar and Rick had sent an expeditionary unit to Mayfield to see if it could be taken. They had not heard back yet.

"We don't know," said Rick, turning around. Skylar grabbed the wheel, then handed it back to Rick.

They saw big numbers of brown and green National Guard trucks, tanks on flatbeds, troops in trucks in full uniform, guns visible. On the news on the radio, the top of the hour reports talked about suspected domestic terrorism planned in Iowa and a national alert.

Skylar switched it to classical, and turned back around in her seat, and they sat in silence, each with their own thoughts blaring.

Kaitylyn read a book on war, looking up every now and then to take a breath.

"I think Prince has his Twitter thing about ready," said Lara.

"Everyone in the world?" said Skylar.

"That doesn't seem possible."

443

"Not everyone," said Lara.

"What's he gonna do with it," said Rick, again turning toward the back seat and pissing Skylar off. She grabbed the wheel and scolded with both eyebrows.

"Not sure," said Lara.

"He's such a twat," said Skylar.

"Not really," mumbled Lara.

"The Prince whisperer," said Skylar.

Kaitylyn looked out her window, seeing her worried self, that overly serious little Hermione she thought she resembled reflected back in her face, and in the background the military vehicles rushing this way and that. She tried to avoid her gaze and could not stop looking.

So, she just looked into her own eyes and figured she would soon be sick all over the back seat.

She thought of fighting. She pictured the fighting on the gym floor after the basketball game between her high school and St. Cecilia's, their big rival. Kids just ran from both sides of the gym right smack to the middle and boom! They hit each other, head on, and swung their fists and growled! And she loved it. The girls and boys both ran down, leaped from the last row of bleachers onto the shiny, hard gym floor and rushed at the kids from across town. Kaitylyn remembered it all in detail, how she picked out a girl in a blue top and bared her teeth and grabbed her hair with both hands and pulled and pulled, and then she slapped her and kicked her legs and the girl just sat down, covered her head and started crying. Kaitylyn dropped her fists and watched her cry and then was jumped by another girl and they wrestled on the floor. This girl was bigger than Kaitylyn and she pinned her and sat on Kaitylyn's chest with her knees on her arms. She laughed at Kaitylyn until she was pulled off by a teacher and Kaitylyn saw her underpants, white and soiled.

She went through her book as well as she could. She didn't like to read in cars, sometimes it made her sick. At each new thing she looked up, out the window as to swallow it, at the military vehicles and the regular vehicles and they both made her sad.

What would they do with the wounded? They didn't have any doctors or nurses or bandages. What does a wound really, really look like? What does it feel like, really? What will it be like to be fighting with one other person and you both have knives, or guns. What will it be like to be all alone, lost, wondering where you are, who is left, who is trying to find you to murder you. Where will they fight? What is Iowa like? Will it be in corn, too tall to see, or in big, open fields, or do they have some woods down there, rivers? Towns? She will need to sleep. If she does not get enough sleep she will be grouchy and mean the whole time, guaranteed. What would it be like to fight in terrible cold, it's getting cold, and snow, rain, sleet, a tornado. What if she decides she doesn't want to kill anyone. Can you say, I quit and walk out. She'd done that on a few jobs. I doubt it. She had read about how many soldiers choose to just shoot over the heads of their enemies because people really don't want to kill. But then they will lose and what good will that do.

Lara thought of Narnia. She never thought of Narnia, not since she was a kid. She searched hard for something, something to justify, to explain, to inspire, somewhere to hide.

Kaitylyn looked down to continue reading and vomited into her lap, a little cat throw-up. Her back humped a little and she deposited in both hands. She tried to muffle and hide, but the smell nudged the others and pointed right at her.

They pulled new helmets out of the plastic and put them on and took them right off as a military vehicle came up beside them, passing them on cruise control and really pissing off Rick.

Skylar worked her phone. This is like Woodstock, she said. Everybody's gonna be in Iowa. Very cool.

"So, where's Korey?" Asked Kaitylyn, wiping her mouth with her sleeve.

"He's getting there on his own," Rick talked back over his shoulder and Skylar tsked him.

"Evey?" said Lara.

"Doesn't she have a kid now? Anybody hear?"

Lara looked toward Kaitylyn, then to the front.

Kaitylyn shook her head and shrugged, Rick kept driving and Skylar looked out her own window.

Skylar decided to draw down her visor to see into the mirror to put on mauve lipstick and Rick looked at Skylar then back to the road.

"Hector? Reuben?" said Kaitylyn.

"Haven't heard," said Skylar.

Kaitylyn and Lara exchanged looks.

"Brooke?" said Lara.

"Wow," said Skylar, "haven't heard from her in a *long* time."

She rolled her window down just a bit to push out some used Kleenex.

"Oh," said Lara, "looks like everything's all set, looking good."

"Yeah," said Kaitylyn, "yeah, great."

They got to Iowa I guess all right and found Bumfuck and were driving around town like a bunch of too-old main street cruisers looking for the big senior keg party.

"There!"

Lara pointed.

"Right there!"

Rick stopped the car right in the middle of main street and there was Jim and Danny sitting in the front window of The Café.

They all made a big deal about Rick driving down the street to find a place to turn around because they would lose them and shit and fuck.

He pulled into the diagonal parking.

They leaped from the car as if it were on fire, stretched so big they showed their underwear and moaned and waved to Jim and Danny, embarrassing the shit out of them, and they were forced to explain to those sitting inside around them that they didn't have any idea who those people were.

Jim and Danny waved their hands and mouthed "go away," "go ... the-fuck ... away."

Lara scrunched her head like the inquisitive cat trying to understand why they were doing that.

Jim flipped her a double bird under the table and that did it.

"Fuck you!" Lara yelled.

"Let's go!" she told the others, grabbing arms and shoulders and leading the others away, down the sidewalk.

"I'm hungry!" said Rick.

"Where we goin?"

"Just move," said Lara, pushing him by the shoulders.

They stopped at the corner.

"They didn't want us in there," said Lara.

"Fuck them," said Skylar, beginning to charge back.

"No!" Lara gripped Skylar's arm.

"No. There's a reason, just cool it. For once."

"Aslan returns," whispered Kaitylyn.

They stamped their feet and pawed at the little snow ghost dust scooting back and forth over the sidewalk, waiting for Jim and Danny to exit La Café.

A red pickup slowed at the intersection. The driver stared at the unlikely group on the corner as he floated through the stop sign.

"We've gone back in time," said Rick.

"This is the 1950s."

The others looked all around without comment, at the water tower, the grain elevator, the bank. Even the cars seemed old.

"I'm not fucking shitting," Rick said.

"That town sign back there was a portal.

"Did you *ever* see 'The Fucking Twilight Zone'!"

"You. Are. Fucking. Crazy," said Lara.

An old pickup made its way slowly down main street. The man driving wore a cap and grey overalls. Five children sat in the back on bags of seed, dangling their feet. One holding a stick, enticing a dog to follow them.

"Oh my God," mumbled Lara.

"There they are!"

Kaitylyn pointed down the sidewalk at Jim and Danny, scuffling out to the street like bishops from the bordello.

"Psssttt!" Lara hissed and waved. "Hey!" she shouted.

Jim and Danny, heads down, hands in their pockets, walked their way. They all shuffled around the corner together and made a huddle.

"This is fuckin' Danny," said Jim.

"He's my sniper."

"Nice," said Rick.

"He was gonna fuckin' shoot me, but now he's not," said Jim.

"Cool," said Rick.

"Listen," Jim said.

They all hunched in closer together.

If you look at Iraq and Afghanistan's situations, they are quickly becoming much like our reservations. They will have puppet governments funded and controlled by a U.S. Government that siphoned off their resources. You don't have to be an English major to read the writing on the wall; I am in here as a warning to others, just like those men who are in Guantanamo are a warning to others — if you stand up you face these same consequences.

I am tired, I want to go home. I want to continue my art work, I want to plant a garden, I want to walk in the forest, I want to walk in the fields, I just want to lie down on the grass and feel the sun against my skin. I want to be able to hold my family close to me and not have someone tell me time's up.

Silence, they say, is the voice of complicity. But silence is impossible. Silence screams. Silence is the message, just as doing nothing is an act. Let who you are ring out and resonate in every word and deed. Yes, become who you are. There's no sidestepping your own being or your own responsibility. What you do is who you are. You are your own comeuppance. You become your own message. You are the message. In the Spirit of Crazy Horse.

— Leonard Peltier

SEVENTY

It was December, soon Christmas.

At the now famous Meeting Around The Corner, Jim had suggested it was too late to start The Big Battle Of Bumfuck. He said they had made friends in town and they weren't bad people, Muggles, but still good folks, he said, and that whenever they were together in town the others had to pretend they didn't know them because that way their new friends would trust them. Fuck that, said Lara.

That same day they drove out to where Jim and Danny thought the battle should be fought, a valley on a river, with a bluff, a cornfield, now fallow, and if you look closely it is lined with deer stands, some in camo color, some just faded plywood. Skylar and Rick said fine, how are you gonna make sure this is the battlefield anyway, and they were going back to Minneapolis and see ya in the spring.

"What about everybody else though?" said Kaitylyn and Lara almost at the same time.

"What about Evey, Hector, Reuben, Korey, Brooke?" said Lara.

"What are they gonna think when they get here and we're not even here?" said Kaitylyn.

"They're coming?" said Rick.

"Yeah, that's true," said Jim.

"We can't stay here," said Skylar.

"Yeah we can," said Danny.

"Everybody stays," said Lara.

"Have you robbed this bank yet?" said Rick as they were walking again to the car after visiting the ice cream shop.

"Not yet," said Danny.

"Well, don't," said Lara.

Jim and Danny took them to the woods.

To a big, no, giant red tent in a clearing, a canvas tent, with cots and desks and chairs inside.

"Whatdya think?" said Jim.

"No fucking way," said Skylar.

"Who stays here?" said Kaitylyn.

"You guys do," said Jim.

"Me and Dan got the house."

Three minutes later they all crunched shoulder to shoulder in the living room of a little house about fifty yards from the big red tent, in front of an old fireplace, warming themselves.

Jim explained that they thought it was probably abandoned, but that it worked. They had made some minor adjustments, like relieving themselves in the woods, but it basically worked.

"We'll stay here," said Lara.

"I wonder why it was abandoned?" said Kaitylyn.

"Beats me," said Jim.

They used the big red tent as a guest house, for storage, to get away from the crowded little house, the wood smoke, the cans of kipper fish that Danny liked to eat. First, they let the others know they were planning to wait until spring for the battle. Skylar had a call in to the United Nations to negotiate a truce through the winter that never got returned. Korey eventually turned up at the front door of the little house in the woods, and a bit later, maybe the same afternoon, Evey, Hector and Reuben were spotted by the lookout in a tree stand, lost in the woods.

"I lost the baby," Evey said when Kaitylyn asked, after they got inside and were taking off their coats.

"Oh my!" said Kaitylyn.

"I'm so sorry," said Skylar.

Rick hugged Evey around the shoulders.

"Gotcha!" said Evey.

"Joke!"

"That's not funny," said Kaitylyn.

"Not cool," said Skylar.

Evey hung her coat and drooped her head.

"I guess I'm not used to being around people," she said.

"This is going to take a while."

"Ahhhh, Evangelina."

Kaitylyn, Lara and Skylar rushed in for a group hug. Rick quick fetched a short glass of whiskey and handed it to Evey.

They settled in, hanging out, talking, arguing, going to town, watching the military trucks passing through looking for the rebels, quite a few at first and later not so much.

They trained, some pushups, some situps, some karate and target practice, but basically life became a matter of endurance, it was just getting through the day, counting the days, hating the grey, hating Iowa, then hating it more and more and wanting to kill something, to walk into the woods and the snow and keep going and never come back, watching the crows, listening to the crows, wondering about individual crows and crow culture, naming the crows, wondering where are the crows today, where will they be tomorrow, the next day and the day after that.

For a while Jim, Danny, and Reuben got interested, obsessed is more the word, in UFOs and Bigfoot after somebody thought they saw or heard something I guess one night while out pissing off the porch.

And so, they already had these walkie talkies that somebody found in a box in the basement of the house/cabin and some fucking batteries that worked, and yeah, they went out and sat in some tree stands, not too far from each other, watching for UFOs and listening for Bigfoot, each shivering in his own misery, and pissing and shitting off the side, perhaps, perhaps not. Some crows would know.

"Fuck that," said Korey when they asked him to go, and he went off to the kitchen table to play Kings Corner with Hector and Rick and Lara. Kaitylyn, Evey and Skylar were off somewhere else doing some other shit.

So, who was it?

Oh, yeah, Jim, Danny, Reuben, out in the deer stands in the middle of an Iowa winter. Well, by this time they were about half crazy, and the cold probably relieves a little bit of depression, is what I understand.

They talked back and forth on the walkie-talkies, at least for as long as the old batteries lasted. That's the story I've been told, that I found out, in my ways, not important.

Anyway, I think it was Jim who mentioned:

"We're here because of Geronimo, you realize that."

"Who's Geronimo," said Danny.

"That's not why," said Reuben.

"Yes it is. Think about it."

"I'm leaving," said Reuben.

"Don't do that. That's all it would take?" said Jim.

"Wait? What was that?" said Reuben.

"What?" said Danny.

"I heard something," said Reuben.

"It sounded like Gerry!" said Reuben.

"You guys are crazy," said Danny.

"That's what I been fuckin' tellin' you, man," said Jim.

They lived by chopping wood, rabbits, melting snow on the stove, and scrounging cigarette butts in town.

"I wish Max was here," said Lara.

"Remember his writing?"

"Zim, Joe," said Korey.

They sat and stared, feeling the fire on their faces.

On Christmas Eve Day they exchanged homemade cards, made a snowman, put up lights they found in the basement over the door. After dark they went to the little front porch to drink Danny's homemade mead he'd been working so hard at brewing in the basement where he had taken up refuge with a sleeping bag and some books, also savoring the store-bought cheese and crackers, taking their time tearing the plastic and pealing it from the delicacies.

While they chewed, they thought about dying, who will care, and remember them, at least I would, that's what I would be thinking about at that time.

Rick offered this, I know for a fact:

"When you get old, past a certain age, I forget what it is, forty, you could have a heart attack any second, fall over dead. You never know. You walk around all the time knowing you could be dead. It's terrible. Right?"

"I don't know," said Skylar.

"I might like ...," began Kaitylyn.

"No, really," Rick continued, "trust me, it would suck, big-time. This is better. This is good. Yep. Good."

They watched it snow and checked their phones, looking for Prince Hope's promised big Christmas message to the world after he had gotten "everyone" to subscribe to his Twitter account.

Skylar got them to sing that "all the treasure buried there," song and Hector and Reuben exchanged hurried glances.

"Fuck," came the worldwide Twitter text from Prince Hope.

"oops," followed quickly.

They waited, looking up at the sky for reindeer crossing the moon, maybe. I liked to do that.

"I'm goin' to bed," said Jim, "g'night."

"What's that!" said Skylar.

"Fuck you, g'night," said Jim.

"No! Right there, lights," she pointed.

"Get the fu ...", said Jim, looking back over his shoulder, one hand on the screen door.

"What the f ...?"

Danny grabbed his gun from two feet away, as did Skylar, Rick, and Kaitylyn. Lara rushed inside for the giant cop flashlight they'd found in the basement.

They watched down the narrow, snow-packed lane, which meandered through the trees, down the hill, as some sort of vehicle was definitely crunching toward them. They could run. They could fire. They could wait. They decided that Danny and Jim and Korey would go into the woods with their AR-15s and cover their flank while the others waited in the snowy Christmas eve in the woods on the porch like the Romanovs waiting to be murdered by drunken young Iowa men. That's what Kaitylyn's diary told me.

A black SUV pulled up, short, about thirty yards from the porch steps. Men in black felt coats crawled from all doors and stood in the snow, showing no weapons.

"Maybe they want directions," said Rick to the others.

"I'll go talk to them."

"No," said Lara.

"I know who it is."

"Hello, Mike," she said, hardly loud enough for all to hear.

"Lara," said the man standing by the driver's door.

He walked toward them, followed by the others.

Special Agent Mike Braxton stood at the foot of the steps, all in black, a nice black hat on his head, the others the same, facing up to the shivering rebels on the porch.

Lara shined the light right in Braxton's face.

He did not blink or look away. He smiled.

"You're all under arrest," he said.

The rebels gripped their guns tight and gritted their teeth, raising the barrels just an inch toward the F.B.I. men.

"Just kidding," said Braxton.

"It's Christmas Eve. How do you like your accommodations?"

He explained briefly that the house had been used in the past as a hideout for F.B.I. assets before court or by agents needing to get away.

"We thought you'd find it okay."

Lara looked accusingly at Jim then back to Braxton. She dropped the light from his face.

"Well," said Braxton, tipping his hat.

"Merry Christmas."

They turned to walk back to their vehicle.

"Merry Christmas," said Evey, just before Braxton disappeared inside his door.

On a Wednesday, it says in Kaitylyn's diary, some of them ventured, or were driven by boredom and despair, to sit in The Café, hear people talk, TV, smell bacon and eggs.

"Pie?" said the waitress.

"How much is coffee?" asked Skylar.

"Okay, coffee's," she looked at the others for final approval.

"Coffee."

It was wonderful, apparently, the sounds, somebody else's cough, smells, oatmeal, the lovely clatter of dishes, and laughter.

They stared in silence, amazed that things had not changed. There was "The Price Is Right" on the television, somebody told a coarse joke over in the corner where they thought nobody could hear. And, at the table right next to them, four men talked about "those fuckin' faggots."

A military advertisement blared on the TV.

Lara began to talk, fairly loud, to nobody and everybody and Skylar reached to hush her, this was not the time, wait for the battle, we are just visiting, this is not our world, stay out of it — while Kaitylyn, Rick and Reuben reached below the table for their handguns and knives. Hector clutched throwing stars in both fists and leaned over with just his mouth like an amputee to sip his coffee one last time.

"They fight just because somebody tells them to," said Lara.

"They feel they have to, pay taxes for war because they have to ... we don't have to be here, but we are here. ... have to sign up for the military or can't go to college, get loans, get a job, have a life."

It wasn't very clear what she was saying, too complicated, says Kaitylyn in her diary, but what the fuck? It wasn't what they were used to hearing, the guys at the next table, and it was enough to get their attention.

"Fuckin' faggots," came the antiphon from the other table.

"We're the prols who do not know," came Lara's rejoinder.

"Revolt of the prols," said Kaitylyn.

"There's an e. Proles," said Hector, who must have known Kaitylyn kept a diary.

"No. Prols," said Reuben.

The rebel's phones buzzed and they looked down.

It was Prince Hope's second try at his grand worldwide text.

"Peace on Earth ... was all it said," Skylar looked straight at Hector and Reuben, smirking.

"You know what Max would have thought about this?" said Kaitylyn.

"I don't fuckin' ... care ... what Ma ...

"What?" said Rick.

"He would have said what a privilege, that's exactly what he would have said. To be down here, among people, walking right here, in the middle of the action."

"Down here?" said Skylar.

"On fucking earth," said Kaitylyn. "From way up there, zoom right down here."

"That's a movie," said Hector.

"Prolly nine movies," said Kaitylyn.

"Men in Black," said Reuben.

"No," said Skylar, "It's a Wonderful Life."

"Shut ... the ... *fuck* ... up, all of you," said Lara, "yes, please," she said to the waitress, holding a pot of fresh coffee.

From the "other" table came "conspiracy theories," "vote fraud," "fake news."

Lara was about to stand, to either fight or offer some form of correction when Skylar grabbed her arm and sat her down.

"Goddamn it," said Skylar.

"At least now we're talking about that."

"You really believe that crap, don't you," said Hector, laying his stars on the table to grip his new, warm coffee with both hands and bring the treat to his mouth.

"Oh, God," said Lara.

"Gimme strength," she whispered.

They sat in silence, looking around. The other table threw out money to the middle for a tip, squeaked chairs, mumbled epithets and left. "Price Is Right" changed to "Family Feud," as the rebels put together enough change to get more coffee and one small order of fries.

These are the days, you'll remember.
— Natalie Merchant, 10,000 Maniacs

... a rural community of ten thousand, buried half the year under a leaden sky and heavy snows and all the year under the weight of its large and intransigent ignorance.
— Frederick Exley, *A Fan's Notes*

SEVENTY-ONE

"You guys hear anything?"

Korey asked Jim about their night in the deer stands.

"Some howls and shit."

They celebrated Danny's birthday with a cake, home brew, a nice fire and strawberry ice cream.

"Looks like blood," said Korey.

"Why do you do that?" said Evey, frowning up at him.

They wore the birthday party hats they had found in the basement. The F.B.I. had thought of just about everything.

A group stood with drinks in front of the fire talking group home shop talk.

"You can't ride the lift," said Korey.

"You can," said Evey, "you're not supposed to."

"I did," said Kaitylyn.

They talked about how sometimes things disappeared.

"Like *here*," said Korey.

Korey then said something about somebody at the kitchen table.

"Don't do that," said Evey.

"I hate that."

"You do it, too, miss perfect," said Korey.

"Yeah, right," she said.

He sighed big, turned and walked to look out the window alone, then went right back when somebody began re-telling an old story he knew.

Another group had formed at the kitchen table to play cards.

Danny showed how he could cut the deck one-handed.

"It's just us," said Lara.

"We all imagine we are super heroes. Don't we? I do."

"Wonder woman," said Reuben.

"No," said Lara.

"And that's normal. But at the end of the day, we're just us, and that's cool."

"Keepin' it real, sister," said Danny as he began to deal.

"He hasn't said that much all year," said Lara, nodding toward Korey.

"So, why are you here?" said Lara to Danny.

"Cut right to the chase," said Danny.

She didn't stare, but kept her point on Danny.

"Well," he said.

"This might sound bad, but for me it's all about being a hero. I want to be a hero, somewhere, somehow. I think it's my destiny and I haven't really done it yet."

He told a story about being a crossing guard as a kid on a busy street, and how it was cold and dark in the winter and he had to make the decision about when to stop the big cars, to walk out there and hope they stop so he could get the kids over from the other side of the street.

"No," he said.

"Nobody got killed, or hit, nothing happened, nothing bad, but it could have, and I found out I liked that. Every day when I walked back to the school and everybody was okay, I felt good, but not quite a hero. I was just doing my job. It wasn't quite enough. I wanted more."

"You were in like second grade," said Reuben.

"Right," said Danny.

"Yeah, well, what happened since then?"

"I don't remember," said Danny, "stuff, this n' that, but what I remember is that crosswalk. I need more. That's why I'm here. Glad you asked?"

He looked at Lara, chewing the rubber strap under her chin.

She looked at her cards and fanned them in her hand.

"Yeah, so what are we gonna do now?"

Korey had wandered over from the other group. He stood behind Lara looking at her cards and pointed at the ace of diamonds. She folded so he couldn't see.

"Do now?" Evey asked Korey.

"Ummm, the war?" said Korey.

"Oh shit!" said Lara.

"You didn't forget," said Kaitylyn.

"You're just chillin'. We got time."

Lara asked Skylar to take her spot and walked to the counter where she found a pen and paper and began to make notes.

"So."

A bit later Rick walked over to Lara still writing.

"What are we going to do now?"

Lara looked up smiling, her hands full of pages.

"We," she said, "are going to sing happy birthday!"

She walked to the card table and led the others in singing for a blushing Danny.

They began making preparations for battle: communications with the other rebels around the country, training, maneuvers. Skylar baked cookies, lots and lots of cookies, placing them gently into plastic bags and packing the freezer.

Each day they sat around the kitchen table just like they had done back at the group home.

They scouted the town and the land around for a good battlefield. Danny saw some names in the doorway of the funeral home on a marquee, the people who had recently died. He crossed himself and didn't say anything, but Lara noticed. Kaitylyn read war strategy and history books out loud.

"A great place to die," Korey liked to say, making his own Iowa license plate motto, and nobody liked to hear that.

Hector, Reuben, Evey and Skylar went walking one day in the woods to make sure government troops did not already have them surrounded and get away from the house.

"Life is just a bunch of rationalizations, excuses and lies," said Skylar as they walked.

"How so?" said Evey.

"No offense," said Skylar, "but look at you having that kid, and he's not even around anymore. And then you killed that Rachel. What kind of mental gymnastics do you even have to do with yourself each day just to keep going?"

They stopped and everyone just stared at Skylar as she kept walking until she also stopped.

"What?" she said.

"I'm sorry, but it's true."

"You didn't need to say that," said Hector as Reuben mumbled a curse in Spanish.

"No," said Evey.

"It's true. I think about that, a lot.

"I'm probably OCD about it. I don't know how to figure it out, it's true."

She looked over and Skylar was leaning against a tree. Evey ran to her just as Skylar slid down to the ground, where she sat, flat in the snow, sobbing, her arms up around her head.

Evey knelt next to her.

"I'm so sorry!" cried Skylar.

"It's like Geronimo said," said Skylar, gulping her breaths to talk.

"Why can't we just help people."

"Rather than kill them and steal from them," Evey helped her with the familiar refrain they all recalled from Gerry's repertoire of catch phrases.

"It's just all so *fucking* heavy," said Skylar.

"It's not you, it's me," she said.

"It's all of us," said Evey, hugging Skylar.

Hector and Reuben let them stay for a short while as they nervously scanned the area.

"We gotta go," said Hector.

He and Reuben helped Skylar and Evey to stand and head on back to the cabin.

"Who's Brooke?"

Danny asked Lara one day as they sat at the table together.

"An old, old friend," said Lara.

"Where is she?"

"I have no idea."

Danny stayed and watched as Lara drew sketches of a battlefield, charges, flanks, reinforcements.

"It's hard," said Lara.

"It's getting so close. People are gonna die and people are going to kill. It's hard to imagine."

"Be professional, polite and be ready to kill everybody you see," said Danny.

"That's what the Fallujah commander said.

"All military are willing, ready, prepared to kill and we honor them with the highest praise, generation after generation."

"Yeah, you're right," said Lara.

"But still."

"It's only interesting if something happens," said Danny.

He offered a factory made cigarette to Lara and Lara shook her head.

"It will," said Lara.

"Yeah, but," said Danny.

"Life.

"Can you imagine a guy living a life where he does shit, not trying to be safe. Shit."

Lara looked at him and thought of that most interesting man in the world TV commercial, smiled and went back to her work. She told Kaitylyn about it later and Kaitylyn asked Lara how old she thought Danny was.

The last thing he heard was probably NPR, so sad. He turned on the light, looked at the burner on the stove and boom.

The little cabin went flying in every direction, the chimney straight up and the fireplace out, bricks, boards, frozen cookie shrapnel, books, everything, everything that wasn't stored in the big red tent.

It burned and they threw handfuls of snow on the fire and then let the embers be, pulsing like a heart on fire.

"He was a hero," said Jim, later when they were all together again in the big red tent.

"Who?" said Rick.

"Danny."

"He was a fool," said Hector.

"Don't fuckin' say that."

Jim turned on Hector.

"Don't you realize?

"He was F.B.I. All the way, all the fuckin' time."

"We knew that," said Lara softly but firmly.

"That's how they found us," Jim continued.

"That's how we found this place. He knew that house was a gas bomb. Either he did it or he knew who did, maybe when we were all in town or walkin' around. And he went in there anyway. He saved us."

"Nobody does that," said Skylar.

"Who would do that?"

"That's your story and you're stickin' to it," said Reuben.

"Fuckin' A-Ray," said Jim.

SEVENTY-TWO

Bix,
I use all this alloted energy out here in the mornings, for videos before 8 A.M., or to begin it is before the 14th of a month. After a 14th of a month I have difficulty doing much online except reading, or emailing.

At this date something is at Sane Progressive new, wasn't there at seven o'clock. Full scale USA war in Syria. Ah, perhaps. I have to catch it tomorrow morning early enough.

I do not comprehend, how can USA jackoffs know more than I do. I believe the entire USA fleet of airplane carriers can be sunk with mini-nukes inside two hours or what is it. But zero contest, airplane carriers are obsolete. Russia has state of the art. Less slobbery, general pig waste.

Russian technology does such as freeze an airplane's control. I suspect Hillary and Joint Chief's of Staff sit on their commodes believing they have buttons and switches for them to control Earth.

What ever happened to them. Mystery abounds in America. Hell, our official leaders tell big lies daily.

Oh well. I have some pot. Not bad stuff really. For now I take rest and preservation, nutrition. Next book from Novak I read is THE PLOT TO KILL KING, the Truth Behind the Assassination of Martin Luther King, Jr. Which is by William F. Pepper who beat the F.B.I. in court and this has been kept out of the media. It was granted in court the F.B.I. killed King. And how many of Dick, Jane, and little Sally know this. Run Spot, run. How many Blackbirds know this? Ah, none. Forget Bill. Bill is coming on.

Further Out,
Bill

When we look back on this sad, pathetic period in American history we will ask the questions all who have slid into despotism ask. Why were we asleep? How did we allow this to happen? Why didn't we see it coming? Why didn't we resist?

... There will be rebels. They will live in the shadows. They will be the renegade painters, sculptors, poets, writers, journalists, musicians, actors, dancers, organizers, activists, mystics, intellectuals and other outcasts who are willing to accept personal sacrifice. They will not surrender their integrity, creativity, independence and finally their souls. They will speak the truth.

The state will have little tolerance of them. They will be poor. The wider society will be conditioned by mass propaganda to write them off as parasites or traitors. They will keep alive what is left of dignity and freedom.

Perhaps one day they will rise up and triumph. But one does not live in poverty and on the margins of society because of the certainty of success. One lives like that because to collaborate with radical evil is to betray all that is good and beautiful. It is to become a captive. It is to give up the moral autonomy that makes us human. The rebels will be our hope.

— Chris Hedges

SEVENTY-THREE

She sat in her corner of the tent, on her chair, holding her tea in her lap with one hand and writing in her notebook with the other.

The new rebel camp, The Big Red Tent, showed from a hundred yards away in the still-dark early morning in the woods like a Soviet colony on Mars.

Kaitylyn saw it and wrote it down, like Max would have, after she returned from her walk, before anyone else had risen.

They had found the perfect battlefield and it was almost spring, a time to water the new flowers with young blood. She wrote that and erased it, not getting it all. Someone who cared enough to look would find it.

But how to get it to happen there.

There was a cornfield, and a river, a large pasture, a run of trees, and a ready made cemetery off to the side waiting.

Korey gave an interview to the local newspaper and radio station. They came out to the camp. CRUSHER snipers made sure they weren't followed. Korey made sure to tell them about Geronimo and the shred room and the ticket, despite the rolling eyes all around him as he sat with the reporters.

"That doesn't prove anything, does it?" asked the reporter.

"It's a ticket from one of those plane flights," said Korey.

"It shows that, umm, somebody wasn't on it. That person was not in that hole."

"Yes, but," said the reporter.

"Yeah, I know," said Korey.

"I just always thought it was a deep meaning that would end up being the big answer to everything and I still don't get it.

"You either, right?"

The reporter shook her head.

The reporters asked about the coming battle.

Korey told them where the battle would be, gave them a map.

After the young news people left, Korey posed the question to those gathered around the main table in the middle of the tent: "But why would they want to kill Gerry? I mean, face it, a retard. What the fuck? What's he gonna do?"

"I killed him," said Kaitylyn.

"I killed Gerry. I gave out meds that night. I thought this way he could be a real hero, the founder of a movement. It worked."

"You did? Woah," said Korey.

"No, of course I didn't," said Kaitylyn.

"The government did, or the F.B.I., or C.I.A., or somebody. And you want to know why? It's because just what we always thought. It's that plane ticket you and Gerry found in the shred room. It was from the Shanksville flight. Gerry was talkative and smart and people loved him and Prince Hope knew about him and he was going to get Gerry on TV, on some afternoon national fucking talk show with his ticket and Gerry was going to tell the whole fucking country the truth about 9/11, because he knew what the truth was, that retard knew, and they couldn't let that happen. That's why they killed him and that's why we're here."

"It's called rabbit turds," said Rick.

"What!" said Lara.

"C.I.A.," said Rick, "or, umm, what is that? Squirrel sucking."

"Sheep dipping!" said Kaitylyn.

"Skunk works," said Skylar, "and no, that ain't it. You people are so fucking crazy."

"You people?" said Lara.

"Shit," said Korey.

"I didn't know that."

"You didn't know that!" said Lara.

"We all knew that, we talked about it!"

"Nope," said Korey, "nobody tol' me."

"That wasn't even it," said Skylar.

"Nope," said Rick.

"Don't you remember?" said Skylar, for some reason going all Valley Girl.

"How it happened?"

"We were all pissed about cars that broke down and paying rent and no raises and we were like all gonna quit and start a union. You don't remember that?"

Lara shook her head, as did Korey. Kaitylyn nodded.

"Working weekends?" Skylar continued.

"Oh, that shit," said Jim.

"Oh, yeah."

"Oh, yeah?" roared Skylar.

"What the motherfuck! I can't believe this."

Well, the reporters took it, the map, and printed it in the newspaper.

"Well," said Lara when she saw the story.

"Maybe it's going to be that simple. We just show up and maybe the other side does, too. I guess we'll have to see, huh?"

They waited, yet longer, while aching to be free of the woods and the site of the blown up house and the pieces of Danny showing up every now and then.

"When it's not so muddy," said Lara.

"Aren't we afraid the F.B.I. will just meet us about a mile from the battleground, arrest us and it's all over, no battle?" asked Evey.

"No," said Lara.

"Korey gave them a fake map. Ta-da! Not a fake map, just a map of some land a few miles away. I think we'll be able to get there and they will be close enough to find us. It should work. It's in one of your books, Kate, Napoleon did pretty much the same thing."

"No he didn't," said Kaitylyn.

Every day they tested the ground to see if this day would be another of interminable length, more plans, cards, quoting dead generals, drills they no longer trusted to prepare them for much of anything, or would be their death day.

Each day they, the worker bees, watched the queen get up, get dressed, pass through the tent flap, then followed her as she stood on the little path, testing the ground with her bare toes.

"It's time," she said one morning.

Like a hive just fallen off the truck, busted open at a valley of wild flowers they went to work.

They initiated the newest thing, the Ham radio, the whole Morse code communications system passed down by Actually and modified by Hector and Reuben and Sara. Lara was able to notify the stateside units and also contact supporters around the world they were preparing to move.

They arrived at the scheduled battlefield, hoping to be first.

They found no one in sight.

They heard a hiding bird.

"That's a quail," said Jim.

"Fucking meadowlark," said Kaitylyn.

"They'll be here," said Lara.

She explained the plan, as dreamed by Jim and Danny, to break out of prison, or the local mental hospital, the man who had written the letter to the editor.

She pointed.

"See. There it is. Look."

And they crowded behind her to sight down her arm to her finger to the farm house.

"He lives in a farm," Korey stated.

"Cool."

"No, dickhead, sorry."

She touched Korey's shoulder.

She again stretched out her arm and pointer finger and purple fingernail. They gathered behind her left shoulder and looked as she ever so slightly raised the finger up over the farm house roof, over a field, to a something in the distance.

"Woooaaahh," said Reuben.

"Oz."

"No, dickfeet," said Korey.

"Narnia."

Lara shook her head.

"It's the state hospital," she said.

"Mental institution, nut house, crazy farm. We scouted it. It's gigantic, red brick, very old. This farm house used to be part of it all. The nuts used to raise cows and ducks, I guess. They had a tunnel, under the farm to get to and from in the cold weather and so nobody would wander off, prob'ly.

"Nobody's in the farm now. We're gonna plant bombs, blow it up at the right time, voila! win our battle, save the world, all that shit."

"Right here," said Skylar.

"Right here," said Lara.

"I thought we said no bombs," said Kaitylyn.

"Cool plan," said Korey.

"If we blow up the house, won't that blow up the tunnel? Just asking," said Skylar.

"Good question. It's a thick door, possibly steel. Everything will come down around it. In fact (she raised one finger into the air, pissing off Skylar probly) the explosion will make it super easy for us to get right to the door and it will probably blow it open perfectly so we can get right in," said Lara.

"Of course it will," said Skylar.

They stood in the dirt road surveying the bloody scene.

The land was rolly, pasture land as smooth as a golf hole, tending up to the west, the green grass of the front yard of the abandoned home guarded by some trees on the north side and a pond on the south.

"Bloody Pond," said Jim.

"Don't say that," said Korey.

An American flag was painted on the side of the red barn, fading. A few black and white cows grazed next to two or three rolls of hay and one big tree almost right in the middle. Kaitylyn pointed out the broken gate of an old cemetery was visible on the far side. The section was lined on two sides by trees and from the looks of it, almost all around with rusty barbed-wire fence on ancient wooden posts.

"It's perfect," said Kaitylyn.

"Yeah. I guess," said Evey.

They found a gate and drove in.

They rode in back of the pickup like a farm family, Lara walked along, ahead, to make sure the land was not mined. Somebody followed with the SUV and the trailer, finding the land more bumpy than it looked. They pointed and oooed at each cow pie. "Where's the corn?" someone said. And someone else pointed to a nearby field. They found the dip, a miniature valley, and began to set up, unpack, stack sandbags and dig personal foxholes.

Lookouts reported somebody stopped on the road, locals, gawkers.

Feeling a little like Civil War re-enactors, they put out the CRUSHER lawn signs.

Lara called a meeting, pointing to her map and assigning locations for where they would all be with their troops when they fucking got there.

"Evey, you are here, by the grove, Korey by the cemetery, Rick, here, Skylar, Kaitylyn, Hector, Ruby, me. We're going to give them the farm house and surround it."

Spotters now reported hundreds of bicycles on the road. Apparently they had chosen for the battle a point on the annual bicycle ride across Iowa. Spotters were asking Lara if they shoot the bicyclists or take them prisoner.

They were still meeting when their first troops arrived, followed by another vehicle, then a caravan, many of them veterans of the battles of Mayberry, Cicely, Mary Tyler Moore.

"Hey!" shouted Hector when the meeting looked to be breaking up. "We've got a little surprise."

Reuben ran away and returned dragging the two large bags everyone had remarked about when they had arrived at the cabin before Christmas.

"With our brothers — and sisters — we will share," he said.

"You found it!" said Skylar.

"Not exactly, not that," said Hector.

"We're not always digging up there, and we've been up there a long time."

"We noticed," said Lara. "We wondered what was in those bags. They weren't Christmas gifts."

"Well, we knew how much some of you liked that whole Narnia thing, which is weird, but, we had time to make these," said Hector.

"Pooosturing, bluuuffing," said Kaitylyn.

"Aaawesommme."

"And also theeese," said Hector, pulling out some big coffee mugs from the bottom of the bags, white with red "Uff Da," imprinted. He passed them out.

"Nice," said Rick.

They waited at the big rock where they had that first planning meeting, checking in troops, assigning them to battalions, divisions, units, whatever. Before nightfall each general took their troops to their locations to spend the night and await the battle in the morning.

Troops continued arriving through the night. Kaitylyn advised Lara that parking was becoming a problem and they were almost running out of T-shirts, orange with "CRUSHER" and Geronimo's image and the year.

For a while it was quiet, but nobody slept. they lay awake looking up at the giant sky and the stars, listening to the hoots of the owls, the cars on some distant highway, the cow moos.

At dawn Lara sat alone on the big rock sipping her coffee listening to Military Polonaise in her ear buds, still no sign of the government. More bikers rolled past, some few teenagers rushed along, throwing up smoky dust, honking, drunk from the night before, headed home, in big, big trouble.

Lara set down her white Uff Da mug, slowly, keeping an eye on the sky. She listened hard, holding her breath.

Wapwapwap. She thought she heard it.

She listened and looked there, over there. There.

Wap-Wap-Wap.

There it was a black bug about three trees high aiming straight for her forehead.

The black helicopter kept coming over the fields, the road, the farm house, the proposed battle ground, dropping low, low, moving fast, whoosh, right over Lara's head. She saw the pilot and the other guy. It was loud. She smelled it, oily, greasy. They banked, sped off and disappeared again.

Everyone gathered around her and the generals at their locations texted and called like crazy though they were supposed to use the walkie-talkies, the Morse code and the Ham radio system communications thing that Rick was trying to be the headquarters for from the SUV.

"They're here," said Lara.

"Where?" said Skylar.

Lara watched the road.

Thousand-one, thousand-two, she counted.

She got to one thousand forty-four and saw the first dust on the road and then the first SUV, followed by a string of more, and from another road another dust storm rising, with military trucks. Helicopters now swooped in from two directions.

The bikers and gawkers disappeared from the road.

CRUSHER spotters reported roadblocks set up around a two-mile perimeter and the highway shut down except for military and government vehicles.

On the news on the regular radio it said that Iowa and federal law enforcement agencies were attempting to negotiate with a terrorist group, "apparently radicalized on the internet."

On the Ham radios/shortwave Rick heard from Norway and Sweden that moderate ET activity focused on Iowa was being reported.

Lara ordered all troops to battle stations. At the big rock headquarters, surrounded by sandbags, vehicles, barricades made of barbed wire and fence posts, Lara ordered everyone to arm themselves and prepare for battle.

The few cows in the field raised their heads from grazing.

Lara got a text on her phone from Special Agent Mike Braxton.

"He wants to meet with us," Lara texted Skylar and Kaitylyn.

"No, you should go," said Skylar.

So, Kaitylyn began walking out from her position, in her orange T-shirt, camo pants and boots, camo cap, her rifle slung over her shoulder as Lara did the same, making her way from the big rock, toward the big tree.

Braxton and two other men started out from the farm yard, which they had converted to a headquarters and which was laced with bombs, in the house, the barn, the garage, the chicken shed.

They headed out from the three directions to the big tree, Lara having to go over some rolling hills, Braxton's crew in between some cows, not bad.

"Look!"

Evey pointed up from her post to the sky, nudging the person next to her.

"An eagle."

It carved out a circle high above a big tree.

Lara arrived first, then Braxton, Kaitylyn.

"Beautiful day," said Braxton.

Braxton and the two men with him wore sunglasses, F.B.I. black caps, handguns and T-shirts with the American Gothic image of the older couple, the farm house and the pitchfork.

"Funny stuff," said Lara.

"I see CRUSHER is still sponsored by professional wrestling," said Braxton.

Braxton introduced himself.

"You killed Morgan," said Kaitylyn.

"You cut off her hands and sent them to her mother," said Lara.

"To make certain of identification," he said.

"Her mother was heartbroken," said Kaitylyn.

"She was a terrorist," said Braxton.

"We were there to protect that town. You had totally taken over. Is that supposed to be democracy. Listen, you and I both know you are only here to get attention. It's an easy gig. You don't have to get up in the morning and go to a real job. Morgan was a murderer. We had evidence from informants and photographs."

"Judge others by yourself," said Lara.

"Displacement," said Kaitylyn.

"Actually," began Lara.

"I feel like someone should flip a coin," said Kaitylyn.

"Projection ... Listen, let's get up to speed, shall we?" said Braxton.

He removed his sunglasses, held them in one hand at his side.

"This doesn't have to happen.

"It's all in your hands."

"Okay," said Lara.

"It's in my hands. I say you stop doing what you're doing."

"Stop what?" said Braxton.

"Stop what," said Lara.

She turned and began to walk back to the big rock. Kaitylyn began to back up toward her position, holding her rifle at her chest, keeping an eye on the agents, watching them as they made their way over bumpy ground, around Bloody Pond back to the farm yard.

The rebels dug deeper, put up more rocks, smoked more cigarettes.

They watched more trucks rumble down the roads. Their dust formed low-lying clouds. Helicopters continually wapped around.

The morning joined the afternoon and they made the fucking night.

When it was dark they still were forced to listen to the sound of heavy machinery. They could no longer hear the traffic on the highway. From the farm house those rebels stationed nearby heard loud talking, laughing, then loud gun shots spaced about five minutes apart. That lasted about an hour or so, and then they cranked up the music, the Sesame Street theme, over and over and over.

"Do you believe in miracles?"

Jim asked the guy from Duluth sitting with him on the wood bench in their foxhole. They bumped fists.

At dawn all was silent.

Then birds chirped, now chattered.

A hint of sunrise glowed over the edge.

"Moo," said the cow.

Rick drank coffee and worked the communications system in the SUV.

Lara stood at the big rock, rifle on her back, cap pulled tight to her eyebrows.

She texted.

From the rebel positions around the giant field came the chant:

"Four dead in O-hi-o.

"Four dead in O-hi-o.

"Four dead in O-hi-o."

It continued, at low level, on and on.

Lara held her coffee to her lips with both hands, closed her eyes, just like the fucking Folgers commercial, listening to the chant, like classical on her headphones, in stereo, so understated and deadly, like a million Zulus in the corn.

Like an alarm clock suddenly blaring, the sun popped over the trees, shining its light over the field, the big tree, the cows, the farm yard filled with vehicles of all kinds, the big rock HQ, the grid of land and dirt roads, the perimeter set up to keep the public away, the onlookers already filling the roads for miles around, the Lion Heads in the trees on the north ridge.

That had been Reuben and Hector's big surprise, Lion heads they'd found in a store in Hibbing, some mascot for some sports team, and stilts, enough for three giant fearsome lions to stand in the trees, looking out at an Iowa pasture. The cows seemed to take notice for a moment.

"Four dead in O-hi-o."

"They hear us on the road!" Rick shouted to Lara.

"Good," she said, preoccupied with her next move, Braxton's first move and her second and third.

"Oh shit," she said.

She grabbed the binoculars resting on the rock, smacked them to her brows.

She smelled diesel fuel, saw tanks, troop carriers, a line of soldiers forming in the ditch to her far left.

"They could just bomb the shit out of us. Why don't they do that?" shouted Rick from inside the SUV.

"I dunno," said Lara, barely loud enough for Rick to hear.

"Maybe they want to see us die close-up, like horses, prove something, I don't know."

"Or wait," said someone else at the Big Rock HQ dip in the field.

"We don't have hardly any food."

"You're right," said Lara.

"I didn't really think about that."

Government troops in pitchfork T-shirts began stepping through the barbed wire, climbing over, cutting the wire down and heading into the field.

Lara ordered Evey to move out on her planned flanking maneuver to the north.

Generally speaking, no one knows who fired the first shot, but after the first exchange of fusillades from AR-15s, M-16s, Berettas, Rugers, bows and arrows, rocks, with puffs of smoke drifting over the field, Reuben lay on his back squealing and crying, trying to keep his arm attached to his shoulder. Two other rebels lay dead with perfect holes in their foreheads.

One government soldier crawled back toward the road, making a pale red trail, unable to walk because of the rebel arrow in his hip.

Evey's battalion reached its landmark, knelt and fired at the soldiers trying to make their way across the field. Evey aimed over the heads. It was her decision. She wasn't going to tell anyone.

Helicopters buzzed the field, shooting at the rebel tree lines.

"Jim? Korey," said Lara, like a director, using the megaphone they were going to just try to see how it worked in a real battle.

"Where are you?"

The men and women in Reuben's battalion worked on him and texted Rick to get some goddamn help up here.

"This won't work," Lara said to herself as she texted Skylar to try to coordinate some help to Evey who was trying to come in behind the farm house headquarters. Evey had the detonator for the farm house. She needed to be within fifty yards, they figured, for it to work.

"Oh, shit," said Lara.

She rushed to one of the pickups, rummaged through the front seat and the back bed, finally finding the flag they had meant to put up. With tools in her teeth she knelt on the hood to attach the flag to the antenna, then slid down just as a bullet popped the windshield. She sat on her ass and hands, smiling, watching the flag, skull and bones, that they'd found on special at Savers, flutter in the breeze.

She pounced up like a gymnast, found her megaphone and again shouted at Jim and Korey as another helicopter swooped them all.

Lara had sorta figured that the idea would be to hold off the main government troops with fire from the long line of trees while Evey went around and blew up the house and Rick tried to get help from Sweden and Norway, and overall public opinion and some fucking help from the rest of America on this revolution thing, and some sense of whether extraterrestrials would really come help when things got hot, which she in no fucking way subscribed to, but some of the CRUSHERs were huge fans of Actually and he had made them promise to try that no matter what, if he wasn't around, and he wasn't.

Anyway.

Evey's group, battalion, had moved way behind the farm house, up the hill and around more trees, out of sight, and had encountered heavy opposition coming from the shelter belt guarding the yard.

"Sky, can you get up there?" Lara texted.

"On my way."

"Whoosh!"

Lara jumped, startled at the sight and sound, how close, and big and loud it was, the shoulder-launched rocket fired from the rebel-held tree line and boom! it collided with an olive-green helicopter right over the field. The 'copter exploded into a fire ball and crashed thirty yards from the big tree, where three cows lay on their sides.

As Skylar's battalion, unit, patrol, whatever scratched and clawed, hunched over, trying to get close to Evey's group, Jim and Korey fumbled with the shoulder-held rocket launcher CRUSHER had received from Colombia.

"Slow is fast and smooth is slow, remember that," said Korey.

"That's not it," said Jim.

"Smooth is slow and fast is smooth."

"Shut the fuck up!" said Korey.

"Life is hard and then you die, Bud," said Jim.

"My name's not Bud, Zeke," said Korey, stopping everything to stare at Jim.

Kaitylyn hunched in her personal foxhole she had dug. She had hung a mirror and necklace and some drawings her nieces had made in school. Next to her she heard the rocket launcher's whoosh and she almost felt the thunk of the rounds that smacked the trees near her. She wrote furiously in her diary, now that she was finally away from Lara. It was all loud, too loud. She smelled her hair, like creosote and two-stroke oil. She remembered the smell from going to her brother's moto-cross races. She fumbled for her ear buds and rammed them in her ears. One fell out and she thought of just going with the one, but did the two. With her feet she felt the extra pens, with glitter to see them in the dark is what she had thought when she bought them at Target. She wrote at the top:

This is so that you will know the true history, not the false, phony, crap. I look at the world through one prism, somebody said that and it's true for me too: how it affects me. Okay, I saw a man in the Tarshay parking lot. I was waiting in the car because I didn't want to go in, too many people. He was a young guy and behind him walked his wife.

What I mean is the look of a young guy a week before Christmas going through the Target parking lot carrying a baby thing, not stroller, carrier, from the car, probably SUV, and it's freeking cold, the look on his face. He's got to get that baby inside Target before a certain time or his world will end. That look.

That is the look I saw on one of the men standing behind that head F.B.I. guy. He was scared, scared of us, and it made me scared, to think we were scaring him that bad. I think I might be on the autism spectrum. I just never said it, wrote it down. True story.

Red-maroon goop plopped onto her page. She wiped at it with her fist and looked up, all around.

She continued.

I am super hero person. No, it doesn't work. I say it, but I don't believe it. I don't understand us. How about this. The slaves in the south. You make sure they have nothing and still they come up with music. The

Bronx, devastated, poverty, and they invent hip-hop. People are gonna do it. CRUSHER, we have nothing, TV, bars, crappy apartments, crappy food, cigarettes and we get this going. Strip people down to nothing and they will still come up with something. Why am I interested in Bigfoot, UFOs, conspiracies? Because I am not a normal person. I think that's it. But still I think other people should be interested. It's like they don't do their work. They don't try hard enough I don't know. Gotta go.

Kaitylyn got up and shot glances at the Big Rock HQ, around her area, back, forward. She sat back down in the cold clay, her knees up for a writing desk. She wrote:

I'm back. I want to start a business, a chain. It will be called Taco Bill. It's so loud. She saw on the clay floor the flag she was supposed to have attached to a tree so that Lara could tell where the Kaitylyn Brigade was. She thought about attaching it now, but didn't, not a huge priority, she decided. And then she wrote, her hand gliding over the page, so scribbly. She just had to get this last thought down, and then maybe one more: I have always, not always, sometimes, tried to control the world by my letters to the editor, at least my town. I would tell them things they otherwise would not know, and then ...

Hector headed toward Bloody Pond, on this side of the farm yard.

"Blake's here," Lara group texted.

"Yay Blake," came the one response, from Skylar.

Skylar Brigade had almost reached Evey Brigade when a bomb exploded in the middle of Evey Brigade, a grenade or rocket, or maybe someone stepped on a mine.

"Evey's hit," Lara tried the megaphone then tossed it away. She texted Skylar.

"Evey ... or her brigade," asked Skylar, not getting an immediate response.

Kaitylyn climbed from her hole.

"Oh, shit," she said, seeing all the dead bodies, and how the red blood looked when blended with the orange CRUSHER T-shirts, the crushed, torn apart lion's heads and stilts.

While the battle raged in Iowa, in Washington, D.C., The Big Kahuna, Mr. Important Master Of All High Stuff, Funny Guy, Nice Suits, Giant Car, Helicopter Rides From The Front Lawn looked out of a high window at the city.

He looked out on the big lawn and the roads and the people walking, some standing at the guard shack, waiting. A robin perched near his window and looked at him for a quick second before getting away.

Behind him, already set up were the cameras pointing at his desk.

He turned, wandered over, slid out the chair and sat at the desk.

He put his fingers on the papers and rearranged them, then back to where they had been. He looked into the cameras, moved his mouth as he thought he might later. He touched his tie again and his hair. He scooted his chair making a squeak. He fingered the various buttons in the different colors on the desktop that he could push if he wanted to, reached to almost touch the ones he was not supposed to.

Son Of The Most High, Chief Executive, Commander in Chief, turned where he stood and looked out the window from there, couldn't see much.

The Chief Of State, POTUS, scratched his behind as he needed to pee, but spotting the Prince Hope book of golf jokes, he was drawn to it. He paged through it, looking up now and again at the television showing "The Price Is Right." Covering the rounded walls were photos of himself with other people, awards he had won, university degrees he had received for doing nothing, the head of a mountain sheep from somewhere, and in a glass case a complete set of pristine trading cards from "Full House," his favorite show.

Lara picked up the megaphone and shouted. Nobody heard her. It was too loud. She called her generals, texted them. Nobody answered. She grabbed her weapon, ducked low and took off across the field toward the tree line. She dived in and flattened, arms out, to avoid the bullets smacking trees and shredding leaves and branches. She crawled and reached a slope where she could stand and look around. She clutched her chest with one hand at the sight, bodies everywhere, moaning, bleeding figures with no one to help them, steam rising from the ground.

She moved on, keeping low, sweat in her eyes. She wandered. The battle sounds dropped off the edge of the earth for a second. She flopped again to her stomach as a helicopter thumped over.

Lara opened her eyes and saw she lay in a cemetery littered with CRUSHER bodies amid the old headstones they must have attempted to use for cover. For a moment unaware of anything else she plodded, one slow step at a time, her rifle hanging almost loose in her hand. She read the names, black plaque on white stone, WWI ... GEORGE ROBERT STAND ... Iowa ... US NAVY ... World War ... WALTER ... Medal of Honor ... S SGT U.S. Army ... U.S. ARMY KOREA ... VIETNAM ... PVT LEE TAYLOR 1st Iowa Infantry, Battle of Wilson's Creek Missouri.

A headstone exploded, as if someone inside finally busted out, sending dust into her eyes and she ran, tripping over a body, out of the cemetery, across the slope to where she blended in with a group of rebels firing from the trees. Lara steadied her arm against a tree and began shooting in the general direction of the enemy.

She stopped and listened, thinking she heard someone.

"Are you fucking kidding me?"

"Reuben?" Lara hollered.

"Lara?"

Lara scrambled, tripped, crawled on all fours through the bushes and fallen branches.

She found Reuben sitting against a tree, one arm drenched wet in blood, trying to make a tourniquet from the T-shirt of the dead man lying next to him.

Lara began to help, her hands quickly covered in blood.

Hector and his brigade made their way along a winding, nearly invisible weedy creek, toward Bloody Pond, in order to be positioned to massacre those government troops who would be fleeing the farm yard and house when Evey detonated the planted bombs inside.

Jim and Korey continued to struggle to make the rocket launcher work, occasionally getting off shots at the helicopters, but not yet able to duplicate their earlier success, as Kaitylyn tried to make sense of the battle field through the smoke, the noise from everywhere, whether over there was the Big Rock HQ, or there. Feeling so alone she lay burrowed into a thorny bush down low, shoved her ear buds as far into her head as she could, turned up the music and using her backpack for a pillow, curled her knees to her chest and closed her eyes.

The Pres'dent, The Leader, The Best Person We Have, Yes Children You Can Grow Up To Be As Good And Perfect As This Guy, Our Hope, the head of the gub'ment, the CEO of every prison, who had every prisoner's life in his hands, the CFO of billions of dollars of weapons-making industries, the COO of the IRS and Wall Street scratched his ankle with the side of his shiny shoe.

"Are you effing kidding me?" he whispered to himself, looking at the time on his gold watch. They should be here by now. He hurried now to the window and saw his family almost running down the long driveway, in their long coats, hats, carrying all sorts of bags and suitcases, now over the big grass as if on ice. "They must be going to the grocery store," he said out loud to himself. He checked his wristwatch and the big Lincoln face clock high on the wall with Lincoln's hands moving round and round and pointing to the different numbers like a game show bimbo.

All at once, like actors to a stage, they entered the big semi-circle room from many doors, heading toward where they knew they should go, some nodding at The Leader, most not and started to move and fine-tune all the equipment. His helpers and handlers and directors came in, directing him again to the desk, telling him again to please keep his hands off the knobs. They sat him where he needed to be and allowed him to put on his button, small as it was nobody would see what it said: Mr. President.

He folded his hands on the desk, wishing his family could see him. A few aides gathered together at one of the windows, nervously pointing at the street.

"My fellow Americans," he said, smiling wide, then remembering to display gravitas, as a bang rang out, loud enough to be heard on air.

The nation saw the reflection in the glasses of The Leader Of The Free World, as off camera, some aides rushed out, to see about a guard having shot someone in the crowd gathering on the sidewalk.

In the SUV by The Big Rock HQ, Rick, with a small cadre of rebel infantry surrounding him, worked the shortwave radio, his cellphone, the internet, everything all at once, as one of Actually's disciples had taught him. It was actually coming together, he thought and he smiled. People in the world were hearing about them, understanding, and the scouts around the perimeter just a mile or two away reported the crowds on the dirt roads growing as well. He had to tell Lara. He crawled out of the SUV, stretched big and dived behind the big rock as a jet screeched right overheard. Rick found the megaphone and while sitting down against the big rock, shouted for Lara, stuck an ear into the air, listening for the response as if at the Grand Canyon on vacation.

He heard a sound he had not heard before, to his knowledge, insistent, fast, very serious.

"What the fuck?" he said, rhetorically.

The rocket hit Rick and The Big Rock HQ, destroyed the SUV and the cadre, leaving a hole in the ground, scattered parts, rock dust, but left the pirate flag, tattered, still blowing.

At the same time, Skylar and her brigade made their way across the back field to Evey's location, where bombs had apparently gone off and they were under intense fire.

"Evey!" she yelled.

"I'm coming!"

She stopped for a moment, tried to contact Lara, Kaitylyn, Rick, nothing.

"Fuuuuck!" she yelled into the air as a government rocket landed in the middle of her brigade, tossing everyone, all their equipment backpacks, rifles, into the air, as if a roller-coaster had crashed.

Skylar, big girl that she was, still floated, on her back, turning, head up, head down, her stomach spraying its contents around and around like a loose hose. She stuck the landing on her head and neck.

The fighting, like a water park on a weekend, shut down after dark.

The rebels heard some of the government troops, volunteers, walking to their trucks over gravel, doors slamming, pickups roaring off, to go home, to family, TV, food, rest.

Lara stayed with Reuben and talked to Evey, Hector, Jim and Korey where they sat.

"Skylar? Skylar?" Lara called out on her phone and then stood to shout it into the night.

"Rick? Rick!"

Lara sent her scouts through the wires, across the roads. She found that Jim and Korey were out of ammunition, getting bored, that Hector was in position at the pond, and that Evey had lost half of her people, that she was nursing a wound that she would not tell exactly what it was, and that nobody had heard lately from Kaitylyn.

"We've lost at least half our people," said Jim.

"What're *you* gonna do?"

"I don't know, smart-ass," said Lara.

"What are you gonna do?"

"You're the leader," he said.

"You know that's not true, how did that happen?" she said, by text.

"IDK," he responded.

Through the night the rebels of CRUSHER enjoyed an '80s & '90s mix that Actually had put together. They played it loud on speakers in the trees, to dishearten the government troops and drive them crazy, as Korey said.

Through the night the CRUSHER rebels, veterans of the battles of Mayberry and Cicely and Mary Tyler Moore talked about the skirmishes of the day, legendary after these latest long hours that must have been days, months, years, this battle in the big Iowa field, the skirmish of The Hornets Nest, The Goldfinch Tree. Some talked of a rainbow spotted at some point during the afternoon, and how they figured that must have meant something very good, then not so much.

They made plans for the victory of tomorrow as four pit bulls that somebody had brought along and spotters and snipers kept the government scouts and spies at bay with pot shots and one million candle flashlights from Gander Mountain.

They talked and talked and realized there would be no fucking victory tomorrow.

No fucking way.

They would all die.

"Hector," commanded Lara in a tone of voice in her text that he right away did not like.

"You take Evey and Reuben and go home. The scouts say they can get you through. Go now."

In Spanish translated by Reuben, Hector told Lara to go fuck herself and then to go fuck her whole family.

"Listen, Hector, Evey has a child. Think about that, about your parents. Evey and Reuben need you. Think about the future. If you do not leave now, by this time tomorrow Evey and Reuben, and probably you, will be dead. Life will be over. If you leave now, there is more life, more chances. You can keep us going, keep Geronimo going, CRUSHER, all that shit. Just think about it."

"OK," came the text back from Hector.

She showed it to Reuben.

"I think it means OK he will think about it, not OK-OK," said Reuben.

"Blake, you, too," said Lara.

So they sat and watched into the night for Mike Braxton to rush at them with a knife and cut off their heads. They definitely wondered about that, as the spotters and snipers kept busy, but finally getting tired, crawling down and sleeping at the foot of their lookout trees.

By this time Jim had crawled over from his area to where Lara sat with Reuben, trying to keep him from bleeding to death. Jim raised his rifle when they heard someone coming. Before they even knew it — they wouldn't have been able to do anything anyway it turns out, they would have been dead — Korey stumbled into their little camp.

He held up a head by the hair.

"Is this Rick?"

Lara swatted it down.

"God!"

"Skylar, dead," he said.

They said nothing. What could they have said. They scrounged, each in their own personal misery trough, because it's over, so over.

"I got this," said Korey after awhile, handing Lara the white and black skull and bones flag.

She stuffed it into her jacket pocket.

"They were good people," said Lara in true revolutionary bravado meaning practically nothing, just as another person suddenly appeared standing over them.

"God-damn it!" said Jim, jumping, propelling himself backwards by his hands and feet like a backward grasshopper or some shit.

The figure sat down, Kaitylyn, rubbing her eyes.

"Hey," she said.

"Hey," said Lara, "where the *fuck* have *you* been?"

Kaitylyn explained she had just woken up and in her waking giddiness talked about how she had been writing and she had not felt so relaxed in probably years.

"I'm happy for you, hon'," said Lara, petting Kaitylyn's hair, keeping to herself for now the recent news of Rick and Skylar.

"You needed the rest.

"That does it," said Lara, just as her Purple Rain ringtone rang through the night.

"Hey, Lara, Hector."

"Yes."

They talked and hung up.

Lara relayed Hector's message, that he would go back, with Evey, Reuben, Blake if he wanted to, and whatever other rebels that wanted out, and they could also probly take the wounded out tonight.

"So," said Lara.

They began to make preparations, as quietly as they could, as well as they could in the dark.

Lara grabbed Korey by the shirt as he was going past.

"You, too," she said.

"No way," he said.

"No fucking way."

"You're a soldier," she said.

"I'm your fucking boss. You are fucking being fucking deployed elsewhere."

Hector arrived with Evey. She had bandages on her head and arm. By the glow of a Kmart lighter behind somebody's hand they talked. Evey told Lara, or whoever was going to do it, how to blow the farm house.

"We got to go," said one of the scouts.

"It's gonna get light."

Korey said something to Jim.

"Right on, bro," said Jim.

They all hugged and cried and said they would see each other later, and then the line of CRUSHER rebels marched out, toward the wire and the road as the sniper and the spies behind the lines made a ruckus on the other side of the field, behind the government lines, with gunshots, fireworks and scattered megaphones talking trash.

They stood and watched them go — Jim, Kaitylyn, Lara — in their boots and camo and CRUSHER accouterments, in the dark, their hands and faces dirty, mud, blood, knives and handguns on their belts, warriors, rebels, actual revolutionaries, in Iowa.

They thought none of that.

What they thought of as they turned away from watching their friends go was what to do with Rick's head, somehow find what they needed in the dark, their backpacks, ammo, weapons, little handmade maps, phones, batteries, all the little shit that if you don't have it when you go on a trip you know it's going to drive you crazy, and then try finding it all in the goddamn pitch-dark and you've been fighting for your life all day and have not slept.

They sat on the low edge of the tree line, the slope, to smoke. They lounged against trees, cross-legged, on their backs looking up at the stars.

Kaitylyn would take Evey's old position. Jim would go to Bloody Pond. Lara would move back toward the big rock in a blocking position when the government troops tried to pin down Jim's brigade. Kaitylyn would blow the farm house. Jim would slaughter the troops who ran his way trying to escape. As Lara blocked, Jim and Kaitylyn would enter the tunnel, go get the fucking writer, bring him out and that's as far as they had time to plan for now.

They looked at each other, helped each other get on their gear, painted each other's faces, made sure the knives and handguns and ammo were in easy to reach positions and shoelaces tied.

At the exact moment, the perfect time, not just before dawn, but a little before that, they bumped fists and moved out with their people, making sign motions, two fingers to the eyes, pointing this way and that, like third base coaches in a prison softball game.

Kaitylyn made her way to the rear of the farm yard without encountering government troops, through the little swampy area she was surprised and pissed to find.

She sent two scouts into the yard to check things out as she checked out the detonator mechanism.

Jim made his way through some definite swamp that he *had* thought about, spread his troops around the pond in the pussy willows or whatever. Some wanted to go into the water and submerge themselves and wait, but Jim said that was fucking stupid.

They waited, watching the possibly autistic, reticent sun pushing itself up over the edge.

Lara with her command of twelve brave souls, five women, seven men, were attempting to move forward in line, though Lara, having been in marching band, knew that was one of the toughest maneuvers. She wanted to try anyway. They got to pretty much where Lara thought they should be. She called them together and again explained their mission. She asked each of them where they were from, why they were here. They whispered, excited to be asked, they crowded together. And then Lara explained again the history of CRUSHER, and Geronimo.

"He was just the neatest guy," one girl said.

"Yeah, I guess so," said Lara.

"He would have wanted to be here," said someone else.

"He is here," said the young woman from Baltimore.

"Yep, you might be right," said Lara.

"What the?"

She received a text from her mother asking how she was doing "since there's all this on the news."

"I'm fine," responded Lara.

"Love you."

This was at just about the same time as Kaitylyn pissed her pants and Jim had what he thought was probably his first panic attack. He squatted and concentrated on his breathing, in, out, as the thought ran through his head that there was no way he could do this. Jim fought to put that thought out of his mind and it was hard, because the thought was not irrational. He took deep breaths, let them out slowly. I'm not gonna die even though this panic attack is telling me I'm going to die, which is crazy, he told himself. But it wasn't at all.

From a distance. You've heard that song. How's it go? There is harmony, everything looks fine, great, running smoothly, everybody doing jobs they love and being great to each other and it all just hums along, spins like a top.

And that's where the movie starts. Actually, probably about twelve movies that I know of start that way, and then you zoom down from the continents view to countries, cities, towns, fields, roads, trees, houses, horses, people, hearts, eyes.

And you are right in the middle of the action.

Like it or not.

Kaitylyn's scouts returned.

"Nobody there," they both breathlessly spurted out.

"What? Nobody?"

"Negative. Nada."

Without another word Kaitylyn turned, pushed down, blew it.

Well, the sound and sight of an explosion is so much more than can be described. It is so loud and so quick and even if you are expecting it, as Kaitylyn's Brigade was, it surprises the shit out of you. And especially in the almost dark. The light and the flames shot straight out and straight up. They ducked and put their arms over their heads to try to protect against the showering boards and splinters and brick. "Ooof!" Somebody got hit. The pieces plopped into the swampy areas and thudded against the dry land.

Fire engines and sirens sounded a far ways off as Kaitylyn and her brigade gathered themselves with all intention of charging toward the farm yard area.

"God-damn it!" said Jim, mostly to himself, as he discovered across the pond, by the light of the explosion, that government troops were crouched right the fuck there.

"You guys don't have fuck all anything else to do than goddamn sit there and wait until morning, you fucking pussies. Get up an' fight!" he said, standing, shouldering his weapon and firing on the government troops in the camo and face paint and expensive Ranger-type fucking hats over there.

Lara's group heard all of that, saw it, tried to keep from looking back over their shoulders, to keep their eyes forward in the relative calm of their area.

"Spread out," Lara sent them out along the tiny ridge in the general area of the big tree and the big rock and the three large shadows in the dark by the tree, that she wasn't planning to mention.

"STOP! HALT!"

Bright lights shined in the faces of Kaitylyn's brigade, a circle around them.

A military voice barked commands, telling them to put their hands in the air, behind their heads and lay down face-first in the muck.

"NOW! ASSWIPES!"

Jim laid down six sweeps of his weapon across the far side of the pond, spraying up water and brush. Cries and moans and grunts filled the new day and a dark film began pushing across the water.

Special Agent Mike Braxton, dressed in full night camo gear, face paint, the works, called out to the rebels on the ground, asking which one of them was Kaitylyn.

"When it gets light, Kaitylyn, I'll find you. I know what you look like, dear. Don't go to sleep. It's not night. It's morning."

Jim and his brigade exchanged fire across the pond, each side taking losses. Jim knew he had ten men and each time somebody went down, became a floater or knocked back off their feet into the weeds, he tried to keep a count while watching his own ammo and the position of the opposition, all with the sun right in their eyes. Excellent planning, he would have said to Lara had she been there. He shot a quick look left to try to see how Lara's brigade was doing, but there was too much brush and too much going on.

Kaitylyn and her troops lay in the mud, arms and legs stretched out to form X's as they had been ordered. They listened to their captors trudging around them, making jokes, cussing, calling them names.

"Kaitylyn! Kaitylyn!" Braxton called out.

"Whoever tells me which one of you is Kaitylyn will be a hero. The rest of you will be able to go home tonight, go to McDonald's, take a hot bath."

"I'm Kaitylyn," a young woman from Arizona called out.

"I'm Kaitylyn," said a young woman from Pittsburgh.

"I am Kaitylyn," a young man from Valentine, Nebraska, turned his head in the muck to call out.

Kaitylyn struggled to breathe as she felt a boot on the back of her head. Mud went into her mouth and nose and she fought.

She gasped and shot up to sit as the boot was removed.

"Kaitylyn Anne Bridge."

Braxton stood over her.

His rifle pointed at her head.

"I'd know those dolphin earrings anywhere."

She scooped mud and grass from her mouth and eyes, her heart preparing to detonate, and hoping her diary found its way into friendly hands some day.

Lara and her brigade continued to stare into the harsh dawn light, beautiful as it was, signifying nothing, continually snatching looks behind them, watching Jim's bunch fighting valiantly, not being able to see Kaitylyn for the smoking, burning farm house and flashing emergency vehicle lights, helicopters now humming into position to shine spotlights on the captured Kaitylyn Brigade.

Jim fired his last burst and called as loud as he could to get his guys over with him.

They were four.

"We don't have much time," he said as quickly as he could.

"Ka-bars," he said and they grabbed their knives from scabbards and handguns from the holsters. The four hunched down low as the enemy had ceased firing, searching for them. They heard rustling in the weeds, water moving like somebody trying to make their way across a pool. Some had entered the pond.

Kaitylyn was yanked to her feet by both arms, hit in the stomach with the butt of a gun, begun to be dragged off to the woods.

Braxton stepped in and stopped it.

He barked some commands, and the soldiers began ordering the rebels to stand, as they were gotten into a line and marched through the farm yard toward the road.

Jim and his four crawled around the pond to get as close as they could.

They pounced. Jim shot a guy in the head, kept shooting. He heaved the gun away into the pond when it ran out of bullets, and in the same motion he grabbed another guy's hair and cut his throat. The blood spurted like a pig in a slaughterhouse. Jim caught sight of something big in his peripheral vision and turned just in time to have his knife kicked from his hand. He heard it slice the water.

He squared off with a large man who had lost his helmet in the fighting, a man Jim thought resembled the Russian in one of the Rocky movies. He put up his hands and they circled each other, each step a muck suck. The giant Russian guy lunged at Jim and Jim jammed his pointer finger bent at the knuckle into the guy's Adam's apple. He dropped, face-first into the mud, gagging.

A crowd of men rushed at Jim, threw him down and beat him.

An older man who looked to be in charge said STOP.

"He's the only one left. From the fuckin' tattoo he's one of the top dogs. We'll save him for hanging."

"What do we do, there's nobody here to fucking fight?"

One of Lara's bunch hollered over to her.

"There's fucking nobody over there by the fence. We can actually leave. Let's go, c'mon!"

Such language, thought Lara.

Three of them ran, over rolling hills, past the smoking, smoldering SUV, they ran over the pasture. A machine gun rattled, throwing up dust as they fell on their faces, their backs, rolled around a bit, then stopped rolling.

"Let's go," said Lara, not asking for ideas.

She led them back, through the woods, down the slope.

"Fuck the tunnel," she gathered them around her.

"We're heading right for the building."

They crouched low and marched off, over a rugged, picked corn field, getting to within a few hundred yards.

Lara took off her backpack for her binoculars. She zoomed in on the mental institution, seeing some guy in a window.

"That could be him," she said.

"Who?" said one of her fighters.

"The writer," said Lara.

"The writer?" said someone.

"That's why we're here?" said someone else.

"What the fuck! What does he write? Comics? What is this?"

"Didn't anybody brief you on this mission?" said Lara.

"Nope," one of them said as two others shook their heads.

Lara looked again through the binoculars, now up to the roof and saw snipers in camo, aiming their way.

She herded her people down into a draw just as shots rimmed off the edge, throwing up clods.

"You are gonna die here and you don't know why?"

"Not really. I don't care. C'mon, let's go, lets fuckin' get the writer guy, what's he write?"

"You care!" said Lara.

"Jesus! Fucking Skylar! What the fuck?"

She lifted her head and shouted into the growing clouds.

Lara dug the dirty pirate flag from her pocket and tied it round her rifle.

"No. This is important!" said one of her troops.

"Yes. It is," said Lara.

"It doesn't mean it's over.

"You are just going to not die today."

She instructed them firmly to make a show of tossing away their weapons, raise their hands into the air and follow her.

It began to rain.

They marched in single file, their heads and clothes sopping wet, having to yank each foot from the clingy ground as they marched, soon surrounded by Jeeps with machine guns and foot soldiers with rifles and officers screaming instructions at their men and at the prisoners, funneling them toward the dirt road.

Lara was pushed in the back of an F.B.I. unmarked car, next to Jim and Kaitylyn. They leaned forward with their hands cuffed behind their backs.

The rain fell harder, pounding the roof, making the muffled shouting and troops and trucks outside just a bad dream.

"It's over," said Jim.

"We gave it a good try. We done good."

Lara had to maneuver her body in the tight space to stare right into Jim's eyes.

"This isn't no fucking movie," said she. "It ain't over, until I say it's over, and it ain't over."

"Look," said Kaitylyn, "look."

She motioned with her head as best she could.

"What?" said Jim.

"Right there," said Kaitylyn.

They all ducked down to see out the side windows, through the rain, at the faint rainbow in the distance.

Note from the narrator:

From The Prince Hope Show ...

This portion of our program is being provided to you by the good folks at "The Next Big Thing" — New Apps for your phone, more stuff for you to do while you are doing that boring driving thing.

Well, folks, hold on to your hats because this new app is gonna rock your world.

It's the application that allows you to understand that UFOs, Bigfoot and Conspiracies are ... Real.

Download it today ... well, maybe tomorrow, we're working on it.
The folks at "The Next Big Thing" ask you to ...

Be careful what you hope for, huh?

What happens the day Barack Obama and George W. Bush and his father are walked out of the golf course in handcuffs charged with prior knowledge and hiding information about a felony – the attacks of 9/11 — and a thoughtful U.S. Marshall puts his hand on George Senior's head so he does not bump it on the door and we get the final public sneer or that career criminal? And it appears on the front page of the New York Post and Time Magazine and Rolling Stone.

What happens when the talk about UFOs and Bigfoot and the Wellstone murder are about details and where and when and how rather than a rolling of the eyes.

What happens when we have actual names and court cases and confessions and Newsweek and Wall Street Journal and New York Times front page stories about the trial of some still living principals in the JFK, RFK and Martin Luther King Jr. murders.

Our whole world will be rocked.

And somebody will need to make an app. for that — in a darn big hurry …
… but thanks to the folks at "The Next Big Thing" – it's all already in the works, guys.
Things will be different.
Our whole perception of life and what we should be doing in life will be changed forever.
That might be scary, but it's where we need to go.

Down the rabbit hole, folks.
Step right up.
Don't be shy.

SEVENTY-FOUR

Geoffrey,
Glad to hear. I was turned onto William Blum some years back, shortly after I got the computer for Xmas.

A writer friend now passed had sent me an autobiographical novel of Blum's, some years old but with Blum's email address inside. I still have this interesting book, have to dig it out of stuff inside the closet in the kid's room here, forget the name of it right now, and still have the book Bloom sent me then, as he immediately answered my email. KILLING HOPE, is large, famous. a sordid biography - horror - of C.I.A. brutality in Latin America. Ah, am incorrect, Bloom and I had some correspondence via email, but KILLING HOPE I received a bit later from Mike Novak. You can see in Bloom's email, he has written other well known books, on the C.I.A. etc., I have not read. I may have read KILLING HOPE twice, it would do to read it twice. I could give it to you, maybe when you can visit.

Sometimes Bloom can be cranky with me. He did not care to get the Postings. He calls me "the other Bill," so we do fine. He is a couple years older than I and it has amused me he had become a politico in the Bay Area when I was there an acid head. He is a socialist, in early years had a career and some decent occupation in Washington, before he became too alarmed or disgusted.

He has avoided the 9/11 issues. Certainly he feels he has plenty to do. He sees the senseless mayhem in the excuse of 9/11, the bleeding of our nation to please the insane who rule to conquer.

He has been seriously ill recently, some cancer I think. He may be alright by now, is certainly awake.

When Mike and Bonnie returned with stuff from Lyla's house, I was given maybe it is 3 or 4 boxes of my stuff, and I have so little space living in a trailer that I have hardly looked into them, thus have them in this closet of the kid's little bedroom, but a lot of books, some were not even originally mine. Hopefully, there still are these one sided papers of a stack copied by the mentioned late writer friend, of the Marine General who after World War One stopped a coup on the USA government, General Smedley D. Butler. This is quite the story, rather blotted out in USA history. As it goes, Smedley D. Butler is more known for a book, WAR IS A RACKET. This is really a thin little booklet, a copy of which did come from the deceased writer, whom I knew from the ULA, Underground Literary Alliance - Lyla had surprised me by getting my plane fare to this meeting in New York where Jack Saunders and I headlined. I have WAR IS A RACKET in this room visible on a shelf. Tried to get Mike Blackbird to even peek at it.

WAR IS A RACKET has become quite famed by now, one classic. Bix and Hatch read it and Hatch who wants to hear no conspiracy theories dug it so much he ordered copies to hand to others....Interesting, Hatch yet makes not further connections....Now this you have time to read. Sidney Butler a decorated Marine had much experience in USA rape of Latin America, when he was too busy to think directly about it all. But he did, start thinking. He passed just before the USA entered the Second World War. He pointed out we should have not been in that war either. Same old corporate shit and greed. Example, if he was the first to say so, the fascists had no way to get over here to get us.

What an astounding, horrific world.

Love,

Bill

Hey Bill,

Thanks for passing on the Anti-Empire Report. Blum makes sense to me.

Geof

Bix,

Thanks for all this, some interesting pieces of present times. I have been a wee out of it with computer shit, which today has fixed itself, to my surprise. This early morning I nearly did not turn it on.

I think, it is about this setup I have, if I look at videos my juice runs out. I can look at videos before 8 AM, then, and had been getting by, but I think lately I used up so much before 8 AM, I had a day or so I could not do email on the computer. But this early morning I was back, could do Sane Progressive videos, other sources like_jamesKessler.blogspot.com. And I have one week before return of full power.

I like Oliver Stone, and he does tread carefully. Sure, he is a Truther. I did also read one article just then of all this sent, that top one, on possible USA fascism. This guy treads yet more softly. We are in fascism now, and that author of course knows this.

Not being much for movies - except past years accidentally on tv - my heart of ONE EYED JAX. FARGO - or the entertaining one of the two girls who run off and avoiding authority - ah, SELMA AND LOUISE - drive off a cliff. I would go see SNOWDEN. I saw this trailer this morning. This acting is decent. Let me say so. Most movies are too stupid for Billy Frank.

I refuse to use a definition of "political" in my own case. Mike Blackbird calls me this. He votes, of course Democrat. Very funny.

My understanding is the voting in USA is fixed, for Killary.

I have been bored with Trump, or Killary or by now Obama. Trump is the inserted bogyman. The election is rigged for Clinton, who is worse than Trump. Am quoting Debbie Lusignan, a delight of brilliance, theater, rage, love, humanitarianism, a superior intellect - way superior. Hey, one can look at her in her flowing blouses or full t-shirts, hey. SHE IS REAL.

I have no inkling where this is heading.

Probably, we have enough angry nation who identify as heroes we old fellers will be fine.

Love,
       Bill

And even though it all went wrong I'll stand before the
Lord of Song with nothing on my tongue but Hallelujah.
— Leonard Cohen

SEVENTY-FIVE

They say, the process of learning is never-ending ...
"Electricity moves through wires passing the charged electrons to the destination, getting around by flowing either through air, liquid or solids ..."
That still doesn't really explain it, in my opinion.

You ever notice? These guys drop F-bombs like Dresden, as this one guy said.
Well, there's more, but this is what I have, so far.
Oh, yeah, Mayfield.
They were searching for THE house, you know, the perfect house on the perfect street and inside the perfect family.
They did get to a house, in Ohio, and what did they find? An historical bronze plaque that said this was one of the houses where filming was conducted and/or shown in the opening of the show.
"There are other houses also involved in the production, in California, Florida, Indiana, Connecticut."
And so, this thing isn't over, yet.
Does it smell like updog all up in here?
What's updog?
Not much, what's up with you?
According to Actually, I sure miss him, this is Jesus and his disciples talking before the meal at The Last Supper, according to the Gospel of Meh, recently uncovered under a pile of laundry in South Bethlehem.
And Brooke.
She was with The Special Unit, you know, The Red Shoes. You might have guessed what they were about? Or not. Sort of an einsatzgruppen, death squad, mercenaries.
Well, not quite, more of a Life Squad, IMO.

495

I believe there are three right now in operation. You know of one.

The one sitting outside in three, four vehicles, outside the office where Brooke now works, with their recording devices of course. I'm not really sure what kind of an office, but she seems to be putting down roots, or maybe she's still spying, I haven't really heard.

The Red Squad, unit, whatever records practically everything that goes on inside that office with Brooke in it, and then at some point, usually later than sooner, I hear about it.

Well, as I said, there's more, but this is what I have so far.

I was supposed to hand all this over, give my report as it were.

But I'm not.

I'm not going to tell anyone.

Only you.

I'm watching out my window onto the street in Saint Paul trying to get people to turn around. Also attempting to speak telepathically with some of them, just smart-ass stuff, but I think there's potential here, that whole staring at goats, MK Ultra thing that the real people have not been told about cuz we are the goats.

This whole place is The Great Hall of Lenin.

You come in the morning, walk right up to the paintings and photos and watch them until noon into the afternoon and all night. You stand there your whole life and still you don't understand. This ... whole ... fucking ... place.

Unless. Unless you get lucky. You find someone, someone like me perhaps. Or these CRUSHERS. They are the most interesting thing there is, these rebels and these C.I.A. and these F.B.I. and these aliens, Bigfoot. There. I said it but it's true.

Look around you. Reach all around you in every direction. Is there someone like Lara or Jim or Kaitylyn or Mike Braxton and all the rest of 'em?

I'm watching some Roswell videos on YouTube.

I know it's true. Not the government weather balloon total bullshit, but the first thing they said.

And I'll show you how I know.

And I know that the 9/11 government story is not true. And I know that what they have told us about Oklahoma City and Waco is not true. And I know that the government stories about what? how many are there now, hundreds? San Bernardino, Aurora, Tucson, oh yeah, Boston, Sandy Hook, the most famous ones. They tell us lies. Have you read, like Kaitylyn, about how the C.I.A. did these highly creative black operations to circumvent the good guys in all these other countries. They do it here, too. Especially here. Really. That's what intuitively pissed Geronimo off, is what I think. He had limits and he knew it and couldn't stand it. But what limits have you got? Your fat butt?

And I'll show you how I know. *(This is when the C.I.A. steps in or Mike Braxton and my car goes face-first for some odd reason into the center field wall at the high school stadium with me in it during the seventh inning stretch. But it won't happen to me. I'm not stooooopid. I'll be fine and I'll tell you and both of us won't be stupid. I promise.)*

Not now. I got shit to do.

Oh, here's something.

Something just in from The Red Unit.

I guess it's Brooke making friends for real or for show with her co-workers. This particular transmission is being transferred to me live.

You can listen if you want.

This is Brooke. It sounds like some sort of a coffee break, you picture it, I can, they are either in a break room, sparse with sign-up sheets to bring crap to a potluck and napkins and creamers, or they just sit at their desks, pull their stuff from their drawers.

There are Brooke For City Council lawn signs on the floor, leaning against furniture in Brooke's area. She is trying so hard.

Whether she is still a spy or whether she has finally decided to be June Cleaver, I haven't heard.

The talk goes around and you have to join in, you have no choice, it's worse than a Tiger Cage interrogation. If you don't fit in, say the right thing, you die ... you fade away, you lose your apartment, your routine, your life. These thoughts are there just as you giggle and smile and sip your goddamn drink, looking over the top at your adversary contemporaries like an outlaw over the ridge.

Or not.

Maybe you're a normal person.

Well, Brooke, I won't go into it all here, but people are talking about college and of course, Brooke went to college and so she's right in her crowd.

They know someone who worked at Walmart and someone who worked in a group home, and Brooke sits silent as Judas at a hanging.

"Yeah," she says. "... oh yeah, group home workers, what a sub-culture that is."

To be fucking continued.

ALLISON HEALY - ARTIST

Raised in the Northwoods of Minnesota, Allison developed a deep connection to the natural world as well as a great attention to detail, a theme that carries through much of her work. She left high school two years early and received an associate degree in liberal arts, with a focus in literature and fine art at the age of eighteen. Earning a Bachelor of Fine Arts degree in illustration from the Minneapolis College of Art & Design, she also spent some time abroad intensively studying illustration and graphic design at the University of Brighton, on the south coast of England. Her work has appeared on a range of publications, including but not limited to: book covers, children's books, magazines, album covers, greeting cards, and several applied graphics for various products. She is currently living and working in Boston, Massachusetts, where her studio is now based.